Lauren Keegan is an author and psychologist living on Dharawal and Gundungurra Country (Wollondilly, New South Wales). She has worked in perinatal and infant mental health for fifteen years, has two young girls and drinks more tea than is sensible. She is the author of *All the Bees in the Hollows*, which was voted Best Debut Fiction at the 2025 Indie Book Awards and longlisted for the ARA Historical Novel Prize 2025. This is her second novel.

This book deals with intimate partner violence. While the author has taken great lengths to ensure the subject matter is dealt with in a compassionate and respectful manner, it may be troubling for some readers. Discretion is advised. If you or someone you know is experiencing intimate partner violence, please call: 1800 RESPECT

THE WOMAN IN THE SEAL SKIN

LAUREN KEEGAN

affirm press

affirm press

First published in Australia in 2026 by Affirm Press,
a Simon & Schuster (Australia) Pty Limited company
Wurundjeri Woiwurrung Country
Level 3, 162 Collins Street, Melbourne VIC 3000

Affirm Press is located on the unceded land of the Wurundjeri Woiwurrung peoples of the Kulin Nation. Affirm Press pays respect to their Elders past and present.

New York Amsterdam/Antwerp London Toronto Sydney/Melbourne New Delhi
Visit our website at www.simonandschuster.com.au

10 9 8 7 6 5 4 3 2 1

NATIONAL LIBRARY OF AUSTRALIA

A catalogue record for this book is available from the National Library of Australia

9781923293328 (paperback)
9781761822452 (ebook)

Cover design & illustrations by Emily O'Neill
Typeset by J&M Typesetting in 12/20 pt Garamond Premier Pro
Printed and bound in Australia by the Opus Group

FSC www.fsc.org MIX Paper | Supporting responsible forestry FSC® C001695

To my husband, Ryan: my biggest champion.

‘There is human time and there is wild time.’

Clarissa Pinkola Estés – *Women Who Run with the Wolves*

Part I

Haul Out

One

Malie, Orkney, 1695

I will never truly know the boundaries of this island. It never looks the same from one day to the next. Right now, the mighty serpent releases its breath, blowing the sea onto shore. The land shrinks. The sea steals the land, wave by wave, breath by breath. Father says he's seen one: a sea serpent, the length of a man but not nearly big enough to draw in the tides with its breath. I edge back from the shoreline. At ebb tide the serpent pulls the energy away from the shore, releasing its grip on us, expanding the island outwards. It will be many hours before the serpent sucks the tide back in and retreats from the land. Puts everything right again.

It's as if the wild storm that blew in from the North Sea yesternight was nothing but a turbulent dream. She'd been in a right temper. Aye, dusk to dawn, the roar of her wrath shook up the island, the swells tormenting the western coastline. Wind blew seafoam up to our house; the corn crops and barley field were overblown with sand. Half the crop was ruined, maybe more, in one night. I lay alone in my bed, imagining the ocean swallowing the boat in one expansive gulp. After weeks at sea, gone would be my husband, father and brothers. Devoured by the deep dark depths of the ocean.

'A day 'atween the weathers' is what my father calls a day like this. A quiet or peaceful period in between bad spells of weather. Yesterday it was a ferocious downpour and today it's calm and clear. Tomorrow, well, who knows?

As I meander southwards, I glance back at the old red sandstone cottage and the purple-flowering moorland creeping down to the sandy bank. It's the home I was born in but I live there now with my husband, Johne. The hill dyke behind it must have been hit by the storm as the sheep have escaped. The flock, with their squat stature and shaggy coats, graze on the tawny-coloured seaweed purged from the sea overnight. The kelp keeps them plump in the harsh winter conditions. I count fifteen: that's about half of the ewes. The rest are likely up in the moorland. I must check on them soon. With damage to the crops, we'll need them healthy and strong. We lost four of our ten lambs in the colder-than-usual spring. At least we have the sea and its infinite bounty.

Astern, the harbour is still. No boat, no men. I might see them come through the Sound, once I reach the Point. The wind tangles my hair, and the salty tang of the sea is on my tongue. As I tread along the shoreline, my bare feet leave impressions in the patterned grey sand. I find limpets nestled in the seaweed, thrown out in the storm. I collect as many as I can and drop them into the caisie. I will smoke them on the peat fire with dried seaweed and it will make for a salty, chewy treat. It's best to keep busy when the men are away and not be thinking too much about when they will return. *If* they will return.

'Nothing but danger at sea,' Father always says. He forbade me to go into the water once my mother, Nava, left. Mother said the ocean tells a story; it moulds to the shape of the person in it. It *remembers*. The sea is gentle and mysterious – not to be feared. I know not what lies beyond the shore, nor do I want to. Bad things happen at sea: men drown, ships sink, women disappear. She is unpredictable. Ferocious. She took my mother, and she took my friend. Neither could resist the ocean's call. The wind whips hair across my cheek again, and I pin it back against the nape of my neck. A shiver travels down my spine.

Nae. It's safer on land.

Yet, despite the danger, I am still here. I am drawn to the sea. Like Father to his boat when he sailed the seas. Like Mother to the swell of the tides she swam. I teeter on the edge, neither a sailor nor a swimmer. At least, not any more. I come here looking for *her*.

Beside the sandy bay, amid the rock pools, a herd of seals sprawls upon the rocks. After a storm, they haul out to rest. I scan the glossy, slippery figures but I don't see what I'm looking for. I don't see her. I'm tempted to dip my toes in the water, edge forwards for a better view. The stream is fast flowing as I approach the Point, the southernmost tip of the island. It's wilder than back in the harbour. Ahead of the Point is the last cottage in the parish and a narrow pier which juts out into the ocean. A rickety square sterned dinghy is moored there. It's made of clinker construction, where the edges of the hull planks overlap each other. Everyone on the island has one for inshore fishing, but only my father possesses a Yole: a twenty-foot double-ended vessel used for Haaf fishing. The Yole navigates open waters up to ten miles offshore, but almost always in sight of the island. It's a family business: one my husband is now a part of.

A man strides along the pier with a young boy scurrying behind him. Henrye Sinclair. He stops and looks sharply in my direction. My breath catches and I leap back from the water's edge. Henrye touches his hat with a slight dip of his head, and, with an armful of kelp, he continues up the sandy bank towards his home. His son scrambles across the sand behind him, silky seaweed dangling from his peedie arms. He's grown so much. I continue to the Point. I know if I were to get up close to Henrye I'd see grief lines carved around his eyes, eyes that have dulled in the three years since he lost his wife. Beatrice was my childhood friend, only one year older. She came across the Pentland Firth from Scotland with her family in the summer after Mother left. She was the only person who didn't treat me differently. She didn't treat me like a selkie's daughter.

Adjusting to the harsh conditions of the island proved difficult for her parents: they were keen to see Beatrice married so they could return to their homeland. Beatrice married Henrye and their son, James, arrived soon after that. James was just four years old when Beatrice drowned. It was the longest day of the year, when the sky was bright and the sea was calm. It was cruel that she should be taken on such a beautiful day. I remember her limp body and the smell of the sea on her. Henrye's grave face and James's sobs. Even now, I still don't know what she was doing at sea, but her death was a timely reminder for women to stay away from seducing waves and murky waters. I'd married Johne soon after – a welcome distraction from my grief.

The sea took his wife but Henrye, like all of us, still relies on it for food. The pull to the sea is so great that all twelve farmsteads in our parish run in a wide belt along the bends of the harbour. Henrye's home is before the Point, then mine, and the next five houses heading north towards the harbour belong to my father and my four brothers. Beyond the farms and crops, the turf-mounted hill dyke loops around the fields, separating grazing animals from crops on the rising moorland. There is a scattering of other huts and houses beyond, close to the port where three sturdy piers extend into the harbour to cater for the visiting fleets. Our property runs from the highest point in the hill to the lowest stone in the ebb: nestled between land and sea.

'Malie.' A timeworn voice from behind whips my focus from sea to land. 'Are ye a'ight, love?'

'Bessie.' My hand clasps my chest, heart pounding beneath my ribcage.

'Didn't mean to startle ye.' She links her arm through mine and nestles in close. She smells of earth and the wild thyme found scattered across the moorland. 'Lost in the past, ye looked like. No good will come of that.'

'Nae, just worried about the men. That storm ...'

'Aye,' Bessie says, firm but kind, much like her nature. 'They'll be back, don't ye worry.' She slips a piece of cloth into my hand: creamy silver wool, softened over time by frequent handling. She closes my fingers around it. 'Hold on to this and yeh husband will get fair weather. He'll be home shortly before ye have yeh supper.'

I breathe out deeply and pocket the cloth, my hand still clutched tightly around it, the wave of worries I'd struggled in since the storm settling into a calm swell. My mother and my best friend were taken by the sea; I cannot let it take my husband too. I can't bear the thought of being left behind, being left alone on this island. 'Thank you, Bessie, that's kind of you.' Bessie has a knack for these things. Father has never thought kindly of her. Thinks of her as a lowly widowed peasant, living in a peedie hut at the northern end of the township. It became our little secret, mine and Bessie's – she'd visit me with a warm pot of food and stories of the sea when Father was on a fishing voyage. I was left to care for my four brothers, but as the boys matured, one by one, Father took them out fishing with him, which left me alone for weeks on end with nothing but the crashing sea and blustery winds for company. After my mother left, I worried something bad would happen to the rest of my family, that I'd be left behind. I fretted day and night, praying for their return. I'd never defied my father before, but the loneliness was unbearable. Bessie mothered me when no one else did.

'Be prepared, love. After a storm like that one, the men may never be the same again,' she says, and with that, she squeezes me against her in a brief hug. She pulls away and shuffles across the sand, following the path trod earlier by Henrye. She must be off to see him. A pang of guilt pulls at my chest. Since that day on the shore, him cradling Beatrice's lifeless body, I've not been able to bring myself to talk to him, let alone visit. Even if Johne would allow it.

Pale clouds drift across the horizon. The wind is gentle, remorseful for the thunderous gale of yesternight. The tide will carry the boat in, I know it. Sail back in on the serpent's breath. Back to shore, to me. To *us*.

My hands spread across my stomach. I am bursting to share my news with him: something to make us a true family. Finally. It has been more than two years. My four brothers' wives have all conceived and birthed bairns, but not me. The year I married Johne, all four of them were expecting at the same time.

I thought I did something wrong. From the moment I could walk my mother swept me out of bed from dawn. Don't sleep in, don't be still. Little girls were meant to be on the move. This, she assured me, would one day bless me with an easy delivery of my own child. After she left, I stopped swimming. I didn't move as swiftly. The grief seeped into my bones and hardened like stone, making movement slow and burdensome. I was busy caring for my brothers, but it did not come easily.

Nae, nae. There's no use worrying about all of that, now the bairn grows within me. Johne will be happy and all will be good between us again. Like those early weeks of our marriage. I sidestep across the sand, like a crab, just to be sure. Shuffle, shuffle. Keep moving or else the birth will be a long process.

A seal howls from the east and my heart knocks against my ribs. Tap, tap, tap. There she is. *My* seal. Nestled on a rock in the shallows. Her bloated belly spills across the rock; waves crash and splash her mottled grey coat. Her human-like eyes are on me. Eyes dark as my mother's. Dark like mine.

Moss-covered rocks surround her as though she's a tiny island in the sea, near the rocks spilling out into the Sound. Seals are a social mammal, frolicking in groups with their herd. My seal likes to escape for a quiet moment, away from her rowdy family. As a girl I liked to escape my brothers too, but once Mother left the island, there was no evading my responsibilities. Father reminded me of this often enough. It has been twenty years, and I still wonder if he cannot bear to look at me because I am so alike my mother. While I cannot change the way I look, I promised myself I'd not cause Father any further pain. I'd already lost my mother; I couldn't bear to lose my father too. I vowed to stay away from the ocean.

A seagull circles above, squawks in greeting. The large great black-backed gull has a heavy yellow bill and flesh-pink legs. Seals are the eyes of the sea, but gulls are the eyes of the sky. Wherever there's a seal on shore, a gull is not far away. When it's pupping season a seal nursery will fill the rocky coastline. The gulls will stalk the herd and swoop at first sight of the afterbirth.

Satisfied that Henrye and Bessie have gone and with no husband or father here to tell me otherwise, I tentatively step towards the sea. It calls me. The bairn in my belly gives me the courage to dip my toes into the freezing waters. The waters I so much loved as a child, though I only dared enter them when the serpent breathed out, knowing the sea would always take me back to shore.

'Always keep something for yourself,' Mother told me. For her it was the sea. She'd swim every day, no matter the weather, cold or rain. It drove Father wild, but she did it anyway. Who could blame her? It was in her nature. My feet sink into the cool water. I glance back. My footsteps have been washed away, and I get a little thrill from knowing how fast the sea hides my secret.

She's still here, her docile eyes watching me. As though she can see me, see through me. Right into the life that has formed within. She shakes and barks, a joyful bark. She nods back to the water. *Swim*, she dares me. *Swim, like you did as a child.* I shake my head. Water laps at my ankles. It feels like chains, heavy chains that could pull me under at any moment. The sea was freeing for my mother, but for me it incites nothing but fear. Uncertainty.

I could never. It is forbidden.

Still, I step towards her. Drawn by her energy, her silky skin and her docile eyes. The seal sings and it's mesmerising. Keep moving. I shuffle forwards, closer and closer, water now lapping at my knees. If I went further, would my body remember how to stay afloat? I inch forwards, always moving, so as not to let the worries settle too deeply on my conscience.

Flapping wings and the trance is broken. The gull soars overhead, circles the seal. Screeches a warning. A masthead penetrates the blue of the Hoy Sound. I exhale in relief. Father's boat! The men have returned on a fair wind, just as Bessie predicted. I bring the silver cloth to my lips and kiss it. 'Thank you, Bessie.' I inch forwards and then stop. I shouldn't be here. I cannot greet them in the water. What am I thinking? Nae, I must get back. I wave goodbye. My seal dips her head. I flush with shame at her disappointment. I am not as brave as I once was, not like my mother. Things are different now.

I tiptoe back to dry sand, where the earth is firm and solid and safe. Predictable. My feet are numb and tingly. They wear the thrill of the sea. I scramble back up the sand banks to home. To wait for my husband. I banish all thoughts of cold water tugging at my ankles. The seal's knowing gaze. Eyes so familiar, as if looking at my own.

Out with those thoughts. Nae, I must not become like my mother, yearning for the sea. Wanting what she could not have without sacrifice. Her betrayal is imprinted on my skin like an invisible scar. Each day since she left us, I have vowed not to make the same choice as she. I would always choose my family over the call of the sea. I will not succumb to the wildness. I will not lose control. I will wait for my husband as a good wife would do.

I sit upon the stone bench and salt tingles my skin, and I wait.

Two

Malie

Something is wrong.

Feet stagger on gravel and hoarse, anguish-ridden voices carry on the breeze. I dash outside towards my husband. Johne's arms drape across the shoulders of my father and my eldest brother, Patrik. Johne is limping. Something is tied around his leg and a dark patch is swelling outwards. He's badly hurt. That wretched storm!

My brothers Jerome, William and Adame trail behind with the other fishermen, heaving a wagon of fish. They've walked all the way from the harbour wharf like this and brought the smell of the sea with them. There's something glossy and grey in the wagon, too. My stomach churns as my seal tumbles back into my thoughts. Could it be her? The surge of panic brings me to a standstill.

'Malie!' Father bellows and the thoughts recede. A rush of anxiety propels me forwards, my gaze snagging on Johne's leg and the bloodstained breeches. I mended them before he left. A rope is tied around his upper thigh, and I glimpse a flicker of curved ivory protruding from above his right knee. Is that a fishing hook?

'What happened?' I ask. Johne lifts his head; heavy eyes flicker open and closed. His face is as pale as a seal's belly.

'Make space for him, Malie,' Father says through gritted teeth, hauling Johne higher up on his shoulder. 'Ye'll need to remove the hook.'

I retrace my steps to the solid stone structure I was raised in. A simple house, made of stone with a roof of turf, built to withstand the wind. I slip inside before the men, Mother's words ringing in my ears. *Be the first out of the house, the first one back in, don't linger at the doorway or a long delivery will follow.* I must do everything right, especially now I have conceived. I haven't forgotten anything my mother told me when I was young. Her words circle on a loop in my mind because my memories are all that is left of her. When Mother was carrying Adame, she'd say worrying wasn't good for the bairn. But what am I to make of this? Something bad happened at sea. Bessie warned me the men may never be the same again. She was right: Johne is hurt. How could she have known? The blood, the hook. I shudder. Try not to worry. Don't upset the bairn.

My hand involuntarily cups my abdomen. Eyes pressed shut. My news must wait. I draw in a shaky breath, open my eyes. I clear the stone bench on the left side of the room and flick a sheet upon it. I can't believe I even considered swimming in the sea. I don't know what overcame me. I have responsibilities! My husband is badly injured and if I'd not returned when I did, I may not have been here to help him. What then? I shake off the worries as I collect Johne's pillow from our bed, plump and soft, filled with seabird feathers. Seventy-two birds it takes to fill a pillow for my husband's heavy head.

The men clamber in. The crunch of boots echoes, and there's the thud of a body on the solid bench. I focus on what I need. Pliers, bandages, whisky. I collect the supplies from the stone cupboard carved by Father for Mother. What else did she use that time Patrik fell and spiked his lower leg on an oyster-ridden rock? Part of a shell had broken away and lodged deep into his skin.

Bird fat. Aye, to dress the wound. I collect the stone jar from the shelf and remove the lid. The men are sweaty and salty, tall, broad-shouldered, filling the space. This room was so big when my brothers were younger; now they loom in all the gaps. My breath catches. There's not enough air for us all to share. In this moment I long for the open seaside. Father withdraws a glinting knife and cuts away a square panel in Johne's woollen breeches before throwing it aside and tearing the linen braies underneath. I must patch those later; we do not have enough flax to make a new pair.

I clasp Johne's hand and sweep damp hair from his forehead. He's awfully pale. 'Johne, what happened out there?'

He grunts and groans. 'Selkies.' He spits and then his eyes roll backwards. I look sharply at my father, but he only shakes his head. *Nothin' but danger out there ...*

'Ye got everything?' Father asks.

'Aye,' I say. 'Aye.' Feet shuffle beneath me: keep moving, don't stay still. I inspect the wound, and my four brothers gather around the table, the three older fishermen Angus, Bernard and Duncan lingering at the doorway. I inspect Johne's leg. It's one of the older hooks, hand-carved from whale bone; the sharp point has pierced through layers of flesh, the splintered barb tearing the leg downwards.

It's hard to breathe. *Focus.* I draw on an image of the expansive sky, the space and fresh air. Mother told me if you feel closed in, *restricted*, go to the sea, even if only in your mind. This soothes me now. If I'm there, then I can keep moving. The wild ocean is more freeing than the stifling blood and sweat of the men-filled cottage.

I loosen the rope and blood pulses out the wound. Father clears his throat. Aye, not the right thing to do. I tighten it again, but I don't have the strength to do it as the men had before and blood swells out of the wound. It stains the sheet. Johne's head sinks into the down pillow. I collect the whisky, tilt my husband's head and tip it into his mouth. A couple of snifters of whisky will stimulate circulation. He coughs and splutters but lifts his chin for more.

I squeeze his hand. 'This part will hurt.'

I pour the whisky onto the wound. He writhes and groans as I press down the cloth to soak up the blood. Jerome and Adame step forwards to secure him: I hold his knee with one hand and grip the hook with the other.

I close my eyes and imagine the swell of the sea. The rise and fall imprints in my mind and when I reopen my eyes I no longer see the men. Just something that must be done. Something that must be done well.

One. Two. Three. I twist the hook free in one slick movement. Muscle and flesh tears and Johne roars. His leg convulses and blood spills out, more spilling with each pulse. Like the flooding of the banks as the tide comes in. I clamp down on the wound with the cloth. 'Pass me the sewing kit.'

It is my younger brother, Adame, who hands me the needle and linen thread. Jerome continues to hold Johne down. No one else steps forwards to help. They just stand there watching me. I bend the needle into an arc and douse it in whisky. I must suture the muscle layer and damaged tissue first. 'Hold this together while I stitch it.' His gulp is loud, his breath unsteady, but Adame does as I ask, as I know he will. I've been a mother to him since I was six years old. He was not yet four when our mother left. While the muscle laceration is not deep, it will affect Johne's mobility and is at risk of infection.

I move on to the skin layer. Pinched flesh, jagged lines; not a clean cut. Johne's scar will not be bonnie – something he ain't likely to let me forget. The needle pierces the skin, down and back out the other side. Johne groans and the men hold him firm. I steal a glance at my husband; his teeth grit together and his eyes are pure fury. I am inflicting pain on him, humiliating him in front of his kin. I grip the needle. Nae. Nae, he's not angry with me. I'm helping him, saving him. He's angry at the pain, that's all. I push away all thoughts of those eyes and his large hands, what they might do after the men go home.

There's a low chatter as the men avoid looking at Johne, as the needle pierces and releases with each stitch. It takes longer than I anticipate because my fingers slip with the oozing blood. Adame leans in and dots the blood away with the red-stained cloth. It makes no difference: the sea of blood spills over again. I focus on the needle going in and out, in and out until I reach the end of the gash. I tie it off twice and step back. The stitch is good. Aye, it's the best I can do. I smother it with bird fat, bandage the wound and then Adame slides a rolled blanket under Johne's leg for elevation.

I breathe out, breathing out the ocean I'd been holding onto. Now, my hands shake – better now than earlier. They're covered in blood. Under my fingernails and up to my elbows. Down my chest and all over my clothes. I lift my head. We are a sorry sight. Bloodstained, weary men. For one fleeting moment I feel I am one with them.

Adame whispers in my ear. 'The sea spirits have left us. They were gone, Malie. The fish are gone. Not just in the shallows but in the deep too.'

My brother's words are a winter mist, lingering in the air between us. The fish are gone. The fishermen rely on the sea spirits, whom they cannot see, but who watch over them. There was a decent catch in the wagon. Not as much as previous trips but certainly more than none. There has been nothing in the nets since early spring. The men have left for longer voyages since, venturing further and further into the North Sea. Father's Yole is not ideal for distant fishing grounds and the frequent storms have made their work even more challenging.

'The storm damaged the crops, too,' I add in barely a whisper, careful to avoid meeting Father's eyes.

Father growls as he brings his fist down on the stone table. Even Johne flinches, and he is barely conscious. 'A'ight,' Father barks and Adame steps backwards. 'Out with ye.'

The men scramble, addressing my father, Neill, by name as they leave, eager to retreat home to their wives and bairns. They too will be fretting after the storm.

Adame holds my gaze. He looks at Johne, dozing on the bench, and back at me. 'Take care, Malie.'

'Send a message if you need me.' Father leaves without a word more, knowing with no children and an injured husband, I have no means to send a message unless I deliver it myself.

Adame's home is nestled between mine and Father's with my other three brothers beyond in a neat line towards the harbour. Adame chose to be the wind break between Father and me. He has always been protective. He looks to Johne one final time before he marches out of the house. Then we are alone. The cottage had felt full and stifling but now it feels empty and cold.

The wagon is dragged back up the path. A bucketful of fish was left by the hearth to be cured and smoked. It dawns on me that the bucket – and not the wagon – is our ration from their fishing expedition. Six herring? The men were gone almost a month. I hold the stone wall to steady myself. How will we survive the winter? Not to mention our bairn. I finger the cloth in my pocket, the one that brought my husband back to me. Is it because I wanted a bairn so badly? I wished, I prayed, I begged to the heavens. God answered my prayer but is his price our crops and catch? Will the water, the sky and the land punish us?

My stomach is covered in my husband's blood. Instinctively my hand shields it. It's flat but I feel full, swollen with the news I must share. The metallic smell makes my stomach churn, and I swallow back an acrid taste in my mouth. Now is not the time to draw attention to myself.

I shake out a barley-coloured sheep's wool blanket at my husband's bedside; I'm startled by the grip of Johne's hand on my arm. 'Finnfolk did this. Yer nothin' but trouble,' he spits. His eyes lock on mine and I hold my breath.

Don't stress the bairn, don't stress the bairn.

'Leave me be,' he says, and I breathe once more. He releases my arm and his head lolls to the side. I cannot move him from the table. I tuck the seabird feather pillow back under his head and cover him with a blanket despite his groans.

Yer nothin' but trouble. I shiver as I pull a blanket around me and warm my hands over the peat fire. What did he mean about the Finnfolk? Was he blaming them for his injury or the missing fish? Both? And what of the selkies? Is it possible my mother has returned?

Hand to belly again. Mother's words whisper in the breeze. *Keep something for yourself, Malie. When you're married, when you become a mother, keep something for yourself.*

I can't keep it to myself forever, but as I watch over my husband shivering and twitching in a light but confused sleep, I have a thought: I will keep *this* to myself, for now. I can share it with Johne tomorrow. When he feels better.

Mother won't mind if I keep more than one thing to myself. The wee bairn in my belly. And my seal, the one who sings to me. My thoughts return to the slippery grey skin in the wagon and my throat tightens. Nae, it cannot be her. Not my seal. I would feel it in my body if she were gone. Besides, the men all know better than to kill the seals. An expectant one at that. Or they'd face an untimely fate. Aye, if it'd been a seal they'd killed, they'd all be drowned and the boat lost.

A niggling thought: how did a hook end up in my husband's leg? The men may not have been lost but something bad *did* happen at sea.

I drag inside the bucket of fresh water that Adame collected from the loch behind his property and left for us. I should get my dress and the cloths into some cold water before the blood sets. I get to work, scrubbing. I try to wash the worrying thought away, but it returns again and again like the unwavering tides of the sea.

~

Our front door is made of patched-together driftwood seized from shipwrecks or rejected by the sea and thrown up onto our pebbly shores. The door edges inwards and Bessie, bathed in silver light, startles me from troubled thoughts. She shuffles inside, a pot and a jar tucked in the crook of her elbow, and nudges the door closed behind her. With a fleeting glance at Johne, I scramble towards Bessie to relieve her of the load.

'A pot of broth for yeh husband, and ale for both of ye.'

'Oh, Bessie, you shouldn't have. It's late and cold out – you'll make yourself ill.'

Bessie chuckles. 'Och, I'm as strong as an ox.' Shuffling with a slight limp, she scoops up two stone mugs from the shelf above the cupboard and with a twitching hand splashes ale into both, slurping hers back before passing me the other. I suppose there will be none left for Johne, but I accept it anyway.

'How did you know about Johne?' I ask, grateful for the warning, not that it prepared me any for the scene that unfolded since.

'How did I noo? Henrye told me, love.' Bessie sighs. 'He'd been in toon and seen the men at the wharf, said yeh husband was in a bad way. Thought if he's sick, and senseless, it'd be safe to visit ye.'

Before I can say I was asking how she knew *before* the men came ashore,

Johne mumbles and groans from the table. I sip at the ale, which tastes nothing like the namesake of the grain used to make it. Meadowsweet makes for bitter ale, but it warms my throat and loosens my tongue. 'I'm worried, Bessie. He's badly injured, but there's something else too. He's talking about selkies and the Finnfolk and the sea spirits being gone.'

Bessie clucks her tongue and sets her mug aside. She warms her hands together and then circles them above Johne's bandaged leg, as though she were moulding a beremeal dough. I step closer and stroke my husband's shoulder. Bessie lays a hand upon his injury and Johne shivers beneath my fingertips.

Bessie scrunches up her face, deep in thought, and after a moment she pulls back. 'He's not going to die, Malie. He'll be a'ight.'

'How can you be sure, Bessie?' I'm thinking not only of my husband but the bairn, and how we both need him to pull through this. To come back to us, whole. I'd do anything to start over. Things were fraught between us before he left.

'I just noo.' She claps her hands together. 'Must be off now.'

I realise this is her first visit in the two years since I've been married to Johne. Her secret visits when I lived with my father ceased when he moved into his hut and Johne moved in with me. I have missed her. 'Here,' I say, pulling the silver cloth from my pocket. 'This is yours.'

Bessie's eyes crinkle. 'Nae, you keep it.'

I shake my head, tucking it into her hand as she did with me on the shore. In this cloth, she gave me both hope and dread. It brought my husband back to me, but with this terrible injury and a new anger he thinks I've caused. 'I cannot keep it.'

She tucks it into her coat and opens the door. A blast of cool air whips through the house. 'Be back in the mornin',' she calls over her shoulder and hobbles away. The crunch of boots on gravel drowns in the waves of the wind.

Three

Henrye

'Hold it tight,' Henrye tells his son. The drift net, spun from flax, was dropped from the pier in the early hours of the morn, where surface fish such as herring, mackerel and sprats once passed through frequently. The corks attached to the top of the line keep the net buoyant and the stone line sinkers weigh it down so the bait is not stolen by shallow feeders. 'We'll pull it in together.'

James grips the rope with an expression of fierce determination that traps Henrye in a cross sea of pride and angst. The pride comes from the great strength he sees in his son, a perseverance and resilience so necessary on this island. The angst is over his son's incessant need to please him; he wishes he didn't try so hard. His love for James is unconditional.

They haul in the net and sprawl it out on to the pier. There was a time when the line would be up to a mile long, and snoods with a hook were dropped off the net, baited with fish or shellfish. There were hundreds of hooks per line and it would take many early morn hours to prepare them. Most of the fishermen had ceased this method; it was too much work for too little reaping. Henrye rocks back on his heels. Empty. He has come to expect this, even though they're more than halfway through herring season. There had been a time when the fish would get tangled in the nets by their gills, and all he had to do was collect them. A colony of seagulls squawk in flight but they don't bother to circle the pier. Henrye keeps a neutral expression so he won't worry James but, as usual, he underestimates his son's cleverness.

'Again? There's nothing here. Papa?'

Henrye rests his arm on one of his knees. 'Hmm.'

'I can't remember the last time we had a catch. What will we do?'

He lifts his gaze. 'Don't you worry about that James. That's for me to figure out.'

'What if the fish never come back?'

He grunts and pushes up on to his feet, dusting the sand off his knees. Henrye's father was a fisherman, Henrye is a fisherman and so it goes that James will be a fisherman too. But how can one be a fisherman if there are no fish in the sea? Not in the shallows and not in the deep. They are surrounded by an ocean devoid of food.

'We keep on doing what we're doing. We focus on the kelp. Just like my Papa told us.'

It may be the only thing that keeps them alive during winter. He hopes to get his son off this island. One day. Somewhere not so isolated and dependent on the seasons. There is no future for them here.

The MacDuffies returned nearly empty-handed after rough seas and a ferocious storm. He'd seen the commotion when they'd disembarked. Something happened to Johne but he didn't dare get close enough to find out what went on. Bessie told him about the injury when she brought them supper last night. He might've feigned disinterest but he did listen to every detail of her prattle. He couldn't help himself. She'd planned to call round Malie's on her way home. He'd not been keen on the idea, and told her so, but Bessie had her own mind and there was nothing he could do to convince her otherwise. A small part of him is relieved Malie has someone to check in on her. He worries about her when the men are away and she's up in that house all alone. But he worries about her more when she's not.

Henrye shakes off the nets, and all thoughts of Malie, of the past. He forces his stiff face into a smile and pats his son on the shoulder. James is his future, that's what he must think of. 'Son, let's go home.'

Four

Malie

Bessie arrives at dawn with a pocketful of stones. They clatter together like old Fergus Grahame's teeth in the cold. He, like Bessie, lives alone in a hut at the northern end of the harbour, and they have equally little land and standing. I suspect she checks in on him regularly, just as she does with Henrye. The sea called to me all night, so it is a good thing she's here, snipping the invisible thread that pulls me to the shore when I should be here at my husband's bedside. I've not slept a wink. Every time I closed my eyes I saw that grey seal skin in the wagon; agonised over whether it was my seal. Adame's whispers of missing fish. Johne blaming the Finnfolk. Selkies. I rose hourly to check his fever, frequently placing the back of my hand on his warm, dry forehead and encouraging him to sip water. Even now, after a fitful sleep, he remains pale, febrile and senseless.

Bessie lays her hand upon Johne's injury once more and shakes her head. ''Tis the sea spirit lying upon him. We'll fly it away.'

'Sea spirit? Adame told me they were gone.'

Bessie shakes her head. 'Nae, they haven't gone. We've just forgotten how to listen.'

'Can you help him?' I ask, clasping my husband's hand. Whatever he does when recovered, I am desperate to see him healed. I will keep my vows, I will make things right.

Deep-set wrinkles encircle her eyes. 'Aye. I brought these.' She retrieves the stones from her pocket one at a time. She holds up the first: speckled grey with a shiny finish. 'A stone from commonty,' she says, meaning the communal grazing area beyond the hill dyke. She places it beside Johne on the table and then from her pocket retrieves another: this one is large and shrouded in moss. 'A stone from the seashore.' She sits it beside the first and pats around in her pocket for the third – reddish pigment and a rough finish – which is set alongside the other two. 'And this is from the kirkyard,' she huffs. She must have trekked to the western side of the island where the kirk and burial ground overlook the beach. In winter, it is often heaped high with mounds of seaweed and crowded with flocks of seabirds.

My hands tremor as my fingers brush over them. I've heard stories about the three stones, how one can use them to cure sickness or evade death. Devilish witches preying on the vulnerable. A wave of nausea crashes upon me and I clasp my hands on the table. Bessie is fussing with a pot on the hearth, mumbling, and while she is distracted, I compose myself. Blurry vision gives way to clarity. My husband's pallid face and uneven breath reminds me that time is against us, and while the stones are seen as devilry, they are also said to work. Again, I put thoughts of consequences aside for later.

The water bubbles and spits in the pot on the fire as Bessie drops the stones into the vessel one by one. We kneel before the hearth watching the flames crackle and dance, the peaty earthy smell circling us. Bessie hums an old tune in Norn, the Old Norse language of my forefathers. Mother knew a little of the language, but Father forbade her to teach us, speaking only in Scots. Humming gives way to silence while Bessie examines the pot. With a grunt of approval, she wraps the folds of her dress around her hands, removes the pot and then disappears outside to drain the water.

'What do we do now?' I ask as she re-enters the house and places the pot on the ground between us.

She uses the silvery wool cloth to scoop a scalding stone from the pot and places them both in my hand. 'Put this stone behind the door.'

I don't want to take part in this ritual and I am about to refuse her when Johne's ragged breath from the bench quietens the fear. I must help him. Besides, the stone is too hot to dwell on, and so I do what Bessie tells me. The first stone is tucked behind the door, the second in the nook of the hearth and the third, now cooling, is tucked beneath Johne's injured leg. Bessie pockets her cloth and instructs me not to touch the stones until she returns at nightfall. Then she leaves again.

~

My oldest brother, Patrik, and the youngest, Adame, visit midmorning. Adame places a pot in my hand and a warm linen bundle, sweet-smelling of bere bannock. 'Elinor made brose: she wanted you to have it, knowing you'd be busy caring for Johne.'

'Och, that's kind of her.' The men lift Johne and move him from the stone bench to the bed where he will be more comfortable. Oh! Do they see the stone I put under his injured leg? Not wanting to draw attention to it, I place the pot and the bread bundle on the stone cupboard positioned against the wall. I remove the lid and inhale the delicious-smelling food – a mixture of peas, beans, kale and barley. Overcome with hunger, I realise I was so caught up fretting over Johne that I forgot to eat last night. I unwrap the linen bundle and break open the end of the flat bread to savour its sweet nutty flavour.

'Give my thanks to Elinor,' I say, with a mouthful of bread. Adame chuckles while Patrik grimaces, repositioning Johne's legs at a more natural angle on the bed. They've removed the torn woollen breeches so he'll be more comfortable. I will repair them tonight with patchwork, so they are ready for him when recovered. Elinor is a young bride and gave birth to their bairn in the spring. Nicholas is a sweet wee boy with round, dark eyes like Adame's and fair skin like Elinor's. Father wouldn't allow me to marry until all my brothers were wed. Adame, not even twenty-one, engaged the help of our brothers to build a modest stone cottage on the next property, securing a wife shortly afterwards. I suspect it was to free me of my duties and allow me to find a husband of my own. I'd waited long enough, and options were scarce. I was married the next spring at the age of twenty-three.

'We'll repair the sheep dyke on our way out,' Patrik says. 'You've lost a couple of lambs in the storm.'

'Och,' I say, swallowing the bannock. 'How many?' In all the fuss I've forgotten to check the dyke after seeing the sheep spilling out onto the shores to scavenge the seaweed. The corn is ruined, and we'll lose more than half of the barley come harvest. With so few fish in the sea, we'll need the sheep to survive the winter. I wrap the linen back around the bread, feeling another layer of appreciation for Elinor's generosity.

'Three,' Patrik grunts as he departs the house. My stomach drops. That leaves only three lambs, twenty-six ewes and one ram. When we were married, Father gave us fifty sheep.

'Will ye be all right here, Malie?' Adame asks. His face hardens when his gaze lands on Johne's sleeping form.

I link my arm through Adame's and guide him away from my husband. 'Aye, I'll be fine here on my own.'

Adame makes a sound at the back of his throat. 'I mean, once he wakes up, will ye be all right? He can get into a right temper, ye know.'

I purse my lips together. 'He'll be merry to see me, I'm sure. Ye were gone for weeks.' He'll have missed me and will be grateful for everyone's help – I'm sure of it. Then there's news of the bairn. 'We'll be all right. We will,' I assure him.

Adame pauses at the door, allowing me to slip outside before him, a habit formed when we were children. 'Has Johne said anything since we brought him to you?' he asks, cocking his head back to the house.

'He's been mostly senseless. I wish he could tell me what happened.'

A flicker of emotion passes over my brother's face. 'Aye, nothin' to worry about. Just a terrible storm, and Johne was in the wrong place at the wrong time.'

'I don't understand how a hook could've gouged him so deeply. What was he doing at the stern of the boat in that storm? Why didn't he move somewhere safe?'

Adame pauses. 'I saw all those marks on yeh arms over the summer, Malie. And on one of your eyes before we set sail. Father shouldn't have let ye marry him.'

I suck in a breath. What has this to do with what happened to Johne on that boat? 'Och. Don't worry about me, brother. We'll be all right.' I place a hand over my stomach. Adame is kind to worry about me, but once Johne has recovered, we can start anew. Those thunderous moods will be behind us.

I try not to think about the night before he left. He wasn't himself.

'Adame!' Patrik calls impatiently from up the path.

My kind younger brother wraps his arms around me in an awkward hug. It takes me by surprise as he hasn't done so since my wedding day. 'I'm sorry,' he whispers, releasing me and turning to trudge along the path towards Patrik, leaving me confused about the nature of his apology.

'Thank you.' I wave but neither brother turns back. A wind whips up from the sea and a white-tailed eagle circles above the flock, eyeing off the last three lambs on the hill. My brothers will be sure to herd them into the dyke before they go. I let out a shaky breath as I retreat inside, shutting out the wind.

I pick up the feathery pillow from the stone bench and gently lift Johne's head, nestling it beneath him. As I'm lured across the room towards the sweet-smelling bannock, my gaze rests on the stone on the bench: the reddish-tinged stone Bessie brought from the kirkyard. As if it were boiling in the pot once more, I juggle it between my hands and tuck it back under Johne's injured leg, and draw the woollen blanket over his limp body to hide the devilish stone beneath.

Nightfall can't come soon enough. I circle the hearth like the eagle in the sky, reliving my brothers' movements from the bench to the bed and their subsequent hasty escape, returning again and again to the same agonising question: did they *see* the stone?

~

Bessie returns after sunset with a pot of food which she sets outside the door, declaring: 'That's for Henrye and peedie James. I will see 'em when I'm done here.' She marches off with a vessel tucked under her arm before I can ask anything of her. An hour later, she's back with the hem of her dress dipped in damp sand and the vessel filled with salt water that sloshes over the rim and splashes down her front.

'Here, let me help you.' I take the pot from her shaking hands and place it on the cupboard. She has walked from the northern end of the village, traipsing back and forth along the shore to see me. I must do something, if only to keep myself busy.

'Ye have a dead lamb out there,' Bessie says.

'What? Another one?' That leaves us with only two lambs! No fish, damaged crops and dwindling livestock. My breath hitches. How can we go on like this?

'Aye, the eagles are picking them off up and down the coast. Don't leave no meat behind either.'

‘Eagles?’ I groan. ‘Och, there was one circling the flock earlier.’ I must dispose of the lamb before Johne regains consciousness.

I pour Bessie a mug of whisky and usher her to sit for a moment. She accepts the mug but not the offer to rest. ‘Nae, we must begin,’ she says, draining the liquid and wiping her mouth with the back of her hand. She glances at the empty bench and then to the bed at the rear of the cottage where Johne remains in the same position as my brothers left him. ‘Did you move the stone, too?’

‘Yes.’ I do not mention it was moved as an afterthought. ‘Will it still work?’ I’m still uncertain what it is we’re doing.

‘Aye.’ She looks at me then tilts her head. Shuffles closer and sniffs the air. ‘Yer with child,’ she states.

My mouth drops open. ‘How did you know?’

A flicker of fear shadows her face. ‘Och. Does he know yet?’ She glances at Johne and shakes her head. ‘Nae, I suppose he doesn’t. Let’s hope he takes good care of ye now, lass.’

‘Now? Bessie—’

‘Bring me the three stones.’

I hastily gather them and place them on the cupboard beside the water vessel. They are cold to touch.

‘And now,’ she says, ‘drop them into the water vessel.’

The greyish stone from the hill sinks to the bottom; the moss-covered seashore stone sinks too, the water clear and still. When I drop the reddish-tinged stone from the kirkyard into the vessel, the stone sizzles and turns as though it was plucked from the fire. ‘What is it, Bessie?’

She clucks her tongue. 'A spirit troubles ye husband. We must cleanse him.'

'Do you mean the sea spirit, Bessie?'

She ignores my question, scooping up the vessel and kneeling at Johne's bedside. She plucks the silvery cloth from her coat pocket and soaks it in the water. She washes Johne's face, his arms and the skin around his wound, all the while whispering in Norn, the Old Norse language. Hairs prickle on my arms while anticipation and fear thrum beneath the surface. Johne is limp and dozy but breathing at a more regular rhythm. I don't want to think about what will happen if he wakes to Bessie's chanting and the stone-washing. She towels him off and redresses the wound while I shift my weight from foot to foot at the end of the bed.

Satisfied that he is now both cleansed and dry, she empties the vessel outside the cottage and leaves it by the door, where she trades it for the pot of food. 'I'll get this over to Henrye and James and then I'll come back.'

'All right, thank you.' I wring my hands, feeling both relieved and bereft by her impending departure. 'Bessie. What happens now?'

She shrugs but does not meet my gaze. 'We do it again and again until your husband is healed. Then it is done.'

I nod as she departs. We'll do it again and again. All right: we have a plan, and this plan gives me something to focus my thoughts on. We'll cleanse him until he heals. Ignoring the niggling question about *what*, exactly, will be done.

Five

Malie

They tend to haul out at dawn, just as I do. Out of bed, no time to linger. At the Point, glossy, grey-skinned seals laze about. No pups yet: too early for that. I can't see her. She could be hidden among the swollen grey figures, but I sense she's not ashore. It's impossible to hide on these islands – you must be in the sea. Rolling hills of green fields slope down to the waterfront. Although the skies are often shades of grey, the land is craggy, damp and green. Not many trees due to the Atlantic gales, and with only pockets of stunted woodlands, we rely on stone or driftwood and imported Norwegian pine, larch, deal and fir for our boats. The land is mostly low and exposed; the only shelter from the wind is the sandstone cottages in their autumn hues of grey, red and yellow. Each stone is quarried from the shore and laid partly sunken into the ground to form a barrier against the harsh winds.

The sun peeks out from the horizon and rays of light pierce the ocean. Shadows dance on the waves like a candle flickering in a darkened room. I'd best get back. Aye, it's easier to come here when the men are away. Bessie will return soon. She came at noon for the second cleansing ritual but when she came back before supper for the third I sent her home. She could barely keep her eyes open. Told her to return in the morning: we'd do the third cleansing then. Besides, I was worried my family might see her walking back and forth across the island. Here I am partially hidden by the curve of the shore which tucks me out of sight of Adame's house. Elinor will be busy with the bairn. Only Henrye, were he out in the peat bog, could see me.

As a child, I'd creep along the rocks and watch the seals and their playful antics, more interesting than the rough-and-tumble play of my brothers. It was a place to escape the boys. The men. I'd nestle in the rocks and observe the seal nursery, pups barking and clumsy and falling into shallow pools as they learned to swim. I recall my own awkwardness when Mother tried to teach me how to move in the water. How to breathe. The strokes, coordinating both arms and legs in unison, moving through the cold water, holding the breath and then releasing it. Our daily lessons in warm weather felt useless: I just couldn't get it. I felt incapable of swimming but as much as I was clumsy in the water, I was always happy to be there. To feel buoyant and free, to share something with Mother that no other could. My lessons were a secret, so Father wouldn't find out.

I could not swim, until one day I could. The strokes, the coordination, the breath, it came together all at once. I was graceful like a selkie, like Mother. My muscles twitch at the thought of moving my limbs and the grace of it all. How freeing it was to glide through the water like a seal. A seal with no seal skin.

Mother was the only woman on the island who could swim with grace, as though she were born from the ocean itself. I suppose that's because she was. She came to the island with a pelt, and she left in one too. Sometimes I'd forget – she seemed like a normal mother to me. But then I'd see her at the kirk or in the village with the other mothers and realise my mother was not like them at all.

It's a strange memory to think about now as I meander back along the shore, the Point behind me and the curved shore dotted with houses ahead. Now my toes sink into sand so I tiptoe, tiptoe so as not to leave behind my footprints. I follow the sound of waves and the knocking of a boat against the rocks. It's him again. The fisherman: Henrye Sinclair.

I flush with shame. I shouldn't be here. I should be tending to my husband, not checking on the seals. Henrye leaps off the boat and ties it to the narrow, rickety pier leading him from sea to sand. I quicken my pace so that our paths do not cross but his stride is long and we meet on the moorland. I lower my gaze and he dips his head indicating that I should go ahead of him. I charge forwards, clutching my boots, feeling the nakedness of my feet under his scrutiny. Johne would not be happy at all.

Henrye clears his throat, and I run on. He does it again and I stop to spin around, only to find him close to me. His woollen breeches are baggy at the knees from frequent crouching or leaning on the ground. His jacket has a patch unevenly sewn by the shoulder. Henrye's throat gulps and he looks down, taking off his hat before meeting my gaze. Heavy brows, an untamed beard and gentle eyes.

'She's, uh, she's all right,' he says in a deep timbre that isn't the usual booming tone for an Orcadian contesting the wind; rather, it is a warm undertone that hugs the breeze. I suppose he doesn't have many opportunities to speak. Henrye has mostly kept to himself since his wife died. Guilt crashes into me like rough waves against rock. It's true I've avoided him since Beatrice drowned. It hurt too much to see the grief on his face, to feel it in my heart. Again.

'Who?' I ask as an unwanted image of my mother comes to mind.

His cheeks flush and he nods back at the inlet. Bites on his windburned lower lip. 'The cow. The one you come looking for.'

Anger ripples through me and I brace myself to deny it, but it is quickly doused by relief. 'Where is she?' I ask. I was worried about her, even if I didn't want to admit it.

'She hauled out up there with the herd and then dived back into the water. She's easy to spot with that speckled pelt of hers.'

I gnaw on the inside of my mouth, wondering how, in this moment, Henrye, a near stranger, can know more about me than all the men in my family, my husband included.

'She was lookin' for ye, too,' he murmurs.

'For me?' I ask. Another flutter. She was there for me yesterday, too. I knew it. Henrye has seen more than I realise, which means I have not been as careful as I thought. If Henrye knows, then it's possible Johne – or my father – knows what I've been up to as well.

Henrye tilts his head, studying me. 'I remember how you and your ma played together in the water. I was envious of that. When my pa took me out fishin', I was never allowed to play with the seal pups.'

A memory rolls in, like waves on the shore. 'You're ready, my girl.' Mama rises from the sea, slicks back her dark hair. Wipes salty water from her sun-kissed skin. Her eyes twinkle.

'Ready for what?' I ask, paddling in the shallows.

'See the land?' She points into the distance. The shore was not familiar; we were not near our home. We'd taken Father's boat. We were somewhere up on the northern tip of the island.

I see it then. Like a seal bobbing in the ocean, a glimpse of an island that wasn't there before. I forget to tread the water, and I slip under the surface before kicking back up and blinking away the salty water. It's still there.

'We'll swim across the sea until we're halfway here, halfway there.' Mother is awestruck.

I shake my head; hair flicks in my face. Dark with red undertones, so different in the sea than on the land. When dry it's curly, buoyant and auburn. Silken and slick against my back when wet. The water transforms everything. Sand, hair and even the way we move, shifting into an altogether different being.

'It's too far.' I glance back at the shore, anxious my father will appear. 'And the undercurrent is too strong. It's dangerous.' Mother taught me to swim, but Father taught me how to read the tidal currents. I see that two great masses of water rage in opposition like two male orcas rivalling over a mate.

'No, Malie. Can't you feel it? You belong in the sea. We both do.' She dives into the water, disappears beneath the waves. I tread water as I wait for her to resurface. A minute passes, then another, and then, when it feels as though I cannot hold back my panic any longer, she rises from the sea and sucks air deep into her lungs, her face basking in the sunlight.

Mother has always belonged at sea. Her skin is more supple, clear and plump. Over the preceding winter, it had peeled and flaked, her hair limp and thin, her skin pale. But here, in the sea, the warm air, the salt, the water and space, she is restored.

Mama waves and when I smile back, her grin widens – bigger than I have even seen it in the weeks since we have taken to the water every day. It's as though she's preparing for something. I asked her why she was swimming so often, even though Father didn't like it. She told me, 'It is time, and therefore I must.'

We lock eyes and my heart swells, and I can feel what she feels. The sea does feel like home.

Mama waves me over to her. And she dives back under, her feet bonding together like a tail as she slips into the sea. I tread water. The smile falls from my face as she disappears once more. The distance stretches between us. Is she swimming towards me, or away? 'Mama!'

'Malie?' Henrye's voice is laced with concern and the memory is pulled away like an ebb tide.

'Nae,' I say to him now. 'Nae, I only swam with my mother. That seal, it was only after she was gone ...' I was drawn to the shore, looking out at the horizon, waiting for Mother to come home. Not long after that day, my mother waded out to sea and never came back. But my seal did. She'd haul out on the rock as the tide came in, year after year. As though she was looking for me too. So, it couldn't have been the same seal.

'Aye, my mistake then.' Henrye places his hat back onto his head. 'She was lookin' for ye, nevertheless. I thought you'd want to know she was all right.'

I swallow but my mouth is dry from the salty wind and the confusion. Henrye's boy appears and leans into his father's side. James looks a lot like Henrye: thick brows, full lips and freckled skin. His eyes, though, they are his mother's sky blue. I blink back tears. James is just a little boy, a boy without his mother. He'd be about seven years old now. Only a little older than I was when I lost mine.

Henrye takes off his son's hat, ruffles his hair and replaces it. His freckle-dotted cheeks redden. 'James, say hello.'

Father was not as gentle-natured with me after Mother left. There was no time or place for grief: we just had to get on with things. I had to look after my brothers, as my mother once did. I can see James is well cared for; Beatrice would be so proud of them both.

James scuffs his boot in the sand. 'Hi, Malie.'

He remembers me. The guilt and regret sit heavily on my heart. 'Hello, James.'

'Is your husband all right?' Henrye asks. 'Heard he was injured at sea.'

I blink. 'Johne? Aye, yes, he will be. At least, I do hope so. He's not been well.' The sun sits higher now and tension courses through my body. 'I must get back before he wakes.' I'm late. Bessie will be there by now – what if Johne's already awake? 'Bye, James. Good to see you.'

Henrye taps his hat and the connection is broken. Our shared history, our love for Beatrice is hidden in the shadows. Back to passing strangers on the shore. I turn and run, feet sinking into dry sand and then sludgy grass, one foot in front of the other. Retracing my steps home.

~

Voices carry on the breeze, and I pause at the threshold of the cottage. Johne is awake! I hope Bessie is already gone. In my head, Mother's voice reminds me not to linger at the doorway as the bairn may get stuck during birth. I steady myself against the stone wall and prod away Mother's voice so I can focus on the exchange.

'You saw it, didn't ye?' Johne asks, an edge to his voice.

'Aye, I saw it.' Another gruff voice says in response. 'Finnman. *Selkie*.'

My breath draws in and my head swirls as though I'm being tumbled about in the sea. It is not Bessie but my father. He has come before I have tended to my husband. Did Bessie not come? Oh God, I hope she wasn't here when Father arrived.

'Bad omen,' Johne says. 'He's driven away all the fish.'

'What are we going to do, Father?' Adame asks. Och, he is here too. His presence goes a little way to settling my nerves.

'We'll do what we must.'

The hairs on the back of my neck stand on end.

'Nae, we can't kill him,' Adame protests. 'It's bad luck. We can't kill a Finnman. Or a selkie.'

'We can and we will,' Father says in a tone that leaves no space for negotiation.

'But what about Mother?' Adame asks, his voice breaking.

A long pause. 'Do not speak of her. Your loyalty should be with me. I'm not the one who left. It's been twenty summers, son. She's long gone.'

'What if you take her?' Adame pleads. 'Or her bairns?' He shakes his head. 'Pups, I mean. What then? What if you take her away, forever?'

A fist slams down on stone. 'I said,' Father's voice deepens and darkens, 'there will be no speak'n of her!'

All is quiet for a moment, and when my father speaks again he is back in control. 'Now that Johne has recovered, we'll go back to the sea and hunt the Finnman. We'll leave tomorrow. For now, we'll stay close to shore. Keep searching.'

A huff, heavy feet and then Adame is in the doorway, brimming with tension. His red-tinged cheeks are smoking like the peat fire.

My head still swirls, and I can't be sure whether it is being with child or what I've overhead that has me off kilter. 'What is it?' I whisper.

He shakes his head and elbows past me. My tongue feels heavy as I try to find my voice. An unwanted thought: I should have gone through the door first. 'Adame?'

He scuffs his boot on the gravel path. 'I'll come by and check on you before dusk, all right?' Then he's gone.

Inside the cottage, my husband sits upright on the edge of the bed. There is colour back in his face.

'Johne, you're awake. I was so worried about you,' I say, sidestepping Father who, like my brother, is filled with tension. His forehead is deeply creased, his eyebrows knitted together as if he were wound up in knots. 'Let me clean your wound and replace the bandage.'

Johne's expression darkens upon seeing me. 'Already been cleaned,' he growls, and I freeze, the true meaning of his words hitting me with force. I step backwards. Bessie was here. What if he woke while she was cleansing him? Och, he'll be furious that I wasn't here and that someone else tended him while he was ill and weak. He is about to speak again but his gaze flickers towards my father, and his face softens, though he still speaks with a gruffness that does little to hide his irritation. 'Where've you been, Malie?'

'I'm sorry.' The words come out in a rush. 'I needed fresh air. I was so worried about you, Johne. I went for a walk while you slept and collected some herbs for your wound. Let me change your bandage again.' I place the freshly picked cockalowrie onto the table and kneel in front of him to unwind the bandage. 'The daisy roots infused in water, or whisky if you prefer, will aid the healing process.'

'Aye, whisky.' Johne leans back against the stone wall, closes his eyes and groans.

Father clears his throat. I feel him watching me, noting the salty tang on my skin, the damp sand on the hem of my woollen dress. He knows where I've been. He *knows*.

Johne sits upright and flinches. The wound pulses again: trickles of blood spill out between the linen threads. I'd pulled it tight but just like the sea blood oozes and trickles into every crevice. I dab it with a clean cloth and soak up the dried specks of blood. Johne flinches but doesn't say anything in Father's presence.

'The ships will come through soon; we expect them any week now. We'll have nothin' to trade.' Johne doesn't like to be still. An injury won't prevent him from taking to the seas. The vessels usually come in the first week of summer, but the winter lingers into spring, delaying travels. Sea ice chokes the harbours, the Dutch coast and the Denmark Strait, in recent years. We'd heard Iceland is exceptionally severe.

'Aye,' Father says. 'We must purchase oak. Build a bigger boat. The Norwegians make them for the deep sea.' Johne agrees, telling him to fetch him tomorrow for the voyage but father doesn't respond. He wants Father to leave now. I want him to stay, eager to delay the questions about Bessie, the tension, a thick fog lingering between us. 'You didn't tell me what happened out there, Johne,' I say. 'How were you injured?'

Johne grunts and leans his head back against the wall. Father speaks for him. 'A righteous storm, Malie. Johne attempted to cut the nets free, but the wild weather threw him about and he got caught up in a longline.'

I frown, thinking it must have been with some force that a hook wedged into my husband's leg. Johne scoffs. 'I saw 'em out there. The selkies. Diving in and out of the sea without a care in the world. And as soon as I'd seen 'em the sky turned dark and stormy. They brought the weather with them to send us back to land. *They* did this.' He says *they*, but his eyes pin me like an eagle pins their prey. 'And then there was the Finnman in that long, narrow boat.'

'Finnman?' I ask. Selkies in the sea and a Finnman, too. Aye, one and the same. Selkies slip from their seal skins and seduce lonely fishermen, but a Finnman takes the form of man and seduces lonely wives. Men, women and the sea, all at their mercy.

'Aye,' Father says. 'I saw him.'

'We won't survive the winter if we don't fight back,' Johne insists.

'Aye, we'll do what must be done,' Father says in that tone that means there's no changing his mind.

'You can't mean that, Father.'

He turns his back on me and moves towards the door.

I tie up the fresh linen on Johne's leg, but he shrugs me away. 'Leave me to rest.'

Father nods and exits without a word more. Soon Johne's head lolls back and he begins to snore. I am grateful for this moment of peace – and to avoid explaining the stone ritual and Bessie's presence. Not when he's already so angry about the storm and the selkies and the injury.

I sweep the sand out of the cottage. Sweep it out, out, out. Tomorrow it will be back. It always comes back. Sand on the floor, salt on the skin. I can always rely on the tides to come in and out, and with it the winds bring the sand, sprinkling gold dust across the island. No matter how much I try, just like Mother, I cannot be parted from the sea.

Six

Malie

Her song stretches through the thick of crashing waves and deafening wind. At the Point, I break away from the group of women, my brothers' wives and their children, to study the herd. She's there, on her own. Her piercing eyes serenade me. Is this how Father felt the day he met Mother: powerless before her charms?

At the approach of footsteps, I kneel on the damp sand and collect three long and narrow razor clams that have washed ashore after another storm. They clink against the others in the caisie. The heather is wearing away and the open-weave holes have stretched so that any smaller clam may fall through the gaps. I will make another before the baby comes.

'Malie, how is Johne?' asks Elinor. Her bairn, Nicholas, just a few months old, is fast asleep in a basket on the sand facing the hills, unbothered by the rising breeze. Elinor came from Eday, up in the north isles, and had left behind her family and a small village to join the MacDuffie clan. When my brothers wed the population of our peedie parish expanded quickly, especially once the bairns came along. As lovely as a growing family is, there is now a considerable demand on our provisions. Less meat, grain and textiles to trade when the fleets disembark in the harbour to replenish their supplies. Anne's two older boys dig around the rock pools while her youngest boy sits on a linen blanket on the sand with Kattrine and Marion's bairns – all born within a few months of each other. Nicholas is the youngest. We met at Anne's earlier in the day, walking south along the foreshore together, scouring the shelled sand for molluscs. The fish have gone but there's enough bait to be found.

I shrug. 'Aye, he's doing all right.'

'He'll be back at sea in no time, I'm sure,' she says with a wink.

'Aye, I'm sure.' I dig around, searching for more clams. I settle on seaweed, shaking the sand loose before adding it to the caisie. I pad it out so the clams stay nestled like shag eggs in a nest. The large, long-necked geese-like birds don't seem to mind the rubbery texture of seaweed. 'Thank you for the food and bread. Your bere bannock was delicious.'

Elinor beams. 'It's the least I could do. I'm sorry I couldn't come by and see ye. Nicholas didn't sleep a wink during that storm – and neither did I.' Sensing his mother talking about him, Nicholas grizzles from the basket by her feet. Elinor gently shushes him, and he settles once more. It has not been easy to see the other wives having babies and not having one of my own. I felt I was letting Johne down. He has no family left. I know how much it means for him to have one of his own. I know he didn't mean to, but he made me feel like a disappointment. Like there was something wrong with me. Until now, that is. I absentmindedly stroke my belly, wondering about the size and shape of my own baby. Half the size of one of these clams, I reckon. Swaddled inside my abdomen, like Elinor's bairn in the basket.

'And you, Malie? Are you all right?' Elinor takes a good look at me, in the same way Adame does, as though they know something about me that I do not. I cannot tell her about the bairn, not until I've shared it with Johne. He was so angry about Bessie; I couldn't bring myself to tell him. Imagine if he learned that the old woman was the first to know I am expecting a child?

After Father left and Johne roused from his sleep, he called me to him. I was preparing his supper and hadn't heard him stir. He saw me flinch, beckoning me closer with a low, steady voice. His leg still bothers him, and he cannot put his whole weight on it for long, so I stood a little way back, the door behind me. An easy escape should I need one.

'How could ye have that devilish witch in our house?' His face reddened, and his fists gripped the edge of the bed, ready to leap. 'What were ye thinkin', Malie?'

I wrung my hands together. 'I wasn't thinking, you're right. I only wanted you to be better, Johne. Can't you see? You were injured and very ill. She just washed you and made sure you drank water, and it worked, didn't it? There's no harm in it.'

'She was saying some kind of spell,' he said, his face twisted in disgust. 'I heard her mumblin' and sayin' somethin' to me in Old Norse, but I couldn't open me eyes. It's like I was trapped in my body. She did somethin' devilish – I'm sure of it.'

'Bessie's just an old woman who wanted to help us. I didn't know what else to do,' I said and stepped forwards. He reared up and I paused a few feet from him.

'Then why did I wake to find that old witch washing me face and me wife nowhere to be seen?' he growled.

'I was out walking.' I picked at my cuticles. 'I thought I'd be back before she arrived. I'm sorry. I should've been here. I'm sorry I wasn't.' I wanted to move towards him, wrap my arms around him, but just like the sky before a storm, his face was dark, clouded and unpredictable. I kept my distance.

'Yer lucky I sent her away before your father came,' he muttered, uncurling his fists and leaning back against the wall again. The colour drained from his face, and I saw it then: the truth behind his anger. He was ashamed. If Father came while an old woman was caring for him, he'd have not liked it. He is not one to show any weakness. I felt a rise in tenderness for him in that moment. I cannot imagine how hard it must be to have your body restrict your movements, so you could not do what you could normally do. I don't like to keep still much either and, aside from Bessie, I don't let people look after me; I've always looked after others. That's how it's always been. With the fight gone from both of us, I moved to him, nestling into his side. He'd been in such a bad temper before he left: maybe this would bring us closer together. It was a long moment before he nudged me aside so he could wrap his arm around my shoulder. We sat there for a long time, so long I should have told him about the bairn.

'Malie?' Elinor asks me again. '*Are* you all right?'

I bristle. 'Aye, I'm fine. I'm not the one with a hook in me leg,' I say, and regret my tone immediately as her face falls. Elinor is always kind to me, even when many others are not.

'No, of course.' She laughs it off but it does not reach her eyes. 'Had me worried, though,' she says and then speaks in a louder voice to the group of women as they gather around, caisies brimming with limpets. 'That storm, I wasn't sure they'd be back.'

'Och, it was a wild storm,' Kattrine says, gripping Marion's arm as she surveys the sky. 'I took the bairns to Marion's house. I don't like staying at home on my own when the weather is that wild.'

Wild, yes, but we've had far worse. Though, to be fair, severe storms have become more frequent, even for summer. Island storms are different from what the sisters are used to in the Scottish Highlands. Father arranged marriages for Jerome and William to Kattrine and Marion through their father, whom he'd met in Inverness. It's a busy Scottish port and market town. Their dresses are cut different from ours, tailored to fit their waif-like bodies. We make our own clothing here. Even after several years, the two women have not acclimated to the island weather nor the dangers at sea. Not to mention they speak so softly; we have to strain to hear them over the roaring wind and sea.

I do understand their trepidation though. It is a risk every time the men go to sea: the fear that no men from the MacDuffie family will return. Kattrine and Marion have one child each, and Patrik and his wife, Anne, have three. Like my mother, she had one after the other, the eldest now almost four years old. Anne has always been a practical type of woman; she gets things done. Born in Westray, she is the sturdiest of us all, her corpulent body made to brace against the ferocious Arctic winds. She clicks her tongue. 'Nae, it's in their blood to navigate a storm. They got the instinct for it. No need to worry.'

'What about the Finnman?' I ask. 'The one they saw but could not catch? The men say he swept away the fish in the sea. He hasn't left us anything.'

'Silocha nan Ron,' Anne mutters. *Children of the seals.*

I flinch. Kattrine glances at Anne, wide-eyed, but Anne, unheeding of the shared looks, has found a limpet and digs it up, slipping it into her caisie. Marion gasps with what sounds like delight. She often brings gossip and news from the letters she receives from her friends and family in Inverness. I can only imagine what she tells her childhood friends about the lore of our island, or what she says about my family. Elinor shifts closer to me. Though there were few of them, children in the town occasionally tormented my brothers and me, calling us children of seals. After all, I am the daughter of a selkie. The children looked at us with a mixture of awe and caution. I suppose it could have hindered my marriage prospects but Johne had never cared about all that. I am also a daughter of a fisherman, from a family of fisherman, and that meant something to Johne. Until now, of course.

We all watch on as Anne turns away, the overflowing basket clattering against her hip. Last year, there was a sighting of a Finnman off the coast of Westray, and Anne's parents wrote to her and warned her about our family: that our selkie kin may have returned. She told Patrik, who told Adame, who shared it with me. I rub at the hardened skin on the palm of my hand, the calluses. Selkie hands. Stories of my childhood swirl like a whirlpool in my head, and I am dizzy again. I grip the caisie tighter, regaining my balance.

The women disperse, their attention back to scouring the shoreline. I find myself inching further south towards the Point, where the expectant seals have gathered. Always drawn to the creatures of the sea, those who do not judge me, do not expect anything of me. My seal worms on the mossy rocks. I skim across the sand, drawn closer to her, not wanting to dwell on Anne's cruel words. It's best to keep moving, edge the worries out of my mind. It's the best thing for the bairn.

I collect whelks, the shellfish Johne uses for bait. He's eager to get back out to sea but Father delayed the voyage until he is steadier on his feet. The fleets will arrive soon and we have no fish for the visiting Norwegians, who supply us with timber for the boats. If we're low on fish, we must trade more mutton, but our flocks barely survived last winter. We have little linen after the crops were damaged in the wild storms, and I'll need to keep some for the bairn. Only half the crop is flourishing with blue flax flowers popping up in recent days. Flax usually grows so easily here; it needs a short growing season, which has worked well for our long winters and short springs. It's the ferocious storms that are the problem.

Though Johne's leg is healing nicely he's not been up and about as he usually is. If he can go fishing again then he'll feel more like himself, more open to my news about the bairn. I must tell him soon before he notices, or, worse, someone else discovers I am with child. If Bessie guessed then maybe someone else could too. My breasts feel fuller, my hips wider, and even my scent has changed. Something new in the salty air, something primal. I will tell him soon.

Her song pierces my thoughts, the other seals shifting away as mine makes space for herself on the rocks. Her dark eyes meet mine. I am a child of the seals. I want to scream it aloud, so that Anne and everyone else can hear me, but I don't. I remain silent. No use causing ripples when there's so much strain in the village already. I draw in a deep breath. Life will soon change for the better. I'll have a bairn and I'll be just like the other wives. There will be nothing to set me apart. We'll all be the same.

Mother's words ring in my ears. *Keep something for yourself, Malie.*

~

The day 'atween the weathers is the last time we see the sun for several days. Autumn arrives early with overcast and mostly cloudy days, skies laden with thick grey frosts almost every night. The wind is always in the east and it's cold. It's only early July. Indoors, it is heavy and grey, too.

'Malie, that's enough,' Johne grunts and flicks my hand away. 'No more bandages.' He pulls the mended woollen breeches on over his linen braies.

I sigh. 'I must tend to it, Johne.' He shuffles back and forth across the room, determined to take to the seas by week's end, which is the latest my father will allow. This will be the last time before the fleet is expected to arrive. Johne has still been out rounding up the flock and cutting peat. His wound is crusty and an uneven layer of hardened skin conceals it. It is healing but any nick could rip it back open, the ebb and flow of blood oozing once more down his leg. My nose tingles at the anticipated smell of blood. There's an uneasy sensation at the back of my throat.

'Tend to my stomach instead. That mutton won't cook itself.' My stomach recoils. He's right, the mutton must be cooked today. I have put it off long enough. He plonks down on the stone bench and folds his arms across his chest. 'I'm going to see your father after church this morning. We must get back to sea tomorrow or we'll nae make it through winter. No use waitin' until the end of the week. I'm all right to go. No bandage needed.'

'Church?' It's a long walk to the kirk. An hour or more with his limp. I had thought he wasn't ready for that. *I'm* not ready for that. My chest twinges with guilt at the swell of disappointment I feel. It's just that I haven't told him about the bairn, and it feels wrong to keep it from him. Our presence in church, together, will only fortify the feeling.

Johne blamed the selkies and Father agreed with him. What plan are they concocting? Catch more fish or catch a Finnman? My father and brothers have scoured the shores and there's been no further sighting of him. Is that why Johne is so eager to get back out there? Not to catch fish but to punish the Finnman?

I heat the pot on the fire and, as Johne scuffs outside to check on the sheep, I prepare the leg of mutton, choosing to keep it on the bone for a fuller flavour as it slowly cooks on the hearth while we're at church. The earthy smell of peat entwined with the meat will scent the house for days. A wave of revulsion brings on the nausea. Usually, I'd enjoy the dark, sweetened meat, but all I crave now is fish, which must be rationed. The measly six herring were smoked and cured for later. I hope to keep them for myself.

There's a watery sensation in my mouth; I swallow it back. I'll be sure to avoid Johne and the sheep, as my unusually sensitive stomach will expose my secret. I will tell him when I'm ready. When things have settled, maybe after he's back from sea. Being on the boat will do him good. He's more relaxed there and in the days that follow, in the same way my mother was when she swam. The injury is only a setback.

I collect wormwood from the garden, which is sheltered from the westerly winds by the stone cottage. Unlike the corn crops or the beremeal, of which we'd only salvaged half after the storm, we still have potatoes if they don't rot underground with the increased rainfall.

I am startled by a thin voice on the breeze. 'Malie.'

Panic stirs within me. 'Bessie! You shouldn't be here.' I drag her behind the house where, thank God, we can't be seen from the sheep dyke.

'Malie.' She grips my forearm with a strength that surprises me. The skin on her hand is soft and folded but the muscle underneath is taut. 'Malie, listen to me.'

'What is it? You're scaring me.' She loosens her grip and shakes her head as if to gather her thoughts. She is wheezy and dishevelled. Has she run all the way here? Impossible at her age. 'What is it?' I ask again, gentler this time.

'Malie. I think I've made a grave mistake saving yeh husband.'

'Saving Johne? Nae, I am grateful for your help, Bessie, even if my husband is not.'

She shakes her head vehemently. 'Nae. Somethin' bad is comin',' Malie. Shouldn't have interfered with nature.'

'You mean let him die? I would not have allowed it.' I pause. 'What is coming?'

She swallows. 'A death.'

The wind extracts a shiver from me. 'What do you mean?

'I've seen it. Come next spring, a woman dies at the hands of a man. He strangles her. Right here on this island.'

The meaty smell has reinfiltrated my senses, and I taste acid on my tongue. I reach out for the wall to steady myself. 'Bessie, who is the woman?'

'My dear,' she says, her mouth curling back in regret, 'I think it's you.'

~

My stomach settles as the mutton changes colour from red to brown and the raw scent evaporates, replaced by a sweet and savoury aroma. Even so, I have no desire to eat it. Bessie's premonition has put me off my appetite.

She is always dependable and wise, and she saved my husband from the brink of death. Could this be true? Has she really seen my passing? The bairn is due in spring; I didn't think to ask her if she knew whether I was still with child at the time. She hurried away before Johne could stumble across her. Johne can get into a right temper but surely he's not capable of murder. And certainly not of me. Surely not.

It hasn't been too difficult to hide my secret from him. He's barely looked at me since his return. What happened with my Father is now happening all over again with my husband. When Johne sees me, he sees a selkie. It hurts me, because I have strived all my life to be nothing like my mother. To not remind Father of the pain she caused him when she chose the sea over our family. I've always put family first. It's possible

Johne is just consumed by his injury and his frustration at being incapable of hauling in the fish nets at the piers each morning. They're still empty. Not even the seals have bothered snooping around them.

The last few years have been colder than anyone on the island recalls. More snow, longer winters and shorter growing seasons, which have constrained our crops. We used our limited grains to replant for this year's crops rather than eating them. Our flock is small, and with only two lambs remaining, we can't cull too many sheep or we'll have none to breed. I heard about an island further north where a disease wiped out all their cattle. Adame and my other brothers lost many calves and milking cows over winter. Only one remains. The only livestock thriving is Henrye's geese. Not that I'd draw any attention to that. The geese have a habit of raiding our crops.

A draught blows in the open doorway, swirling and circling the room. I'm shivery but also damp with sweat. I pull the shawl tighter around my shoulders and catch a glimpse of Johne up the hill cutting peat, a fierce expression on his face. My brothers will be down to help soon; more bodies make for quicker work. As I watch him, his eyes flick upwards and he looks at me like I'm a sheep he is about to slaughter. I shiver again and close the door. I hope he can get back to the sea soon. Shift all that tension into something useful. Nae, I'm sure it will all be fine. Bessie must be mistaken.

I return to the bubbling pot and find the smell is no longer appetising but nauseating once more. I get on with it because Johne's belly filled now will distract him from future empty bellies. Outside the wind continues to howl.

Seven

Henrye

Henrye sits with his son on the pew at the back of the kirk. He likes this vantage point. It's like being atop a crag, watching the seals frolic around as the sea crashes against the rocks and gulls circle overhead stalking their prey. From here, he can scan the environment. Observant, patient and persistent; all necessary qualities of a fisherman. His late father taught him that. It was a lesson that served him well at sea but was just as useful on land.

'Papa.' James tugs at Henrye's shirt. 'Will we look for whelks after the service?'

Since his mother's death, James has gone out on the boat with Henrye every day. He couldn't very well leave him alone. Besides, he prefers to keep him close. Bessie comes by to help them out when she can but Henrye doesn't like to rely too heavily on her. They live on opposite ends of the township and she doesn't move around as easily as she once did. 'Aye, we will collect the bait before the weather turns.' Not that there's much point. No fish. Nevertheless, it's good to keep up the skills, and they can feed the bait to the geese. Henrye intends to harvest more kelp while they're out too.

James smiles and kicks his legs for a moment before noticing a frayed edge at the knee of his breeches. He picks at it and the thread unravels, exposing more of his pale skin. It needs patching, again. Not that Henrye is very good at that sort of thing. 'James,' Henrye says, nudging him. 'Leave it be.' He cackles and kicks his legs back and forth. That's when Henrye notices the pants have shrunk. They sit well above James's ankle. How had he not seen this before today? His boy has lengthened no less than two inches over the summer and grown out of all his clothes. Henrye doesn't usually notice these things but now he sees it, he can't unsee it. These are the moments when he misses Beatrice the most, knowing she'd organise James's clothes before he could get the question out. She was a practical sort of woman, liked to get things done. Much like Bessie, the only person he can think of who might be able to help him. Beatrice was too impatient to be a skilled weaver but she did a good enough job. She'd often seek out Malie's help as she had a finer stitch. He can no longer ask his wife or her friend. Nae, he'd ask Bessie for help.

As if the very thought of her is enough to cobble her up in real life, she appears. Bessie plonks down on the seat beside James and squeezes him against her chest. 'Oh, my boy.' James giggles and wrestles free of her embrace but Henrye knows his son secretly relishes the affection. Like Henrye was, his boy is being raised without a mother. It has been three years since he lost Beatrice. Henrye's own mother died in childbirth and his father, though he lived a good life, was taken four winters ago. Whatever disease took hold had pecked away at him like a seabird feasting on a whale carcass. By the time he passed, there was little more of him to bury than bones. Less than twelve months later Henrye lost his wife too. It felt cruel to lose both wife and father so close together.

Henrye does his best to care for and protect his son but he does worry about him. What if something happens to Henrye? No siblings, no grandparents and no mother. James would be all alone.

Bessie turns to Henrye. 'And how are ye? I've made too much soup; I'll bring some around to ye.'

She's a matter-of-fact woman, a little odd at times, sure, but he likes her straightforwardness. He doesn't need to guess at what she might be thinkin'. 'Please, Bessie, there's no need—'

She waves him off. 'You'll be doin' me a favour, you will.'

Henrye sighs. He knows once Bessie has an idea in her head, it's best not to argue with her. Like him, she's widowed, and he thinks caring for them keeps her mind occupied. It's the least he can do and he does enjoy her cooking. It dawns on Henrye he should talk to Bessie about James. *She* could look out for his son if anything were to happen to him. Make it more formal. A fisherman's job is dangerous and it's only sensible to have a plan. Especially with the increasingly wild weather and reduction in supplies and provisions to trade – not to mention whisperings of the so-called Finnman rippling through town, picking up speed like a winter gale. People have lost their minds over far less. Then there's the MacDuffies.

Footsteps crunch beyond the door and Malie enters the kirk as though she's blown in with the wind. Always in a hurry. She tucks flyaway curls back behind her ear only for them to spring back up in an unruly manner anyway. When he was a lad, her quick pace was the first thing he noticed about Malie. It's so unlike the way other islanders move: slow and deliberate. But Malie has always been energetic and a bit impulsive. She was always moving but when her mother was around there was a natural rhythm to it. Now there's an edge to the constant movement, like a fish flitting about in the shallows, wary of a dogfish shark.

Henrye always imagines Johne with a mighty fin on his back. Predatory. Today he looks anything but as he hobbles behind Malie. He stops beside Henrye and snarls. 'Keep yeh geese off me crops, Sinclair.'

Malie looks at Henrye with wide eyes. Bessie stiffens beside him. Henrye shakes his head ever so slightly and Malie's shoulders drop. Johne's leg pains him so he doesn't even bother to look at Henrye again as he shuffles up the aisle. They take their place in the front pew, beside Neill. Her brothers and their wives fill out the two pews behind them. They'll all have travelled inland from the rear of their properties – east to west – traipsing over hills and through thick moorland. The trek has taken a toll on Johne; sweat sheens on his hard features, and the tension in his body gives away the immense pain he is in. Being at the southern point of the island, Henrye has the shortest trek to the church, following the shoreline along the south-west of the island.

The MacDuffies are the largest clan in the parish. While Henrye is a solo fisherman, taking only what he needs for his family, the MacDuffies' Yole is a ten-stroke construction with a twenty-one-foot keel. A bigger boat means a bigger crew, which brings in more fish. At least it did until recently. There are a few other men in the town who work with them: Duncan, Bernard and Angus. Sometimes they get some of the men over on Hoy to help. They all rely on the trades when the fleets come through in the summer, often stopping for two to three weeks to replenish provisions and shelter in the harbour from storms. It's been a lucrative trade but in recent years the fish were less abundant. Now, they'd all but disappeared. He doesn't blame them; the years have been bitterly cold.

Henrye was raised as a farmer and a fisherman, working the land and sea. Rather than sticking to traditional income sources, Henrye adapted to the vulnerable climate. Henrye has a small flock of sheep he keeps for meat over winter, and there're the greylag geese he trades either salted or smoked to visiting fleets or neighbouring islands, not to mention the pounds of feathers which are always in high demand for stuffing mattresses and pillows, or pens. Beatrice was adept at preparing those, but now when the time comes, Bessie helps him and shares a portion of the revenue. Kelp is something new – something his father encouraged him to do. Been told by someone up on Ronaldsay that it would soon be in demand. Henrye is willing to try anything to secure a future for his son. The MacDuffies have become so reliant on fish trades they've had to travel further and further into the deep sea in search of fish, but there is only so far the Yole can travel safely.

He's heard about the Finnman and how the MacDuffies were hunting him. When poor conditions make food scarce, it's only human nature to look for a reason; to find someone to blame. It's just that the MacDuffies seem to make a habit of blaming others rather than taking any kind of responsibility for themselves. Like Henrye they *could* diversify, focus their attention on solutions to their problems; but they'd rather intimidate and make threats to get what they need. While the cows and sheep dropped dead in the cold conditions, Henrye's geese are thriving.

As the Reverend approaches the podium, Neill senses Henrye's gaze on him and he looks back. His brows draw in and he puckers his mouth, turning back to the altar. The hair on the back of Henrye's neck stands on end. Without a word passing between them since he was a child, Neill sends a strong message in that momentary glance: *You don't belong*. Henrye sits on his hands so he doesn't launch himself at Malie's father.

There was a time when Henrye's father got along well with the MacDuffies. He and Neill even worked together at sea for a time: they were neighbours after all. That all changed when Malie's mother left. From then on, Henrye and his father became outsiders and, if he's being honest with himself, that's exactly what he'd like to remain. Being in the inner circle of the MacDuffies is more trouble than it's worth. He's already had enough pain and loss to last a lifetime.

His purpose in life is to provide for his son, give him a good life. A simple life but a good one. One day he'll get him off this island. Henrye watches as Malie leans away from Johne ever so slightly. It would go unnoticed to most people, even Johne himself, but Henrye sees it. He imagines her hands wringing in her lap, as if to warm herself, but it is the movement that keeps the fire going, for what would happen if she stopped? What would happen if she paid close attention to her husband and her father? Really saw them for who they truly are? What then?

Henrye grunts and Bessie looks at him with amusement. It's no use thinkin' about it, because what can she do? There's no escaping them.

They must all live on the island together, no matter their grievances.

Won't stop Henrye from keeping an eye on her anyway. Just to be sure. She fidgets about on her seat, which earns her a glare from Johne. Even though he'd rather avoid the MacDuffies altogether, her safety is important to Henrye. He doesn't trust them and neither should Malie. Not that he can tell her that. Why should she believe him? James shuffles closer to him and Henrye drags his gaze from the bothersome family. Tells himself it's best he keeps out of trouble.

~

The kirk, made of yellow and red sandstone, faces Hoy Sound, which draws both Henrye and James out after the sermon towards the cliff's edge. James enjoys foraging in the rock pools at ebb tide when the sea level is falling, but he's out of luck – the tide is coming now, waves rolling onto the sand, flooding the pools and rocks. The clouds hang low in a perfect horizontal line across the sky, leaving just a sliver of blue sky between it and the sea, just enough of an opening to see the rolling hills of Hoy. It's been a long time since he took James over to Rackwick beach with its giant boulders and its sweeping shoreline of sand as pink as a bairn's bottom. When Henrye was about James's age, a ship sank off Deerness and the two hundred prisoners aboard were lost. Almost fifty of them escaped, and, though most were rounded up, a few of the men hid and remained living on the island. The men don't give them any trouble when they travel across the Sound to make trades with the fleets. Like everyone else, they're just trying to survive. More folk live there now, young families, probably all at their kirk this morning, too.

James runs along the edge of the cliffs, chasing away a seagull pecking at something in the grassy mounds. Henrye senses Malie before he sees her, drifting towards the sea cliffs, pausing at the edge. Is she thinking about her seal? He wishes he didn't stop to talk to Malie that day; they hadn't spoken in so long. He's made things awkward between them. Should have left things the way they were. Now he is punished with a sense of longing to talk to her again. It's just that she looked so forlorn, and he knew she was looking for her seal friend. How could he resist taking away that moment of uncertainty and worry? It was such a simple gesture. Simple, yet dangerous.

She glances sideways at him, a flicker of a smile and then back at the sea, her gaze drawn to the grey seals bobbing in the waves. He hadn't noticed them until now. 'I was worried they'd killed a seal; that's why I was down at the shore after the men had returned.' She speaks in a low whisper and he leans into the wind to hear her, his eyes trained on the glossy figures in the sea. 'I saw something slippery and grey in the wagon. They were so angry, the men, I feared what they might've done.'

Before he speaks, Henrye glances over his shoulder at the townsfolk gathering in the kirkyard. Johne is perched against the stone gate, facing the kirk not the sea. He breathes out. 'Ach,' he says. 'It was only a basking shark.'

Malie turns sharply. 'A shark? Are you sure?'

'Adame told me so. Saw him at the port yesterday. He was telling me about the pitiful haul they brought in, few fish and an emaciated basking shark. Your father kept that one.' He tries to keep the disgust out of his voice but he's not certain he succeeds.

She slumps with relief, her hand at her chest. 'Och, I was so worried. Thank you for telling me so.'

'It's nothin,' he says and drags his eyes from her to the sea. 'There.' He points beyond the bobbing seals to the triangular black fin slinking under the murky waters.

Malie gasps as a moment passes and five gleaming heads and fins surface. She grins at Henrye. 'Orcas. I haven't seen them for some time.'

Henrye chuckles, his gaze trained on the pod. 'This is the best place to see them. I come here often. James loves them.' As he speaks his name, his son joins them, shouting out, 'Whales!'

Malie laughs. 'Isn't it wonderful, James?' And then she frowns as she takes in his clothes. 'Och, Henrye. James has grown so much. I'll weave him some new trousers and shirts.'

'Nae, I don't want to trouble ye. I'll ask Bessie to help.' He feels guilty relying on Bessie as she helps him so much already but relying on Malie would get her in deep water with Johne.

She shakes her head. 'It's no trouble at all. He'll need better fitting clothes come winter. Besides, it keeps me busy.'

Henrye smiles because he knows this about her. Even though he shouldn't accept her help, and he senses Johne is no longer looking at the kirk but at his wife smiling at their widowed neighbour, he agrees. He doesn't want to be responsible for taking away something that brings her joy.

Seagulls swoop the orcas, intent on nipping at their fins, no sense of the threat of the predator below. Henrye, however, knows the feeling. He feels Johne's eyes trained on the back of him. Henrye thanks Malie, and even though he doesn't want to, he turns his back on her and ushers his son northbound. He's promised himself he'll stay out of trouble, away from the MacDuffies, away from Malie. He doesn't look back.

'Papa, can we visit Mama?' James asks in a tone that causes a twinge in his heart.

'Aye, and your grandfather, too.'

James skips ahead to the kirkyard and Henrye feels some of the tension ease with the more distance they put between them and the parish. They follow the well-trodden path between the sea and the neatly aligned burial mounds to their right. To an outsider, the mounds might look much the same: a slight elevation in the earth created by backfilling the graves. The older ones have subsided and vegetation has grown over them, but Henrye will not forget where his wife and his father are laid to rest. Buried a year apart, side by side.

James halts at his grandfather's grave. The mound is low, and Beatrice's sits only a peedie bit higher, both sprouting green grass and pops of purple flowers. Henrye places an arm around his son as they regard the graves. His exhale is audible, expelling all the grief and tension he has carried since the death of his wife and father. It should be him there instead of Beatrice. If he could do things differently, he would. He squeezes his son, who lets out a sound, both a yelp and laughter. 'Papa, you're squishing me.'

Henrye's voice is thick. 'Sorry, son.'

James squats down to pluck a purple flower from each of the graves and pocket them. He smiles at his father. Henrye clasps his son's shoulder and spins them around to take in the view. His darling Beatrice has the rising sun warming her shallow grave at the start of each day. She is wrapped in their finest linen cloth. Malie was the one to weave it. Beatrice brought warmth and laughter to their days and he misses her gentle and jovial presence every morning.

He doesn't know how long they stand there but it is long enough that by the time they make their way back to the kirk, the parish has dissipated. The orcas have moved on and the sky has darkened. Henrye and James trek back home along the coastal path in the rain.

Eight

Malie

A fresh wind grazes my cheeks as I trudge south along the waterfront, leaving the township behind. The sun sits low on the east, its rays like tentacles twitching in the sea. To the west, a short-eared owl with ochre and white plumage and striking yellow eyes flies low over the grasslands, searching for movement, hunting vole or small birds in the early dawn light. The summer days are eighteen hours long, which means I can trek the western coast, a three- to four-hour one-way journey, and be back by nightfall. I used to make the trek with the other wives but it cannot be done in a day with young children and the frequent stops to tend to their needs. I've trekked this coast since I was a child. Johne barely registered my shifting weight as I crept out of bed this morning. I dressed then strung together four caisies in a loop across my chest before setting out into the crisp morning air.

My skirts brush against profuse purple heather, widespread across the moorland. The rich colours contrast against the dark, muted shades of the peat and adjoining green lowlands. The overnight rain coats the earth in a glossy sheen, while the sky is draped in heavy fog. It is difficult to see beyond my own feet but I head towards the Point. I keep moving, relying on memory. Johne wants eggs.

Seabirds nest on the western cliffs where the land sits more than three hundred feet above sea level, overlooking the North Atlantic Ocean. Typically this is a job for the men, but Johne says I am lighter on foot and stealthier than he. I tend to agree with him. Some of the islanders used to climb crags to gather the eggs from fulmars and gannets, secured by a rope staked to the clifftop. It's dangerous work, especially with the increasingly wild weather. I won't be attempting that today. With a bit of luck, I'll find razorbill and guillemot eggs in caves I can scramble to safely, and those we can store for a couple of months.

At the Point, views of the small island of Graemsay are clouded in heavy fog. Glistening grey heads bob in the sea. The weather could turn at any moment. I take note of any sheltered spots along the path in case a storm descends. A little further along I am on the bottom stretch with views across the Sound to the twin peaks of Cuilags and Ward Hill on the island of Hoy, known as 'High Island' in Old Norse. It's a treacherous stretch of water, raging wind and the boom of breaking waves, only to be traversed by experienced and knowledgeable sailors. Thick fog and rain could mean sailing blind and being at the whim of the sea.

In a little under an hour, I reach the kirk on the West Coast. The fog has now lifted. No orcas today but a few otters twirl around in the rising swell. The wind peaks here and so I veer off the coastal path inland for another two miles until I reach a broch, which is abandoned and in disarray. I snack on bere bannock and the last of the dried herring that was preserved last spring. On the horizon, bright white bodies circle the sky, diving headfirst into the waters at speed. What are the gannets feeding on if not fish? How have the bird species sustained themselves? The seabirds appear to be in fine fettle, meaty and thriving. If we cannot rely on the sea or livestock, we must revert to the practices of our ancestors and reinvigorate fowling. Like Henrye with his geese. My father is set on getting a larger boat.

While perched on a stone, I am reminded of my promise to weave new clothing for young James. Back home, Johne had questioned me about Henrye, what it was I'd spoken to him about and why. I'd told him about James needing clothing and Johne had huffed about it until I reminded him that he was the son of my closest, now deceased, friend. He looked bashful, at least for a moment, and conceded.

I tuck the leftover food into my caisie, tighten my coat around me and follow the trodden path through the kirkyard, pausing when I find Beatrice's burial plot. I kneel on the grassy surface, skim my fingers along it, trying to bring her smiling face to my mind. It is harder than I thought. The last time I saw her, she was skittish. We sat upon the pier in the harbour, our feet dangling into the gentle swell below. James was only a tot but was out on the boat with Henrye that day. Beatrice was worried about my marriage prospects and encouraged me to gain independence from my father. Adame was building a house, so I reassured her that when he moved out, my time would come. I squeezed her hand and laughed.

Told her not to worry about me. Her smile in return was strained.

Now I think upon that last tense encounter, the sight the next day of her limp body washed ashore and how Henrye had collapsed upon her in grief. Like the weather and sea, life can change drastically in an instant. A robust wind rises over the cliffs and I tremble. Best keep moving.

From here I push north to the summit, following a grassy, often boggy, path along the cliffs. An old red sandstone sea stack juts out from the sea: an impressive sea stack that may one day collapse to the ocean bed. For now, it holds up against the westerlies. As the wind picks up, I am careful to keep my feet steady on the ground along the cliff's edge. The grassland is a carpet of small purple flowers with a bright yellow centre. I crouch down and pluck a Primula scotica from the ground and twirl it between my fingers as I look out to sea. The coast here is higher than back home, small inlets and nousts, waves crashing against the coast. Large dark brown shapes glide overhead. Skuas, pirates of the sky, glide effortlessly in the air, stalking nests for the same reason as me: to steal eggs. The land angles down towards the sea with a steep vertical drop into the water. Along the cliff face protrude layers less than a foot thick, and this is where the fulmars nest. It's an awkward spot to lay eggs but it keeps them relatively safe from predators. They remain still, to keep their eggs from rolling about. I won't be climbing down the cliff face to collect fulmar eggs. The skuas can have them.

The higher I climb above sea level, the fiercer the gale. My nose feels wind burned, and my head a little light. I pull my scarf up over my ears; the tips of them too are stinging in the wind. There are small burrows along the edge of the cliff and just below is a lip with more nests. Razorbills tend to nest up at this height, preferring more space than the guillemots below. They are sociable and thick-beaked birds. They tend to sit tightly on their eggs, so I must be quiet and patient.

A gale blows off the sea and destabilises me. I drop to my knees on the soft damp ground. This gives me more control as I brace against the breeze, which whips the haze across the horizon. The fog breaks into small islands hovering in the sky. Another colony of grey seals is bopping in the sea. It was a seal song that led a little boy up here when I was just eight years old. He'd wanted to see the seals from above and had slipped from the cliff into the waters below, never to be seen again. His parents were devastated but it didn't stop their next two youngsters from climbing the cliffside to play and whale-watch, with caution of course. Steady footing and balance are bred into us on the islands.

I caress my abdomen, hoping the wind and cliffside walking will brace the bairn in the womb and build resilience for the harsh conditions on our island. Shuffling forwards, I spy a burrow. There's a tunnel; above, a black and white bird with a colourful beak squawks a warning. It's a Tammie Norrie nest. I suck in a breath. These puffins lay Johne's favourite type of egg.

Peering into the hole, I confirm the absence of brooding parents. I reach my hand down the tunnel until my hand pats a soft feathery nest. A single oval-shaped egg is nestled inside. Clasping the egg, I withdraw my arm and the parent bird squawks loudly. The egg is warm and white with faint brown spots. Johne will be happy, but one won't be enough. I skirt along the rocky edge and find another six burrows, collecting the eggs and nestling them in the caisie basket as I go. I uncover a few great auk nests; these penguin-like birds lay a single egg like the Tammie Norrie. I take these too.

After some time, I collect two razorbill eggs, quick to snatch them up as the brooding parent takes a break. They swoop and squawk at me. I cover my head with my hands and squat down low until they back off. A pang of guilt throbs under my ribs as I rob them of their offspring, a thought that has more weight to it now that I will have a bairn of my own. It's early in the season, so they may have time to lay a replacement. I'm thankful that at least my bairn is tucked safely away inside of me. Imagine sitting on a nest and fending off danger!

With twelve large eggs nestled in the caisie, I am certain Johne will be happy with my harvest. I shuffle away from the burrows and nests, easing away from the steep cliffside. The rain shouldn't catch me off guard but it does. I tuck the eggs into the caisies and find myself cloaked in darkness. Heavy, dark clouds hang overhead and a crack of thunder echoes as wind sweeps across the land. I stumble backwards and crouch down to scan my surroundings.

I must seek shelter and fast. Inland is high, flat and open. I make a quick decision to brace myself against the wind, my legs burning against the force of it as I edge towards the cliffside. I tuck the caisies close against my chest to protect the eggs. My stomach rumbles in unison with the thunderous sky. The rain spits and splatters across the rocks as I stumble down a grassy ramp that levels out to a ledge where, on the right, fulmars roost. To the left is a deep cleft in the cliff face, small enough for me to sit inside with my baskets, but not so big that I am left exposed to the harsh wind. Bird droppings stain the rocks and there are remnants of nest materials. It has a warm, musky odour. I burrow in, like a brown hare, nibbling on the last of the bere bannock as I wait for the storm to pass. The wind is hurtling towards the south, creating ripples in the sea as it fights the tidal waves crashing against the rocks below. The three roosting fulmars are watchful but deem the storm a bigger threat than I, as they too move back and lie low on their nests.

The storm passes quickly, petering out to a light drizzle. When the fog lifts I have a clear view of the sea. On the horizon, there's a boat. Nae, slimmer than a boat. I lean closer, eyes squinting, as the foreign object sits in the shadows of the clouds. Could it be a long boat? A strong gale knocks me sideways and I hunker down lower on the rocks so I am one with the cliff. A human figure sits upon the boat but I cannot see whether it is male or female. Only the upper body is visible, the lower body hidden under grey, glimmering like a seal. My heart pounds. Could this be the Finnman Johne spoke of?

The boat looks like it is in rhythm with the swell of the waves; the person is unmoving. No oar or paddle to steer or control – they are at the whim of the sea. A flash of Mother in the water, graceful and at ease. Though she said we should always be wary of the sea, she was never afraid. If we swim with the swell and the tides, the sea will take care of us. If we fight it, then it can drag us down to its depths.

Mother tried hard to be like the others but she lived on the precipice of sea and land. She spoke a different language, with skin and hair darker than anyone else on the island. She was a selkie and selkies cannot live on land forever. I imagine she felt as Johne feels now, yearning for his boat. To do what he was born to do. Just like the fisherman, my mother was meant to be at sea. Perhaps that's why Father didn't want me to swim any more. He thought, given the means to escape, I would leave him too. Never mind: I cannot slip into a seal skin and transform like my mother.

The figure remains still. This person knows the sea and is not afraid of it. Unless ... nae, surely the person is all right. The tide is taking the long boat south but the wind will change and so too will the swell. There's no need to alarm the men. There's something peaceful and harmless about them. This person is not a threat. Besides, I can't have Johne marching out there in his state. He's only just recovered. *Keep something for yourself.* Mother's words echo again. But the *somethings* are mounting and the more I keep to myself the harder they will be to offload.

I creep out of the cleft, careful not to disturb the fulmars. Though I could easily take their eggs, I feel a begrudging camaraderie after waiting out the storm with them, so I leave them and their eggs alone. My feet slip about on the muddy ramp back up to the cliff and I clutch the caisies against my chest. I retrace my steps back along the coast. After several hours I arrive at the kirk as the wind howls again and knifing rain stabs my face. I hunker down again at the cliffs of Black Craig, waiting for the rain to pass, before heading south and then inland, cutting through to the village and escaping the coastal gale. By the time I reach the house, it is evening and with no food remaining except for the eggs I am ready to eat again. I am ravenous.

In the cottage, I find Johne waiting for me. I close the door behind me and deposit the baskets of eggs onto the stone table. He doesn't ask me about my day or seem concerned that I have been caught up in not one but two storms. No point telling him about the long boat because there's a fierce expression on his face. Again. His eyes narrow and flicker like the flame on the hearth. I sigh. My husband is ravenous too.

~

'Did you say you'd seen someone on a boat? A long narrow boat?' I asked Adame the next morning. Elinor pats Nicholas asleep in her arms as she paces around the hearth in their small home.

'Nae, not me,' he says. 'It was our father.' Adame sits beside the hearth, pouring something strong smelling down his throat.

'Hmm,' I say, wanting to ask more but not wanting to draw too much attention to my interest either. 'Could he have been mistaken? Surely visibility in that storm was poor.'

'It wasn't just any storm.' Adame breathes in deeply. He rises, disposing of his mug on the table before closing the door, shutting out the howling wind. It whistles and swirls around the cottage. 'The morning was clear and bright. No sign of clouds. We all expected a good day for our return to the port. The tide was bringing us in, and we would come back on a fair wind.' He looks wistful for a moment. 'Then, something on the horizon. A small boat-like contraption, that's what Father says, unlike anything he'd ever seen. And in the boat, there was a person sitting there. Tall, dark hair flowing down their back. At first it looked like it was going in the opposite direction. There were seals about too. And then the sky turned dark. The wind went in every which direction. The tide was no longer bringing us in but knocking us about this way and that.'

I steady myself against a shelf above the hearth, the heat making my skin feel clammy.

Adame continues. 'It was Patrik who heard stories of the Finnman. There was one seen at the south-end of Eday and another one off Westray. The locals talked of drastic changes in weather and the fishermen got few or no fish after these sightings. They travelled in a narrow, long boat, like the one Father saw, and could travel great distances. Patrik said they came ashore to seduce wives and take them back to their kingdom, Finnfolkaheem. They're too fast, cannae be caught.'

'Finnfolkaheem. What's that?'

'Aye, it's their winter home. An underwater castle, nae city it is, adorned with crystals. In summer, they inhabit Hildaland. The hidden island; a magical vanishing land. It's inaccessible to us humans, so even if we went looking for it, we cannae walk the island. Many folk have tried. I suppose the Finnman we saw is looking for a wife to take back to the underwater kingdom before winter. None of the lads were happy about that prospect.'

My mouth hangs open; the words won't form. Could this be one of Mother's clan?

Adame huffs. 'And Johne claims to have seen selkies bobbing in the choppy waves, but I only saw seals.'

I sit at Elinor's spinning wheel, which my brother constructed out of driftwood and pine he traded with the Norwegian fleet last summer. The linen is tangled around the spindle. I unwind it and begin again. 'Do you think our mother was out there?'

Adame sighs. 'I couldn't feel her. That doesn't mean she wasn't. All I know is I didn't see nothin'. No selkies, no Finnman.'

'Och, Malie,' Elinor says. 'You don't need to do that. I'll get to it soon enough.' She continues to rock Nicholas, who has now drifted off to sleep but she keeps up the easy rhythm anyway. The peedie one must feel like he's swaying in a boat.

'Never mind. I'll just get you under way. I like to keep my hands busy.'

Elinor stands beside me. 'You make it look so easy.'

'I've had more practice than you. You've combed it out nicely.'

'Aye. Thank you for giving me some of the flax from your last harvest. I hope to have my own crop come autumn. Depending on the storms, of course.'

'You're welcome.' Elinor hasn't much experience with linen or wool, and the bairn has kept her busy since spring. But spindles of linen yarn are good for our trades, not to mention keeping us in clothing and bedding year-round. With the prospect of no fish to trade, we must focus on what we can do. We must look towards our future.

'Has Bessie said anything?' Adame asks quite suddenly, making me stumble over the spinning wheel and mess up the spindle. Now it looks worse than when I began. I groan and begin to unwind it again.

'About what?' I ask, careful to avoid his gaze. I don't want to draw attention to my connection with Bessie, or the stone ritual that helped my husband.

'About the sea spirits or the selkies?' he clarifies.

'Bessie?' Everyone is quick to dismiss Bessie's knowledge about the sea and the sky and yet she's the first person they consult for such knowledge. My thoughts turn to the cloth and the three stones and Johne's wrath. Bessie's prediction that the men may not be the same after the storm. That she has seen my death. 'Nae, she's said nothing to me.'

'Hmm,' he says, staring into his empty mug. Something weighs on him, more than the absence of fish. Has he seen the boat too? Perhaps Johne is not the only man to return changed. The wind howls around us. I hope the person I'd seen on the coast was taken back out with the tide. Far, far away from the men on my island.

Nine

Malie

I see the long boat first. It's on Henrye's foreshore and has not been taken out with the tide after all. It's early morning but could just as easily be late at night, with the sun hidden beyond the grey clouds. The mist transforms to drizzle and I pull my woollen coat tighter around me. There's something about the stillness that propels me forwards, an eerie stillness despite the Arctic blow off the sea and the sea spray falling about me. At first glimpse, the boat looks to be abandoned – there's no sign of the Finnman from the day before. Perhaps there was no one there at all. Or they may have drowned. About fifteen feet long by two feet broad, the boat frame is constructed of whalebone and swaddled in seal skins, with a single, narrow opening for a person to be enclosed up to the waist. This must be why, to the fisherman's eye, the person's lower half resembled a seal. My fingers glide across the skin. The hair is densely packed together, making it lovely and warm and dry and waterproofed against the elements. It's solid, silver-grey in colouring, likely from a male seal as females tend to be spotty and lighter.

I glide my hand along the frame from the bow to the stern and it is not until I round the other side that I see the figure curled up on the sand. Not a Finn*man*, but a woman washed upon our shores. Dark-featured, draped in a seal skin, this one motley and pale. The clothing underneath is too big for her small frame. A selkie?

The image of the limp figure ships me back in time to three years ago, where I stood on this pebbly shore and watched, in horror, as Henrye slumped over his wife's body. Beatrice was pallid and unmoving, seaweed tangled around her feet and sand in her hair. A hooded crow stalked the shoreline. I stood numb, silence deafening until the waves roared and everything became amplified. Too loud. I'd dropped to the ground in a heap and that's the moment Henrye looked up at me, tear-stricken, giving an imperceptible shake of his head. She had not made it. Whatever it was she faced out there, in the sea, it had taken her.

Now the sea has cast up something else. No hooded crow but something does circle overhead. The high-pitched whistle of an eagle pierces the clouded sky. I drop the caisie and creep closer, my legs weighted and stiff. There is no movement. The woman smells of the sea. I crouch down, to brush away the hair on her face. Her dark lashes rest heavily on her cheeks. There's something familiar about her features. I lean in, place my hand against her nose, where I feel a faint coolness as she exhales. Alive. Oh, thank goodness, she's alive. I close my eyes for a moment to think. What am I to do with her?

I should tell my father: he'll know what to do. He helped my mother when she washed ashore. But would this woman be safe with him or any of my family now they're intent on hunting the Finnman? Will they change their minds if they discover she is a woman? There's so much anger now, I can't be sure. People say my mother seduced my father, that fishermen are powerless before the selkie's charms. Could this still be true? Will they still be powerless, even with such disdain for the selkies? Nae, not with there being no fish in the sea.

The sound of a boat crashing against rocks startles me. Henrye leaps from his craft and secures it to the pier, with his son trailing closely behind him. I am rooted in the sand, torn between wanting to call for him and wanting to send him away. No time to do either: Henrye catches a glimpse of the boat, the lifeless figure, and then he turns his attention to me. His body goes rigid and I wonder if, like me, he is caught in the rip of his memories.

James pulls on his sleeve and this seems to snap him awake. Henrye mutters something to him and then James runs up the grassy bank towards their home. Henrye approaches, pursing his lips and his throat bobbing as he swallows. I say nothing when he drops to his knees beside the woman. He rests the back of his hand against her forehead, then her cheeks. He leans in close so his ear is almost touching her mouth. 'She's alive.'

Our eyes meet and we both exhale loudly. He scans the shore, apparently satisfied we are alone. Henrye's parcel of land and sea are tucked away and not in sight of my home or those beyond. From land we are safe, but if Father's boat or the fleet sail into the Hoy Sound, we'll all be visible. There will be nowhere to hide. We must do something quickly. Can I trust Henrye? 'She's a selkie,' I whisper.

Henrye gives me an odd look. His brows furrow; his dark eyes are trained on me. He seems to be weighing up his options, whether to help me – or the woman – or not.

'We must protect her, Henrye. I cannae take her home with me,' I say and his face softens. I cannot take a woman just like my mother home with me. I am determined they cannot know about her. Until I know for certain who she is or where she has come from, I must keep her safe.

'Aye.' He scratches his chin. 'I'll take her home.' He glances at the heap of woman and then up the banks towards his home. The eagle continues to circle above. 'Can you help me carry her? She needs warmth, fresh water and food to restore her energy, before she can return to wherever she came from.'

'Aye, I'll help.' My mouth feels dry as I think about how Johne may react if he knew I was going to another man's home. I've been there before but that was when Beatrice was alive. I couldn't go back after she was gone. We've had so little contact and yet, since Johne's injury at sea, we've met three times. The sea brings us together. 'But what about the boat? We can't leave it here.'

'We must, for now.' Henrye whispers softly to the woman: 'We will take you somewhere safe. Somewhere warm where you can eat and rest.' Then he heaves her up over his shoulder, where she hangs limply. Henrye groans under the heavy seal skin and wet clothing but steadies his gait and trudges through the sand. I scurry along behind, flicking off wet hair plastered to her face. The sudden movement makes my head spin and I close my eyes to right myself.

'Are you all right?' Henrye asks, stopping to look back over his shoulder.

I blink widely; we have no time to waste. 'Aye, let's go.'

The eagle tracks us from sea to land. We stop several times so Henrye can readjust the woman before he peels off her hooded pullover and bundles it in my arms. The seal-skin pelt is lined with seal intestines. It smells fishy but is unexpectedly lightweight. Underneath, she wears a woollen top, seal-skin pants with intricate stitching and soft knee-high seal-skin boots, lined with a snowy-coloured fur that is both soft and coarse. What kind of animal is that? It is certainly not wool. It is clear wherever the woman has been is frosty enough for her to need insulated clothing.

I can't imagine removing the pelt helps Henrye but he surges forwards with renewed energy until he reaches his cottage just beyond the moorland. James has already lit the peat fire, gathered blankets and surrendered his bed for the woman. Henrye lies the woman down on the bed as I spread the seal skin over the stone bench beside the fire.

She mumbles something unintelligible as I approach, eyes flickering closed. I kneel beside her and whisper, 'You're safe.' Even though I don't think she understands the words, my voice settles her and she drifts back off to sleep.

Henrye hands me the blankets and turns his back on us so I can remove the woman's damp clothing and chafe her warm with a dry blanket. She barely reacts until I draw up another blanket and tuck it in under her chin. Her eyes flicker open; her lips are dry and pale. Her skin no longer bears the stinging chill of the sea.

'Water,' I whisper to Henrye, who brings a mug with fresh water from the loch. I tilt it to her mouth. She licks her lips and swallows and turns her head away, eyes closed once more.

'I'll leave it here,' I say, placing it on the ground beside her. I tuck her in again and it reminds me of when I did this for Adame when he was young. I breathe out a sigh of relief. She is warm and safe. For now, at least.

My gaze flickers around the home Henrye once shared with Beatrice. I am reminded of how we sat at the table together, sipping on herbal tea, or out in the garden on a warm day. She shared stories of her married life, as her stomach swelled and she prepared for motherhood. I was so happy for her. She was so alive. I blink. Henrye watches me from the door.

'We must do something about her boat.' I swallow. 'The men in my family are talking about killing any Finnman – or woman – they find.'

Henrye rubs his brows with force, contemplating. 'Aye, let's get the boat. It's on my land; I will store it somewhere safe until she can return to sea.'

It will be near impossible to hide such a thing on these exposed lands, but we must do something with it. Henrye instructs James to watch over the woman and then we make our way back down the path through the grasslands. A light drizzle blurs my sight but I sense the eagle has moved on. When we reach the sandy bank, Henrye grabs my arm and pulls me back. I fall into the heather and look at him in shock. He places a finger to his lips and points towards the sea. That's when I hear voices on the wind. Men's voices. We crouch down low and creep forwards and I am not surprised to see Father and my brothers examining the boat. Johne is there too, limping, his face irate. They scan the shore, searching for the owner. We got her away just in the nick of time. Is it too late for her boat? I turn to Henrye. 'What should we do?'

Henrye breathes heavily out of his nose – the only sign that he is ruffled, and his calm presence settles my nerves. 'We cannae do anything now: it's too late. Let's hope they will not think to look for a woman.'

The men's voices rise higher and Henrye's name is caught in the wind; I glance at him and he shakes his head. My husband grabs the bow of the boat and then my father and brothers surround the sides and stern. They heave up the boat and walk along the sand, where they realise it is lighter than expected so William and Jerome pull away, leaving Johne and my father to transport it along the coastline towards our properties. Adame trails behind them, scratching his head and looking out at sea.

'Let's hope they don't destroy the boat, so the woman can still return to her homeland,' Henrye mutters.

'You can't let them do this, Henrye,' I say. 'That boat is yours. It's on *your* land – it's Udal Law. You should have a say.' Father knows better. Udal Law is Old Norse law, which supersedes Scots law and gives us rights of full possession, though the laws are interpreted depending on whom they benefit, of course. By Henrye's land, he has rights to the foreshore between high and low water. The sea creatures – if there were any – in the sea would be his and anything that washes ashore too. If the men move the boat to their land, unaware they are being watched, they can claim it as their own; though if the Crown caught wind of it they would surely dispute it. A long boat may be deemed treasure and treasure always belongs to the king.

Henrye grunts. 'There's five of them and one of me, Malie. I won't get much say in the matter. They'll take it further up shore and claim it as their own.'

'They wouldn't do that,' I say with little conviction, but Henrye gives me a pitying look. In this moment, I see my family through Henrye's eyes and my cheeks flush with shame. They are intent on killing innocent people, stealing boats and intimidating other parishioners. As I crouch down in the heather, I am overcome with disgust. What has got into them? A few failed crops, a dismal catch and they're willing to turn on anyone? Even an injured young woman? I wish Henrye would stand up to them but, as I watch their retreating backs, I understand why he doesn't. They have all the power on this island. And Henrye has so little. And, I realise, so do I. Tears sting my eyes.

'Malie.' Henrye's voice is deep and brooding. 'Go home. I'll go down there. They'll have questions for me anyway with my boat being so close. Go home and act as though you never saw the boat. Never saw the woman. All right?'

I shake my head. 'Nae, I cannot leave you to deal with all of this.' *With them*, I want to say.

'Malie,' he says again, and I realise he is right. If I go down there with Henrye it will infuriate Johne, and my father even more so. Neither have liked him much. They only tolerate him because he was married to my friend.

'Och, all right, I won't say anything.' Another secret. Another *something* to hide from my family. Another thing to keep to myself – but if this woman is like my mother, then I must protect her. Because if she's like my mother, then she's also a bit like me.

'Henrye,' I whisper and he looks back. 'Be careful.'

I scramble back down the path just as the drizzle thickens into heavy rain and walk on unsteady legs to my home. It is not until I am safely back inside, breathing heavily, hair dripping wet, and wondering how I can unsee the woman and the boat as Henrye requested, that I remember the caisie. I dropped it on the sand when I saw the woman and did not retrieve it when we took her to Henrye's. I peel off the damp woollen jacket and dry it by the fire. Goosebumps prickle my arms.

Johne will know I was there.

Ten

Malie

I wait all day for him to confront me about the caisie. My stomach knots with tension as I track his moods. He returns midmorning, heavy footed, retrieving a rope and an axe. He then leaves without so much as a backwards glance. He does not notice me holding my breath as I stir the barley stew in the cauldron over the open fire. The nutty chewy texture of the barley, peas and potato is a nice change from the mutton. I wait until it boils and simmers before creeping out to the highest point of the moorland, where I can clearly see where the sea meets the horizon. Father's vessel, having left the northern pier, sails south past Henrye's strip of land with the force of the wind behind them. They'll be scouring the western shoreline for the Finnman. They won't be back for a few hours, as they must wait for a fair wind to bring them back. I don't dare go to Henrye's to check on the woman, even though I want to.

I weave linen braies and shirts for James – he can wear them under a woollen tunic and breeches I've already blocked out. I'm keeping my hands busy but, even so, I find I cannot sit for long. By mid-afternoon Johne returns momentarily with only the knife, muttering he'll be back to see my father and something about Udal Law. I am certain they will keep the boat, not dismantle or destroy it. Even if they permitted the woman to leave, which is growing more unlikely, the boat now belongs to us. Well, to the men. I suspect it was moved to my father's foreshore. He'll claim it as his own, just as he did my mother. Och, that's an unkind thing to think. I cradle my stomach. Johne doesn't notice me pacing back and forth around the room but perhaps that's because he's used to me always being on my feet.

By early evening, I've all but convinced myself I didn't leave the caisie there at all. I misplaced it elsewhere. Or perhaps they were so distracted by the boat they didn't even notice what I left behind. The serpent's breath likely sucked it in with the tide and pulled it out to sea. A vessel washed ashore, a caisie taken back. A fair trade.

I am wrong, of course. As hope begins to swell and I think maybe, just maybe, it will be all right ... this is when he strikes.

My husband enters the cottage early evening, leaving a heavy downpour in his wake. His hair is dripping, and his limp is worse in the damp air: he looks like a powerful creature who has crawled out of the sea. The door is shut firmly behind him, leaving us alone in the candlelit room, him with one hand behind his back, his broad shoulders shaking with rage. The rain roars down on the roof, but it is eerily silent in the cottage. All but the thumping of my heart against my rib cage.

His face tells me everything I need to know. Everyone saw the caisie and they must all know I was there first. That it was on Henrye's land. I know it is the humiliation, the shame, that fuels his anger now. They had a plan, one that did not include bystanders, and now I have missed the opportunity to explain. The only thing that brings me a sense of relief is knowing Father has left Johne to deal with it, which means he does not see me as much of a threat. He knows I will not confront him. It is not the way we do things.

Johne's voice is low but menacing like the waves before a rising storm. He grips the edge of the stone table. 'What were you doing at the Point this morning?'

I devise a plan: to feign innocence. It won't matter what I say – Johne won't believe me either way. 'I walked to the pier this morning. Visited Elinor and peedie Nicholas on the way.' I say, even though he knows I walk south along the shore at dawn every day. He knows I pass by Henrye's house on my way to the Point to visit the seals. 'Johne, what is wrong?'

Johne pulls out the caisie from behind his back and drops it onto the stone bench. It is light and makes the slightest murmur as it lands on the table, but I feel the weight of it on the surface. The same spot I'd tended to his wound and taken care of him. Now a threadbare woven basket, with a gaping hole – unquestionably mine – lies between us. The small basket feels like it stretches the coastline, prising us apart.

Our relationship sometimes feels like the sea: treacherous and dangerous but also exciting. He feels everything so intensely, his love and his anger. We're pulled away and then drawn back into one another, only for a big swell to crash upon us both once more. The caisie is one of those waves, one that will soon settle back into a gentle swell. I must mould to the water, move with the motions, like Mother taught me. There's no point in fighting it; fighting him.

He steps closer and heat radiates from him like an angry fire. 'Why didn't ye tell me you found a boat?'

My heart pounds in my chest. Mother's voice: *Keep something for yourself.* 'Boat? I don't know what you're talking about, Johne. What boat?'

'Are ye telling me you didnae know?' His accent thickens, his voice low and deep. 'Are ye?'

I shake my head, keeping my voice light, swallowing back the rising lump in my throat. 'I wasn't there. Johne, I was at the pier – you can check with Elinor,' I say, because I know he won't ask another man's wife about my whereabouts. I reach for the caisie. 'I was wondering where this was. I must have dropped it when I was caught out in the downpour.'

I wring my hands together, trying to recall whether I'd told him about the downpour on my return trip inland after collecting the seabird eggs. He'd not enquired about my trip, only directed me to prepare two razorbill eggs for his supper. That was after he'd taken me to bed. Though my clothing conceals them, I feel the thrum and throbbing of the bruises along my arm and inner thighs. Johne breathes through his nostrils, heavy and loud. 'Shame about the clams,' I add, shuffling on my feet and scooping up the basket to look inside. 'They must've buried themselves in the sand. I found some big ones.'

Johne's nostrils flare.

'What's the matter, Johne?' I bravely step towards him. My face is calm like the bottom of the ocean; inside my stomach is choppy like the waves. Something else I learned from my mother; this is how she calmed my father. Do not fight back. Play dead like the voles do when in peril. I look up from under my lashes so as not to provoke him.

'Yer hidin' something, Malie. I know ye are.' He changes tactic, lowering his voice to a tone of disappointment. 'First that devilish Bessie comes here to curse me, then you're talking to Sinclair at the kirk in front of the whole parish and now this ... Ye can't be trusted.'

My stomach churns and I feel nauseated. I did bring Bessie here knowing he'd have protested if he'd been conscious. I did speak to Henrye in front of the whole parish and, even though it was a harmless conversation with a neighbour, Johne doesn't like it when I speak to him. And now, it pains me to be dishonest with him. He's right, I *am* hiding something: I have not been truthful. I share a secret with Henrye which, if Johne were to discover it, would be dangerous for both of us.

I soften my voice and step towards him, my palms flat to placate him. 'Johne—'

He charges forwards, slamming me back into the stone wall. His expression is murderous and for a moment I fear Bessie's premonition may come true. Could he really do it? Could his temper make him go too far? His clenched fist hits the stone beside my ear. I squeeze my eyes shut as my heart roars in my chest. Louder than crashing waves, thunderous skies. I am certain he can hear the pounding. The fear.

I gasp. 'Johne, please. Please don't do this.' He can't do this now, not with a peedie one growing inside me. Things are meant to be different now. How has it all gone so wrong?

'Yer hidin' somethin'.' He grinds his molars together as though he is gnawing on a sheep bone.

I swallow. *Keep something for yourself.* My bairn. My seal. The boat woman. *I can't keep them all, Mother.* I inhale slowly, deeply, easing my heart rate as I trade one of the *somethings* for amity. 'Johne, there is something I've been wanting to share with you. But you were injured, and I wanted to give you time to heal. So that we could celebrate together.'

Johne cocks his head and some of the tension in my body eases. I have his attention but I am not yet steering the boat. First, I must pry his fingers from the helm. I'll keep the seal. Keep the woman safe. Hand him a distraction. Disarm him, for now. I summon up more cheer than I feel, beaming at him. 'I'm with child.'

Johne chokes and his knuckles graze along the stone. Confusion, puzzlement and then wonder flicker across his face. His hands flatten and the tightness in my chest eases.

'We're having a bairn?' He runs a hand over his face, revealing a softer expression.

I clasp his familiar face in my hands. 'Aye, Johne. You're going to be a father.'

He swallows and I hold his gaze before he draws me into his chest, the bairn in my belly nestled between us both. Safe inside, for now. My body sighs against him. The storm has passed and the outlook is clear. Bessie must be mistaken. He might get in a temper but he'd never go that far. He'd never hurt his bairn.

The one problem with Orkney weather is that it's unpredictable and one cannot know when it will again turn.

~

It's a day 'atween the weathers. Johne's stormy mood lulled into a calm. He's all but forgotten the interrogation about the boat and I am pleased I sufficiently distracted him. The fleet is expected to arrive any day now and the men are at the harbour, mending piers and preparing for their arrival. The men, my husband in particular, have been agitated in preparing what little livestock and meat we have for trade on account of there being no fish, while the wives prepare the linen and feathers. With the men busy at the pier, I can slip away to see the woman. The selkie.

Once I hear Johne's heavy tread leave along the stony path, I leap out of bed, dress in my woollen outerwear, gather my supplies and creep into the early morning light towards Henrye's house.

I can hear the seals rousing on the rocky bank. At Henrye's, dim candlelight filters through gaps in the stone cottage. I hesitate on the doorstep. Is it odd that I'm here? Johne will be irate if he learns I am creeping off to another man's house in the darkness, let alone to visit a selkie. Before I can change my mind, the door opens and Henrye appears in the doorway, ruffled and fatigued.

I open my mouth to speak but no words come out and I'm suddenly hit with an intense fear that the selkie woman did not survive. She was exposed to extreme cold and dehydration when we found her. Poor Henrye – and after losing his wife in a similar way. As if reading my mind, Henrye says, in a hoarse voice that catches on the breeze, 'She survived.'

I breathe out, deeply, the relief lightening the heavy feeling I carried here. 'Aye, that's good. Aye. I brought her some clothing and such. And some for James too.'

I feel awkward as I present them to him. Henrye's eyes crinkle and he steps aside. 'Come in.'

Upon entering, I see two sleeping figures by the hearth. Henrye's son is curled up under a blanket and his handsome face looks very much like his father's. A pang of sadness that Beatrice doesn't get to see her boy grow up.

The woman sleeps in a fitful state, twitchy and uneven in breath. She's wearing a woollen sweater in a deep blue like the ocean. I recognise it as one of Beatrice's. When she wore it her eyes glistened. I drop the clothing at the edge of her bed even though it feels like a useless gesture. Henrye has already taken care of it. Perhaps I'll have better luck with James. As he wakes, I present him a collection of new items. James rummages through the pile with excitement, measuring the breeches against his legs. I'm pleased the length is accurate, leaving extra room for him to grow. I made two linen winter stockings, to keep him warm over winter. The woman doesn't rouse even as James squeals with delight.

'Has she been like this since yesterday?'

Henrye stands beside me. 'Aye, only brief periods of lucidity, a little water and broth here and there, but mostly sleeping.'

'Well, that's good, I suppose. She's recovering her strength, little by little.' We watch her twitch and murmur as though she is being chased and I wonder about her experience at sea. What happened out there? Has she been adrift since the storm?

'Aye.' His face is clouded in worry.

'Johne and my father found my caisie beside the boat. They suspect I saw the boat but I don't think they can be sure.' I wring my hands together. 'I denied it, of course.'

He eyes the nervous grasping and looks as though he wishes to press me further. I tuck my hands behind my back and divert my gaze. 'Did you speak to them yesterday?' Then I remember that Henrye went down to greet them while I snuck back to my house. 'What did you say? What did *they* say?'

He eyes me with curiosity. 'They're intent on killing the owner of the boat. No mention of where they found it. I waited until they'd hauled it up to Neill's before heading into town.' He looks sideways at the woman, who remains asleep. 'They're convinced the traveller is male and that he's responsible for the absence of fish on the last voyage, and since then, too.' He chews on the inside of his cheek. 'I'd hoped it wasn't so. I must help her get back home before they hurt her.'

'They wouldn't—' I start to say but I realise I do not know what my father and husband are truly capable of. It's possible they saw this woman on the boat from afar. She may have been adrift for weeks. I am relieved I told them nothing.

My gaze snags on the grey seal skin draped across the bench, drying by the fire. Though I never saw it, Mother had one just like it. She told me so. Its warmth likely saved her from succumbing to the cold and damp when she was beached. My fingers trace across the silky soft skin, and I imagine myself wrapped in it as Mother once was. She missed it. Father told me she found her seal skin and returned to the sea. It was the key to her past and she chose the sea instead of our family. Instead of me. It was her way home. Why didn't this sleeping woman don her seal skin now and return to the sea to regain her strength? Father made it seem so simple. Am I missing something? Does she need a full moon or a fair wind?

'The fleet will arrive soon. Could one of the ships take her away? Get her further north or up to Norway until she has recovered and can return to the sea?'

Henrye frowns. 'To the sea? Nae, in her fragile condition it will be too risky. She must regain her strength. If she has her boat, she can get herself back home – once the fleets have gone of course. She'll be safer then.'

I sigh. 'I will help you. My family will be busy preparing our trades for the market. I can look for the boat, and then, once she's strong enough, she can go.'

He shakes his head. 'It's dangerous, Malie.'

I consider Johne's thunderous mood yesterday and how I'd calmed it to a swell with my words. They don't know a woman washed ashore with the boat. They're looking for a Finn*man*. They don't know anything yet and that's the way it must remain. At least until she's safely off the island.

I must help Henrye, because it is the right thing to do. He's worried about my family, though, and with good reason. I lift my chin. 'Don't worry, Henrye, I can handle them.'

Eleven

Henrye

The woman sleeps most of the day, rousing only once, after noon. She blinks at him in confusion. Her dark eyes and dark lashes are framed by midnight-coloured wavy hair resting below her shoulders. She warily assesses her surroundings, but when she sees his boy, she smiles and drifts back off to sleep. The sight of James is enough to reassure her she is safe here with Henrye.

His heart thumps at an irregular rhythm, like a hen harrier taking flight, frantic wings in the cool sky. It's unsettling, having this woman here. First Malie – keeping an eye on her and that rascal husband of hers – and now, this woman. *I can handle them.* Malie's words churn around in his mind. He really shouldn't let her get involved in this. It's dangerous for Henrye but it's even more dangerous for her.

What good is he? How can he help Malie or this foreign woman? What would he do if faced with the MacDuffie men, or Johne Gray? He can't risk getting on the wrong side of them: he has his boy to care for. It already bothers him that Malie has visited him unaccompanied. It wasnae a problem when Beatrice was here but now that she is gone it could put Malie in a precarious situation. Johne is not a man you can deceive and get away with it. Not without punishment. Henrye doesn't want to see Malie's life become any more difficult than it already is, and certainly not because of him. He couldn't live with himself. And yet, he saw in her eyes how much she needs this. Without intending to, they have both become invested in the castaway.

'Papa?'

Henrye drags his gaze from the resting woman to his son. 'Aye, my boy.' He places a hand on James's shoulder. 'What is it?'

'Will the woman be all right?'

Henrye's gaze rests upon her for a moment, seeing the rise and fall of her chest. 'Aye, she'll be all right.'

James leans against his father's knee. 'She will go back to the sea, won't she, Papa? It's where she belongs.'

Henrye makes a sound at the back of his throat. He must help the woman because it's the right thing to do. But her being here confuses his son. There is too much talk of selkies and Finnfolk and magical islands. His own wife was subject to such spectacle, but he won't let his son believe the tales. He wants him to know the truth. The *almost* truth. 'She can't stay here – you're right, James. We'll make sure she is warm, well fed and rested. Then we'll help her get home.'

A sad smile flickers across James's face. 'Don't worry, Papa, I won't tell anyone.'

Henrye was not much older than his son when he too kept a secret for his father. It saddens him that his son must carry a similar burden.

His heart takes on a wing-like flapping rhythm again and he wills it to still, to soar, without effort, like an eagle in the sky. 'Aye, we must keep it to ourselves, to keep her safe.'

'I understand, Papa.'

And Henrye has no doubt his little boy does understand the enormity of the situation. He knows exactly the world they live in. They do what they must to survive.

~

As the sun settles on the horizon, halfway between day and night, Bessie arrives at his door. For a frantic moment, Henrye considers hiding the woman or sending Bessie away with some excuse about them being ill but as he registers her eager and kind face, he calms. He could actually do with her help.

One look past him and a riptide of concern and excitement lights her face. 'Henrye?!' She pushes past him to inspect the woman closer and, as she does this, the sleeping woman's eyelids flutter open. One blink, two, three and then she holds Bessie's gaze until Bessie breaks the contact and turns to Henrye for an explanation. 'Who in the world is this?'

He closes the door behind them and mutters, 'She washed ashore.'

'She's no driftwood, Henrye.' Bessie's eyes widen and he knows what kind of tales are likely fluttering about in that head of hers, but she's a sensible woman: he can trust her. She gets to work at the hearth, heating a pot he only now realises she had in her hand all along. She's brought them supper.

It's not until they are sitting around the fire, their bellies full of soup, that Bessie finally gives into her curiosity. 'Henrye Sinclair, you must tell me everything – and don't leave out any detail!'

He knows right then and there he's made the right decision to include her in his plan. The only reassurance being that people pay just as little attention to her as they do him. No one else can know. He will not willingly unload the burden on another. God knows he can't let history repeat itself. This is one woman he'll be sure to get off this island: the only difference is, he must figure out how to keep her alive until he can.

Twelve

Malie

The path to Henrye's is lit by a slither of moonlight. The wind changed direction late yesterday and so the men didn't return; they're likely moored somewhere on the western coast until morning. I take it as a sign: I am meant to be here. Henrye ushers me inside, scanning the moorland and the carpet of yellow flowers behind me. He's nervous about Johne and my father and brothers but we're safe and I tell him so. Satisfied I have not been followed, he shuts the door firmly behind him as if a door alone is enough to keep the men in my family out.

'How is she?' I whisper, noting the darkened room. James is asleep on Henrye's bed while the woman sits upright on his, her face bathed in candlelight, rubbing her eyes. 'Och, you're awake!'

'Her temperature settled today. Bessie mixed her up some sort of concoction,' Henrye says with a grimace. 'She roused about midday and ate a bowl of vegetable soup and smoked herring, too.'

'Oh, that's good. We can trust Bessie,' I say, and try not to think about what kind of concoction Bessie has come up with. At least there are no stones lying around. The castaway tilts her head, her dark eyes watching me. She has no idea there are men out there, *my* men, hunting her.

'Hello,' I say.

She lowers her head in recognition but does not speak. I take my time to kneel beside her so as not to startle her.

'My name is Malie,' I say, placing my hand on my chest. 'Malie.'

She studies my face, my hands and then slowly meets my gaze. After a beat, she places her hand over her chest. 'Kûna.' Her speech is different from ours and yet there's also something familiar about the way she speaks.

'Kûna,' I repeat. She smiles and then makes a strange tutting sound which is also melodic and gentle. I glance at Henrye. 'What did she say?'

He shrugs. The woman speaks again, more words tumbling from her mouth that I can make no sense of. 'I don't understand, Kûna, I'm sorry.'

She settles into silence again; pulls the blanket tight around her shoulders. Her gaze flickers to the seal skin draped over a chair by the peat fire. It is scrubbed clean, but its faint salty smell still lingers in the air. Bessie has been busy. 'We want to help you get home.' Kûna smiles but I know she doesn't understand me either. And then a word spills from my mouth as if it's stifling hot soup. 'Iglu.' A word Mother often spoke. Here we live in houses made from stone but she spoke of many different houses from her homeland. Her people, when they took to land in human form, lived in winter huts of peat and rock close to the sea.

The huts were cold and damp. In spring, they'd venture out hunting to collect food for the next winter. They made tents from their seal skins for shelter, or a temporary iglu made of stacked blocks of snow. Mother spent much of the summer in the sea. Her homeland is like some magical place, an island, where selkies over-wintered, just as my brother envisioned. Finnfolkaheem. Mother's people were nomadic, free to move where the food was, always moving, always adapting. She found the settlement on Orkney difficult to adjust to, with only the men leaving on fishing voyages while the women remained home.

Kûna's eyes widen and her whole face lights up. 'Go back to iglu?' I say again. I knew there was something familiar about her language. It is the language Mother brought ashore with her. The selkie language.

She nods emphatically. 'Illu,' she says, dropping the g and emphasising the l sound. She appears more youthful when she smiles. Younger than me, younger than Elinor even, but a woman no less. Her skin is thin on her bones, which makes me think about the lack of provisions in her boat. How long was it since she'd eaten before washing up here?

I try more words from my mother's tongue. I place my hand on my chest. 'Nuka,' I say. Little sister.

'Angajo.'

'Angajo. Big sister.' The words slot into place. 'Like Mother.' She had three sisters, but she became separated from them during the storm that led her to our shores.

Another sentence spills from her lips but the words morph together, and I can't make them out in isolation. Why didn't my mother teach me more of her native language? And then like the rising lochs in spring, excitement mounts … Kûna might know my mother, where she came from and where she intended to go. She might know where my mother is *right now*. We can help each other.

'My mother is like you. She went missing … She went back home. To illu. Henrye and I, we will try to get you back to your home, too.'

She reaches for my hand and pats it. 'Kujanak,' she says, and I assume it means thank you.

We have the same dark hair, dark eyes and bronzed skin. Foreign words slip from our tongues. The only difference is I am safe here and she is not. I want to know more about my mother, but for now, Kûna must rest. I must be patient. Kûna yawns and I encourage her to lie back down as I tuck the blanket around her. 'Shh. Rest and we will find a way to get you home. We'll keep you safe.'

Visibly exhausted from the interaction, she closes her eyes and I tuck the blankets back in around her shivering body. Angajo, *big sister*. She has a family, a younger brother or sister somewhere. Her parents must be so worried. I know what it's like to have someone you love disappear, and how awful it is to live every day with that uncertainty.

Henrye leans against the stone wall by the door. His beard has grown more overnight. 'Are ye all right?' he asks gently.

I smile. 'Aye. She reminds me of my mother.'

Henrye scratches his beard. 'She likes you. She feels safe. That is good.'

'She speaks Mother's language.' I cross the room to him and speak in a whisper. 'Henrye, we must keep her safe. We must protect her.'

'Aye, we will,' he says firmly. He does not care for Udal Law or taking revenge on the Finnman. He will protect Kûna and find a way to return her to her homeland. 'I must go to the port tomorrow. I must make trades to get us through the winter. After the fleet leaves, we'll make plans to get her home. I'll ask Bessie to check in on her ...' He pauses. 'It's not safe for you to come here.'

'I can't believe we've found another selkie,' I murmur, ignoring his concern. Who else can I talk to so freely about this?

Henrye clears his throat; his eyes dart to the woman and back to me.

'What?' I demand as he seems to consider his next words.

'Malie,' he says, his voice rough around the edges. 'She is *not* a selkie.'

I huff. 'She speaks Mother's language. I remember some of the words she taught me. It's selkie language.'

A moment passes before he speaks again. 'It is not selkie she speaks but a Greenlandic language. Kûna is an Inuk.'

I wring my hands. 'Inuk?'

'Aye,' he says. His gaze lowers to my hands, and I stuff them into my pockets. 'She's from Greenland, which is across the North Atlantic Ocean. She has travelled a very long way. Malie, she's a human, like us.'

'Nae,' I say, stumbling towards the table. This can't be true. 'But she's like my mother.'

'Aye, she's like your mother,' Henrye says, in a grave tone. 'Your mother was from Greenland, too.'

My hands reach out for stability, but the room spins and the ground suddenly falls out from underneath me.

~

Father told stories around the peat fire, of sea monsters and sea spirits, of shapeshifters and witches. But my favourite story of all was the one about my mother.

'Father, tell me the story again,' I beg, leaping from the warmth of Mama's lap into my father's.

Father's eyes crinkle at the edges. 'Aye, a'right then,' he says, and I nestle under his arm. 'It was a day 'atween the weathers. A blustery storm came through o'night.'

Mama shivers as she recalls knifing rain on bare skin. How the cold etched deep into her bones and the wind: the howling, chilling, relentless wind. Not a day goes past without it. Orcadians are born to withstand the wind, but Mama was not born here. She had to learn how to brace against the violent storms.

'But on that day, it was clear and blue,' Father continues. 'I went to check my nets. The weather was looking promising, and I expected a big haul. Plenty o' fish to fill our bellies.'

'But it wasn't just the fish you found, was it, Papa?'

Father chuckles as his gaze settles upon Mama. A cold draught slithers into the room like an eel in a dark sea. I quiver.

'Nae, not just the fish,' he says. 'I trudged down the sandy bank and what did I see? A woman. It was as though I were in a trance. Her skin glistened in the sun, her hair as dark as a guillemot, and she lay on the sand, with a heavy, sopping-wet seal skin draped across her. She was washed ashore in the storm. No one or nothin' else could be seen on the horizon. Just blue sky and gentle waves, a soft breeze, and the sand upon which yeh mother laid. The most beautiful woman I'd ever seen.

Her name was Nava.'

'A selkie?' I ask, breathless.

'Aye, a beautiful selkie, who shed her skin ashore. I was at her mercy.'

I giggle and this brings a smile to Mama's face. It doesn't reach her eyes. She strokes her rounded belly; I have a little brother in there. My big brothers, Patrik, William and Jerome, are out in the bustling wind, stacking peat outside the doorway to dry. I can't hear them but I know they are bickering and elbowing each other to be the first one inside, eager to please Father.

'Your mother injured her ankle,' Father continues. 'So, I scooped her up and carried her back home. Tended her until she regained her strength. Promised to take her home once she recovered. I'd never seen or met anyone else like her before. And when it was time to return, well, she decided to stay. She'd be my wife; we'd have a family.' He taps my nose. 'You.'

He has told the story many times before, straying from the original a little more in each retelling. Even so, it's my favourite. Father leans over and gives Mama a firm pat on the knee. 'We've never looked back, have we?'

Mama glances at the door. She gets nervous when she can't see the ocean. I leap to my feet and dance around the room, creating a stir as my brothers burst inside. 'Father tells the most beautiful selkie story!'

I loop my arms around Mama's neck. 'Don't you think, Mama?'

She strokes my inky, silky curls. 'It is a beautiful story,' she says.

A beautiful story, indeed. But was it true?

~

One day, at dawn, Mother kissed each of her children on the forehead and she squeezed me so tight. She told me to be brave and strong. 'One day, you will understand. I will tell you everything.' And then she was gone.

Father returned from the sea and his temper rumbled the stone walls. I told him she went swimming and had not come back. He trekked back and forth from the sea and home all day long. He scoured every shoreline but there was no sign of my mother. The following morning, he sat my brothers and me down by the fire and explained that Mother had taken her seal skin and returned to the sea, back to where she came from. She'd not be returning.

If only ... thoughts tumbled around my mind for hours, days, weeks, months. *If only* I was more courageous. *If only* I swam to the island with her, she may have taken me with her. *If only* we were enough.

Then I became responsible for my father and my brothers. Expected to take on the role of mother: cooking, cleaning and caring for my siblings. Och, I'd felt abandoned. Why didn't she take me? Why didn't she take all of us? Why didn't she come back to visit? But amid the devastation there was something magical about the story, too. She came upon land, fell in love, had a family and then returned to the sea where she belonged. Anyone could see how she longed for what she'd left behind. She loved us but she also loved the sea. In the end, I suppose she loved the sea more.

But if Henrye is right, and Mother's tongue was Greenlandic and not selkie, then why did she go along with these stories? If she did not slip into her skin, transform into a seal and swim into the swell at sunrise, what happened to her? Where did she go? *Why* did she leave?

I think upon this, after Henrye heaves me up from the ground onto the stone bench seat and insists I drink from the mug of fresh water pressed to my lips. Henrye tells me he has heard of Inuit people washing up on Orkney shores before. Finnman. Anne's family had warned her about the Finnman sighted off Westray last spring. There was also a sighting off the coast of Eday a year before that. Henrye had heard about the Inuit from some of the sailors who hunted whales off the east coast of Greenland. They regularly came ashore to replenish drinking water and make trades and connections with the Inuit.

'Are they voyagers?' I ask. This may explain why they take to the seas, why Mother was drawn to exploring beyond land. They may be searching for food.

He frowns. 'For years, ice has surrounded the entire Greenland and Icelandic coasts. Some of them may have ventured farther than usual. But something tells me that's not why they have been found in our waters. Kûna had no supplies, no food or protection. She was not prepared at all. That makes no sense for an islander. We know what is needed to survive the sea, the land and the weather.'

I wring my hands together, to keep myself moving. I am still too dizzy to stand. 'You believe something went wrong?'

'Aye,' he mutters. 'Even with the ice sheets expanding into the Atlantic, it's a long, treacherous journey. One wouldn't choose to do it alone, let alone with so few supplies.'

We both look at Kûna, sleeping. How are we to understand what happened to her so we can keep her safe? The ocean calls for her. Even if she is not a selkie, there is an island far away that is her home. She will want to find her way back. 'Why didn't Father tell me? He must still believe Mother to be a selkie.'

Henrye says nothing. Kûna is not a selkie and neither is my mother. It hits me then. The seal I've felt connected to since I was six years old is just a grey seal. Not, as I'd secretly wished, Mother returning every summer to see me. A tear slips down my cheek and I turn from Henrye to wipe it away. 'I must find that boat. My husband and brothers are out there hunting her. The only advantage we have is that they don't know she washed ashore with the boat – they don't know she's a woman.'

'Aye,' Henrye says again, deep in thought.

'What is it?' I whisper.

'If you do find the boat, tell me where it is and I will retrieve it.' He rubs his chin. 'She will find her way back home.'

'Henrye, let me help you,' I plead. I feel responsible for the danger she is in. It is my husband and my family who want to punish her. Och, she also makes me feel closer to my mother, as though Kûna were my family too. I want to be near her.

'No.' His voice rises, and I step back. He shakes his head and speaks in a gentler tone. 'Malie, it's not safe for you. Ye can't come back here. If you can locate the boat, then leave the rest to me. I'll make sure she gets home. Even if I must take her there myself.'

'How can you be sure?' I ask.

His face is grave. 'I have failed before; I will not fail again.'

Thirteen

Henrye

In the repetitive, laborious task of peat-cutting, Henrye's mind sifts through fragments of his life, breaking them into blocks like the peat at his feet. Since he was a peedie boy, he has felt powerless when faced with the demise of the women in his life. His little sister died at birth, his mother died the following year and then Malie's mother disappeared. So, it is no wonder he didn't allow himself to become too attached to the idea that Beatrice would be in his life forever. In the end, that may just have been her undoing. He could not marry Malie; Neill would never have allowed it. Not with what he knows. He's had to stand by and watch Malie's father tell her lies. He's convinced the whole island of his truth. With Neill's obvious dislike of Henrye, he thought it best to keep his distance from Malie. Beatrice was a safer option. Only he'd been wrong about that, too.

The birth was frightening, and with the loss of his sister and mother fresh in his mind, he was tormented with the thought that he could lose Beatrice too. After James was born, there were a couple of years of comfort: the worry eased. Then his father died. It left him the sole bearer of the secret they'd both shared nearly all his life. He'd been happy that at least his father was relieved of this burden. Grieving his father brought it all to the surface, lapping about like sea foam. Beatrice knew there was something he wasn't telling her, and so, regrettably, he dispensed some of the burden on to her. He wanted to finally tell someone the truth: a mistake he will forever regret. Instead of bringing them closer to one another, it only drove them apart.

It's his fault that his young lad will grow up without a mother, just as he once did. The dreaded cycle of life continues. Now, there is Malie to worry about. Her husband is a brute, but getting through to any of the men in her family is like trying to walk into a westerly wind: impossible and downright stupid.

As Henrye cuts peat from the midge-infested moorland, a daily grinding task from May through to July, he thinks about how much better it feels to do something rather than nothing. Because to do nothing is to accept defeat. And he has never been one to give up.

He doesn't have the biggest peat bank on the hill but now James can manage some of the heavy lifting it is quicker work. Not as quick as the MacDuffies, who worked dawn to dusk before their last voyage, cutting the peat and dividing it among themselves. They work rhythmically from one property to the next.

Henrye keeps one end open to allow his geese to escape should they find themselves in the bog. He flayed the bank a day earlier, cutting off the heather in strips of sixteen inches wide. Now, he uses the tusker – a narrow spade with a four-inch cutting edge – and positions his boot on the step on the side of the wooden handle so he can use the weight of his body to drive the tusk down. With a twist of the handle the peat is broken off in a dense brick, and James picks it up and throws it up on the bank to dry. Then they do it again. There are not many weeks left of the cutting season and they will need the peat to last them until the next. They are down to the fourth layer now, the black bottom peat which will dry to give the hottest fire. Once he's done, Henrye will replace the turf neatly, green side up, at the bottom of the bank to recreate a level growing surface.

As his body endures the repetitive work, his thoughts work in a repetitive nature too. Peat-cutting makes for good problem solving. This time, he'll do it differently. He can't let Kûna meet the same fate as so many other women on this island. There are many things he has no control over, like the sky and the sea and the men, but what he can do is help her. Even if he must take his own boat and see her to safety. Each day longer she remains on the island, the greater is the risk of her discovery. He must protect her from the MacDuffies, even if it puts him in danger.

The wind plays a foreboding tune, reminding him of the other threat to Kûna's escape: winter. If he doesn't get her off the island in autumn, it will be too late, and he couldn't possibly keep her hidden until spring. No one can remain cooped up inside for that long and Kûna, if she's anything like Malie's mother, will want to feel the sand on her toes and the salty water on her skin, not be hidden in the darkened stone cottage.

It's the sight of Bessie that pulls him from his ruminations. He is pleased to see her. She trudges down the path, her right shoulder leaning into the wind, her hand on a thick stick to support her weight.

'You a'ight there, Bessie?' he calls.

'Aye, aye. I just need a peedie help with balance these days.' As if to test her, the wind picks up and even Henrye must dig his heels into the ground to remain upright. He feels a pang of guilt that she continues to traipse back and forth across the island every day to check on Kûna, and, he suspects, himself and James too.

'What have ye brought there, Bessie?'

'Just some food for the lass, to restore her to good health.' She grins broadly. He thinks she quite likes the excitement. She pats James on his head and he grins up at her. 'Hello there, lad,' she says, offloading the pot onto the child and following him back up to the house.

Though it makes his skin prickle to accept the help, he tells himself it's for the best. Kûna needs it. He pauses, sensing Malie down at the bay. He leans on the shovel and brushes salt spray from his beard. It niggles him, that a hunted so-called selkie hidden away in his cottage is probably the least of his worries. Malie is often on his mind.

Just as the seals and the birds and the critters stow away before a big storm, he has a hunch something big is coming. He's not entirely sure he has it in him to brave it again.

Fourteen

Malie

I long to see Kûna but the men are on alert now with the first sighting of a masted ship coming through the Hoy Sound. They have come in on a fair wind, along with a heightened sense of anticipation for the island's merchants. A few weeks later than expected: the poor conditions undoubtedly made the sailors' journey across the North Sea long and treacherous. Our island is their last port of call and they won't stay long – they'll be anxious to be on their way again. When they dock, there will be evening celebrations and dances. Tomorrow, if the weather is good, we'll go to market.

It's best Kûna remains hidden with so many people expected to be about. I think back to the night before Johne left for his last voyage and how out of control he was. I can't even recall what angered him so. What would Johne do if he found out I've deceived him? And what about my *father*? I shrug the thoughts away; they are too horrible to entertain. Nae, I can't go to Henrye's house. Not yet anyway.

Instead, I make my way down to the inlet. I convinced Johne that we must build up other reserves: razor clams, crabs and seabird eggs. This is partly true as we are low on food supplies, but I also want to look for Kûna's boat and above all else *keep moving*. Being stagnant allows the worrying thoughts to take over which is nae good for the bairn. Johne agrees it would be best to eat what is readily available along the shore now and keep the mutton for winter. But he has a big appetite, so a lot of eggs and clams are needed. I can't get eggs now that the fleet is here: the trip is too long and the weather too unpredictable. Besides, now he knows I'm with child he won't allow me to go. And in the absence of a storm, finding clams is not an easy task.

I step backwards along the sand, watching for air bubbles on the surface. Sure enough, foamy bubbles pop out of the wet sand, and I pounce, digging out the clam, shaking off the sand and dropping it into the caisie. I repeat until the basket is full. At least the Finnman hasn't scared these away. I pause. If Kûna isn't a selkie or a Finnman, what happened to all the fish?

From dawn to early morning, I comb the sandy banks, looking for food, looking for treasures. I feel at ease knowing Johne will be tending to the sheep in the fields. A farmer on land, a fisherman at sea. There is always work to be done.

A ribbon of blue unfolds across the horizon, white – not grey – clouds dot the sky, and the sun beams through like holy spears striking the sea. I stop for a moment to soak up the sun and warmth on my face that holds off the cold sting in the air. The seals sing nearby, basking in the sun and bopping in the waves. Eyes closed and head tilted up towards the light, I wonder whether Mother feels the sun's warmth right now, wherever she is. I hope she made it to Greenland, back to her family. I wonder what it is like there. My fingers and toes sting from the chill of the wet sand. I suppose I could wear shoes but I do like the feel of the earth on my feet.

A whistle startles me and I see Henrye's boat pull into the pier. He gestures to his son to secure the boat with rope. James leaps from the boat and pulls the rope taut. Without a second thought, I rush towards him. I'm desperate for an update on Kûna.

Henrye comes ashore. His boots are wet, his nose is red from the chill in the air and there's sea spray on his beard. 'Morning, Malie.'

My breath hitches and I try to remember my manners. 'Aye, morning, Henrye.' James runs up with ropes. Henrye has a net flung over his shoulder full to the brim: not with fish but kelp. 'How is she?'

He nods. 'Aye, she's a'ight. I think she understands she needs to stay hidden, for now.'

I glance up at the cliffside where Henrye's reddish-coloured sandstone house hides behind the billowing heather. He was gone for hours, longer than I have been on the shore. 'What if someone comes to your house?'

He shrugs. 'No one visits me. Except Bessie.'

I swallow. 'Aye.' Guilt churns inside me. 'Any luck with the long boat then?'

He shakes his head. 'I've travelled around the western coast today. Thought they might've hidden it along there. There's nothing there and they wouldnae take it to the harbour. Too open.'

'Aye, and the ships are coming into the harbour now.' I nod at the stretch of water between the Point and holms, where a two-masted brig displaying the Scottish Saltire comes into view.

James comes to stand beside his father, leaning against his leg. 'Hi, James,' I say, and a small smile emerges as he returns my greeting. 'How is your guest?' I ask.

'Kûna is well, thank you,' he says; his eyes widen with excitement. 'We must keep her a secret to keep her safe.'

'That's right,' I say. 'You're doing a wonderful job of taking care of her.' I turn to Henrye. 'I'll keep my eye out for her boat.'

He clears his throat as if preparing to speak but quickly a look of discomfort appears. I turn: behind me, Elinor makes her way along the shore towards us, Nicholas tucked into a basket under her arms. A small caisie hangs from her wrist. She waves and picks up her pace when she sees us.

The sun disappears behind the clouds and the bay darkens. The wind comes up from the sea. James drops to the ground, rubbing his foot. I gasp. 'Are you—?'

Elinor joins us. 'Good morning, Malie.' She pauses. 'Mr Sinclair.'

'Elinor, how are you?' I speak louder against the wind. Nicholas grizzles.

'Aye, good. Shh, shh,' Elinor murmurs to the bairn. He fills out the basket now. He grew so much over the summer.

'I was just combing the shore for clams—'

James groans and hops on one foot. To Elinor, he says: 'I hurt my foot, and Malie was helpin' me.'

Elinor's face softens. 'Oh, that's so kind of her. Are you all right now?'

He grins. 'Much better.' I hide my smile, though I think he is very clever. Sun filters through the clouds again.

'Aye, we must get back then,' Henrye says in a low gravelly voice as he readjusts the net on his shoulder.

'Aye. Have a good day then, Mr Sinclair,' Elinor says.

He tips his hat. 'Ladies. Thank you for your help.'

'Of course,' I say coolly.

'Goodbye,' James calls. As Elinor turns her back on them, he winks at me and I stifle a laugh. I wish I could go with them and see Kûna for myself. Mother always said not to put off what could be done today, but I don't think she meant to do it if it put other people in harm's way.

'Well, then,' Elinor says, gently rocking the bairn in the basket. 'Do you mind if I join you?'

I hesitate, ready to decline her offer when I see something bobbing in the sea behind her. A seal? I squint and see that it is not a seal but a woman with dark hair. Her arms straighten above her head and then she dives into the swell, her feet disappearing under the crest. 'Kûna?'

'Sorry?' Elinor spins in confusion but I grab her arm to keep her gaze from the sea.

'Aye, of course you can,' I say. 'I was walking to the Point, but now I think it will be best to keep the wind behind us. Let's watch the fleet come into the harbour.'

Elinor looks down at Nicholas. 'The extra walking will do us both good. He likes the movement.'

'As do I.' I stroke my stomach. 'I will have a peedie one of my own soon, you see.'

Elinor's eyes widen. 'Oh, Malie!' She draws me in for a hug. 'That's wonderful news. I'm so happy for ye. I know you've wanted a bairn for some time.'

I risk a final glance back at the sea but there's no sign of Kûna. She has not resurfaced. My stomach flips with concern. What if something happens to her out there? Or worse, what if she is seen by the wrong person? But there's something else tangled in the worry: envy. She looked so free, like my mother once did. For a moment I remember what it felt like to be in the ocean and to think nothing of one's responsibilities on land, if only for a moment.

'Come.' The air is thick with salt and sea but the wind has pulled back, so we make our way along the shore. 'Tell me,' I say, drawing in close to Elinor as we walk along the pebbly sand, 'what has Adame said about this Finnman?'

~

Part of me thinks that maybe the men tore the boat apart like flesh from bones and divided it up among themselves. On the other hand, I suspect they'd have wanted to keep it as evidence of an intruder: the Finnman who stole their fish. I brush invisible dust from my dress. Something tells me my father oversaw the boat's fate; it was last seen at his property by Henrye.

With the men down at the harbour, helping the sailors draw stores of water from the well, I am sure I will not be discovered. The only sign of life at Father's home is the bleating from the sheep who graze nearby. I search around his home, in the fields, around the gardens and I find myself looking out to sea. Father has a clear view of the coast. He can't see Henrye's house but there's a glimpse of the foreshore that leads up to his property. Surely they'll not have taken it further north of the harbour and risk Bessie or anyone else in town seeing it? I am about to give up and leave but there's one place I have not yet checked. I enter the hut: it has a musty, earthy smell. A dirty pot sits upon the ashes of the hearth. Ruffled sheets on the bed, a spluttering of mud from the doorway that trails across the room. I sigh. 'There's nothing here. Just an old, lonely man.'

I take the broom and sweep out the dried mud; it grinds along the floor as the hard bits are compacted on the ground. I sweep and sweep until all speckles of dirt are now outside the cottage where they belong. The sea breeze freshens the air in the cottage, fit for only one person. Father insisted on living alone when I wed and Johne had agreed, helping my father lay the final stones on the cottage. My brothers had long moved out, finding young wives and quarrying stones for their houses with their own hands. My eldest brother, Patrik, should have become the landowner of the house where I now live. While he indeed owns the building, he insisted I stay as I still had my father and younger brothers to care for. Patrik chose to build a simple stone house by the pier. Furthest from me.

I sit on the side of Father's bed and for a moment I recall the heartbreak in those days and months following Mother's disappearance. How did he live with himself, knowing she'd chosen life as a seal over her family? I'd heard him mutter it to himself when he thought no one was listening.

It's something I've asked myself so many times. How *could* she leave us? And why hasn't she come back? If she is a true selkie, isn't she able to take on human form whenever she likes? Were we so easily forgotten? I am a fool. Why have I never questioned this before? Henrye's revelation is unsettling, but I am also inclined to believe him. Now that I've met Kûna and seen how human she is, how vulnerable and exposed she was on the shore, I wonder how she could possibly be a selkie? How could my mother? My poor father. I cannot bear to tell him the truth.

I kick at the ground and as my foot swings back it hits stone. I drop to my knees and look under the bed. A large stone sits under it, partially submerged in the dirt. I try to pull the stone towards me, but it is too heavy. I look around the room for something to help lift it and settle upon the broom. I leverage it under the rock. Underneath is a hole, a hole under the bed, meant for hiding something from view. My mouth is dry, and I breathe in, fighting the guilt and fear. Am I violating my father's privacy? Yes, but what if it is something that belongs to Kûna?

I lift the stone and heave it aside and there in the hole is something dark. I reach in, fingers touching something thick, soft and silky. My chest tightens; I know the feel of it. I know what this is.

A seal skin. Just like the one Kûna had when she washed ashore.

It is covered in dirt and hasn't aged well. I lift out the grey pelt and shake it. Dust drifts to the ground. I bring the soft fur to my cheek and inhale. It smells of dust and fish and warmth. And I want to hold on to it forever. Because this is not from the boat, nor does it belong to Kûna. The blood drains from my face.

This seal skin belongs to my mother.

Fifteen

Malie

Clouds hover low overhead, making it feel later in the day than it is. I see her, my seal, basking in the sun. Her eyes are trained on me. Dark eyes like mine.

Kattrine and Marion spoke in excited whispers about stories of the Finnman and how he comes ashore to take a wife. Whether she already has a husband or not is none of his concern. He will enchant and seduce her. It could explain why the men are so intent on finding him, if only to chase him away from their wives. Anne told them it was all nonsense, which made me feel better for a moment, but the stories of the Finnman are no different from the stories about my mother. She was a selkie who seduced my father. Or so they said.

I know Kûna hasn't seduced anyone. If anything, she is keen to return home. If the tales were true, wouldn't she have, by now, seduced Henrye, the widowed fisherman who offered her shelter and safety?

Father had told these stories for so long that not only did his children believe him, he had perhaps convinced himself of them too. Was it to protect us after she left? She may not have left for her selkie kin but she still left and Father stayed. How can I be angry with him about that?

If only Mother had told us her side of the story, perhaps I wouldn't be left with so many questions all these years later. Like a gentle tide, a memory ripples in from childhood. It was the summer before Mother left. From beneath the surface, I kicked up from the sandy ground, my feet together like a flipper, until at last I reached the top, gasping for breath.

'How do you hold your breath for so long?' I panted and Mother chuckled. 'It feels like my eyes will bulge from my face like a herring. It's impossible. How do you hold it?'

'I've had more time to practise, Malie. First you must succumb to the ocean, the feeling of not being in control, and simply focus on remaining calm. The more you worry about being out of breath the more likely you are to be out of breath.'

I frowned. 'Do you mean the ocean will help me if I let it?'

She shrugged and dived under the water in one swift movement before rising again, her hair slicked back.

'But you're a selkie.' I sulked. 'You were born like this.'

A strange expression flickered across her face but she looked skywards, her eyes fluttering closed as the sun glistened off her bronzed skin. I forgot to paddle my feet and slipped under the water for a moment, kicking back up to the surface. I spat out the salty water and rubbed water from my eyes. Mother looked at me.

'You mustn't let life defeat you, Malie. We must keep moving, keep trying. Every day I swim; I never say I will do it tomorrow. Why, when I can begin today? Where I come from, while it is like here, it is also different. The conditions are more challenging: the ice mountains on land and sea tower up to the sky like giants, sending glassy shadows onto the lakes below. It is a daily reminder that we are just small specks in the world.'

'But seals are born to swim,' I said, treading water.

She sighed. 'Seals yes, but not babies. I was not thrown into the water at birth. I had to learn to swim.' She came closer and caressed my cheek. 'I want you to learn everything there is to know about surviving in this world because one day I may not be here. You must be able to survive on your own.'

Panic set in and I paddled faster. 'What do you mean you won't be here? Where will you go?'

'Seals return to the same site every year to breed and moult but the rest of the time they are elsewhere. They travel, learn and explore. We're not too different.'

'Selkies, you mean?'

She sighed. 'No, Malie. I mean people.'

Like driftwood on the shore, the memory is isolated and yet dazzling like treasure. I don't know what to make of it, but I know my head was filled with selkie stories as a child and so anything my mother said slotted into that frame like a stone dry stacked in a wall. If Mother was not a selkie but an Inuk, I must re-examine the memories, the clues about her heritage. I did not want to part with Mother's pelt, but I cannot reveal what I know. Not yet.

Mother may not be a selkie, and my seal is not my mother, but this herd has brought me great comfort over the years. Like an annual gift, a message from Mother, like a thread in a caisie holding us together. I tread carefully towards the smooth, flat rocks where the herd rests. A few heads perk up and I stop on a ledge, resting here so as not to scare them off in their delicate state. She's not with the rest of them but I find her, my seal, a solitary figure on a rock. On the lookout, protecting her colony. She sees me. Pulls herself up onto her front flippers and shuffles about. I wave and she flicks her head. I wish I could wade out in the water, be close to her. She rests on the rock, awaiting the arrival of her pup. We are connected in this way: both waiting.

'All this time,' I whisper, tears threatening to trickle down my cheeks. 'I thought you were my mother. My long-lost mother, returning to see me every year.' I fight back tears to not worry the bairn, but my eyes sting and I think maybe holding back is just as harmful as letting go.

The seal howls and dives into the water. I sob and wrap my arms around my abdomen, my own precious baby. 'If you're not my mother, then where is she? Where did she go? Why did she leave me?'

Tears dampen my cheeks, my neck and chest and it is a few moments before I realise the sky is crying, too. Great big droplets fall from the darkened dome.

The seal rises from the shallows of the water, shuffles forwards. She does not shed her skin and envelope me in her motherly arms but she worms her way towards me. I sniffle and creep forwards. I extend my arm, fingers splayed open as though I am ready to accept a precious gift. I hold my breath as she nuzzles into my hand. Her whiskers tickle my palms but I don't pull away. A rush of emotion escapes in a strangled cry. I stroke her soft face, and she blinks. Her eyes are human-like, curious and kind.

A seagull squawks overhead and the trance is broken. She shuffles backwards, dips her head and returns to the sea. Tears stream down my face. Twenty years: that's how long I have waited for my mother to return. The seal gave me hope. Now, all hope is gone. Did she seek out her family in Greenland? If so, why did she choose that family over ours? And the most difficult question of all: why didn't she take us with her? My throat tightens and my stomach churns with grief. No matter her reasons, it doesn't change the fact that she never returned. Once she was gone, she didn't look back.

Rain falls, gulls squawk, seals howl and the sounds of my cries are drowned out by the sea and the sky and the wind.

~

A wild storm blows in, delaying trades by a day, maybe two. Rubble and items that were not secured on the ships have been blown up on shore by the wind. The sailors are grateful to have beaten the storm to shore and, along with my husband and brothers, are drinking to their good fortune at the inn which opens twice a year to sell ale to passing seamen. With the men otherwise occupied and the weather keeping the rest of the village indoors. I stay tight to the grasslands under the shadows of the clouds so as not to be seen from the shore. I vow this will be the last time I visit Kûna until the men go to sea.

Something scuffles past my feet in the early light; I catch a glimpse of a vole disappearing into the grass. A hen harrier releases a high-pitched squawk from her nest nearby. I hasten through the shrubbery so as not to disturb the wildlife any more than necessary. At the headland, the breeze is gentle – it too is still waking from its slumber. Henrye's dinghy is moored at the pier. It thuds against the rocks. A flock of gulls circle the seal herd beyond, squawking and flitting about in all different directions but never colliding. An organised kind of chaos. Water from the overnight rain has filled the bogs. I hope Henrye has enough stowed away for the winter.

Earthy-scented smoke filters out through a vent on the side of the cottage, a dull candlelight flickers and a shag sits atop the house, sand eels dangling from its beak. I knock on the door and Henrye answers, bleary-eyed and beard scraggly. He's exhausted. Tired from keeping this secret. I know how he feels. Even though I want to learn more about Mother's heritage, we *must* return Kûna to her homeland.

'Good day,' he grumbles, rubbing his brows.

'You look awful, Henrye. Have you had any sleep?'

He chuckles. 'Aye, not really.'

I take a deep breath. 'I believe you, Henrye.' His brows draw in with confusion. 'I believe what you say about Kûna and my mother.'

'Did you find something?' Concern is revealed in his features.

I open my mouth to speak but words don't come out. I did find something and it confirms Henrye told me the truth. 'I haven't found the boat. It's not at my home, or my father's or any of my brothers'.'

'Aye, I have been searching too.'

The house is lit by a single candle. James is perched upon a stone bench with a bowl of steaming beremeal porridge, the toasty aroma lingering in the cottage. Kûna is upright, a steaming bowl in her lap also. Her face brightens upon seeing me.

'Malie,' she says. I like the way my name sounds, with a different inflection from the one I'm used to.

'Hello, Kûna.' I sit beside her on her bed. 'How are you?'

She smiles and reaches behind her, retrieving a stone. She places it in my hands.

'What is this?' I ask, turning it over. It has an engraving of the long boat. I look at Henrye and his expression is grim. To Kûna, I shake my head and reach for her hand. 'We don't know where it is. But we will find it.' I point to the stone. 'We'll find it and you can go back home. For now, you must stay away from the sea.'

Tears spring in Kûna's eyes and I imagine how lonely it must feel to come from afar, to speak a different language, to look and sound so different. To feel so alone. I imagine that is how Mother felt. Is that why she stayed with my father? To feel less alone? And yet many years of marriage, a home full of bairns, and there was still a void no man or child could fill. The void was the sea, her home.

Together we sit teary-eyed and Henrye fusses over James to give us some space. After a little while, we sit in silence and Kûna gently pulls her hand from mine. She studies me for a moment, then places a hand upon my stomach. I draw in a breath and her eyes twinkle. 'Nârtussok,' she says.

And I recognise the word: Mother used it when she was with child. I thought it was a made-up word, but it's not. It is Inuit for expecting a child.

It now makes sense; Mother's traditions were so unlike other Orcadians.

'Yes,' I say. 'Nârtussok. I am having a bairn.'

The air stills as Henrye turns around and sees my hand cradling my stomach. His gaze flicks up to mine and a panicked expression flashes across his face. 'Malie, ye can't be here.'

'It's all right, Henrye,' I say. 'The men are at the inn; I'll be careful when they're back.'

He shakes his head, his voice deeper, more accented with emotion. 'Nae. You must go. I will take my boat around the coastline in search of the long boat. Ye can't come back here, I mean it this time. Ye cannae get caught up in this. Certainly not now,' he says nodding at my stomach, which has begun to bulge from under my dress and coat.

'Nae.' I stand. 'I will come with you. We must get her back to her homeland as soon as possible. I'm afraid of what will happen if we don't.'

'As am I.' He worries at his eyebrows. 'But I'm more concerned about your husband finding out you've been coming to a widower's home when you're with child. How that may look.'

What he doesn't say is that you're expecting a child after your husband has been at sea for many weeks, while also calling upon your widowed neighbour. A shiver travels up my spine as it is no doubt a leap my husband would take if he were in one of his tempers. I hate that Henrye knows this about my marriage.

I stand up taller. 'Henrye Sinclair, I'm quite capable of taking care of myself.'

'That's what I'm afraid of.' He sighs and then grumbles, 'You remind me of your mother.'

Before I can ask him what he means by this, he ushers me back outside and closes the door on me and the rising sun.

Sixteen

Malie

The port is alive with ships: large ships, small ships, long and short. From the Dutch Republic, Denmark, Sweden, Ireland and others I don't recognise. One of the largest is a fully rigged Norwegian ship with a seventy-person crew, stockpiled with pine to trade for boat-making and repairs.

The harbour is bustling. The women are at the stalls, trading leftover cured fish, the vegetables and grains that survived last winter and the recent storms, oil candles and medical supplies, bird and fish fat for wound tending, and seal skins pillaged from the occasional animal that washes ashore dead. Sailors mingle, as they have things to sell and trade too: Norwegian timber, beaver fur, axes and knives and so on. The sailors replenish their fresh water supplies before they set sail.

Henrye walks along the dock with James. Bessie oversees his merchant stall, set up with a barrel of geese feathers, feather quills and smoked geese meat. She has brought her homemade ale and various medicinal concoctions. James greets a captain who is inspecting the pen. There's no sign of Kûna.

Everyone in the parish is here, including my brothers and their wives, a few of the folk from the eastern side of the island, men from Hoy and some from further north, too. The traffic has increased in recent years with the war: sailors avoid the English Channel, and the colder seasons have made it difficult to navigate the open seas. With all these people here it's a relief that Kûna is hidden away – though what if one of these ships is from her homeland? What if they can help her get home? I cannot see any Greenlandic ships, nor have I heard of any making port here.

'Good mornin', James,' I say as I meet him at his market stall. I've left Elinor in charge of our stall. It's her first proper season selling spindles. Adame had mutton and live sheep but those sold earlier in the morning. Ignoring my protests, Johne slaughtered more of our flock, which also sold quickly.

'Hello, Malie.' James grins before turning back to the sailor who tests the quill on the rag paper made from linen and flax.

'Malie.' Bessie hauls me in for a firm, brief hug and is back behind the barrels before I can catch my breath. 'You a'right, love? You keepin' well?'

Henrye dips his head with a sideways glance at the barrels to my right. My husband's back is to us: he is deep in conversation with a tall, wide captain. I catch a Nordic accent on the breeze.

'Henrye, don't you think someone here could help Kûna?' I whisper. 'They could take her on their boat and get her home.'

Henrye worries at his beard, gaze flickering about the port. He says nothing but he is on alert. Will he not talk to me now he knows I'm with child?

'What's wrong?' I ask. 'Is it Kûna? She's all right, isn't she?'

'She's fine,' he grumbles. 'Aye, she's around here somewhere.'

'Here?' I ask, my skin prickling.

'Aye. If anyone asks, I'll say she's a relative from Scotland, came over with the fleet.'

Kûna appears at his side and beams at me. 'Malie.'

I smile back but keep my distance: best people don't see us being too familiar. I feel uneasy but I agree that the fleet's arrival makes for a good cover.

Henrye is rigid. 'I think I should take her back home; something is off—' He stops abruptly, eyeing my husband again.

Another two towering Norse men approach the barrels and Johne shakes each of their hands in turn. They chat in a friendly way. I hear them speak of the shoal fish migrating south since last winter, benefitting the English. The Norwegians invested in timber trades instead. Father joins them and shakes the men's hands, too. One speaks loudly and deep and brings his words to me on the breeze. 'We've lost something that belongs to us. It may have shown up here.'

'Aye?' Johne says, his chest puffed. 'What did you lose?'

'Not what, but whom.' He leans in. 'We were on a very important voyage. We lost a woman.'

Father raises an eyebrow. 'Ain't no woman washed up here.' My heart rate picks up and I sense Henrye's body stiffen behind me.

'No?' The man frowns. 'She was travelling on a long boat.'

Johne and my father exchange a look. My pulse quickens. *She*. They're looking for a woman. Finnwoman. Selkie. Now Father will know to look for a woman, and then Kûna will be exposed. I turn from Henrye to lean on a barrel, feigning interest in the goose feathers. I finger the long grey plumage, my ears trained on the conversation.

Father says, 'I'm sorry, no woman and small boat washed up here.'

Henrye shields Kûna and I hold my breath. Why has Father lied about the boat?

Johne smirks. 'And even if it did, it'd be ours to keep. Udal Law.'

The Norse men grunt. They respect the old laws.

'I must leave, now,' Henrye mutters and I turn just in time to see Kûna's stricken face as she sees the men. *Recognises* them. Henrye wraps an arm around her shoulders to cover her hair and she lowers her face as he ushers her away. James looks back with concern. *Go*, I mouth to him. *Go*. He's a sensible boy and runs after his father. The blood has drained from Bessie's face but she completes the transaction with the sailor. I look back at the scowling Nordic men who are in search of their precious cargo. Johne and Father stand together, arms folded across their broad chests, chins lifted high. They won't give in. No matter what they plan to do with Kûna, they will not hand her over to the sailors.

While they are focused on the Norsemen, I fall back into the crowd and weave my way back to Henrye's house. We must get Kûna away from here.

~

Henrye is not happy to see me but he does not send me away.

Kûna mimes a capturing, hand over her mouth, the other around her neck.

I swallow and bite back tears so I can be strong for my friend. 'They took you. Why? Where were they taking you?'

Kûna blinks, not understanding me. Henrye clears his throat. 'I've heard of this. There was word that Inuit people were being kidnapped and taken to England as foreign curiosities at fairs. The Danes are known for abducting Inuits too.'

'Capturing them? And then what?'

'I've heard from Scottish whalers that there is a long boat on display at the Physicians Hall at Edinburgh. Another is kept in the church on the Island of Burray.'

Bile rises into my throat. 'On display? And what of the people?'

Henrye's expression turns grave. 'I don't know. Some escaped, most perished.'

'Och.'

'Aye,' Henrye says.

Kûna drops her head. Silence descends for a moment, and it's as if the sea knows. It quietens for a moment, too, then rears up again, howling wind and crashing waves once more.

I pace the room. 'So, she was taken from her home. She escaped and they want her back. Why?'

He shrugs. 'Some kind of novelty.'

I click my tongue. 'It's disgraceful.'

Henrye offers me a hot drink but I decline. Keep moving, moving.

Thinking. 'If anyone speaks of her to the Norwegians, she'll be in danger.' Kûna observes us with unexpected calm. She could have been seen at the harbour; she could have been seen swimming in the sea!

'Aye. And so will you, Malie.'

I stop. 'Me?'

'Yeh pa won't be happy ye kept her hidden. Yeh husband won't be either.'

I bite the inside of my lip. 'No, they won't be happy with me at all,' I say. First, I must think of Kûna.

His expression is resigned, and his gaze lowers to my stomach. He doesn't say it aloud, but I know he is worried for me. 'I'll be all right,' I assure him. It's kind of him to care. 'What if there was a boat going in that direction? Not the Norwegians, obviously. Someone we could trust?'

Henrye thinks on it for a moment. 'Aye, there might be someone.'

My chest loosens ever so slightly now that we have a plan. It may not work, but focusing on the next thing keeps the worries at bay. But there is one niggling concern that pulls at my breath, like the serpent slurping up the sea. Kûna is no longer safe on our island, but she was also abducted from her homeland. What if she is not safe there either?

Seventeen

Henrye

Next morning, Henrye returns to the port, alone. He pulls his cap down and his coat up to brace against the westerly gale. There is still time. The crews will wait for a fair wind before disembarking on their return journeys. Henrye left Kûna and James in the care of Bessie, to whom he gave strict instructions to flee at the first sign of the MacDuffies or the Norwegians. There's an unmarked trail behind his home that leads to the south-west coast and a slippery, steep decline to the rocky coast where he has left his boat. Just in case.

He strides through the busy seaport, past the animal furs and grains. There are piles of imported Scandinavian wood used for shipbuilding. He's never seen the port so crammed – it makes sense now the only safe way to cross the Atlantic is to avoid the English Channel and sail north of Scotland, to Orkney.

Henrye cannot trust the Europeans to see Kûna home safely. So, he must take a risk. He steers clear of the MacDuffies and, at last, his ears prick to the desired accent. He approaches the displays and fingers the wool blankets and felt hats, assessing the men. They speak with a flat intonation, and their North American accent stands out amid the Europeans.

One of the crew approaches. 'Henrye!' he says as he punches him on the upper shoulder. 'I was hoping to see you. What have you got for us?'

'Joseph,' Henrye says, clasping his hand in a firm shake. Joseph is with the Hudson's Bay Company, well known for their fur trades. He hails from Ruperts Land, a territory in North America claimed by the English. Last November, Henrye set him up with clean water and provisions and mended the damage to their boat from the storm. 'It is good to see you again.'

'Without your help I'd not have returned to my homeland to see my newborn daughter before winter.'

'And how is the peedie bairn?'

'Oh, she's beautiful. Not so *peedie*, as you say, any more.' He chuckles. 'I'd say she'd be walking by now; it'll be several months before I see them again.' He gazes at the ocean wistfully.

'Och, aye. It must pain you greatly.'

'Yes. Can I repay you with blankets or furs?' His hand sweeps over the hats. 'We have these beaver fur hats – very popular with the British. I do owe you after all.'

Henrye hesitates and casts his gaze around the harbour. The Norwegian and Dutch stalls are bustling so he can't make out the men who kidnapped Kûna.

'You all right, Henrye?' Joseph asks.

Henrye notices the iridescent rock that Joseph rolls between his thumb and index finger. 'Aye. Well, nae.' He readjusts his hat. 'I do actually need something, but not blankets or furs.'

Joseph's eyebrows draw in and he steps closer with interest. 'Aye?' He tries out the Orcadian accent but fails miserably.

Henrye chuckles and, feeling more relaxed, decides he must trust the sailor from Ruperts Land. 'There's a woman ... she needs safe passage to Greenland, so she can return home.'

'A woman, you say. From Greenland?'

'Aye.' Henrye lowers his voice. 'She was kidnapped by the Norwegian crew and escaped. She is not safe here.'

Joseph scrutinises the European boats and chews on the inside of his lip. 'And you think she'll be safe aboard a ship full of *my* men?'

Henrye bristles. 'Can you give me your word she will be?'

Joseph exhales loudly. 'I will do my best. She is someone's daughter and I will care for her as my own.'

Henrye sighs with relief. 'Thank you.'

'We have good relations with the Greenlanders: I can get her there. For now, I'm in need of a new kitchen hand as ours has fallen ill.'

'That will work out nicely. I have half a tonne of kelp ash I can offer in payment.'

'Kelp? What would I do with that?'

'You can sell it. It is used for making soap and glass. My pa showed me how to make it. He used to trade it in Bristol ... but with the war, that is no longer viable.'

Henrye is the only one on the island in the kelp ash business, or at least trying to be, and that's only because the MacDuffies either didn't know what he was doing, or don't care because they have had the stranglehold on local trades for years. After Beatrice died, Henrye resurrected the practice: collecting tang, which grows between high and low waters and which he'd cut by hand when the tide was out. It only brought a good yield every few years. When burned to ash it provided the alkali for glass.

'Is that so?' Joseph thinks on this for a moment. 'You know what, Henrye. I will take half of what you have as payment but I will pay you for the remainder as long as you agree we have exclusivity over the ash in the future. If there's a market for it, that is.'

Henrye stutters with surprise at Joseph's generosity. 'Aye.' This agreement could support him and James through many winters ahead. 'I accept.'

Joseph shakes his hand and then a smile transforms his face. 'Henrye, why don't you join us? We've always found Orkney men to be skilled fishermen and to remain calm in wild weather. You would be an asset to the crew. Your boy could join us.'

He scratches at his beard, tempted by the offer and the chance to get his son off the island. To be free of the MacDuffies and the ghosts of the women he's lost. He could set up a new life. James would get experience on a large ship. Even bigger than the Norwegians'. A job with the Hudson's Bay Company is well respected, indeed. He could ensure Kûna is kept safe on the ship and help her return to Greenland.

'Well?' Joseph prompts. In the distance, Henrye sees Johne. He sighs. 'I appreciate the offer but I can't leave. Not yet anyway.'

'All right. Perhaps I can convince you next year, huh?'

Henrye nods. A lot can change in a year: he knows that only too well.

Joseph holds up the rock and then places it in Henrye's hand. 'You should take this; I think you need it more than I.'

Henrye turns the rock over. It glistens with blue and green hues, unlike anything he has ever seen before. 'What is it?'

'Labradorite. We use it as ballast, to keep the boat steady. It holds a lot of value back home. My people say the northern lights are trapped inside it.'

The glistening rock *is* like the northern lights and Henrye thinks immediately of Malie. How she combs the beach for treasures just like this one. 'Thanks, Joseph – there's someone here who will appreciate this very much.'

Joseph raises an eyebrow and Henrye flushes, rushing on. 'The wind will be fair in three days, so you can set sail then.' He hopes Bessie's prediction is correct.

'I will prepare my men. Bring her to me at dawn.'

They shake on it.

Eighteen

Malie

Footsteps on the gravelly path. My hand stills on the pot on the hearth. The scent of herbs and herring is both tantalising and nauseating. My husband allowed me to cook a fillet of fish, the last of the measly six he brought back from his last fishing expedition, relenting after I disclosed my cravings. The rest were cured.

A knock on the door. Could it be Johne already? He just left for the inn. Ale with the sailors again and to settle the crews before dusk. He must've forgotten something, unless the weather turned sour. My heart quickens and then slows. Johne wouldn't knock. I open the door and step backwards. 'Henrye?'

He breathes heavily and runs a hand through his ruffled beard. My gaze flickers past him and he reads the fear in my eyes.

'Johne is at the inn. That's why I'm here.'

My chest tightens. 'Is he all right?'

'Aye, aye.' His gaze falls on his boots scuffing at the dirt. 'I secured safe passage for Kûna. She will leave tomorrow.'

'Tomorrow?' *Tomorrow*. I breathe out shakily. 'So soon.' There's still so much to learn about Kûna: her heritage, her homeland. My heritage. My mother. Only, to keep her safe, she must leave. My head spins and I grasp the stone wall to steady myself.

'You all right, Malie?' Henrye asks, eyebrows drawn in.

'Och. It's just I was growing fond of her.'

His face softens. 'I know. I'm sorry I couldn't get here earlier to tell you; I wanted you to have more time with her. I know it's important for you to say goodbye.'

Goodbye. He knows me so well. Mother and Beatrice were gone so unexpectedly, but knowing about Kûna's departure isn't any easier – it's still heart-wrenching.

'Who is she travelling with?' I ask, my voice shaky, head still spinning. Wind blows hair across my face and I tuck it behind my ear. I want to invite Henrye inside but it's not a good idea.

'I have a friend. Joseph.' Henrye swallows. 'He's with the Hudson's Bay Company.'

'English?'

'British American.'

'Aye,' I whisper. Not European. That seems our best option. 'Henrye, are you sure you can trust them?'

Henrye presses his lips together. 'We must. I helped them last year, fixed their ship and the like. He will spend the winter trading beaver skins with the Cree and will take her to Greenland in spring. I have an agreement with him, and he's preparing his crew to leave at dawn.'

I trust Henrye, and so in turn I must trust these men. 'All right. When should I meet you?'

He hesitates, and for a moment I think he might change his mind. I know our situation is unusual; that women aren't usually included in any business with the fleet. My father and Johne have always kept me at arm's length. I've always seen them as my protectors, but now ...

'Come to my house when it's still dark. Alone. I'll row her out to meet them before dawn breaks.'

'I'll be there. I won't miss my chance to say goodbye.' The grief of losing my mother and best friend kept me small and helpless for so many years. It made me follow the men, blindly, without question. Henrye is different. He sees me, he understands me.

Henrye nods and opens his mouth as though to say something more but shakes his head, turns his back and retreats down the path in haste. His footsteps tread more heavily on his departure, his shoulders hunched.

I feel weighed down too: by the growing belly that puts me off balance and the mounting secrets I keep from my husband. It is not just my body that has widened but my perspective too. While there was once only fear bubbling beneath my skin, there is something else rising to the surface. Something fierce and uncontrollable. Something wild. Something that simmered in my mother's body too. I believe it's rage.

Nineteen

Malie

Just as I sensed his presence yesterday, he must hear the crunch of gravel under my boots: before I can raise my fist to knock, Henrye opens the door and ushers me inside. Even with the howling wind and roaring seas, Orcadians are attuned to sound. I rush past Henrye to Kûna's bedside, where she sits, warming herself by the fire, awake and alert. Her skin is silky and smooth as though she has bathed in the sea. There is colour in her cheeks. Her flesh is no longer loose on her bones and she looks taller. She leaps up to embrace me and, even after the weeks of being parted from the sea, she still smells of salt. She smells like my mother.

Without thinking, I trace my fingers through her dark hair. 'You look well, Kûna. Your hair is beautiful.' Just like my mother's. A tear trickles down my cheek and I swipe it away. 'Let me braid it for you.'

She frowns and I chew on the inside of my lip. 'Braid,' I repeat. I take her hand and mimic the weaving pattern and her eyes light up. She nods enthusiastically.

'Sit here,' I say and she obeys. She is beginning to understand the basics of our language. Mother was a quick learner too.

Henrye clears his throat and I remember the father and son in the room. 'I hope this is all right?' I ask. We only have a little time before they meet Joseph's crew and I want to savour my final moments with Kûna.

His eyes crinkle and a faint smile can be seen through his beard.

'You could do with a tidy up, too,' I say, pointing to his face. When he laughs it surprises me. It has been a long time since I have seen him smile, let alone laugh.

'Dad says it keeps the wind off his face,' James says.

'Well, I suppose that's true,' I say, separating Kûna's hair and combing it. I swallow back the lump in my throat. Mother liked her hair tied back after swimming. In the sea, she enjoyed it out, floating in the water, but when she came back on land, she wanted it pulled back, in a tight braid. Refined and tamed. After she left, I practised on Beatrice's hair until I could do it on my own.

I recall the pull and sting of having my own hair braided. It's a long time since someone else braided my hair, except when Anne did it on my wedding day. She was rough and pulled it so tightly I could barely move my eyebrows. I miss Mother's adept and gentle hands. They were the gentlest hands on this island.

It was through her language, her love of the sea, her swimming lessons that Mother was sharing with me some of her history. The life she left behind. Only I was too young and naive to understand what she was trying to tell me.

Keep something for yourself, Malie.

I secure the braid with a strip of linen and tie it twice into a bow. 'There,' I say. 'It looks beautiful.'

Kûna's hand slips into mine and I realise tears have fallen onto my dress. I brush them away. The salt reminds me of the sea. I am made of salty tears. Mother says I was born in the salty sea. It will always be a part of me. I have resisted the pull for so long but now I wonder why I bother. Mother embraced the sea, so maybe it's time I do that too.

~

It's terrible weather for setting sail. A storm brews in the distance and heavy charcoal-coloured clouds blanket the sky. The sea crashes and roars. Henrye tells me the North Americans will pull away from the port anyway. They won't delay their departure. Henrye must row his boat into the Sound and meet them, where they will sit tight until the storm blows over. Kûna shivers and Bessie pulls the coat around her.

'I thought you said the weather would be fair today,' Henrye grumbles at her.

'Nae. Not until noon. This is dangerous,' Bessie says, looking skywards. 'It's a warning from the sea spirits.'

'Aye. Going is dangerous but so is staying. The storm will pass quickly and then they'll be on their way at noon. Out with the tide on a fair wind.'

Bessie frowns at the sky and James squeezes her hand.

'Kûna, please don't go. Look.' I point to the dark, billowing clouds hanging over the inlet like the sky has heavy lids and has not yet woken. 'Danger.'

Kûna presses her hands together, her face pained. 'Go.' And then she envelopes me in a hug. We both shiver and shake as the Arctic breeze blows off the sea.

It feels like an age before the ship comes into view, bracing itself against the treacherous waves in the bay. It is handsome and proud at sea. The Hudson's Bay Company. A tall ship, with billowing flax canvas sails and extending about fifty-four feet long, it is magnificent. Kûna will be safe from the storms on this ship.

'We'll row out. The crew have been told to wait out the storm in the inlet where it's more sheltered,' Henrye says. 'Kûna, in the boat. Malie, you stay here with Bessie and James.'

'Nae,' I say. As the wind whips around us and the sky rumbles in protest, I don't care about Johne or what he will think. What he will do to me. I don't care about my father or my brothers or even the sea. I only know I must see her safely on the ship, so I am not left with any uncertainty. Not knowing. This time I must know. I must. The need to do this is utterly overwhelming. 'Nae,' I repeat. 'I am coming with you.'

'No. Malie, you're with child. It's dangerous at sea, not to mention if Johne gets a whiff of you out there with me ...' He shudders.

'How will he know I am here? I couldn't say goodbye to my mother. I would have given her a last hug – I just didn't know it. I just want to make sure Kûna will be protected, that this sailor, Joseph, is a good person. *Please.*' I follow him along the narrow pier.

Henrye gives Bessie a pleading look but she surprises us both when she clasps my hand and Henrye's. 'Take her with you, Henrye,' she says.

'Bessie, ye can't be serious?'

'It is meant to be this way,' she says. 'You must trust me, Henrye. This is the way you come back to your son.'

I don't question Bessie's obscure message but I'm relieved I have her support.

Henrye sighs and turns his back on us. 'Get in.'

While James steadies the boat, Henrye helps Kûna board and sit on the damp seats.

The waves roughen the edges but Henrye's hand, when he reaches for me, is warm and comforting. He nods at his son, who throws the rope onboard and walks back to the shore, joining Bessie.

Henrye's oar sweeps the sea, in and out, in a drum-like rhythm. In, out, in out. The sea crashes against the boat. It begins to drizzle. I clutch at Kûna. Please don't go. Don't go. Please stay. Stay. Words I wish I'd whispered to my mother. But my friend is not safe here: she must go. She must leave, too.

We approach the boat but the height of the waves keeps us from getting too close. The drizzle spirals into a downpour and in an instant we are all soaking wet. Shivering and clinging to the edge of the boat. Father's words haunt me: *Nothing but danger out there.*

'Kûna, don't go!'

'Go,' Kûna insists, and I am torn between wanting to protect her from the island and wanting to protect her from the sea.

Henrye focuses on steering the boat, his oars thrashing in the sea. I see the concern in his furrowed brows and clenched jaw. He knows we are heading towards danger. The rain eases but the weather is our greatest enemy right now. The Sound is treacherous on a calm day; today it is set on terrorising us.

I slip out of my outer coat and help Kûna do the same with her seal skin – they'll only weigh us down if the boat flips. She wears her pants and Beatrice's knitted jumper. She left behind her furry boots.

Kûna says something else but I can't hear her over the roar of the sea and sky. Rumbles shake the boat from above and below. There are no seals in sight. The mist hides Bessie and James from view.

Men call from the boat; lights flash aboard; we can just make out frantic waving and pointing behind them. And that's when we see it. Out of the mist, Father's Yole approaches the larger ship. My heart thumps in my chest and my stomach feels as though it has descended through the floor of the boat, plunging into the depths of the sea.

They're searching for Kûna. I know it in my heart. Udal Law. What washes up on the shores belongs to the island. It doesn't matter if it's driftwood or a woman: it doesn't leave. We never leave. I should have known they were aware of Kûna all along – nothing on our small island ever escapes their notice. Or their control. The clouds erupt again and thick fat droplets fall from the sky. Henrye glances back and with a determined look he steers away from the ship.

'Nae!' I scream. 'We must get her onboard.'

'They know,' he yells back.

'Och, that's why she must leave!' I cry over the crashing waves, the booming sky, the fear in my thudding heart. The Hudson's Bay ship is bigger than Father's Yole and their crew greater: surely, they can protect her from them. Udal Law or not.

Kûna glances worriedly between us. The Yole is now blocking the ship. She pulls me in for a hug and then she clasps Henrye's free hand. She whispers something to him. She holds my gaze for a long, treacherous moment and then she drops his hand. Her skin glistens; sleek and lean. She closes her eyes and draws in a full breath.

And then she dives into the sea.

Twenty

Malie

Swallowed by the sea. Sucked into the stomach of the ocean, like an insatiable whale. 'Kûna!' I lean over the edge of the boat and it tilts with my weight.

'Nae. Malie.' Henrye pulls me back and the boat wobbles but we stay afloat. We are struck by a deluge of rain. My own worry is reflected in his face. He gasps for breath but his grip is firm, solid on my arm.

'Kûna,' I sob and drop to the bottom of the boat. He tries to shield me from the downpour, from the hurt, but it is no use. We are both sopping wet, alone and in pain.

'Can she swim?' His words crackle in the wind.

I recall seeing Kûna bobbing in the sea, diving with the grace of a seal. Her movements were lithe, well-practised. But this? 'Aye, she can swim.' I look at the sea but I do not catch sight of her resurfacing. Has she come up for breath? How could she in these conditions?

A splash just beneath the surface a peedie way in the distance has me leaning back over the side of the boat. 'Henrye, what is that? Is that a tail? A seal?' Nae, the seals took off before the storm hit. Didn't they?

'We must go back,' he yells over the howling wind. The boat rocks wildly from side to side. He regains control of the oars. 'Lie down low.'

With one final glance back, I do as he says. Father's Yole is beside the ship now. Flickers of light in the dark. We must stay out of sight of the Yole. Voices carry on the wind.

A wave strikes the boat, crashes down upon me. One hand grips the side, the other cradles my stomach. What was I thinking coming out in this? I could lose my bairn. I blink away the salt water: my eyes burn. My throat is dry. Henrye flicks his head and pulls the oars towards him in the thrashing sea but one oar cracks and splinters. He loses his grip and it too is swallowed by the waters.

'Let me help,' I yell. He shakes his head and throws the other oar into the boat. It is no use; the weather is too wild and the waves are chaotic. We huddle together, gripping the bench. We bounce and rock and as it leans to the side we lean back the other way. A crack of thunder, shards of lightning and a deluge of rain. The dinghy rocks furiously; we hunker down but the sea is stronger than us. The sea is in control.

I fall into Henrye, who tumbles backwards. I hold his gaze for the briefest moment before the boat overturns and we too are thrown into the mouth of the sea.

Down. Down. Down.

I descend into the dark depths of the water. Eyes squeezed shut, breath held, and I am falling. Water-laden clothes pull me lower. The water hugs me; my mother's arms embrace me. I think I could stay here forever. Like Mother. Like Kûna. It is peaceful here.

I open my eyes and there she is. Mother. *Malie*, she mouths, her hair spilling around her shoulders. Dark hair, silky hair. My hair. *Malie*.

Mother is beautiful; I miss her. For so long I have yearned for her and here she is, at last. Looking the same as on the day she left. I reach for her. I blink salty tears and then she is no longer my mother: her nose elongates, her spotted skin is grey and silky, she has fins and flippers. But her eyes are the same.

Malie. My mother seal and her bulging belly. My hands cup my stomach. *My* bairn. Och. I can't stay here, hiding beneath the surface. I must face what's out there for my bairn's survival. I draw my feet together as if they are one, like a flipper. I flick with all my might. My arms reach out straight, and I am moving against the sea, up, up, up.

The gentle rocking transforms into rough handling and I break through the surface. Gasping at the salty air. I cannot see the boat. No seal. No Henrye. The waves crash over me and I am pushed under again.

I kick myself back up to the surface. 'Henrye!' There's a groan and splashing. I see him. His head dips under water. 'Henrye!'

He can't swim. *I remember how you and your ma played together in the water. I was envious.* Bessie said I was meant to be here – this is how Henrye will get back to his son. She was right. I dive just below the surface so the waves cannot throw me. I rise to breathe and then dive down further where I can glide more freely.

At the surface, a splash and a call. 'Malie!' Henrye is splashing around, barely keeping his head above the choppy waves. And then he is under. I reach for him. He reaches for me. Our hands grip one another and we are rolled into the air together.

'Lie on your back,' I tell him but he goes under again, pulling me down with him. We both kick to the surface: he knows how to do that, at least. He has watched me do it. My clothes are heavy. It's a good thing I've already taken off my larger coat. I lie backwards, pulling his back to my chest. The water crashes over our faces. He is big but not too heavy in the sea. Even a swelling stomach does not pull me down. My body remembers. This is the only way.

I tuck my arm around his chest and his hands grip mine. 'Kick your feet,' I say, and he does. His reckless movements smooth out and I feel him relax against me as we kick in unison. Waves crash over us and I hold my breath until they pass. I kick, and the movement is slow but I keep kicking. We kick together.

The tide is coming in and I trust the sea to take us back towards the rocks where we left Bessie and James. Don't fight it, Mother told me, you will only tire yourself. Mould to it and it will help you. It is dangerous to be thrown against the rocks but there we can catch our breath.

Kick, breathe, kick, breathe. I hold Henrye tight; he holds me tighter. A mirage in the mist; is that my mother? Glossy black hair, glossy grey skin. Tears sting my eyes; I blink and it's gone. Keep moving. Kick, breathe, kick, breathe.

'The rocks,' I shout. The pier isn't far. Henrye looks back at me and I see the gratitude in his eyes. Admiration, too. My stomach flips and turns and then we pull apart.

Henrye kicks free and a wave pushes him onto the rocks. I reach out and grab one, my shoulder hitting a sharp edge, my cheek colliding too, and yet I hold on. Wait for the waves to roll over me. My clothes weigh me down. I press my stomach against the smooth surface of the rock, shielding my bairn from the waves. Almost there, peedie one, we're almost there.

Henrye has hauled himself onto the rocks and he reaches out to me, pulls me up to him. The weather is calming; there is even a glimpse of blue on the horizon. Water drips from his tousled hair and his beard, falling on my face. As I stumble onto the rocks, his hands explore my face, fingers graze across my cheeks, down my arms. His eyes burn. 'Are you all right, Malie? Are you hurt?'

I shake my head but no words come out. I cough. My throat is raw from sea water. He helps me sit upright. I hold my belly. I am battered and bruised but I am alive.

Henrye drops onto his knees beside me. He heaves and gasps. Relief. His fingers weave through mine. 'Malie,' he says through a ragged breath. 'You saved my life.'

I swallow and gaze back at the sea. 'Nae. My mother did.'

Twenty-One

Malie

We survived the sea and the sky and the rocks but we have not yet faced my husband. As the storm retreats and we catch our breath, men leap from my father's Yole into a high tide sea. My father, my brothers and other menfolk, all sopping wet. Bessie and James dart towards us from the shoreline but my husband is ahead of them. His shoulders are tense, hands in tight fists. He kicks through the water, marches across the sandy bank to the rocks. His eyes pierce me, his mouth moves. The wind howls and so I couldn't hear him even if I wanted to. But I know what he's thinking.

You're in big trouble, Malie.

I should stand up, get to him before he gets to us, at least put distance between me and Henrye, but I am too exhausted. I wrack my brain for excuses, anything, to placate him. But my mind is a storm of images.

Rough waves, a glimpse of Kûna in the sea and the torrent of rain. Henrye sinking underwater. The rocks against my abdomen. *Mother.*

How can I explain this away? Weighted down by the water, the ache of my muscles, the bruises on my body. It's written all over his face. No more visits with Henrye. No more Kûna. No more seals. *No more, Malie.* I know my freedom has come to an end.

It would usually stir up tension, kick my instincts into gear. Not this time. The knowing settles heavily upon me, fear smothered in exhaustion. My breath shakes and tears trickle down my already wet cheeks.

Henrye remains on the rocks, too. His breath has evened out and the weariness has shifted into an alert state. Our eyes meet and he reluctantly lets go of my hand.

Who is going to handle it? Handle him? is the question in his eyes.

'Tell him she seduced you,' I say, wheezing.

'Who?'

'Kûna. Tell him.' My breath shakes as I look at my husband. He emerges from the mist like a mighty god, towering over us, spittle flying from his mouth.

'What in God's name, Malie?!'

I lower my gaze.

'What were ye doing out there with him?! In that blasted storm!'

I draw in a breath, Henrye pulls himself upright. Johne's fists are red and pulsing. 'Ye right bastard.' He pushes Henrye and he stumbles backwards onto the rocks with a grunt. 'Trying to take me wife away from me. And me bairn, too!' He raises his fist.

'Johne,' Henrye growls. 'Your wife saved my life. Let me explain.'

Johne turns his fury on me, his fist still raised in the air. Could Bessie be right about my fate on this island?

'We fell overboard,' I say, my voice raspy. 'I swam us to safety.'

Swam. I see the word tick over in his mind and how he stores it away for later.

'Why were you there? Were ye leavin?' My husband's eyes narrow and for a moment I think he may throw me back into the sea.

'Nae,' Henrye says. 'We were trying to help the woman.'

Johne turns his head to Henrye but his eyes remain trained on me. I am still, my face is blank, I give nothing away. Nothing for him to use against me.

Henrye stands up tall, a flicker of pain crosses over his face. 'Ye were after the selkie woman? Isn't that why ye were out there?'

Johne frowns. 'I heard she'd been living with ye.'

Henrye feigns embarrassment. 'She right tricked me, she did.'

Johne opens his mouth and closes it, the tension easing. A little. 'I'm sure that ain't hard to do.'

Henrye ignores the jibe. 'I heard the Norwegians were looking for her and that's when I realised, she had ...' His gaze flicks to me and back at Johne. 'She seduced me.'

I wait with bated breath to see if Johne accepts Henrye's lie. I see how it pains Henrye to feign weakness, especially to Johne. 'I planned to bring her to Neill but she escaped. She wanted to go with the North Americans.'

'It's true,' I say. 'I insisted Henrye take me on the boat, I thought being a woman, I may be able to convince her to come back. But it was too late, she saw the Yole.'

Johne looks at the sea. 'So where is she?'

I exhale. It was so dark, he mustn't have seen Kûna on our boat. The image of Kûna diving into the sea will haunt me forever. 'She couldn't have survived the storm.'

'She's a selkie,' he roars, charging forwards.

'She didn't have her seal skin! Johne,' I say, 'she didn't make it. I saw her struggle and go under.' I hold his gaze. Please believe me. Please leave Kûna alone. If by some small chance she survived the storm, please let her be. I remember the tail. The splash. Did my eyes deceive me? And what of my mother?

He looks between us: he can sense something is off but he can't put his finger on it. Not yet. A beam of light pierces through the clouds. The sun rises, undeterred by the storm. The sky lightens; the waves settle into a lull.

I pull myself up to my feet, caress my stomach and watch as the two men settle their gaze upon it. The bairn is the only thing that catches my husband off guard, as though he cannot decide whether it is a threat or not. Johne's face softens as I take his hand. 'Let's go home,' I say.

Father cracks open the momentary calm with his staunch arrival, his jaw clenched, nostrils flaring and accent thick. 'How dare ye!' He jabs at Henrye's chest, knocking him back on the rocks.

'Father!' My appeal only angers him further.

'It's not enough you got yeh wife killed and now you want to take my daughter too?'

It makes no sense and yet there's a flash of something behind Henrye's eyes. Fear?

'We struck a deal with the Norwegians. Trade the girl and the long boat for a ship. One that will take us to the deep sea. Now look what ye've both done! We have nothin'!'

Henrye drops his head, only inciting my father more. 'Ye will pay for this, Henrye Sinclair. My word!' He clears his throat and spits at the ground. Henrye does not look up. I will him to look my father square in the eyes and yet I want him to say nothing at the same time. I want them to forget about him.

'It's my fault, Father.' He turns on me then, eyes narrowing as though he does not know me at all. A flash of Mother's seal skin comes to mind and it hits me that, as I watch Father's retreating back, I don't really know him either.

'Ye deal with her,' he says to Johne.

Johne turns on Henrye and his face hardens once more. He regains control, grips my upper arm and I flinch. It is the shoulder that crashed against the rocks. 'Let's go.'

'Aye,' I say.

I feel Henrye's eyes on me. I lift my chin and I don't look back. I hope my indifference will protect Henrye from my father.

~

I feign sleep when Johne slips out at dawn. The Norwegian crew delayed their departure due to the storm and their wish to find Kûna. The Hudson's Bay Company is gone. Johne must see the others off now conditions have improved. I lie in a half-wake, half-drowsy slumber until long after he is gone and the sun is high in the sky. I have leaped out of bed at the first fluttering of my eyelids every morning since I could walk. Not this time. I dared not move all night. Just the thought of sitting up fills me with dread.

The beat up from the ocean and the rocks has left my body bruise-stained and throbbing. And then there was the beating afterwards.

I rub my face and flinch as my fingertips graze my eye. Swollen and mucky. At least he left my belly alone. There's a small bruise on the side from where I hit the rocks but it is otherwise clear. I caress my belly. *We'll be all right, peedie one.* We survived not one storm, but two. The worst is behind us, for today is a day 'atween the weathers.

I push myself up and everything hurts. I groan and shift my weight but it's no better. My chest feels tight, grief-stricken. *Kûna.*

I flop back onto the bed. Let sleep pull me under once more. I cannot move when awake, but in the darkness, I can rewrite the story. I dream of Kûna's escape. Henrye. Seals. And Mother's calls from under the sea.

Twenty-Two

Malie

I rouse to a gentle swaying, as though I am lying in a boat upon a soft swell. The calm sea Mother told me about, not the dangerous sea Father speaks of. I am one with the water.

'Malie.'

Johne? He can't be back already. They were out with the Norwegians looking for Kûna. Desperate to keep their deal. Desperate for a bigger boat, to secure bigger hauls, bigger trades. I hope, if she survived, she is far, far away from here. I cover my face and curl up on my side.

'Malie, love.' Not Johne. A woman's voice. I squint through my good eye. *Bessie.*

I groan, tuck my knees up as high as they will go over my stomach.

A tender but firm hand grips my shoulder. 'Are ye all right, love? Is it the bairn?'

'She's all right,' I say. *She*. I know it now; it's in my bones. *She*. I'm having a girl. She met her real father last night. I want to keep her inside me forever. Keep her safe.

Bessie sighs. 'All right, let's get you up then before that husband of yours returns.'

A sob breaks free when she rolls me over. The pain shoots down my shoulder towards my fingertips. Every part of me aches and throbs.

'Oh dear.' Bessie sees my face. She draws in a controlled breath and breathes out heavily through her nose. Mutters something unintelligible under her breath.

I prop myself up and she wraps her arms around me. I feel like a child, but I don't mind her maternal embrace. Tears trickle down my cheeks, the graze on my cheek stinging. My heart aches for Kûna.

'You best be careful around that Henrye, love.'

'He's my friend,' I say. And he's not the one who hurts me.

'I know,' she says quietly. 'He's a good man. And friends are hard to come by out here, but your husband won't believe that.'

He was angrier about that than Kûna's escape. I bite the inside of my mouth until I taste blood on the tip of my tongue. I clench my fists; they are smaller and softer than Johne's. *Why must they take everything from me?*

Father took away Mother's truth, her joy of the sea. He took away the joy of swimming in the ocean and replaced it with fear. *Keep something for yourself, Malie.* I tried, Mama, but there's nothing left. Johne has taken the boat. Kûna. Henrye.

Bessie worries at her lip. 'The men are desperate, love. When men are desperate, they do terrifying things.'

It's the first time since Bessie shared her premonition with me that I truly believe Johne could be capable of killing me. She heaves me up on my feet and I flinch as tender skin stretches and pulls. The soles of my feet are dotted with scratches and scrapes from the rocks.

'Let's take you down to the bay, dip your feet in the sea. It will help with the healing.'

I shake my head. 'I can't go down there. Johne won't like that, not after yesterday.' I must stay away from the sea. Fight the pull, not be like my mother.

Bessie clucks her tongue. 'I will deal with him. Come, it will do you good.'

My stomach flutters and I realise I may not want to go to the sea but my body craves it. My body remembers how to swim; I saved Henrye. I let Bessie guide me as we shuffle towards the door. She lets me go through first and we step out into a rare, clear blue day. No clouds. A day 'atween the weathers. Like the day my husband returned injured, there is no evidence in the sky or the sea of the storm of yesternight. Once again, everything has changed.

~

The sea is surprisingly calm. It too needs time to recover from its treachery. One distant cloud puff on the horizon, a gentle breeze. I breathe in deeply, filling my lungs with the salty air. Bessie ushers me closer.

I am surprised when I see Henrye's boat at the pier, half-submerged in the water. How did he retrieve it? It was badly damaged in the storm. There's no sign of Henrye or James. We don't venture any closer to his foreshore.

'They're all right,' Bessie says, reading my mind. 'Kûna will be, too.'

Before I can ask Bessie how she knows this, Johne marches towards us and Bessie stands close to me. Before he can speak, and there would be nothing nice he was planning to say given the expression on his face, Bessie gets in first. 'Oh, Johne. What a lovely day isn't it? Terrible storm yesterday.'

Johne's gaze flickers to my feet in the water. I am not meant to talk to Bessie. He thinks her a witch! 'Ye should leave if ye know what's good for ye,' he snarls at her.

'All those cuts and bruises from the rocks, don't want them infected. Wouldnae be good for the bairn,' Bessie says.

I glare at the cuts and nicks on my feet. The salt water stings at first but the water is so cold, icy cold, my flesh is numb now. Numbness is better than feeling the pain. If only I could fall into the sea, submerge myself and disappear under the surface. Right now, it hurts to breathe. Beneath my chest is a cracking sensation as it expands and deflates. I can't be sure if it was an injury sustained on the rocks, or at home.

Johne studies me for a moment, he opens his mouth to speak but just as he does chatter from the direction of Adame's place pulls our attention away. Four women come into view; their words fade away on the breeze but their faces and hand signals reveal an animated, urgent worry.

Johne won't want to face all my brothers' wives. Not with what he did to my face. He turns back to me and flinches, seeing the stains of his fists on my skin. 'Don't stay out in the cold too long, Malie. Ye should be keepin' warm.' He looks to say something else: an apology perhaps. But he shakes his head and turns away. Strides back along the bay, back to the port and the menfolk. A flash of my fate, my body on the sand, torments me.

The women join us. Elinor fusses over me, Kattrine and Marion too. Hands caress my stomach. Reassure me I have a tough one growing inside. I want to feel my bairn but I am numb. I feel nothing. Anne heaves my arm up over her shoulder and I wince at the knifing pain in my ribs. She takes most of my weight, her sturdy gait ensuring I do not lose my footing. They guide me step by step back to the house. I let them walk me home, the sea behind me. Kûna, Henrye, Mother.

Bessie falls behind – I look for her but she is gone. The fire is lit with the driest peat, sparking a hot, soaring flame. I am warmed from the outside; inside I am as cold as ice. No one mentions the bruises that are shadows not of rocks but fists, but the women are gentle with me. They stay busy, keep the fire going, warm up the soup, place it in my cold, numb hands. Elinor warms my feet. Anne busies herself with food preparation. I don't care much what it is. Kattrine and Marion chatter quietly about nonsensical things but, even so, it is comforting.

I watch them coordinate duties as if they were a school of fish, moving as one with purpose. They avoid looking me in the eye: instead, they fuss over me as though I am one of their bairns. All except Elinor, who goes to stand by the door. Her gaze doesn't waver.

I see you, Malie. I see you.

Twenty-Three

Malie

The men from the sea return red-faced and furious. I have come down to the port to collect clams and sand eels, arriving at the same time as the men disembark the boat. Father leads the crew, ordering Jerome and Adame to bring in the empty nets, Patrik to throw the rope from the bow and Johne to secure them to the hooks along the pier.

As he comes ashore, Johne sees the caisie in my hand and his eyes narrow. Perhaps he is remembering how I diverted our last conversation about the caisie. I lift my chin. 'Welcome back.'

He grunts, his mouth pulling down at the corners. Is he thinking about the lies? All the things I have kept to myself, all the ways I have deceived him? The caisie, the long boat, Kûna and Bessie. They'd only been gone overnight after some of the men on Hoy alerted them to a sighting of a woman on one of the skerries. My brothers look grim and a surge of hope wells inside me. Kûna might still have escaped them.

Johne's gaze rests on my abdomen and his face softens. His rough beard scrapes against my cheek as he plants a kiss there. The smell of sea salt and sweat catches in my throat. A wave of nausea washes over me, and I sway on my feet.

'You all right, Malie?' he asks, clasping my elbow to steady me. Gentle. Always gentle after the roughness.

'I'm just a peedie light-headed.' I smile demurely. 'It happens sometimes.'

'Aye.' He rubs my arm with affection, and I have a momentary glimpse of the man I agreed to marry. The man who was sweet and thoughtful and caring. He's still that man underneath the gruff, bristly exterior.

As the dizziness subsides, I regain focus. 'Did you find her?'

He pulls away, his face and neck and shoulders pulsing with tension. I shouldn't have said it. I've ruined it. These moments of connection with my husband are so rare now, it catches me off guard. I can't help but break it. It might be that the disconnect, the tension, has become so familiar to me that there is some security in it. Because when my husband is not simmering with tension, I know the next bout is not far away. Sometimes, the anticipation of his temper is worse than the actual storm.

'Nae. We did not find the selkie. Let's hope she drowned in the storm.'

'Aye,' I say. 'And the fish?'

He walks ahead and I scutter behind him. 'Still gone.'

'Oh.' I take bigger strides, panting to keep pace with him.

'Aye. It's a problem, it is. We'll have no choice but to cull the seal pups.'

I stumble. 'The pups?' No. 'Surely there has to be another way?'

He stops abruptly and faces me. I bump into his chest, a stab of pain in my own. His hair and eyebrows are unruly from his time at sea. 'It must be done, Malie. Then there'll be less seals to eat our fish next season. They're all thriving. They have found fish somewhere, and they've left nothing for us. If we cull the pups from the colony at the Point, then we'll have plenty of blubber to keep us through the winter – and to trade with the Norwegians. Neill will get his boat.'

So that's what they've negotiated with the Norwegian sailors. My mouth is dry. How can they possibly kill the seal pups? Father believes my mother is a selkie, doesn't he? That's why we changed our practices. Why would he change his mind now? Unless he knew all along ...

'We can't have you all taking over this island, can we?' Johne snarls, cutting off my thoughts before he stalks away. Father comes ashore, and his gaze settles on my stomach. He dips his head in acknowledgement. That will be all: no talk of the bairn to come.

Johne believes Father's story of the selkies. If they think my mother was a selkie, then what does that make me? It's in my blood; it runs through my veins. And the bairn? I shiver. The men have so easily agreed to hand Kûna over, to cull the seal pups. Is my own baby endangered by their superstition and fear?

A gust of wind blows off the sea, the temperature drops and the sky darkens. Seals howl in the distance. I must protect the seal pups and I must protect my bairn. I only hope it is possible to do both.

Part II

Pupping Season

Twenty-Four

Malie

'They're ready,' I tell Elinor, inspecting the flax stalks lying on the dewy morning grass on the moorland behind her house. I roll a stalk between my thumb and forefinger; it is brittle and crunchy like straw. After the flax is pulled up, it is spread evenly across the field and over the following three weeks the natural fibres decompose so the fibre separates from the straw.

'You think so?' Elinor twitches her nose. It's a mild nutty smell – it has not gone rancid as did much of last year's crop. 'How can you tell?'

'See here: the sun has dried them well enough.'

'Aye,' Elinor says, but she doesn't sound convinced.

'Best bring them indoors. A storm is coming.' The wind had an extra pull to it on the short walk here and I spied flat anvil-shaped clouds darkening on the horizon. Summer is behind us; the flax flowers have died off and the stalks turned yellow and the seeds brown. We harvested the stalks and it was hard work, straining on my back. Even though I am with child, it must be done. Once pulled up, the stalks are laid out for the process of dew retting. As the seasons change, my body is also transforming. Four months along and my abdomen swells beyond my clothes. Not to mention it is early autumn, which means pupping season is upon us. I've tried hard not to think about it. Redwings glide through the air, sped up by the wind behind them. There's a chill in the air, a niggling reminder that winter will be with us soon.

'Thank you, Malie,' Elinor says. 'This is the first good crop I've had since I've been on the island. I'm grateful that you've shown me what to do. Without any fish to trade, I hope to sell enough spindles of linen yarn to get us through the winter. I want to help in any way I can.'

'As do I,' I say. Not that Johne cares much for the yarn. Without fish and so few sheep available for slaughter, he is set on culling the pups. I shiver, pulling my coat tighter around my shoulders. Elinor made me a linen belt to tuck under my breast to keep my tunic wrapped tight around my growing waistline. The sewing is imperfect but it's a thoughtful gesture. I help her haul the flax indoors, stacking it in a pile in the corner of the room furthest from the hearth.

I am grateful for Elinor's good-natured friendship since we lost Kûna; my only company aside from Johne. Anne and the sister wives Kattrine and Marion have kept their distance from me, likely suspicious of my attempts to help a selkie escape the island. It was an odd change in direction after they'd been so nurturing and kind after the storm. I suspect my brothers, who will want to stay on Father's good side, have warned them to stay away from me. The wives have been pleasant enough at church but beyond that there is little to be said. Elinor's attempts to mediate between us have been far less successful than her solid flax harvest. At least preparing the spindles for the returning sailors who will want warm clothing for winter will keep my mind busy.

I think about Kûna often. Where she may be, if she even survived. I hold on to hope. The not knowing is, as I feared, the most difficult part of it all. It's just like losing my mother all over again. I'm always carrying a sandstone rock in my stomach: that's how heavily the dread sits within me. The only certainty I have is that I will not leave this island. I will have my bairn and I will not know what happened to my mother or Kûna. I also know if I disobey, I will be punished. If not by my husband, then by my father. I must do whatever I can to keep the bairn safe. The bairn is my priority. That, and the seals.

As we bring in the last of the flax, a gusty wind blows up off the harbour and we sink lower into the ground, lean into the wind so the flax doesn't blow out of our arms. 'Would you like to come in for a hot mug of broth? Warm you up after being in the wind?' Elinor asks just as my nephew's screech elbows through the open doorway.

'Och, I best get back before the storm.' I steady myself against the stone wall to catch my breath.

'Ye all right, Malie?' Elinor frowns. 'Yer looking pale.'

'Aye, I'm fine.' I've not been as able to keep up with the physical work as I usually can. Though it probably doesn't help that yesterday I pulled in all my own crop of flax on my own. Johne was busy up the back repairing the sheep dyke that toppled on one of the sheep in a storm two days ago. The poor thing was trapped for God knows how long and was barely conscious by the time we discovered her the following morning. Johne put her out of her misery and got to work skinning her. It means we have an abundance of the one food I can not stomach. It does keep Johne happy, which is a small reprieve for the loss of the sheep and our dwindling livestock. We now have twenty-five ewes, two lambs and one ram: half of the herd we started with when we wed. We'll give some of the meat to my father: best to keep him happy too. He's not been able to look at me since the day at the inlet when I pulled Henrye ashore. His disdain is glaringly obvious in the way that he speaks only to Johne despite my presence. Even with my growing girth, I've become even more invisible.

Elinor sends me on my way with a freshly baked bere bannock, which I accept greedily, plucking off a chunk as soon as I set out for home. The wind gains strength, so I steer clear of the coast and make my way across the moorland to the house. That's when I see Bessie coming towards me. Like the wind, she picks up speed and she pulls me in for one of her firm but short embraces. 'Malie, love. How are ye?' Before I can answer she continues. 'I've just been to see Henrye, to tell him the good news. This has worked out well, bumping into ye out here. Is yeh husband about?' She surveys the moorland.

My heart thumps a little faster knowing Johne will be angry if he stumbles across the two of us. There have been fresh whispers about Bessie's witchcraft around town. He's warned me away from her. With the rumours about me helping the selkie, it won't do me any good to be associating with the old woman. I've been trying my best not to upset him, but I am curious about the good news and so, despite the danger, I ask her about it.

She clasps my hands together and grins. I didn't notice it before but she has a tooth missing on the bottom left. Is that new? Her tongue nestles in the gap. 'There's been word of a woman sighted up north. Not the first time I've heard it either, but I didn't want to get your hopes up. Now it's been confirmed by one of the McAlisters, who were visiting family in Bergen over summer. Then there's old man Bernard up on Rousay: he says it too.'

My skin tingles in anticipation. 'What woman? What are they saying, Bessie?'

'After a wild storm in mid-summer, a woman was seen on a small island off the Mainland. Had long dark hair. Up north near Rousay. They're sayin' she's a selkie.' At the mention of a storm, the sky crackles overhead.

'Och?' I try to picture it but I've not been up north since I was a child.

'Don't worry, lass. No one could get close enough to be certain. If it is Kûna, she's a clever girl. She'll keep out of their way.'

Clouds rumble and without any further warning a heavy torrent bursts from the sky. 'Ye best not stay out in this storm, Bessie.'

'I'll be right, love; I'll head back to Henrye's until it passes. The woman, it's Kûna. I'm sure of it.'

Bessie's words lighten the stone of dread in my stomach. Softening it slightly, making room for hope. 'Are you certain?'

Bessie squeezes my hand once more and then drops it. 'We must go. I'll have a better sense of whether it's true if I can get close enough. You know I can feel these things.'

No doubt she could and though I'd like to go north and confirm Kûna survived that storm, I cannot leave. 'You know I cannot go with you,

Bessie. Johne will never allow it.'

'Your husband will be out on the boat two days from now. When the weather clears. Your father is taking them out. They'll be heading east on another useless fishing expedition. They'll be wanting to catch something to lure the pups when they wean.' She clucks her tongue in disgust. 'But that means we can take my boat up the west coast and he'll be none the wiser.'

I pull the coat tight around me. Firstly, I do not know how Bessie knows this about my own husband when he has not said a word to me. Secondly, the women will stay behind and surely they'll inform on me. Thirdly, her boat is far from a sturdy form of transportation. 'Bessie, how do—?'

Bessie yells over the roar of the sea and the sky. 'Tell him you need to keep watch on the seals. For the pups.' She gives me a knowing look. 'Tell him what he needs to hear to let you go. Let him think you're on his side.'

I open my mouth to protest but close it again in resignation. We both know the curiosity and that small chance of hope are all I need. Kûna is like my family. I won't be at peace until I know she survived that storm. Perhaps a part of me also needs to know there's a possibility of escaping this island. That there's somewhere safe I could take my bairn, if it ever came to that.

~

The mutton stew is hot and thick and fills my chest and belly with warmth, while my skin remains cool to touch. The fire flickers in the draught of the strong gale circling the cottage. There is ice in the wind.

Johne slurps the soup, his mind elsewhere. He has been distracted for days. Or maybe it is me who is distracted. I clear my throat. 'How is the stew?'

'Aye. Good.' He grunts but does not look up.

Wind howls, ringing in my ears. The flame flickers but holds itself against the draught. 'I must leave early tomorrow,' I say. 'Earlier than usual.'

He looks up, his light brows drawn in.

I lift my chin. 'To check on the seals.'

His eyes narrow. 'Nae.'

'Nae?' My heart races. Nae? I must go with Bessie. I must know if Kûna is safe.

'Nae.' He lowers his spoon, his fist tight with tension. I will not forget those fists and what they can do. I must avoid becoming the body on that beach.

I swallow back the lump in my throat. 'Johne, it's nearly time,' I say, hating myself. I hate that I am using the seals as bait. 'It's nearly time for the pups. They birth overnight and early morning. I want to be there when it begins.' I say this knowing we are a couple of weeks from the first pups being born, but Johne does not know the seals as I do and I am relying on that fact right now.

He mulls this as he swallows and I force myself to hold his gaze. 'We must get the timing right, Johne. If I know exactly when they will be born then I can tell you when they will wean from their mothers.' I grit my teeth together, knowing I must give him what he needs to hear. Like

Bessie said: let him think I'm on his side. 'I want to make it up to you. I know you owe the Norwegians and you must nurture the alliance. And get that boat for Father.'

He sucks his tongue as he thinks. The wind howls. My heart raps against my chest, as loud as the howling wind. I will it to quieten, my breath to return to its usual rhythm, to hide my nerves. He will feast on them. I tuck my hands under the table, wringing them together, to move while being still.

He weighs up his options. He cannot have eyes on the seals at the Point when he is heading out with the crew. He knows this. After a moment he slurps back another spoonful of soup. 'Aye. Ye check on them and when we're back we'll prepare for the cull. Trade 'em in November when the fleet returns.'

'Aye.' I exhale, releasing my hands and picking up the spoon again. 'That's a good plan.' My chest tightens as I think of my seal. How will I save her? And the pups? It's impossible.

I sip the stew, the tension in my body softening in its warmth. First Kûna. Then the seals. One problem at a time.

Twenty-Five

Henrye

A disappearing island? Henrye lifts a stack of dried peat bricks and takes them up to his home. A layer of turf covers the storrows to protect them from the rain. He's let James sleep in: he's been working his young body hard this season.

Henrye finds it hard to believe the whispers around town. Why would he? Sightings of Finnman and selkies and sea spirits – none of it is true. Just stories told to justify actions taken by men. There's always another explanation. For instance, Kûna is not a selkie: she was kidnapped from her homeland, Greenland, and after escaping was adrift at sea on her only means of transport, her long boat. Why can't the rest of the town see this sense? And now Bessie is getting in his ear – and probably Malie's too – about Kûna being up north. On some island, a disappearing island between them and Rousay. He'd never heard of such a thing. There was no point getting caught up in the hearsay. He drops the stack by the front door and returns to the peat bogs for more.

No point trying to squash the slab of regret in his gut, the one that reminds him he failed Kûna. Joseph sent one of his men ashore to apologise that another of his crew betrayed him, alerting the MacDuffies to Kûna's escape. He was deeply sorry and would help him in any way he could. Henrye asked Joseph to continue searching for her as they pulled away from the island. Henrye won't learn of any news until Joseph's crew returns in November. With the pelt trade booming, Neill won't jeopardise his alliance with them.

Bessie may be convinced Kûna survived but he was in that storm. He was in that sea, and it was wild. How could she have survived it? Without the help of Malie, Henrye wouldn't have made it. He owes her his life. Henrye desperately wanted to see her after the storm, to thank her again for saving him, but he couldn't risk further angering Johne. So, he kept his distance, watching her from afar. From the back pew in the kirk, from the moorland when she beachcombed along the shore. Reassured by the sight of her, that she was alive, only to be thrown back into fits of worry the moment she was out of his sight.

His thoughts rile him, knowing the strain she must be under living in that house. Not to mention her father – and then there are her brothers, who have all remained infuriatingly silent. He's sure Adame checks in on her from time to time. He's a good lad but the other three should be ashamed of themselves. It's like she's living her mother's life. Bairn after bairn. Living with a brute. Staring out at the sea. It pains him to see her struggling as Nava once did.

As if he's conjured up the sight of her, Malie, with a bundle of caisies draped across her body, bustles across the shoreline towards the Point. It's low tide and the water rescinds from the sand. She abruptly turns to face the sea. Her feet are so close to the clawing tide as it is pulled back towards the horizon, threatening to take her with it. He can sense the desire brimming underneath her tension. She wants to be *in* the sea. Just like her mother. Neill and Johne will stop at nothing to prevent Malie from following in her mother's footsteps. It makes Henrye so angry because she deserves to be happy.

A flock of pink-footed geese fly overhead, migrating from the north. Their high-pitched yelps snap Malie out of her reverie. She steps back from the sea and continues up the shore, where Bessie awaits her. Bessie and her rickety, absurdly unsafe boat. He's not had a chance to repair it, let alone his own. 'What is she thinkin?' he grunts, standing upright to get a better look. Yes, they've got caisies with them, bundling them into the boat. Is she getting Malie off the island? His chest prickles with mixed emotions. Relief that she will be free of Johne. Disappointment that he will not see her again. That she did not say goodbye. He scratches at his chin, which is bristly and rough.

Only a few caisies – no other essential items like peat to make a fire or a blanket for a newborn. Nae, they mustn't be escaping the island, only taking a daytrip. The MacDuffies departed only moments before: their masthead is still to be seen in the Sound if he were to meander further south along the coast. So, what are those two up to?

Henrye picks up another stack of peat bricks and then drops them at his feet. The island. That's where Bessie is taking her: he's sure of it.

He wants to intervene but he holds himself back. Malie can make her own decisions. There are already enough men telling her what to do. He gathers up the peat again and focuses on the trek back to the house. Keep himself busy. He'll keep out of it. Let Bessie handle it. She has a lighter touch than he does.

Twenty-Six

Malie

Rowing from the Point is slow as the Sound is more treacherous than the bay. We pass the grey seal colony. The cows are heavy but there's no sign of the pups yet, just as I expected. I see her. The sun hides shyly behind low-lying clouds, like a toddler caught up in his mother's billowing skirts. My seal basks on the rocks in a shard of light and watches me. The herd flap and moan and howl as they find themselves comfortable positions in the rare light. Together, they are playful and noisy, sometimes rough, like a family gathered for supper after consuming too much whisky.

There's a pleasant ache brewing in my arms and legs from bracing the oars in a circular motion. I'm already out of breath. I'm grateful the wind is behind us. Bessie struggles with the oars but refuses to rest and let me take the lead.

A flock of seagulls sound an alarm, 'ha-ha-ha', a chorus as they circle and swoop, settling on the rocks below, white speckles among the grey seals. They are never far away when it's pupping season. They forage intensely among the seals, waiting for the fluffy white pups to slip from their mothers' wombs. Benign opportunistic scavengers, they pounce on the afterbirths, squawking and fighting over the nutrient-rich placentas. They are a nuisance to the seal colony and I've seen mother seals abandon their pups if they don't feel safe. Self-preservation over maternal instinct. It's in their nature to abandon their young.

I shudder at the thought of having hungry predators circling me at my own birth. I massage my stomach, eager to get the peedie one moving, so when the time comes I will have a fast delivery.

'Bessie, what will we do? We can't let them kill all those pups,' I say as we journey up the west coast, the seals in our wake.

Bessie grunts but offers no solution. My mouth feels dry and I knead my stomach. Get moving, peedie one. Come on. But it's not just the bairn who must get moving. 'We only have a few weeks, at most. Do you think we can move the seals? Get them somewhere safer before they birth?' Even as I say it, I know it's an impossible task. How could I possibly move all these tonnes of vulnerable cows away from the rookery? Away from the place where they come year after year to give birth, raise their pups and mate?

Bessie grabs my arm. I flinch and she drops it. 'Don't do anything, Malie. Not yet. You must think about the bairn – and your bairn will need her mother.'

I feel torn. Between my bairn and hers: my seal. My mother and my father. My husband and my friend. Why must I choose at all?

We drift past the coastal cliffs and the seabird-lined crags where I'd plucked eggs for Johne's hungry stomach. The wind is constant and inescapable aboard the compact vessel. We continue north. Every so often, I must scoop out water to stop it pooling at the bottom of the boat. While most of the boats are made from imported Norwegian pine, Bessie's never had the means to buy the timber. Her boat is made entirely of driftwood tossed onto the sand over the years. Henrye has done his best to smooth it out and seal the holes but there's one pesky groove letting in the water when the sea laps high at the boat.

While the journey is slow and the boat is unsteady, the sea is calm and the sky is clear. 'There's Birsay,' I say, pointing north. 'And a small island off the coast. Could that be where Kûna hid?'

The wind becomes fiercer and the waves crash against the boat. Tidal flows recoil, drawing captivating patterns on the surface. Bessie shakes her head. 'Nae, that's Brough of Birsay. We must go beyond that, to the northernmost part of the island, and then head east.'

'Are you sure we can make it, Bessie?' Dark clouds gather in the distance. There's a reason so few people venture this far north. We're exposed out here in the North Atlantic. With half the day behind us, I'm worried we'll not make it back before dark. The days are shortening.

'Aye, not long to go. We'll hug the coast and pull in near Swannay. We'll walk the rest. It's about five miles.'

I sigh. I'm impatient to arrive, to escape the dark clouds and to know what happened to Kûna. As we approach the edge of Swannay, the sea rises and rocks the boat with a fierceness. A headwind is blowing and we can no longer go up against it. Besides, my arms are tired. 'Time to get off now, Bessie,' I say, eager not to be caught up in a storm at sea again. I've already lost Kûna; I don't want to lose the old woman too.

'Aye,' she says and I jump into the shallows, pulling the boat towards the rocks. We secure it with the rope and then trudge up the hill and follow the grasslands east for several miles.

Bessie, having starting to dawdle, suddenly darts forwards. The dark clouds have dispersed, the sky is flawless and the air is pure. She lets out a laugh. 'Look, we're just in time. Stand right here or we'll miss it. This is what I wanted to show you.'

I follow her gaze. In the distance, as far as can only be seen on a clear, cloudless, mist-free day at low tide, is land. The disappearing island. Adame told me about it but I've never seen it for myself. Or have I?

'Hildaland,' I whisper.

'Aye,' Bessie says, awe-stricken. 'The Hidden Land.'

I grasp her hand; her eyes twinkle.

'Isn't it marvellous?'

I remember when Mother pointed at the land on the horizon. The troublesome white water of the Sound. *Let's swim halfway here, halfway there.* Hildaland. I had begun to think I'd imagined the whole thing. Truth and reality blurred over the years and I did not trust my own memories. Now it comes to me. How we coasted along our island in a boat, just as I did with Bessie. Mother was determined to show me something special. I thought it was just another swimming lesson.

'Malie. Look.'

The sun is glaring and I have to squint but, on the nebulous edges of Hildaland, I can make out a figure. She has a mane of dark hair. 'Kûna!'

'She's alive.' Bessie's laugh is thick with emotion. 'She's alive.'

I sigh in relief, tears in my eyes. It was dangerous coming here with Bessie but it was worth it. Kûna survived the storm and escaped my father. I can put the uncertainty to bed.

'You did it Malie.' I drag my eyes away from the magical land and Bessie squeezes both of my hands. 'You saved her.'

It's a narrow channel of water where the Atlantic and North Sea are at perpetual war, but somehow Kûna was able to navigate it. Hope flares inside me. Mother may have gone there too before continuing to Greenland. A little voice tells me: I can follow them. I could go too, start anew. Nae. I couldn't leave my husband, my family. How would I raise a bairn on my own without any means to support myself? I break away from Bessie's eager gaze and turn back to the horizon. My eyes blur and I blot away the tears with the back of my hand. I blink, searching for the island. A light mist has blown in.

I blink and squint. Nothing. It's gone. No sign at all of the Hidden Land.

~

After the sermon, the townsfolk spill out into the golden kirkyard, arms spread wide, chins tilted towards the skies, drawn to the warmth like a shag with outstretched wings, drying in the sun. Autumn is particularly wild and unpredictable and we know we must make use of the good weather when we have it. It does feel good to bask in the golden rays after so many days of dark skies and mist. Today the view to Hoy is clear, reminding me of the stolen glimpse of Hildaland – was Kûna hiding out there, safe and alive? Or had she travelled further?

Johne, Father and my brothers huddle together by the kirk. A heated discussion ensues. Adame stalks away, joining me and Elinor, who has Nicholas cradled in her arms. The other wives are chattering at a short distance. 'What is it, Adame?' I ask, even though I already have an inkling what the men are saying.

He shakes his head. 'Ye don't want to know, sis.'

My hands tremor and I wring them together to get my nerves under control. I lower my voice so only Adame and Elinor can hear me. 'It's about the cull, isn't it?'

'Aye, I'm sorry. There's no changin' their minds, Malie.'

My throat is dry. 'You must try, Adame. Please. They will not listen to me.'

'I will be no part of it. If I cannot stop them, I will not join them.' Adame folds his arms across his chest. Elinor touches his shoulder and his face softens when his gaze lands upon his son.

He knows of my affinity for the colony. How it's kept me connected to my mother in all the years since she left. 'It's barbaric.'

'Aye. But we need food and Father desperately wants that boat. Thinks it is the only way we can continue to fish in these conditions. We have nothing else to offer them but the seals. What else are they to do?'

Anger flares within me. 'So you agree with them? This is the only way?'

'There's no fish in the sea. Everyone has suffered from crop loss with the weather. Our livestock are dropping dead. How will we survive?'

I step forwards and grip his arm. 'This isn't just about survival, Adame, and you know it. This is about revenge. Nothing good will come from culling the seals. Something bad will happen, I'm sure of it.' I want to tell him about the seal skin under Father's bed. About what happened to Kûna and what Henrye told me about our mother. About Greenland. There is so much to share but now is not a good time. Not with my brothers' wives within earshot, and Father nearby.

'Och, Malie.' Adame pulls his arm back. 'Now you sound like Bessie. You shouldn't be spending so much time with her – you know what Father and your husband think about her.'

'She's a kind old woman who has cared for me since I was a child,' I say, my voice rising so I catch the attention of Kattrine and Marion. I clamp my mouth shut so as not to say anything else in haste.

As I turn from my brother, Elinor catches my arm and whispers. 'Anne said Bessie petted one of her lambs last week and it dropped dead the next day.'

My hands curl into fists; heat rises in me again. 'Nae. Don't believe that. It is purely a coincidence.' The town is turning on itself.

'I know, I know. Malie, I'm only telling you so you can be careful.'

'Aye,' I say. Because I do know. I wanted to believe the selkie stories because they kept me close to my mother. They explained why she left, why she chose the sea over her family. Without the selkie stories all I have is unanswered questions. Confusion. Mother left and Father lied. While Adame accepts defeat.

'Just be careful, Malie,' Adame says over his shoulder as he makes his way to the kirk. Elinor follows and with one final glance back they continue up the hill towards home. I sit upon a broad reddish-sandstone rock by the cliff edge. I think about the three stones, the cloth and Johne's response to Bessie. Perhaps my brother is right. I should keep my distance from Bessie, keep her away from my family, from the MacDuffies. It may be the only way to protect her. My stomach churns at the thought of losing another friend. I have lost Beatrice. Kûna. Henrye and James. And Bessie, too?

I watch them: Bessie laughs with James while Henrye looks on with a serious expression. Always careful, aware of his surroundings. He doesn't look in my direction but I know he knows I'm here. I fight the urge to join them as they look out at the Sound. A gannet soars overhead and dives into the sea, emerging a moment later with something in its beak. What can be wrong with me: feeling pulled towards a family that is not my own? Feeling that I can be more myself with them than with my husband and brothers? With my family, I keep a part of myself hidden, like a seal pelt under a bed, waiting to be dusted off and reunited with fresh air, sun and the sea.

It settles the tension in my body, knowing both Henrye and Bessie watch over me, even if I cannot be with them. That I'm not alone. There's a subtle fluttering in my stomach and I collapse my hands over it. Little bairn. We're not alone.

'Malie.' Johne says my name like a command and I rise without taking my eyes off the sea. 'Time to go.'

I follow him back to the kirk and the path beyond. I follow and do what is expected of me. My body does what it's told, but in my mind a plan takes shape. The men may be set on culling the seal pups but I am just as intent on saving them. I now realise my place in my family is precarious at best, and that even if I am obedient forever, Johne or my father could be in the wrong mood and punish me for something completely irrelevant. Even kill me, if Bessie's prophecy is to be believed. If it's not safe to follow the rules, why follow the rules?

The only problem is, I'll need the help of the two people my family wants me to stay away from: Bessie and Henrye.

~

A cold snap sweeps through the island in early October. There's frost, snow and sleet, propelled by continuous northerly winds. It was lucky Bessie warned me of it so we harvested the beremeal early, the reaping small but gratifying – not that I shared Bessie's prediction with Johne. Two days later north-westerly gales hailed in off the North Sea. For two days and two nights, gigantic waves collided with rocks along the west coast and hostile gales lifted loose sand from the shores and flung it across the island, coating livestock, crops and every house in the parish. We did not lose any sheep and our bere crop was pulled up in the nick of time.

'How did ye know?' Johne asks when the sea has settled into a gentle swell and the wind has weakened so we can go outside and inspect the damage.

'Remember that big storm we had last October? I didn't want us to lose it all again. The sky had the same colours in it as the days before that storm. Turns out I was right.'

Johne's eyes remain trained on me for a moment longer than feels comfortable, but he then drags them away and surveys the lands. Relief passes over his face and I know that even if he is suspicious of me, he's happy we didn't lose the crop.

Keep something for yourself.

Twenty-Six

Malie

The howling and yowling from the herd startles me from a deep slumber. The wind whistles around the cottage, conveying the sounds of the sea. The sun has not yet risen but it is time. Careful not to disturb Johne, I roll out of bed. He snores, his mouth slack. I slip my woollen dress over my linen undergarments and then my winter woollen coat, which is all I'm left with since I lost my lighter-weight one when the boat overturned. I pull boots over my stockings and then push open the door: it groans but the sound is swallowed in the wind. Johne continues to snore. I don't bring a candle as I don't want to disturb the colony.

The air is wet; a light drizzle falls from the dark sky. The moonlight guides me across the gravel, down the grassy path to the sandbank. I reach the rocky shoreline and under the luminous spotlight of the moon I see the colony. My heart races as I near. Dotted within the herd of grey bodies are a few small yellowish-white creatures. Pups!

I creep forwards, careful to stay on the outskirts so as not to worry the birthing mothers. I am overwhelmed by a sudden urgency to see her – my seal and her pup – to have reassurance they have both survived. I locate her speckled pelt in the herd and she lifts her head, perhaps in recognition. I lower myself onto a flat sandstone rock where I'm in her line of sight. She lies awkwardly on her side, her swollen stomach resting on the rocks. One flipper pointed up to the moon, her back flipper and tail on the mossy sandstone. The sea crashes against the rocks, splashing sea foam into the sky, and then it falls upon the herd like snow.

She is panting rather heavily. In the shadows, I cocoon my own bairn within my hands as I wait. She moans and pants. Then her abdomen hardens, her body lifts and both her flipper and tail levitate. I hold my breath. After a moment, her body softens and she melts into the rock. I exhale as though I have experienced the spasms myself. There are several more contractions and she rests between each of them. On the fourth, a pinkish bubble emerges from underneath the tail. I lean forwards, breath held, hands clenched together. A moment passes. On the next contraction, the bubble – the amniotic sac – releases a little more of the pup who is cocooned inside, motionless.

The mother has only a moment to breathe before her body hardens and stiffens again and again. Until, at last, the sac slips from her body and breaks upon the rocks, releasing the pup in a gush of fluids. I gasp and clutch at my chest, fighting back the urge to rush to her side. Sitting still does not come easily to me but I don't want to scare them. If she feels threatened, she will abandon her pup. The mother turns instantly to sniff and nose the newborn. It noses her back. This will begin the bonding process. The peedie fluffy pup will not leave her side for the next eighteen to twenty days.

She is perfect.

The mother wags her tail and lies back down. It is hard to believe that after all her hard work the mother will not eat in the weeks that follow. She will dedicate all her fat reserves to nursing her pup. She will lose energy and weight in a bid to nourish her offspring. She shifts aside, taking long heaving breaths as her pup nestles closer to her. My body sighs in relief, storing information away for my own impending labour. The rising, haunting call of a curlew penetrates the night sky. This has all taken place in just a few minutes but it feels as though I have been holding my breath for days. I ease my lungs back to their natural rhythm. I am so intent on my seal and her pup I do not hear the footsteps until they are upon me.

'I thought I'd find ye here.' I look sharply at my husband, only to find he wears a warm smile.

I rub my belly, hiding my disappointment. This is my moment with the seals. I don't want to share it with anyone, especially not Johne. 'Soon it will be me.'

'Aye.' His voice catches as he drops down beside me and wraps a blanket around my shoulders. 'Aye,' he says again.

We sit together, listening to mother seals grunting and roaring at other mother seals who get in their way. After a while, I speak. 'There are *so* many pups. Aren't they beautiful?'

Johne grunts and pushes himself up to his feet. 'I best get back and tell yer father.'

My stomach is leaden with dread. 'Tell him what?'

''Tis time. We must prepare for the cull.'

'Cull?' I can't disguise my fear. Och, how can he say that now after taking in all their beauty? I bore witness to my seal's transformation from expectant to new mother. Today is the beginning of her pup's life: could it also be the beginning of the end?

'We'll wait until the pups are nice and plump and separate from their mothers.' He faces me. 'Then we'll attack.'

Johne drops a kiss on the top of my head, oblivious to my distress, and retreats from the shore. My gaze falls on the beauty of innocent, fluffy pups nestled into their fatigued mothers. In three to four weeks, there will be a bloodbath on these shores. A massacre. Bile rises from my stomach. Tears slip down my cheeks: they come so easily now.

It is quiet but for the wind as the birthing mothers and their pups rest. Those yet to birth reserve their energy. The sun stirs on the horizon and the herd is bathed in sunlight. The light is always on them. And from the silence come the deep, hoarse calls of the great black-backed gulls: circling above, eyeing the site before they swoop and invade the herd.

My seal lifts her head, checks on her pup and lies back down. Her body becomes rigid again; her flipper and tail lift off the rocks. On the ground, the gulls raise and lower their heads, stalking her. Two come near the mother and her pup and she roars at them. They settle behind her tail, waiting for their meal. I am on my feet, so tempted to run towards the rookery and shoo them all away, but I cannot. This is nature, I remind myself. Natural predators. There's nothing to be done.

They peck at the pup's slick coat. The pup noses in under her mother, where her eyes, at least, are protected. The gulls repeatedly raise and lower their heads, giving out long, trumpeting calls. Impatient and demanding. A hooded crow circles overhead.

The mother heaves and blood oozes out. The gulls swoop in. The mother flaps her tail and attempts to turn towards them but she is having another contraction. She stiffens and then, with one last push, the afterbirth is released. Exhausted, she shuffles back onto her stomach and noses her pup. The gulls pounce on the bloody sac, pecking with bloodstained beaks.

The mother seal turns to the sea birds and roars. They are unruffled, pecking at the bloody sac with even more vigour. The mother does not let up: she barks at them and they edge backwards. Then she yips at them, wild and roaring, until at last they retreat a little.

From a safer distance they squawk at her, but the mother remains in defence of her afterbirth and her pup. They charge forwards, not ready to give up. Then with one, final, defiant howl she consumes the afterbirth herself. She eats it all, hiccups and then resettles on the rocks with her pup. The gulls' heads bop up and down, squawking in protest, before they stalk away to bother another. I drop to the ground, the tension easing. I wrap my arms around my abdomen.

My seal protected her pup from natural predators. She has won this time. But what will happen when the men descend on the colony? A shiver travels up my spine and I wrap the blanket tighter around my body. They nestle in with one another, and I stay watching them as the sun rises over the sea.

Over the next three weeks, the seal pups will fatten up on their mothers' milk. When they've weaned, the mothers will leave them to fend for themselves. The pups will laze about on their fat reserves until finally hunger drives them into the sea. On these days, when they're alone, they will be vulnerable to predators: natural hunters at sea and in the sky. But, for the first time since my mother arrived on our shores, the pups will also be vulnerable to predators on land.

I think about these pups later as I harvest a handful of baby potatoes and a head of cabbage that can't be left in the ground much longer as they'll be ruined by the cooling weather. I'll cook them tonight with the remaining mutton. The turnips will need to be planted soon, before the soil cools too much.

Nothing is ever wasted on the island. If a pup or a seal dies after being caught up in a fishing net, it doesn't go to waste. The meat is eaten, the skin repurposed into winter wear and the fat used in oil lamps – but there have been no deliberate killings in my lifetime. Father put a stop to it – he had that kind of power. And now he has changed his mind and the townsfolk have stood by him again.

At least with the men's focus on the pups, they are less concerned about the Finnman. Kûna. I hope this means she can make her way back home safely.

I straighten and massage my lower back. It is strange to have a body so off balance, tipping forwards and straining muscles this way and that. I flick dirt off my skirt as my thoughts drift back to the pups. The crunch of gravel startles me again. Johne limps past me at an unusually hurried pace. His leg is almost completely healed but he complains of a twinge here and there. He says the pain intermittently shoots down his leg, painful enough that he keels over, groaning. I've noticed how he favours the left leg, like he drags the weight of the whole maritime ordeal behind him. I still can't understand how that hook wedged into his leg in the first place. Adame's recounting does not make sense. If the Finnman and selkies aren't real, what did Johne see? What really happened at sea?

'I'll be down at the port,' he says without a backwards glance.

'The port?' I call. 'Are you planning to head out again?' I hold my breath, waiting on his response, pushing down the relief that he won't be near the herd of vulnerable pups.

'Could be,' he mutters, continuing. 'Depends on the weather.'

I scoff at his retreating back. No chance of that. The clouds have dropped low and are picking up pace as the gale strengthens from the east. They won't make it past the break. I sigh as Johne disappears. Why the sudden urgency to get back to the sea?

Twenty-Seven

Malie

I'm at the bay before dawn. I woke early and could not get back to sleep: Johne snored and elbowed me aside. He didn't go to sea on account of the storm, just as I predicted. I was restless and fidgety. Old habits of leaping out of bed upon waking are hard to change, even if I am slower these days. The familiar noisy piping calls of oystercatchers trill from the shore. In the early morning glow, I can just make out their red eyes and long orange bills.

It's cold and windy but I like to watch the herd from the shadows. The bulls are present, patrolling their breeding groups, but they aren't involved directly in the care of their pups. My mother seal is with her pup, who is now clean and white and fluffy. The pup is clumsy on land, but she will struggle with the cold if she enters the sea now. She won't brave the open waters until she sheds her baby coat, though she may still paddle or roll about in the shallows. For now, she is warm enough snuggled against her mother. She will gain thirty kilograms before she weans, while her mother will lose just as much. I can't imagine what it is like to birth and then live on fat reserves in the weeks that follow. The bulls will lose weight too – they cannot risk going to the sea to feed as they might lose their place with the breeding group. A young ambitious male might see it as an opportunity to position himself in view of the cows before the next mating season.

I remember Mother being ravenous after Adame's birth. It was as though he was permanently attached to her breast and I would bring her fish broth, clams and seaweed I'd collected from the shore for her to snack upon. She would light up when she saw my reaping, inhaling the scent and devouring it as if she'd never eaten such a thing in her life. In my mind, I can still see the way she closed her eyes, savouring the flavours while Adame suckled at her breast.

The mother seal is in a slumber now until her pup nudges her. Then she rolls on to her side rather ungracefully, so the pup can latch on to her teat. It guzzles the rich, fatty milk. I watch until the pup is satiated. They are both healthy and safe, at least for now.

My stomach protrudes from my dress. I knead the firm skin, as Mother used to do. This will be me, soon. Come spring, I will have a bairn of my own suckling from my breast. I massage my stomach until it feels tender: I must keep up this pummelling until the baby moves on its own. There's danger in stillness.

~

I don't notice Johne by the sheep dyke until I am upon him. I am wind-whipped and elated from my visit with the seal pups but I rein it in quickly as my husband stands, eyebrows furrowed as though deep in thought. That's when I notice the blood on his hands and the dead ewe at his feet. The wind hurls the meaty smell towards me.

'What happened?' I ask.

'No fish,' he grunts. 'We need the meat until we cull the pups. The pups will keep us goin' through the winter.'

'We have lost so many already, Johne. We must think of the future. We need enough ewes to breed this season. She could have been carrying a lamb!'

Johne stands up taller. 'We need the meat.'

I suck in the cold air through my nose, willing myself to calm down. A little more than twenty ewes left. Livestock is dwindling across the island. Our crops are failing to flourish and, of course, there's no fish. It makes sense to use what we do have but how will that sustain us through future winters? If we cannot breed our sheep there will be no lambs to raise and breed the following season. Why can't he see that?

'Caught a couple of those greylags in my corn again. Killed them too.'

I gasp. 'Henrye's?'

'Aye.' Johne chuckles. 'We'll eat well until we get those pups.'

I say nothing. It is best I don't show any allegiance towards Henrye.

'How long do you think we have?' Johne asks, sweat beading on his forehead as he leans against the dyke.

'How long for what?' My hands instinctively cup my stomach. Though I want to meet my bairn, I am happy she is tucked safely inside me.

'The pups. You know them better than anyone,' he says as his eyes drop to the wet hem of my skirt and the wet sand on my boots. I reach for the wall to steady myself. 'You're down there watching them often enough.'

I swallow and my gaze settles on the distant bay. 'Yes, I like to watch their comings and goings.'

'Aye, you'll continue to keep an eye on them for us. How long 'til the pups have weaned?'

My mouth is dry. 'There are still more pups to come but it'll be up to three weeks until they wean from their mothers. Then a few more days until they take to the sea. Their mothers, and the bulls, will remain close by until then.' Keeping watch on their vulnerable amateur swimmers.

A grim smile. 'Good. That's when we attack. When the pups are nice and plump and weaned. It's your responsibility to let us know when they're ready.'

'Aye, I'll keep watch.' I pause. Johne's face is drawn in a thoughtful expression. Not angry, not fierce. When I speak, he meets my eyes. 'Johne, is culling the pups necessary? Would it not be a better food source to cull just a few of the adults. Fathers? Mothers?' The suggestion of killing any other seal in the herd makes my stomach churn. But the pups? That's a whole generation in one colony. They can't even fend for themselves. It's cruel.

His eyebrows draw in as he leans against the shovel. 'Nae. The mothers won't be any good. They'll have lost all their fat. They're of no use to us after they've birthed.'

Johne returns his attention to the dead ewe. His words settle on me heavily, like a stone-laden warning. I knead my stomach, massaging the firm skin. Move, peedie one, start moving. I turn away from my husband, collecting parsnips and kale before slipping into the house to prepare the soup. My husband's words circle my mind: *They'll be of no use to us after they've birthed.* I have a bairn in my belly: that means something to Johne. It must. But what happens afterwards?

I have a sudden urge to prove my usefulness.

Twenty-Eight

Malie

'Elinor has gone for a walk with Nicholas,' Adame says when I arrive at his cottage the following morning, just as it begins to drizzle.

Escaping Johne's raucous snores again, I slipped out of bed into the blustery dawn breeze. I stopped by the Point to see the seals, and when I was no longer hidden in shadow, I left them to bask in the early sun rays. I crept back past Henrye's house and mine, up to Adame's, certain Johne was yet to rise. He complained of a cramp in his gut the night before, which I suspect was from overindulging in the freshly cut meat.

'He was awake a lot overnight. It was so quiet last night – I think he's grown used to the wind.' Adame laughs. He has dark circles under his eyes and he rubs at them roughly.

'Aye. I couldn't sleep either.' I bite the inside of my cheek. 'I came here to speak to you, Adame, not Elinor.'

He looks up. 'Aye?'

I hesitate. 'I'm worried.'

His expression turns from weary to grave. 'Are you all right over there with Johne? I thought his leg had healed well. Has he been in a temper again?'

'He's fine,' I say, dismissing that concern. 'I'm fine.' Adame had never been fond of my husband. Unlike my siblings, I didn't have the luxury of scouring other islands in search of a mate. There aren't many options here, and Johne was kind when we first met. He'd come from Hoy to work with my father. He has no family of his own: they were all struck down by the plague.

My thoughts drift to Henrye, bushy-bearded with kind eyes. I've known him my whole life, not well, but he was familiar, at least. There was a time when I thought maybe he was someone I could marry. But Beatrice was keen on him and came of age before me and of course my father wasn't letting me marry until all my brothers had wives anyway.

I shake my head. 'Adame, what's going on? You all came back and everything changed. Father wants to hunt selkies and seals. Johne wants to cull the pups—' My voice breaks. What I don't add is that I'm having a bairn in all this violence.

Adame runs his hands roughly across his short, dark beard. We're dark-haired, which is not uncommon here, but there's no hint of amber as in our father's hair. Our skin is not as fair. I realise we've always been different – not because we're descendants of selkies, but because our mother is Greenlandic.

'Aye, it's a mess,' Adame says and I knew I was right to come here.

Of all my brothers, Adame and I have always been the closest. When Mother left, I was like *his* mother. I recall, as he grew, he asked me many questions about her. What did she sound like? What did she look like? As the youngest, he had so few memories of her, and it was hard not to feel angry with her for leaving him, leaving all of us. To Adame, Mother had always been a myth, whether selkie or woman, who was spoken about but not seen.

'What really happened at sea? When Johne was injured.'

He tenses. 'It was a riot storm, that's what it was. Turns out it wasn't a Finnman at all. But a selkie. That woman who washed ashore, that's who they blame now.'

'Adame, you can't truly believe that, can you?'

He shrugs. 'When we dropped a line in the sea after the storm passed, all the fish were gone. There was nothin' left, Malie.'

I shake my head in disbelief. It's a wild story, but I've heard wilder. The sea is unpredictable, menacing and fierce. Maybe it was not selkies, but the sea spirits? Maybe it was a warning? They have treated it poorly and now it will not share its bounty with us. Father always said the sea was dangerous, but it also brought my mother to the island, and Kûna, too. It saved them. It can't be all bad.

'Is it possible there were fewer fish because of the storm, Adame? It's been terribly cold. I overheard the Norwegians saying the fish had migrated south. They could've swum to warmer waters.'

He shakes his head. 'Ever since we've heard about the Finnman sighted off the island, there has been nothing to harvest. It makes sense.'

'But it wasn't a Finnman. It was a woman. Think about it, Adame.

Why would she need a boat if she is a selkie?'

Adame shakes his head. 'She's a selkie,' he insists.

'Do you honestly believe what Father says about them?'

He pauses for a moment. There's a flicker of vulnerability, and a glimpse of his boyish face comes to light. 'Sis, do you think our mother could be back?'

'Adame,' I say in a rush, stepping closer and speaking in a whisper, 'Father told us our mother was a selkie. A seal who could shed her skin and transform into a woman. He's made us believe that our whole lives. But what if there is another explanation?'

Adame frowns. 'That's why she left us: she went back to the sea. What other explanation could there be? Maybe our mother was just one of the good ones. Maybe there are more dangerous, evil selkies out there who want to punish us.'

I swallow, studying my brother. Can I trust him? He's always been protective of me; he wouldn't tell anyone anything that puts me in danger. 'What if our mother was not a selkie? What if she just came from a faraway island? Not Hildaland but somewhere farther. *Greenland.* What if the Finnman – Kûna – is not a Finnman but just a person at sea, someone from far away?'

Adame stares at me. I remain still, as though any movement could unravel my words, unravel me.

I press on. 'I spoke to the woman. Her name is Kûna. She was kidnapped from her homeland and escaped in her boat. She is not a selkie. She is not trying to punish us. She just wanted to get home. She didn't seduce Henrye. I tried to help her—' My voice catches.

After a long pause, Adame shakes his head. His dark hair falls across his forehead. 'Nae. That's nonsense. Mother is a selkie. The woman who washed ashore is a selkie. After we saw her there were no fish in the sea. There could be more of them about. That's how it is, Malie: we can't be looking for other explanations when the signs are so clear.' The hard edge to his voice reminds me of Father.

It's as though a wave has crashed over me, tumbling me about in the sea. I am rattled, weakened. I have no allies in my family. No one will see reason. If I have no ally, how can I possibly save the seal pups?

'You're right, brother,' I mutter as tears spring in my eyes. 'Silly me.' I'm overcome with the sudden urge to escape. To *move*. 'Say hello to Elinor for me.' I push past him into the knifing rain.

'Malie!' Adame calls out but the wind throws the word back in his face.

Twenty-Nine

Malie

I am the only one to see them leave. From the port, the boat departs under filtered moonlight; they catch a fair wind as the serpent sucks in its breath, carrying them into the Sound. Their voices are faint, the wind whistles and waves strike rock.

One final voyage before the cull, to scour the seas for fish, Finnman and selkies. Father has pinned all hopes on a bigger boat but I think it's time they give up on the sea. We must focus on land. On our livestock, our crops. Each other. We still have linen and feathers.

But the fishermen can't be kept from the sea. It is all they know and they are determined to fight it. To take back what they are owed.

For the first time, I'm not anxious as I send them off into the unknown, but relieved. With the men gone, I am free. Free to roam the coast, to be with the seals ... even to swim in the sea if I want. Swim! 'Nae, not swim,'

I mutter as I follow the coastline along sludgy marsh back to the harbour. Though I cannot forget the feel of Henrye against my chest as I kicked us back to shore. The buoyancy of the water, holding us both like a mother holds a bairn. The taste of the sea lingers. I am hungry for more.

As my boots squelch and groan and my lower back throbs, that memory snags in the tension. A memory of the sea and the water cocooning my body and the blissful, terrifying feeling of letting go. Trusting the sea, the waves, to keep me afloat. I imagine how it would ease the mounting tension in my back.

The moonlight shines bright across the bay. Mother swam in the sea when she was carrying Adame, her swollen belly hidden in the water. 'Is swimming good for the bairn?' I asked her.

She beamed at me. 'It feels wonderful. I am light and free.'

I arch my back but it brings no relief, only stretches and itches my stomach. The walking, the movement, feels good. When I stop, it aches, so I keep moving. A gale blows back off the sea and I stabilise my feet on the earth. My centre of balance having changed I must relearn how to brace myself against the wind. Relearn how to be on land.

I kick off my boots and leave them on the nearby rocks with my coat. Tiptoe towards the tidal line. Heads pop up from the seal colony, not alert, but curious as to my presence. They are relatively quiet and there are many more white fluffy pups interspersed between resting mothers. That looks like the last of them.

I locate my seal among the herd. Her gaze is on me as her pup nuzzles into her side. Does she miss the sea like my mother? She spends weeks in the rookery, not eating or hunting, rarely swimming: she devotes every bit of energy to her pup. Does she feel empty? Or dried out? That's how Mother said she felt, and it was obviously true. Her skin turned from dry and flaky to glowing again after one dip in the sea.

As I pick at a dry patch on the side of my hand, peeling it off in a sliver, my back spasms in the chill. I step closer and the water spills over my toes. I gasp at the shock of it. It's not an unpleasant sensation. It's cold on land; it's cold in the sea.

The pup flops on its belly, nudging towards me. Curious and fearless. I remain still as water laps at my ankles. The mother seal calls her pup back but the pup rolls onto her side and splashes in the shallows. I think my mother seal trusts me but I don't want the pup to become too trusting of humans. I shoo her away and put distance between us. The sea beckons.

'Come,' I hear Mother's call. 'Come in.'

And so I let her lead me into the freezing moonlit water. Just this one time. Just once. I step further, and further, water lapping at my ankles, knees and then hips. My woollen dress protects me from the bite of the water. As it laps over my stomach, I let the weight pull me down, squatting with feet steady in the soft sand. My skin stings but I also feel light and carefree. My back doesn't ache. Seaweed caresses my legs. I breathe in fully and breathe out, raising my face to the sky. And for a fleeting moment I understand. I know how it felt for Mother to escape the land, surrender to the sea. To feel no pain. To have her skin soften and hydrate once more. She didn't need to be a selkie to desire this contact with nature.

As the water teases my neck, I draw in a deep breath and I let myself drop to the sea floor. The way Mother taught me. Grounding myself on the seabed as I do on land to brace against harsh winds. Pebbles massage the arches of my feet. A heaviness comes over my legs and my body as I sink to the bottom. I count: one, two, three, four, five ...

I push up. I reach the surface and gulp back the air. Salty tears trickle down my salty skin. Oh, how I miss my mother. I lean back into the swell and savour the feel of my body at one with the sea. My lower back relaxes and the ache dissipates.

I am reluctant to part from the water and this connection with my mother, but I think this is all I can manage for the first time. *First* time. I laugh through chattering teeth. I am not silly enough to think I will do this just once. Of course I need more, in the same way my mother needed more. And now I can see why she sacrificed so much, including my father's approval, so she could return to the sea repeatedly.

I emerge with an inner strength I have never felt before. I lift my chin as I return to the sand, adjusting again to the weight of my body. The buoyancy is replaced by the heavy, sticky feeling of wet layers of linen and wool against my skin. Feet grounded against the wind, I dust off the sand blown onto my boots and slip them on with trembling hands, wrap the coat back around me and shuffle up the sandbank. The shakes come on quite suddenly: chattering teeth and wobbly legs. My heart speeds up but despite the quivers I feel so alive. Free. As I reach the pebbly path, figures emerge, but I am shivering so violently I can't make out who they are.

'Malie!' The moon is now faint and the sun lights up Elinor's face. 'What happened?'

I swallow but cannot speak. My coat covers most of my damp dress but my hair and hem are wet. There's no hiding what I've done.

'Malie!' Elinor repeats. She's in front of me; warm hands cup my cold face. She looks under my coat. 'What happened? You're drenched.'

Henrye and James appear. I swallow, teeth chattering as I find my voice. 'I, uh.' I glance at Henrye. 'I was checking on the seals. I slipped into the sea.'

Elinor gasps. 'Oh dear, are you hurt? You're frozen to the bone.'

'Nae. I'm fine, honestly,' I say, trying to control my chattering teeth. 'I feel fine actually – just cold.' I feel wonderful. Can I tell her that? Soaring, in fact, like a gull above the sea, as if I were born for this. Nae. I cannot tell her that, though I think Henrye already knows. Did he see me in the sea?

'Let's get you back,' Elinor says. She is startled when her gaze lands upon Henrye and James.

'Is everything all right?' Henrye asks me, though I know he heard what I told Elinor.

'Malie fell into the sea. Can you believe it?' Elinor says in a high-pitched voice. 'It's the coldest autumn in years and she's fallen into the sea!' Elinor doesn't believe me, I don't think, and yet she wants to convince Henrye of it anyway.

Henrye watches me. He wants to say something but he won't with Elinor here. I feel our easy conversations are no longer appropriate with an audience, though I cannot say why, exactly. I want Elinor to get on her way so I can talk to my friend again. 'We'll see you at the kirk, then?' I ask, because I want to say something.

Henrye nods but does not speak and I feel the loss of hearing his voice. A tremor passes through me; the chill setting in.

'Malie, we must get you back and warmed up,' Elinor insists. 'We cannae have anything happen to the bairn while Johne is away.' She says it in kindness but there's a hint of fear in her eyes.

She wraps her arms around me and I shuffle past Henrye and James with downcast eyes.

Now I really am shivering and chattering and cold to my bones. But I am not thinking about being warm: I am thinking about Henrye and James. Bessie. About my friends who are lost to me: Beatrice and Kûna. How I have lost my mother. Why do the people I care about disappear? Why do they leave? Why must I have so much grief in my life? The sea, for a moment, gave something back to me. I could reclaim what was taken. It's why Mother went back to the sea every day. And why I will, too.

'Come,' says Elinor as she ushers me inside my house and tends to the peat fire. 'Don't worry about the baby, Malie. It will all be fine.'

My thoughts drift back to the sea, even as Elinor mumbles repeatedly, 'It will be fine.'

Thirty

Malie

Elinor invites me to stay with her and Nicholas while Johne and Adame are away. She is worried; thinks I am fragile and could shatter at any moment. The truth is, I feel stronger than ever. I have the sea to thank for that. The companionship would be nice but it would also hinder my movements and I'd not be able to visit the seals or the sea freely. Strangely, I don't feel lonely with the men away. I suppose I feel less alone with the bairn in my belly.

As I stand on the threshold between sand and sea, bracing myself against the howling wind, I consider the conditions. I won't be able to swim this winter. Mother did, but even summers past have been too cold for swimming, and this winter is expected to be especially icy. I caress my stomach. Nae, it will not be safe then.

I can't see my seal among the herd. She doesn't pop up her head: not many do now they are used to my presence and saving their energy reserves to feed their pups. Some of the pups are rolling about in the shallows. It's been a week of early rises, observing the seals and then preparing myself for the bitterly cold water. Johne will be back in a day or two and so I must take to the sea as much as I can. I step away from the puddle of boots and coat. The water stings at first but I've learned the best thing to do is to dive straight in immediately. Not give myself time to talk myself out of it. I hold my breath, raise my arms and dive under the wave, like Mother, like Kûna, feeling it crash down overhead.

The sea has always felt wild but underneath it is calm and peaceful. As I break the surface, I draw in a deep breath. The distant call of seals, the swell of the sea, the absence of backache – it's exhilarating. Freeing.

A guillemot drifts nearby. I float on my back, closing my eyes and relishing the warmth of the sun on my face. Water laps at my ears, blocking out the curlew's call, the throaty sounds of the seals and the constant howl of the wind. I drift with the tide; the serpent breathes me back to shore.

A ripple in the water and a splash startles me. My feet reach for the seafloor. Something travels beneath the surface; it's coming towards me. Lithe and fast. A seal? I ground my feet. Seafoam sprouts up and clings to my hair and face. I wipe my eyes and see it's not a seal. 'Kûna!'

She grins. Her hair is dark and silky in the salty sea. Kûna dives with the grace of a seal and holds her breath longer than I can ever imagine is possible for a human. A laugh escapes me. She dives under and I follow; we are two seal pups frolicking in the sea. We glide through the water, and when my muscles begin to tire, I tread at the surface and wait. She pops up and laughs. Water laps at our faces as we bob like seals. From afar we might look like seals: dark-haired, glossy-skinned and playful, at one with the water.

We don't speak the same language, but we do *swim* the same language. No doubt Kûna needs this as much as I do. I feel like a kid again, with Mother, in the sea. *Free.* I wish I'd never stopped. Father's words echo in my ear: *Nothin' but danger*. The fierceness of his attempts to stop Mother swimming. There was always a reason not to swim: her responsibilities to her children. Swimming is inappropriate. And then she left ...

I think of Henrye's wife drowning in the sea. If she'd had the opportunity to learn to swim, like my mother and me, perhaps Beatrice might still be here. Swimming is not dangerous; it is a lifesaver. The fishermen do not agree. They believe it is best that if a boat goes down, the fisherman goes down with it. The icy seas would only kill them anyway. A quick death is preferred over a long agonising one.

I have so many questions to ask Kûna. What happened to you? How did you get to Hildaland? Why have you come back? But for now, I am happy she's alive and well. We communicate with water. I am at peace. As the sun shimmies higher up into the sky, we emerge. Droplets trickle my bronzed skin and my dark hair trails down my back. As I saunter onto land feeling alive and strong, stories of my childhood come to me. How the selkies enchant and seduce. How humans are at their mercy. I can see now how a lone fisherman might perceive a woman emerging from the sea as otherworldly. As not-human. As something to be possessed.

How would Johne feel if he saw me now? Fear or awe? Attraction or disgust? I shiver. I can imagine his surly expression. The anger. He'd be irate that I have exposed myself to the sea, the land and anyone with prying eyes.

I lift my chin. Well, Johne isn't here.

Kûna and I lie down on the pebbly shore, coats drawn over our bodies, as the sun rises overhead. My muscles feel deliciously achy.

As the wind picks up, I whisper to Kûna. 'I am so happy that you're here. I have been worried.'

There is no response and I wonder if she is thinking about what is to be done. We must find her someplace to hide. Somewhere safe. She cannot return to Henrye's. If there is any suspicion about whether she survived or returned to the harbour that will be the first place my family will look. Bessie's will be the second. I sit up. 'How is Hildaland?'

I roll over to face Kûna. Only it is not Kûna but the seal pup rolling around. I glance up: my seal is not far away. The seals and their pups have moved up the shore, venturing further afield, pups lapping in the shallow swell of the tide. The pup noses me, inquisitively. I look around. 'Kûna?'

I leap to my feet, spinning around; my damp clothing sticks to my legs and hinders my movement. Kûna is not on land and she is not at sea. Where is she? 'Kûna!'

The pup edges backwards. Henrye appears up on the hill, his hand shielding his face from the glaring sun. Could she have gone to see Henrye already? Surely he'll know where she's gone. She wouldn't leave me, not yet. Not after being parted for so long.

Thirty-One

Henrye

Henrye knows something is wrong. He sensed it in her distraught calls from the shore. His back twitches in the tension. She is frantic, looking about as though she has lost something important, but she looks physically unharmed. Malie runs towards him, her hair damp, curly wisps framing her face. Her dress, also damp, is pulled taut across her growing body.

He makes a noise at the back of his throat. 'Dammit.' He throws down the shovel. Will she say she fell in? Elinor may have fallen for it but not him. Swimming in the sea is dangerous. The men are away but their wives remain. There's always someone watching. Nothing escapes people on the island. Henrye moves towards her, meeting her at the fold where the pebbly shore meets the grassland. He wants to get closer, but fear holds him back. He must keep his distance.

‘Kûna?’ She leans forwards to catch her breath. ‘Did you see her?’

‘Eh?’ A tremor travels up his spine and he stands up taller. ‘Nae, Malie, I haven’t seen her since —’

Malie points to the sea. ‘She was right there. In the sea.’ She puffs. ‘And on the sand.’

Henrye says nothing. Considers his words. Bessie told him about their trip up north. They believe they saw Kûna but he’s not so sure.

‘Henrye, I saw you up here – you’d have seen us both. Please tell me where she went.’

Henrye’s face grows warm. He’d hoped it wasn’t so obvious that he’d been watching her. He just wanted to look out for her, make sure she was safe but also keep his distance. He would only get involved if she was in grave danger. Then to hell with it. He’d do what he must. But Kûna? He’d not seen her. Nae, he’d only see Malie swimming in the sea. Malie sunning herself on the sand. Seal pups dotted about her: they trust her like she’s one of their own. ‘Malie, I didn’t see Kûna. I didn’t see anyone else but you and the seals.’

‘No!’ Malie steps towards him. ‘No, she was there. You must have seen her. Henrye! She was real—’ her voice cracks.

Henrye puts his hands in his pockets to prevent himself touching her. ‘Malie, are you feeling all right?’ With all the talk in town about Bessie, he wouldn’t want rumours about Malie, too. He remembers she claimed to have seen her mother in the sea when they were caught in the storm. Said she saved them. The way he remembers that day is that *Malie* saved his life. There was no one else there. Now, she’s seeing Kûna when Kûna isn’t there. ‘Can I get you a mug of water?’ he asks but wishes he didn’t.

The look on her face – the betrayal – is enough for him to want to take back those words. Start again.

'Water?! Nae, I don't need water. I saw her, Henrye. Kûna is alive. She swims beautifully,' Malie says as she looks back to sea with a wistful expression. From this vantage point, the seals are scattered all along the coastline. They've moved up from the Point, nudging onto his shores. Unknowingly moving towards the town, towards the danger that lies ahead.

'All right,' he says, because he doesn't know what else to say. He wants her to take a deep breath. He doesn't want to scare her away. Not when she's like this. 'You saw her. She's gone now. Let's keep this between us. Yes?'

She focuses on his face, her breath coming under control. Her hair is wet and there's sand on her feet. She pulls her coat around her. 'Och, all right. She must have gone back to Hildaland.' She sighs. 'It's not as though I can tell anyone else anyway.' Her face pales and pity twinges in his chest. He can't imagine what it is like to be surrounded by such a large family but feel so alone. Henrye has so little and yet he knows his son and Bessie are loyal to him.

She opens her mouth to speak but she looks past his shoulder and fear flickers across her face. He follows her gaze to the Sound. A masthead pierces the sky. He sighs. 'Ye best get home, Malie. Change into dry clothes and warm yourself up.'

Her shoulders slump and he takes a little comfort in knowing she feels the same way about the arrivals as he. The MacDuffies are back.

Thirty-Two

Malie

My skin is damp with sweat as the peat flames grow in strength. Anne diligently rouses it at any hint of a change. She keeps the door shut to protect the flame and save on peat. Her home is filled with treasures from the sea. She and Patrik live closest to the port, which is where Anne finds knick-knacks left behind by the visiting ships. My fingers trace across mermaid tears, peedie coloured glass, a spoon and a bottle. I've not seen any other house like it. So many things, not for use, but decoration. Mother was a collector too, but she would use her treasures to create something anew. From seashell necklaces to pumice stones which she used to exfoliate her skin in the winter or when she was kept too long from the sea.

We have come together to weave and sew stockings from linen or wool. The fleet will return before winter settles upon us. The stockings are a valuable export; we sell to the sailors but they also take them home to their families, near and far. I run my hand over the smooth and glossy pair I've completed and set them aside. My mother only begun to teach me these skills and with Bessie's help, I gained confidence in testing new patterns and techniques of my own. A closer stitch is better suited to our climate. The women now model their patterns off my own. It feels very much like winter is here already. The air bites at exposed skin, leaving behind a stinging, raw sensation. On my walk over here, the mist had settled on the sea like snow. On land, the heather was hidden behind clouds. I could barely see a foot ahead of me.

I stand and arch backwards, enjoying the stretch along the lower curve of my spine. I step away from the fire, closer to the cool draught coming under the door. What I'd give for a dip in the sea right now.

'Are you all right there, Malie?' Elinor asks, stepping away from the other wives to check on me.

'I'm just a peedie hot,' I say.

She chuckles. 'Aye, your body is heating for two now.'

I smile and glance down at my stomach, which balloons under my woollen dress. I had to sew in a triangular gusset on each side to accommodate my growing belly. It's hard to think of it as a baby just yet. I massage my stomach again. No movement, only back pain, nausea and fatigue. And worries about the future – the birth, and what comes next. What will happen in spring? How will I get to the sea when I have a bairn to care for? The longing is all-consuming. It's as though I can think of nothing else. A constant swirl of thoughts: swimming, sea, movement. Keep moving. When I'm moving, I don't fret so much over other things.

It must have been like this for Mother. That's why she left.

'Aye, I do overheat often,' I say. I don't tell her my body has adjusted to cooler temperatures, that these cold days bring more comfort than the heat. I wipe away the beads of sweat from my forehead. 'I think I'll just step outside for a moment.'

'Aye. I'll join you,' she says. As Elinor opens the door, a blowy gale comes through and teases the flames. Anne frowns. 'Just getting Malie some fresh air,' Elinor calls. I am quick to pass through the doorway before her. The birth is some time away but Mother's advice is always near. Anne watches us until Elinor pulls the door closed.

The sounds of women chattering, babies babbling and toddler footsteps fall away. A house full of sisters and nieces and nephews, and soon there will be one of my own joining the clan. Even though the island has always been my home, I've never truly felt I belonged. Despite our differences, it is of some comfort to be among women after growing up in a house full of boys.

'Johne looked as though he was back to his usual self when they returned,' Elinor says, leaning against the stone wall. I step past her, away from the entrance. Can't hover near doorways.

'Aye.' I lean back against the cold stones. 'Apart from the niggling pain he complains of the wound has healed well. He was keen to get back on the boat with Father.'

'Even Adame was getting rather irritable. And that's not like him – he's always been a good-natured man. Can't keep them away from the sea for too long or they become whiny like the peedie ones.' She rolls her eyes.

I laugh. Adame is good-natured and so is his wife. He may not be on my side about the selkies and the pups but he is a good man. Irritable Adame is a far cry from irritable Johne. While my brothers scuffled and played roughly as children, they loved each other and never harmed me. The way my brothers were with each other was the only rough handling I'd known until I met Johne.

He wasn't always this way. Father hired him as he was a reliable fisherman, focused and hard-working. Johne lived with his own father on Hoy until he became ill and died. Johne described him as a tough fellow, with little affection between them. In those early days of course Johne was kind, and somewhere along the way it was decided that we would marry and he'd join our family. There weren't many other prospects on the island, and I wasn't getting any younger. Besides, I wanted a family of my own. So, we were wed.

It was only subtle at first – a snide remark here or there. His anger flared up and he'd shove me or bang his fist on the table like thunder. He's just exhausted. He's frustrated. These were the things I told myself. Father had similar moods, dark and brooding, but he could also be affectionate and kind. I know how to tread water in the rough seas until it's calm again. But as the hope of having a bairn was denied month after month, Johne's resentment of me grew.

There was one time where he'd come home with so much anger in his eyes. He'd accused me of deliberately making a fool of him. I couldn't think what to say. He'd been away for days, and I'd eagerly awaited his return. I placated him, tried to smooth the rough edges, but his anger only grew. It rose like the heat of the fire: his face reddened, his eyes darkened, his fists tightened. Bang, they went on the table. Bang, they went against the wall beside my cheek. I closed my eyes tight and when I opened them he was gone. There was no talk of it the next day. It was as if it had never happened – only it did, again and again. Worsening with each time. The night before he left for that fateful voyage, before he'd been injured, was the worst. He'd hurt me badly; I could not get out of bed for two days after. Like he had planned it that way: for me to be captive in my home while he was at sea and my brothers weren't there to see. I'd been afraid, truly afraid of his return, but then I discovered I was expecting a bairn … It was the first time I felt hope. I still believe it will be different when the bairn comes. I must hold onto hope.

'Malie?' Elinor says now. 'You all right?'

I blink and Johne is gone. 'Och. I'm all right. My mind went elsewhere.'

She rests a hand on my shoulder and I'm sure she can feel the thunderous beat of my heart. 'Getting cold out here; let's go back inside.'

'Aye,' I say, though my skin feels hot and my body is alert. I slip past her, entering the house first. Can't have anything going wrong with this bairn, God knows what Johne would do then. Nae, must keep us both safe, do everything right.

The women gather around the table with bowls of steaming mutton broth. Though I can't bring myself to eat, the quiet of the women and the children brings me some comfort, even with the stifling heat of the fire. Elinor slips me a linen bundle under the table. I unravel it and smile. It's smoked herring. It must be her last one. I tuck it into my dress. 'Thank you,' I whisper.

By winter's end there may be no more mutton to eat. The sheep may not survive. Not if Johne keeps slaughtering them. As though she could read my thoughts, Marion voices my concern. 'I hear many people on the smaller northern isles are migrating south for the winter. It'll be the worst one yet, people say,' Marion says. She is often vague about who these people are that she talks about, but she enjoys knowing details of other people's lives. She's not from the islands, though: she's used to living in a city. Surrounded by people, not the sea.

'I've heard it too,' her sister, Kattrine, adds. 'Do ye think we'll be all right through the winter? I worry about the children.'

'Aye, we best be prepared. That's all we cannae do,' Anne grumbles, bringing the conversation back to practicalities.

Kattrine frowns. 'And there's been no news about that woman that washed ashore? The one who seduced poor Henrye?' She speaks to the group, not meeting my eyes. I have not spoken to anyone about Kûna – except Adame – but I cannot be certain he withheld our conversation from Elinor.

Elinor shrugs. 'She didn't survive the storm. She's no threat to us.'

My skin tingles. She did survive. I saw her. She's beautiful and can swim as graceful as a seal. She is just like my mother. But I don't say this because the look on Henrye's face that day worried me. If he had seen Kûna, surely he'd have run down to greet her. He'd have taken her into his cottage, cooked for her, cared for her until she could get home. He'd make plans with Joseph to get her off the island – I know he carries the guilt of seeing her lost at sea. He'd not have just kept on digging at the peat bogs, would he? Surely not. Surely, if he'd seen her, if he'd seen us together, he'd have come. He'd have said so, but he didn't. She *had* been there; I am certain of it. She seemed so real to me. Like my mother who helped guide me and Henrye out of the sea in that storm.

Is my mind tricking me? Making me see what I want to see? What I have longed for?

'Did you know Malie fell into the water a few days ago?' Elinor interrupts my thoughts. 'I couldn't believe it when I saw her. The wind was incredibly strong that day – must have pushed her right off the rocks.' Elinor gives an answer to a question no one has asked. She bumps my shoulder affectionately, but I shift on the seat as all the women look at me.

'Oh!' Kattrine says. 'Malie, you must be careful with the bairn. The water is dreadfully cold.'

'I'm all right,' I say. 'I'll be more careful next time.'

'Aye,' Elinor says and then steers the conversation away. 'Then Henrye and James came along. He was going down to the bay with the lad. Had their fishing gear. I feel a bit sorry for him, being up there all alone and then being deceived by that woman.'

I see what she's doing. She's spinning a tale, taking control. Veering it away from me.

Marion sucks in a breath. 'He probably wanted the chance for a do-over. Especially after what happened with his wife—'

Anne cuts her off. 'Aye. The whole thing was very odd.'

'In what way?' I ask, my voice steelier than I'd have liked.

'An unaccompanied woman staying with a widowed man is odd enough but keeping her from the town and then paying for her passage with the Hudson's Bay Company. No wonder your father got into a temper.' Anne shakes her head and blows on the soup. 'It's not the way we do things.'

I square my shoulders. 'Anne, Kûna was a young, injured woman – not a selkie – who needed shelter and kindness. There's nothing odd about taking care of someone in a time of need. And what would my father have done if he'd found her? Or your husbands? Would you want it on your conscience if they harmed her? Or sold her back to her kidnappers?'

Anne lowers her spoon and it clinks against the bowl. All is quiet, except for the thudding of my heart. I shan't bring more attention to myself. There are the pups to consider. If it gets back to Johne or my father that I was defending Kûna and Henrye … I swallow; the air crackles with tension. 'Forgive me, I have spoken out of turn. It must be my condition …'

Elinor's hand clasps my arm. 'All is forgiven. I've been there: I know how it is.' She glances around the room, Kattrine and Marion busy themselves with their soups. Only Anne holds my gaze.

It's as though she has been waiting for me to slip up. Is she testing me? Has Patrik put her up to this? Johne assigned me to seal-watch, and perhaps Anne was assigned to watch me. Does he know I was not there to help Henrye but to save Kûna? My heart beats in a fast rhythm and my thoughts race. Hair prickles on my arms. Nae, if he knew, I'd have known. Och, my body would have known. I'm sure of it.

I cannot trust anyone in my family. My time with the women has made this clear. They are suspicious and if the women are suspicious then the men will be too. I now understand why Mother left. For the first time in my life, I too think about leaving the island. Getting far away from my family, from the deceit and the blame. I think about what lies beyond the shore – what is out there for me? For my bairn?

Thirty-Three

Malie

The pups look nice and plump, just as they should be. They look good enough to eat.

The men are down at the port, securing their boats. A storm brims on the horizon. They are not at sea, but I cannot stay away. It's the only thing in my life that accepts me for who I am. I strip off to my linen underclothes, leaving my coat and shoes on the rocks. Clouds hover on the horizon, clustered together like a flock of muddy sheep.

I must see the pups safely into the ocean before my bairn comes. Mother always told me not to put off what can be done today. I knead my stomach, thinking the men make it very difficult for me to do what must be done. Gliding thumbs across my abdomen. Come on, peedie one, start moving.

I see the mother seal shuffling along, her pup beside her. I come out of the shadows and onto the rocky shoreline. She's taking her pup for a walk but she doesn't look as agile as usual, and she's shed a lot of her weight. Her pup's coat is darker.

I step into the water. It is bitingly cold but my skin feels alive. I'll be quick. Johne won't even know I have left the house. I dare hope for another glimpse of Kûna. I don't think too much about the cold as I plunge into the water. My body adjusts to the low temperature after a breath or two. I rise and find my footing. Seaweed circles my feet. I lie on my back, my stomach floating above the water. That's when I feel it. 'Oh!' My bairn is moving.

My stomach is firm and round under my linen dress. I hold my breath and wait – there it is again. I laugh. I touch my stomach lightly; no more kneading. The bairn has got the message. 'Oh, peedie one, once you start moving, you won't be able to stop. It's how you are made.'

Rain falls from the muddy clouds and the wind comes down from the Arctic, roughening up the sea. I should go but I feel light and free in the water. Just a moment longer.

My seal releases a howling song. Her dark eyes are on me. Always watching. I tilt my head back and howl, too. The wildness of it: it's invigorating. We are in tune, a harmonious tune. One mother to another. As if we are kin.

There's a wildness in Johne when he loses control. But I feel it within me, too. I must be careful. Remain in control.

~

Seagulls peck at a red-stained pup by the lapping waves. My stomach churns. It is hard to say whether they had a role in the baby's death or if it was already dead when they found it. I turn away. All the seals now have pups. It is difficult to distinguish the pups from the mothers now that they have shed their white fluffy coats and gained so much weight. There are seals bopping in the sea. The mothers have fasted for many weeks and will be weak and hungry. Johne's words echo in my ears: *No use once they've birthed.* Their job is not complete – they must prepare their peedie ones for life in the sea. If only they would prepare them to fight.

My seal and her pup are moving about more now. She takes a dip in the sea, in the shallow pools around the rocks. The pup is awkward and flaps about but looks to be enjoying itself. It is gaining strength vital to its survival. I recall my own time flouncing about in the waves, trying to remember to move my legs, my arms, keep my head above water and breathe. Her mother, like mine, teaches her in a patient but firm manner. When the pup protests, she barks back at her and the pup tries again. And when they both tire, they shuffle back on to the rocks and sprawl out together for a nap.

The ease of their relationship, their roles in life, spreads warmth through my body, bracing me against the icy breeze. Will it be like this with my own bairn? Will I love and nurture her the way this seal does her pup? Will it be instinctual? Like how Mother was with me ... that is, until she left.

Fear grips me. The pup must also learn to be without its mother. The mother seal will soon leave her pup: it's a fact of life. Her mother will teach her all that she knows, she will test her, and then she must survive on her own. As I once did.

As the bairn grows within my womb, I feel a fierce sense of protectiveness. I will never leave you, peedie one. I will not abandon you. The protective surge is like a wave of longing for the sea. Responsibility is set against freedom. I could go right now. I could go to Greenland. I could take the bairn away from here and start afresh. Live a different life. Find Kûna. Find my mother.

My chest tightens, torn between here and there. My family on land, the unknown family at sea. The tug of the longing is like a boat thumping against the rocks it is tethered to. I don't understand why Mother left us, but I'm beginning to understand why she may have wanted to leave this island. Why she chose the sea.

Part III

Mating Season

Thirty-Four

Malie

When Adame weaned, Mother cried for five days and five nights: one day for each of her bairns. Milk patches dampened her linen shirt. Father tried to comfort her, drawing her into him, but she'd shake him off. Wanted to keep moving. It was as if her skin was crawling with midges: an insatiable itch. She was restless and unable to be still. Nursing kept her tethered to the land. When the ties were cut, only the sea brought her relief. Salty tears mingled with the salty sea. She'd been expecting or nursing her bairns, one after the other. 'No more,' she told me. I thought she meant no more children.

It is different for grey seal mothers. The moment their pups wean, the bulls advance on the cows. Their pups become independent and, with that job done, the mother must prepare for the next. My seal wades in the shallows. Her body rises and drops with the swell of the gentle waves.

Her partner circles her, lazily, and then rolls onto his back. His pelt is solid and dark. She lifts her head and nuzzles him. They flip onto their stomachs and then back again in a playful way.

'I thought I'd find you here.'

I stiffen as Johne's arm closes around my waist and he pulls me into his side. The deep timbre of his voice used to fill my stomach with flutters but now it fills with tension. I think of the pups. Of my fate. He plants a kiss on my temple. 'How are ye feeling?'

There may be a wildness in me but I am not free. I am like the seal, circling her mate. Learning how to survive. Knowing when to yield to power.

'The pups have weaned,' I say. 'The cows will leave them in a day or two.' The smaller seals frolic in the sea but they always haul out on the rocks to rest. 'Two,' I say with finality. It gives me more time to figure out how to send them away from here. They're vulnerable. I'll give them another day. 'Now, it's mating season,' I whisper.

Johne makes a sound at the back of his throat and my skin prickles. The seal couple lazes about in the shallows, rolling with the waves in unison. My seal drops under a wave and the bull shifts on top of her. He grips her with his fore flippers and then her spritely body stills. He settles himself atop her, nipping the nape of her neck. His weight pushes her under so only his round dark back is seen above water. Waves crash over them and they disappear. A moment passes and then another, and then she lifts her head to draw in a breath before she is sucked back under. Their coats fuse with the dusky shade of the water.

Johne grips my side tighter, his thumb pressing against an old bruise.

I remain still, like the cow. I hold my breath as if I too am underwater, biding my time. Another moment passes before they emerge above the water, this time apart, rolling from front to back again. The cow moves closer and pats the bull with her flipper and the male nuzzles her. The tide carries them out. He will move on to another soon enough.

'The day after tomorrow,' Johne speaks and I startle. 'We'll cull the pups.'

I stiffen as he leans in, his breath on exposed skin beneath my ear. He nips my neck and chuckles as he strides across the shore towards the port.

The cows will return at winter's end to moult. They will shed their worn-out coats, shed their skins, revealing new glossy ones underneath. Mother shed her skin time and time again. She shed her history, her origins, her language. So much so that her skin began to flake off. When she dove into the sea, the salt repaired what was lost: the part of herself that had withered and dried. I pick at the callous on my palm, the skin flaking on my fingers. I will not allow myself to dry out, or become an empty shell tossed about in the shallows. I must stand on my own. I must save my mother seal and her pup. And then, I must save myself.

~

I wake to an empty bed. The room is silent without my husband's deep snores. Even though it is dark and the sun has not begun its ascent, something isn't right. Panic grips me, every inch of my body on alert. Oh! I throw back the covers and dive out of bed.

I am too late. I thought I had one more day. He said the day after tomorrow! I rub my face with my hand and a raised callous scratches my cheek. Johne lied. Of course he did. He knows I don't want the pups harmed. Johne wasn't giving me time: he was giving *himself* time to cull the pups without my interference.

I pull my dress over my linen shirt, my stockings, my boots and coat. Throw open the door and dart through the moorland, into an icy wind. I see wandering candlelight near Father's house accompanied by low chatter among the menfolk. I shiver. My family is on the move. The massacre is in motion. I race past Henrye's house towards the Point. The wind is behind me, urging me on. *Hurry, Malie.* I should have got Henrye to lure the pup and her mother away, net her – anything! Mother always said not to put off what could be done today. I should have acted sooner.

The tide is coming in and I run towards the rookeries, to the seals. I kick off my boots and step into the ankle-deep water. It is icy cold but I don't mind. 'Go!' I urge in a low tone. I don't want to alert the men. 'Shoo.' They pay no attention to me and continue to snooze on the rocks.

My arms flail about, my voice is high-pitched and my breath comes fast and quick. 'Go!' I say, louder this time. They lift their heads. Bark in annoyance.

'Shoo. Go. Get!' Yelling now as tears spring from my eyes. A pup worms closer, inquisitive. Rolls on its side and flaps a flipper playfully. It is my seal pup. I keel over, draw in a breath. They know me too well. I've become too familiar and they have no reason to fear me. To fear any of us. Shadows and flickering lights advance.

'Go!'

My seal barks and howls in confusion. Seagulls overhead are skittish, squawking their warning.

'Now!' I see the moment of recognition in her eyes. My seal knows what is at stake. She understands now.

Heavy footfalls on the sand. The men have arrived, armed with clubs, turf spades and glinting knives. 'Go!' I shout, no longer caring if my family hear me. 'Go! Now!' She yowls and then she leads the way, her pup close behind. The colony disperses, sloping into action. She plunges into the water with her pup close behind her as the men charge at them. Seals bounce and rock towards the rock edge, diving into the sea, and foam splashes up around us. They will be safer in the sea. The pups are awkward and inexperienced but they follow their elders' lead. Some may not survive but they have a better chance than if they stay. The men bellow and curse. They realise they no longer have the lead. Chaos ensues.

'Malie.' Father grips my arm and yanks me towards him. Pure fury in his eyes. 'What have ye done?'

Johne heaves and huffs beside him. Men yell and curse. My older brothers are furious. There's no sign of Adame. I lift my chin. *Keep something for yourself.* 'I'm sorry, Father, I think we're too late.'

Father raises his hand and it evokes a memory of him standing over Mother in the cottage. She urged me and Adame to get somewhere safe. He had the same expression on his face as he does now. Father's hand whips across my face and I fall in a heap on the slippery, hard ground.

~

From that day onwards, I am forbidden to leave the house. Bessie stops by briefly while Johne is out and does her best to disguise her fear. Her body, usually soft and rounded, is tense and on edge today. She doesn't want to cross paths with Johne and I don't blame her. It is a risk that she is here at all.

'Are ye all right? Are ye hurt?'

I lift one shoulder in response, wincing and tucking my arm against me. Just when my rib had finally healed. 'He was out of control but he spared my stomach. I am grateful for that.'

Bessie's eyebrows draw in and her breathing becomes laboured.

'I'm all right, Bessie. I deceived Johne again. My father too. I am lucky, after all I have put him through, that Johne stays by my side. I can't have him abandon me now, not when the bairn will be here soon.'

Bessie swallows. 'He doesn't deserve you.'

'Don't say that, Bessie. I do not wish to speak ill of my husband.' I have been careless, impulsive and selfish. Disappointed both men in my life. They told me so. We owe the Norwegians and without the pups we'll have nothing to trade. Have I ruined everything?

After a moment, Bessie clears her throat. 'The seals haven't come back, love.'

'They haven't?' I ask, taking my time to get to my feet. Everything aches and groans when I move. I cannot bear to think about how many were injured or of the pups who may have been separated from their mothers. I hold onto hope that they left before the men got to them.

'They've sought safety. Hidden somewhere.' Bessie pats my shoulder gently. 'You did it, lass, you did it. It's done. You can rest now.'

Hidden. Where have they gone? Could they too be in the Hidden Land? Hildaland. For now, they're safe, but the battle is not won. I'm afraid I won't be able to save them next time. And what of my own bairn? How will I protect her if I stay? Not to mention what they owe the Norwegians.

A surge of energy flows through my weary body. I cannot give up. Not yet. 'I must see,' I say, reaching for my coat and wincing at the sudden movement. I must see with my own eyes that they have gone, that my seal and her pup are safe.

'Nae, Malie. You must rest. Regain your strength. You'll need it, for the bairn and … such.' Unsaid words are left hanging in the air like mist. Bessie's premonition lingers between us. *You'll need your strength to survive the spring, and your husband.*

There is too much at stake now: I cannot lie low. I must keep the bairn safe. Johne wouldn't do anything to hurt her. Would he? If I lose the baby, he will blame me, but outside these stone walls, he will feel the blame of our people. He won't want to carry the humiliation. Nae, as long as the bairn is in my womb, we will be all right.

I pull on my coat. My shoulder pinches and I wince. I have fresh bruising on my arms. My muscles feel worn, exhausted. I want to crawl back to bed. Nae. Must keep moving.

'Malie, please.' Bessie rests both hands upon my shoulders. 'Please stay.'

'I'm sorry, Bessie, there's somewhere I need to go.'

'Go? Go where?' she calls as I stumble into the icy breeze.

Thirty-Five

Henrye

He hasn't slept a wink when he hears someone call his name. It is low and urgent, fighting the howling wind. The peat fire crackles and James hiccups in his sleep. Henrye leaps from his bed and flings open the door.

'Malie? God, what are ye doing here?' Her hair is windblown and her face is flushed from the cold air and whipping breeze. The bulge of her stomach escapes her coat. Against his better instinct, he pulls her inside, out of the wind and the cold, into the warmth of his home. Into his arms.

He steps back as she catches her breath. There's a faint bluish blemish on her neck and tension surges through his body. *Johne, that bastard!* Henrye wants to send her away. She shouldn't be here. It's too dangerous. But he also wants to keep her here, keep her close. Safe. Her eyes are wild and she reminds him of her mother. She looks just like her mother did the night before she disappeared. On that night, all those years ago, when she arrived on their doorstep and spoke to his father in low, urgent tones. She begged him for help and his father reluctantly agreed to get her off the island.

Henrye ushers her towards the peat fire. 'Please, sit here. Warm yerself. Ye will catch a cold.'

She shakes her head, pacing about instead. 'The seals have gone. Are you sure?'

'Aye,' he says. He couldn't believe she'd got them away. First him and now she has saved the seals, too. She is incredibly brave but there's no doubt she has suffered the consequences of her actions. 'For now.'

She lets out a long, shaky breath, deflating like a sail in a wind lull. She sits on the stone bench beside the fire. 'Good. That's good.'

'That's why ye came. The seals are safe,' he reassures her. 'Can I offer you a hot drink?'

Malie wrings her hands together. 'If Kûna made it safely to Hildaland, maybe the seals went there too.' She gazes up at him through damp lashes.

He wants to crouch down and hold her hands, steady her. Instead, he sits on the bench beside her. He runs his fingers across his beard. 'I don't know.'

She turns to him. 'First Mother, then Beatrice, Kûna and the seals ...'

A strangled voice comes from his mouth as though someone were wringing his lungs. A stranglehold of grief.

'Henrye?'

Malie's gaze is drawn to the hand on his chest where he grips at his shirt. He releases the hold but the pressure remains. 'Aye.' This is why he prefers to keep to himself. To stay away from everyone. Focus on his boy and his livelihood. He enjoys predictability. After a lifetime of uncertainty, he wanted – nae, needed – certainty. Malie's family is trouble. He doesn't want to get on the wrong side of Johne or, more importantly, Neill. Yet here he is.

'I miss her.' Malie sniffles.

'Kûna?'

'Beatrice.' She looks up at him.

Henrye feels the tug at his chest again. He wills himself to remain still. 'Och, me too.'

'Is it wrong that I sometimes feel angry at her?' Malie frowns. 'I lost my mother and she knew how much that hurt me. Why would she go into the sea? She couldn't swim. I know her death has nothing to do with me – it is selfish to think so. But I feel angry that she died.'

'Aye.' Henrye's voice catches in the back of his throat. 'I feel angry sometimes, too.' Only, his anger isn't directed at Beatrice. It's at Malie's family for all they had taken from him – what they'd taken from Malie, too.

'And now the seals have gone. Everything I care about leaves the island.'

Henrye sits beside her. He thinks, I am here. I haven't left you. He says, 'The seals will be back. They'll return at winter's end to moult.'

'I know, but I can't wait that long.' Malie draws in a deep breath. 'I think I should leave too. Can you take me there?'

Leave? Panic surges through him. He can't take her away. It's impossible. Pleading eyes that remind him of her mother's; so too does the fading bruise above her cheekbone. The only difference is that Malie is expecting a bairn. She will need the women's help to birth and care for a newborn. 'Nae,' he says gruffly.

'Henrye, please.' With her hand on his forearm, his pulse beats at an irregular rhythm. A yellowish bruise spills out from her sleeve. His chest tightens but loosens a bit when he notes the fear, the urgency, in her eyes. Could he live with himself if he doesn't help her? He swallows. Probably not.

She reads his silence as agreement. 'I must go, now. Henrye, please. Far away from here. Take me to Hildaland and after winter I'll find passage to Greenland. I wish to be reunited with my mother and Kûna and the seals.'

He stands up and her hand drops away. 'Now? Malie, we can't go now. Winter is almost upon us. Your husband will be looking for ye.' His eyes flick to his son.

'Something bad is coming. Bessie warned me. I must go now.'

He grips his chest. 'James is sleeping. It's impossible.'

Her gaze softens. 'Bring him with us.' She stands and collects blankets and coats as though she is the lady of his house. Does she not know what she asks of him? If he takes her from here, he will never be able to return. And then what of his son?

She turns at the door. 'Well, come on then.'

'Malie—'

'I know where it is, Henrye.'

He blinks. 'Where what is?'

'I've seen Hildaland,' Malie says, eyes brightening. 'I can show you the way.'

He stares at her, mesmerised by the twinkle in her eyes, as if she were the Hidden Land herself. As though she may vanish before his very eyes.

He feels torn. He wants to set her free, but he must consider this carefully. She is with child! 'Nae, Malie. Nae. We cannae go in winter. It is unsafe for you and the bairn.' He pulls his gaze from her to James. He must be the voice of reason. 'And my son. You lost your mother to the sea, Malie, and I lost my wife. Hell, the sea nearly took us both in that storm. My boat was damaged; it won't take us that far. I won't risk our lives again. I won't leave my son with no one.'

Malie huffs but her demeanour softens. The bruises on her neck remind him of what is at stake. It is not just the sea that endangers them. 'The seals are protected at sea, for now. And if Kûna made it to Hildaland then she is out of harm's way too. We wait until the time is right. Joseph offered me a position in the Hudson's Bay Company. I will repair my boat and we can set sail for Hildaland. Then join their crew when they return in summer. We could all go together. We'll leave after winter, when it will be safer for you and the bairn. All right?'

'Fine,' she says and he sighs, knowing full well he has not actually won this battle. He won't let her convince him, though. There is no way they can travel any earlier and survive it. 'We'll go at the first sign of spring.'

'Spring.' Her face dulls, as though spring engenders not hope but resignation.

Thirty-Six

Malie

The Norwegian fleet returns for only a few days in November. They are outraged not to receive the seal blubber and skins they were promised. Father blames the weather and the storms; says the furore chased them away. Johne and my brothers slaughter almost all the livestock to keep the crews fed on their return journey, confident they'll get the blubber and skins before their next visit. They will not back down from their plan, leaving us with just six ewes, two lambs and a ram. Johne does not let me take the new spindles of linen yarn stockings to market. He doesn't want me anywhere near the crew. As far as I know, there are no other ships in port. Joseph did not return. Likely they are elsewhere, bracing themselves for a cold winter.

Outside, the world changes. By December the sky and land are blanketed in white, clouds and snow. I don't recall much snow when I was a child: the wild winds lashing across the island whipped away anything in their path. But the winters have been colder, colder than in my childhood.

Underneath stretched and thinning skin, my body transforms too. Organs shift aside for the bairn, who now kicks with all her might. I whisper to her on darkened evenings about the land and the sky and the sea.

Johne snorts and stirs before slipping back into sleep. He has nowhere to be. There is little daylight, so our mornings start late and we venture out momentarily, only for the sky to darken soon after so we retreat indoors. We have returned to our previous rhythm of spending day and night together, not seeing much of my family. Father accepts visits from Johne but refuses to speak to me.

With Johne not venturing far from home, Bessie no longer visits. News of the death of Fergus Grahame, the old man who lived alone in the northern hut, finds its way to us through Adame and Elinor. Johne says Bessie was the last one to see him alive. He says it in a way that holds Bessie to some kind of account, even though she was the only one in the parish to care for poor Fergus.

Johne is vigilant about checking on the sheep, having kept them in the dyke over the coldest months. Three days in a row he's found a dead ewe, frozen during the icy night. The days are quiet but for the howling wind. I miss swimming in the sea. I miss Kûna. I miss visiting Henrye and James. I miss the seals. But I must bide my time, follow the rules, until I can leave with Henrye in the spring.

I think of Kûna, alone in the Hidden Land, out there in the cold. I hope she remains hidden from the men who seek her. What if there is no food or shelter for Kûna? What if she dies there, alone and cold? What if it is not magical, as I'd been led to believe, but barren and wild? Tears sting my eyes.

I ache to return to the sea and rest my eyes upon the seals: I know some have returned to the Point as Elinor has told me so. She saw them bopping in the waves on a clear day. But they don't dare haul out: they're still wary. The men will wait for the seals to return at winter's end. When the seals moult, they will laze about on the rocks to stay warm under the sun's gaze. They will be vulnerable and exposed. They will think themselves safe. That's when the men will strike.

Sometimes I feel like one of the herd. I'm rounded like a seal's belly, exposed and vulnerable as the hunters circle me. Johne has kept his fists to himself, his touch careful and tender when he reaches for me under a blanketed sky. The fear in him has subsided for now. After all, there is nowhere I can go.

I've always felt safe on solid ground, but now my weight is off kilter, so too is my relationship with the sea. It calls to me again. I feel myself leaning towards it. Inhaling the salty scent, devouring it. Yearning for it.

I pick at the flaking skin on my hands, which has spread to my arms and feet, too. My eyes feel dry and gritty and my energy stores are low. Something strange is happening. I peel off a flake from my thumb and watch as it floats to the ground. I'm drying out, like Mother did. Little by little, I will flake away.

I lean against the doorframe. Outside, snowflakes drift onto the white ground. I shift away, circling the room. Don't linger in doorways; don't be still. I must have a quick and healthy delivery, see my bairn safely into this world. I tear off a bite-sized piece of the dried herring Elinor had pilfered from Anne and press it against my tongue. It calms the nausea that still comes and goes. Salty, fishy. My only taste of the sea.

~

On Sunday there is no snow or rain, only mist suspended in the cold air. We shuffle into the kirk. It is dark inside but the air is clear and visibility improves.

'Is yeh father coming?' Johne asks, barely looking at me. 'I need to speak to him after the sermon.'

'I believe so,' I say, my gaze snagging on Henrye's in the back pew. I may be imagining it, but his shoulders relax when I slip inside before my husband. James glances back and grins. I hide my smile with my hand. 'He should be here,' I say. Everyone will be here. No snow, no excuses.

Johne ushers me into the second row. 'Aye.' I haven't seen Father since I sent the seals away. His eyes registered the yellowish bruise on my neck then he looked away. It's hard to know whether he wanted to pretend he hadn't seen it to spare me, or if he just didn't care. The bruising from my husband has now gone, but I feel the sensation under my skin, as though a slight touch could bring it all back in an instant.

Elinor sits down beside me with Nicholas on her lap. He is big-eyed and alert. Elinor smiles when she sees my stomach. 'Ohh, look at ye. How do you feel?'

'I feel ... different, I suppose.'

'Aye,' she says, eyes glinting as Adame joins us. I miss my brother, my ally. 'Ye look well,' she says and I know what she means: your skin looks well. There's no sign he has laid a hand upon ye. Only I am not well, and my skin is shedding, bit by bit. My soul sheds, too.

As the Reverend clears his throat, I pick at my thumb. It's raw and bleeding and there's an open wound on my knuckle. On my tongue, the blood tastes of salt. The pull of the wild sea is strong. Johne glares at me and I tuck my hand under my legs.

I sense Father's presence behind me. When he is angry, the air shifts, like it did when I was younger. Like when Mother swam or did something else against my father's wishes. Everything darkens around him and it is best to keep out of his way.

I glance back and our eyes meet. Without words he asks: *How could you do that to the seals?* I silently respond: *What did you do to my mother?*

The Reverend speaks and I turn away from my father. I can't make out what is said; my mind is swirling like whitewash. I am here and yet I am different. I think back to last winter before I knew there was a bairn in my belly, before Kûna, before I knew the truth about my mother. Before I looked at my father, my husband and my brothers differently. Before I saw them all clearly. Before I saw the lies. A sea of deceit. I must bide my time.

~

Snowy days lead to wild weather and strong winds, and the air chills me to the bone. My skin sheds, little scales dusting my blankets like snowflakes. The rain turns the snow into slosh; the peat bogs around the cottage become waterlogged. Johne is at Patrik's, so I make the most of a clear day and venture outside. Keep moving when I can. Today the sky is an intense blue and the landscape glimmers in the winter sun.

The daylight hours in winter are short but the uninterrupted skyline lights up the island. I lean back as I walk down to the Point, feet sinking into the ground, bracing myself against the wind. Grey seals, unbothered by the gale, are tossed about in the waves. Otters tumble about, looking for their next meal. The sky is full of birds in flight – greylag geese and gulls.

I scan the horizon for a tail or flipper, hoping to sight a pod of orcas that passed by last winter. They eat fish, ducks and seals. They prey on seal pups, but with the colony away they've probably moved on. I don't see orcas but I do see Henrye Sinclair. He tips his hat in my direction and strides along the rocky shore up to the path that leads to his home. James trails behind, trying to keep up. He waves enthusiastically and I wave back. It is as though all those months of friendship don't exist. My heart feels like it is being pulled from my chest, as though it wants to chase after him, like his son. I miss Henrye's friendship; he is the only one who knows the truth of it all. The only person who has not lied to me.

But he is afraid, too. Afraid of Johne and my father and what they may do to him – or me – if we are seen together. He must consider James's welfare and that I can understand. If something happened to Henrye, who would care for James? I risked a great deal visiting him but I cannot risk it any more. I must bide my time.

As Henrye and his son retreat, my unanswered questions hang in the air like the rain. Will you still take me to Hildaland? After winter, will we still go?

I keep walking: must get back before Johne. My daughter kicks me in the ribs and I keel over from the shock of it. She shifts about and settles as I stroke my abdomen. *I haven't forgotten about you, peedie one.* Waves collide on rocks, sea spray clings to my cheeks and the tide spills onto the land. Sea and land entangled together. How could Father ever make my mother choose between them?

I am desperate to be free, to find Kûna and my mother, but how can I leave this place when I am to become a mother? I am heavier, feet sinking into earth. Anchored to the land.

As I approach my home, sleet crunches underfoot, but in the moorland, I spy tufts of green. It's the first sign of spring. A wave of nausea hits me. The change in season means my getaway with Henrye nears. Unless Bessie's premonition proves to be true.

Thirty-Seven

Henrye

He will not take her to Hildaland in spring. Nae, it's impossible. Not with his peedie dinghy, not even now it is repaired. The tidal currents up north are too strong, too unpredictable. Maybe Neill's Yole would get them there but he can't very well steal that. The turmoil claws at his heart, like a white-tailed eagle crushing a water bird in its talon. He wasn't thinking clearly when she asked him. He knows how desperately she wants to get away from her family, and if he is being honest with himself, he is relieved she wants to break free of the MacDuffies.

Her husband's fists, the hatred in his eyes, the bruises on her face, the way she curls inwards like a periwinkle tucked in its shell. It physically pains him. Neill's behaviour did not soften towards Nava after she had children – it worsened, as Henrye suspects it will for Malie.

The disappointment on her face when she discovers the truth. He cannae take her: it wouldn't be right. He can't risk her life, or that of the peedie bairn. If he takes her to sea, they could be swallowed up by the waves again, and in her condition, he can't rely on her saving either of their lives. And what if Joseph is delayed and they are stranded on Hildaland? They are barely surviving here; how will they endure a smaller, uninhabited island? He must consider the children, Malie's bairn and his son.

Nae. He'll convince her to wait until the Hudson's Bay ship returns in June. He'll have the protection of Joseph's crew and can take them all away from here – to Greenland if that's where Malie wants to go. Henrye, James, Bessie, Malie and her bairn. He will have a job to support his son and Bessie can help Malie.

Until then, he must keep Malie at a distance; it's for her own good. If it means he can protect his own heart, too, then that works for him.

With Kûna gone, and Malie's confinement nearing, he must focus on the future. He must be practical. Joseph didn't come back in November – there was too much ice to navigate so close to winter– but Henrye holds on to hope that they'll come back this summer. They must all wait until then. If they made it through the dark, cold winter, surely they can all survive spring?

'It's for her own good,' he says aloud, trying to convince himself. 'Her own good,' he repeats.

Thirty-Eight

Malie

With a caisie and a measly harvest of clams resting upon my stomach, I rejoin the women on the sandy banks. Our diminishing flock has meandered down to the shore, the sheep feasting on the kelp thrown out by the waves. Three ewes and a lamb dropped dead over winter but one lamb survived and so did the ram. We have only three ewes remaining and remarkably all three are in lamb. We might get through another year yet.

Elinor eyes the seals out past the rocks: a herd of twenty or so are tumbling about in the waves. My breath catches. They've come back! Pulled back to the place where they were born and where they birthed their young. Seagulls circle the skies. A few seals have hauled out on the rocks, upright and alert. On duty.

'I think ye did the right thing. Those poor pups, Malie,' Elinor says. 'Sending them away. I can't believe they were going to slaughter them all.'

Her voice wavers and she smiles at me. 'I know your brothers and their wives aren't happy about it but I think it was the right thing to do.'

Tears prick my eyes as I keep them trained on the seals bopping in the waves. They've come back to moult on the rocks, and the men are still set on their plan to cull the herd by half. Pups, cows, bulls; they no longer care. They just want a bigger boat. I don't think my mother seal is there. I want to see her but it's best if she stays away. I can't lose her, too. 'Thank you, Elinor.' After a moment, I ask: 'What does Adame think about it?'

Her shoulder leans against mine. 'Well, he's not happy that yeh father is not happy because that makes all our lives more difficult,' she says with a sad laugh. 'But Adame is a kind man and he will always look out for his big sister. He didn't want any harm to come to the seals – or you. You must know that.'

She holds my gaze, and in her expression there are many things left unsaid. I don't talk to Adame or his wife about Johne, but I've never felt completely unsafe, because I know my brother has always kept an eye on me. 'Aye.'

Kattrine and Marion join us. Kattrine clucks her tongue. 'Do ye think Beatrice is out there?' She squints at the bopping seal heads in the water.

My body stiffens at the sudden mention of my friend, and Henrye's late wife. 'Beatrice?'

She shrugs. 'Ye, you know how it's said that when someone takes their own life they come back as a selkie, a fallen angel?'

'Och,' Marion says, brightening. 'I heard about that back home.'

I bristle. 'That is not what happened. Beatrice drowned.'

'Well, it's obvious, isn't it?' Marion says, brimming with energy while her sister averts her gaze. 'She had a tough time when her boy was little. Why else would she have gone out there? Your father said she had a weak mind and that's why she did it.'

'My father?'

'Aye, she wasn't herself after James was born,' Kattrine adds half-heartedly.

'How would either of you know?' I spit. 'Or Father? Did any of you ever visit her, care for her as I did? You weren't even here.'

Kattrine stumbles backwards as if I've set a gale upon her. 'Sorry, Malie. Didn't mean to upset ye. I know she was your good friend.'

Anne appears then. 'That's enough, both of you,' she snaps, and the sisters straighten as though reprimanded by a parent.

'She didn't want to die,' I add quietly, but I'm not entirely sure that's true. I know she wouldn't have wanted to leave James. She loved him. But she was not herself before she died. She was angry and distant. Come to think of it, my mother was like that too before she left. Maybe there was something stronger tugging at her. The pull of the sea. Maybe love isn't enough. A lump forms in my throat and I pull away from the women.

'It's just sad, that's all I'm saying,' Kattrine mumbles. 'She left behind her son. A little boy without a mother.'

A shaky breath escapes as I turn back. 'Yes, and I know what it is like to lose a mother, to hear rumours and gossip about her. It is hurtful. Leave the poor boy and his father alone, Kattrine.'

Kattrine's face pales. 'Malie—'

I turn my back on the women and march up the sand, not as fast as I'd like because I'm heavy, and the wind is against me, and it frustrates me I can't escape them with haste. The stories and the lies. I can't escape anyone, stuck on this island in the middle of the North Sea. I long to be a seal who can come and go as she pleases. I long to be anywhere but here.

It is Elinor who catches up with me; even with Nicholas in a sling across her chest she is more agile than me. But I don't mind too much that it's her. We walk back home in silence. Even so, my thoughts won't quieten. One niggles at me about Mother's disappearance. She longed for the sea but Father forbade her. If she is not a selkie who returned to the sea, then what really happened to her?

The gentle breeze sweeps away the tears threatening to overspill. I push down the thoughts and the worries but I know I can only do that for so long. There is only one person who can tell me, once and for all, about what really happened to my mother. Before I leave the island, I must speak to my father.

Thirty-Nine

Henrye

A roaring wind startles him awake. Henrye sits upright as his eyes adjust to the darkness and his son's sleeping form beside him. It roars again, only it is not the wind, but a man. Henrye hears his name. He strides to the door but before he reaches it it is thrown aside. The air is still but the man is crackling like lightning. His face is pure fury. 'Johne?'

'You!' Johne lunges at him, and they topple to the floor. Johne's weight on his chest; a crack of his ribs and Henrye cries out. James screams. Johne pummels his fists into Henrye, who can only think of the pain and force and how if Malie can brave it then so can he.

He pushes Johne off him. 'What are ye doing here?' he pants. He can't still be angry about him being in that storm with Malie, surely? Has this brute of a man laid low all winter only to surprise him with the wrath of his thunder when he least expected it? Has he planned this all along? Or has he learned of Malie's plan to escape to Hildaland?

Johne is quicker to his feet, though he is off balance, his leg bothering him more than he lets on. 'Ye lost ye selkie wife and so ye try to steal mine?!'

'What?' A wave of fear comes over him. 'Malie is gone?' He thinks of Hildaland and her fierce determination to get there. Has he failed again? 'What have ye done to her?'

'I havenae done anything. She's gone.' Johne pants and looks around; James whimpers on the other side of the room and Johne registers that they're otherwise alone. 'I thought she was here.'

Henrye staggers to his feet, brushes dirt off his pants. 'Why would she be here, Johne? She's *your* wife.'

Johne growls. 'I *know* she's my wife. And you better not forget it.'

How can anyone forget? Henrye thinks. 'She's not here, Johne.' He waits a moment for the words to settle. Where could she be? He should've taken her away from here, got her away from Johne when he had the chance. Henrye hopes he's not too late.

'Where is she?' His voice cracks and for a moment Henrye thinks Johne might cry, but the moment passes just as fast as it arrives. He turns his back on Henrye.

Henrye looks past Johne, outside to the lit-up sky. The moon is at its fullest and brightest. Tonight, the entire bay will be lit up, and the Point, too. He thinks of the seals who keep returning, day after day, knowing the dangers and yet unable to stay away. He thinks of Malie next and sighs. 'I think I know where she is. Wait here for me, James,' he says to his son.

'Papa?'

'It's all right, son,' Henrye assures him.

Henrye collects his coat and waits by the door. Johne eyes him before finally he relents and pushes past him, out into the night sky. With one final glance back at his son, Henrye closes the door behind him and takes the lead. Henrye braces himself, hoping Johne won't tackle him again, but a shift in the air brings him comfort. Some of the tension has eased. And when he looks back at Johne, he is satisfied the fight has gone from him, at least for now. He trails behind Henrye like a pup following its mother at sea. Henrye draws in a deep breath and reminds himself not to let his guard down. He knows the storm isn't over. Nae: the worst is yet to come.

Forty

Malie

The sea sparkles under moonlight, and while the air is crisp at the Point, there is a rare lull in the wind. This makes shedding my clothes only a little more bearable. I hesitate at my final layer, a linen shift, and wonder how it would feel to swim bare. I have spent my whole life clothed and covered, but now my body has stretched and reshaped itself I have a primal urge to bare it. A flitting image of my mother creeps in, washed up on the shores. Without her seal skin she was vulnerable, her choices taken away. If only she had known she did not need the seal skin to become her true self.

I keep on the linen shift, yawning, and sink my feet into the cold, squishy sand. I couldn't sleep, the bairn kicking my bladder and my ribs at an irregular rhythm. I crept past my snoring husband and found myself here. I gasp as water spills over my feet – the winter chill lingers. The tide is coming in. It is the safest time to swim when the serpent breathes out:

it will always take me back to shore. Someday soon I'll make sure when it goes out, it takes me far away from here.

The cold triggers a current in my body, blood thrumming under my skin. My instinct is to pull away, run back to shore, but childhood memories of Mother's gentle but firm encouragement to push past the unpleasant feeling re-emerge. It is agonising; it is good.

Unbothered by my bulging abdomen, the water slips over me like a seal skin. The temperature change awakes the bairn, who only just stilled on my swaying walk here. I laugh. 'It's all right, peedie one. We are coming home, back to the waters where your grandmother swam while I was in her belly. It will make you brave, so you too can join me here one day.'

I sink into the water and paddle as a swell folds over me. I have missed this. I have waited all winter to be reunited with the sea. I paddle over pebbles and seaweed. My heart pounds as the water darkens and sea creatures and kelp brush against my legs. Even though I cannot see beneath the surface, I feel safer here. Safer than I do in my own home, where there is nothing hiding and no place to hide.

Once I reach deeper waters, I sink beneath the surface. On land my body feels heavy, foreign, but in the water, it feels light and familiar. The pressure I've felt in my pelvis and lower back eases. I sink; the icy sea stings my nose and my ears as I go under. One, two, three ... I count to thirty before my feet push me back up to break through the surface. My lungs remember – they've strengthened. My face feels numb. I cannot feel a thing and yet I feel everything. It is wonderful. I am close to Mother here. I sense her with me. The water laps against my skin like a gentle caress. She calls to me, *Come*, and I sink beneath the surface once more.

One second, two seconds, three seconds … a minute passes. I launch upwards and suck in the air, deep, inflating my lungs. I tilt my head back, breathe in the night sky. I am buoyant, pain-free. Euphoric.

I am wild. Free.

I sense their arrival before I see or hear them. Two men run along the shore, calling my name. The sight of them together is more of a shock than the icy temperatures. What is Johne doing here? And why has he brought Henrye?

The buoyant feeling is replaced with dread. I am no longer free: ensnared on an invisible fishing line, hauled in like a herring. Dragged in from the sea onto land, where I cannot breathe, cannot survive. For the first time since Mother abandoned me, I do not feel sad. I am envious. How did she find the strength to leave? To cut the lines and break away? Did she find her freedom? Was it worth it? The line tugs me backwards. It is too taut, too inflexible, too strong.

I slip out of the water, my seal skin. The ground once steady feels shaky beneath my feet, as if the sea and land have become so entwined I cannot see one for the other. One thing I can see clearly is the intensity of the men's expressions. One is concerned, the other furious. It is not difficult to guess who is which.

Henrye steps up but Johne pushes him out of the way. He charges forwards and then stops. I realise it is not anger. Fear? Is he afraid I will leave him like Mother left Father? Or perhaps he thinks I will try to drown myself?

'What are you doing?' he asks, the force of his words dying out as he speaks.

The linen dress clings to my skin; the moon behind me casts odd shadows on the ground. Johne steps backwards and that's when I realise. He is not afraid I will leave him. Not for the sea or even for Henrye. Och, he is afraid *of* me.

For all his tough talk about the selkies and hunting Kûna, faced with a possible selkie he is scared. I see it in his eyes. Confusion, fear. I am his wife. I have slept beside him for two years. He thought he knew everything there was to know about me. And yet. He looks at me like I am a stranger. Och, he is a stranger to me, too.

He will punish me; I know he will. But just as my father tried to keep Mother from the sea, he couldn't take away the longing, the yearning. The power of the sea. Johne will hurt me but he cannot take away the feeling, the power it gives me. I lift my chin. I will do whatever it takes to recapture that feeling again. I know I'll get off this island. I will be free. I will be brave like my mother.

Johne growls. Henrye's face displays something else. Awe?

The peedie one in my belly kicks once, twice. My heart swells. She feels the power too.

Forty-One

Malie

The feeling is short-lived, as Johne hauls me away from the sea, across the sand and up the grassy banks. His fingers claw into my upper arm as if trying to separate skin from bone. Skinning a ewe.

'Think of the bairn, Johne,' Henrye calls from behind us. 'Don't do anything ye might regret.'

Johne's grip tightens as he turns, holding me close to his side. 'Ye? Ye would know all about regrets. Yeh wife died in the sea. Ye of all people know what can happen when yeh wife loses her mind!'

Henrye shakes his head. There's pity in his eyes but he doesn't disagree with Johne. Is it possible Beatrice did choose her fate? Am I losing my mind?

'I am thinkin' of the bairn,' Johne continues as though Henrye has protested. 'The only way to keep it safe is to keep me wife away from the sea before she does somethin' *she* regrets!'

My skin is numb but my heart thaws as if struck by fire. It beats furiously in my chest. Keep me away from the sea? Keep me captive? I squirm but his fingers dig in harder. 'You can't do that to me. Father did that to Mother and look what happened to her! Is that what you want? To drive me away forever?!'

Johne bares his teeth and shoves me backwards. I hit the ground with a grunt and my shoulders sink into the damp sand. Henrye cries out but my vision is blurred and I can no longer see him. Johne drops a knee between my thighs: his hands close around my neck. 'Ye think you can just defy me and get away with it?!'

His thumbs press down on my throat. I choke. Gasp. 'Bairn.' A hoarse whisper escapes. My arms thrash around in a panic but I don't have the strength to push him off. 'Bairn,' I say again. Fatigued, I can no longer see his face but I see us both from a distance, as though I am looking down upon us. His hands on my throat, me taking my last breath. Everything quietens around me. And I think, this could be it. It's spring; we're here on the sand. I am at the mercy of this man. Bessie warned me. Johne is going to kill me. My eyelids droop and my body goes limp. Everything quietens.

Then there's a thump and the grunting sounds of both men. Henrye. The pressure on my throat eases. The sea comes back to life, roars in my ears. I suck in a deep breath, but it doesn't feel like it can ever be enough. Henrye sinks by my side. His gentle fingers on my neck, my face. 'Malie. Are ye all right?'

'Aye,' I say. I'm both grateful and embarrassed that he is here. That he was witness to such fury, to my fragility.

Johne huffs and Henrye pulls back. Johne's eyes rove over my sea-drenched, heaving form. The swell of my stomach. The anger falls away and the fight goes from his voice. 'Get yerself dressed, Malie; you'll catch a cold.' He storms off.

I choke back a sob. He's just left me here with Henrye. It is not the reaction I expect. Henrye helps me sit up, wrapping my dry coat across my shoulders. His expression is a tangle of relief and concern.

'Malie,' he says, his hands clasping mine. 'Come back with me, Malie. I'll call for Bessie. Or Elinor.'

'Nae, Henrye. I can't,' I whisper. I don't sound like myself. My throat is raw, painful.

Henrye's voice catches. 'Please don't go back to him. I couldn't bear it if he tried that again.'

My fingers trace the uneven cut of his beard. There's a trickle of blood from Henrye's eyebrow and red raised skin around his eye. I know what that is, because I've borne it: the imprint of Johne's fist. He pulls the coat tighter around me.

'Thank you, Henrye. But I must go back. He won't try it again. I think he scared himself. It will be worse if I leave.'

He doesn't press me further. A pang of guilt hits me when I realise I'm disappointed. Do I want to go with Henrye? Nae. I must think about the bairn. I thought her safe as long as she stays inside me, but I realise I've been deluding myself. In the briefest of moments, he could take everything away from both of us.

'I'll ask Elinor to check on ye,' he whispers. 'I'll go now, and I'll make sure she brings Adame. Be careful, Malie. Please.'

My throat is too raw to respond. He squeezes my shoulder and strides off. The heat brought by the men dissipates, and my body shivers and trembles. I am still in shock about Johne's retreat. I must get home to the fire.

I should be happy Johne didn't take it any further. His fury may be terrifying but there's certainty in it. I know he will hurt me and then the sun will rise and all will be right again. At least for a little while. The storm has diverted but the dark clouds still hang overhead, a reminder that I am never truly safe. He can't keep me from the sea but he will find some other way to punish me.

~

Bessie finds me in the garden. How she knows when Johne is not home, I will never understand. I pluck a leafy kale from the peat-ash-enriched soil and shake off the roots, setting it on the pile of harvested leafy greens. The stone wall Johne built around the garden in November has sheltered some of the crops from the icy winds. Most of our crops failed last winter due to the harsh conditions and arctic temperatures. This time we were prepared. Bessie's hands clasp either side of my face; she inspects the faint bruising on my neck. She frowns and shakes her head.

I gently lower her hands. 'I'm all right, Bessie.' My voice remains hoarse.

'Is it the bairn, then?' she asks, her voice shaking with concern. 'Did he hurt her?'

I smile. Bessie thinks it's a girl, too. 'Nae. We're both fine. He hasn't laid a hand on me. Not again, anyway,' I say. Henrye kept his word. He sent Adame, who had strong words with Johne; threatened to take me with him if Johne tried that again. The MacDuffies pulled rank, and Johne has fallen into line. At least for now.

'Isn't that worse?' she asks. 'With Henrye stepping in, he won't let ye get the one up on him again, he won't. I worry about ye, Malie.'

'I know.' With her gaze intense upon me, I shuffle my feet. She takes my hand and tucks the silver cloth into the palm, then curls my fingers around it just as she did that day Johne came back injured from the voyage. Maybe things will be different. He could learn to keep his temper in check. I could help him. Och. Am I seriously thinking of staying here? It's a constant battle of fear keeping me rooted and anger urging me to act, to leave. I hate that Johne makes me second-guess myself.

Bessie reaches out again and her hands hover upon my stomach but she pulls back, a pained expression crosses her face. I catch her hand and guide it back to my stomach. The bairn kicks in response and a strangled laugh erupts from Bessie.

'Oh, it's so precious.' Her damp eyes hold mine. 'I was with child once.'

'Oh?' I always wondered why Bessie didn't have children: I know it just doesn't happen for some women. Up until recently, I thought I was one of those women.

'My husband ...' She pauses. 'He got rough one night and I lost the bairn. I was in my final month, like you are now.'

'Oh, Bessie, I didn't know.'

'Had to give birth to her and everythin'.' She swipes tears from her cheeks and her gaze settles on the green landscape. 'I still dream about all that blood and the way he looked at me. As if it was *my* fault I'd lost her.'

I swallow a lump in my throat. The baby shifts in my stomach and I stroke her, gently, reassuring her. She is an active bairn now, except around Johne. Already learning to make herself invisible when he is about. 'I'm terribly sorry, Bessie.'

She sniffs and shakes her head as if to dislodge the awful images from her mind. 'No use thinkin' about it. Can't change anythin', ye know? And he's gone ... so there's that.' Though he died of pneumonia, I think about the clattering sound of the three stones in Bessie's pocket.

I pat her hand. 'Of course. I see why you were worried about me. But the prediction didn't come true, Bessie, not entirely. I didn't die. Henrye saved me.'

She shakes her head again. 'Nae, Malie. Something doesn't feel right. There's more to come. I know it. There's a reason so many of ye young people left this island, Malie. You mustn't stay out of obligation to those men. Ye should get away.'

'Bessie, please. There's no need to worry. You know things will settle for a little while. They always do after a storm. That will give me some time to think about what I do next.'

She looks at me squarely. 'You're a lot like yeh mother, Malie.'

'What do you mean?' I ask, a peedie bit of pressure easing from my chest. I am like a seagull circling the colony: any little nibble of information about Mother and I devour it. 'In what way?'

'She didn't bother too much about your father's beatings, either. It's as though, after a while, she was immune to it. Like she had thick skin.'

She chuckles. 'Seal skin.'

'Nae ...' I start to protest but an unsettling feeling overwhelms me. I know it's the truth. I remember how Mother excused the bruises on her face and arms. Father's stormy tempers, how he'd punish her for choosing the sea over us. The sea over him. I found myself in a marriage just like my parents'. How did that happen?

The wind howls. I thought she'd abandoned me. That she did not care for me. The sea had called her away, at least that's what my father had led me to believe. But maybe it wasn't the call of the sea; maybe it was Father who drove her away.

'Do you think that's why she left?'

'Aye.' She sighs. 'I do.'

Part IV

Shedding the Seal Skin

Forty-Two

Malie

I feel it deep in my bones, the moment my husband executes his revenge. At first, I think it is the howling wind or a wailing infant. Sounds carry off the North Sea, whirring past me in the early hours as I make my way towards the bay. Johne and the men are at the harbour, repairing damage to the boat from the winter storms. In an instant, I realise it is not the wind but the haunting sound of the grey seals. They're back, and I suddenly know my husband is not at the harbour.

'No!' I run as fast as my bulging figure will allow me, ignoring the pressure on my pelvis and the shortness of breath. Panting heavily, I reach the grassy rise above the Point, and I see. The rocks are packed with motley bodies. Some seals have emerged from the sea, beached themselves in the warming sun to moult.

Then I see the men. My stomach is laden with stone. My men and many more. Their boats are moored nearby, surrounding the rookeries and blocking the sea entrance. Just as the bulky, black and white orcas prey on the seals, the men have herded and trapped them.

I cannot move. The men are like thunder: loud, menacing and intense. Clubs and spades in their hands. It's the brightest of bright post-winter days and it seems cruel that the sky can be so magnificent when something so terrible is about to happen. I scan the herd, searching for my seal. Even though I know she is not my mother, she is still a part of me. I can't let her go. I won't.

Threatened by the looming presence of the men, a few of the bulls rear up, waving front flippers and calling out. The cows howl. The fear in their calls curls my toes.

Some of the seals and pups stampede to the sea but the men charge: only a few seals escape. They hiss and snarl and flap their flippers, climbing atop one another. Crushing each other. That's when I see Henrye racing along the shore towards them, a glint of metal in his hand. I find my feet. Toes slip into sand, dry and soft at first then damp and firm, wet and sludgy. The hem of my dress trails in the foamy whitewash as I run behind Henrye.

The seals' desperate pleas echo across the landscape. I can't bring myself to look. I know it has begun. I surge forwards. Keep moving. Seals roar and howl, men yell and grunt. Splashing and crashing as one or two escape into the depths of the sea. On land they are vulnerable. As am I.

My feet reach the rocks and I force myself to look up, to face the horrific scene. Bloodied seals, moaning and groaning, men in a fury. My father, husband and three of my brothers, all wielding weapons. The fishermen, too – Angus, Bernard, Duncan and more I do not recognise. So many of them, but no Adame, not that I can see.

Henrye reaches them first. 'Stop!' he calls but his voice is lost in the rumble of the waves crashing against the rocks, the seals' cries and the men entangled in a fight.

'No!' I yell. I see her, my motley mother seal. Johne has her cornered; there is no pup in sight. Her partner has fled. She is alone. 'Johne, please! Let her go.'

Johne's eyes flick in my direction but it's as if he doesn't recognise me. He's overcome with fury.

'Please! Don't do this. Not to her.' I feel the twinge of guilt at saving her life over the others but she is *my* seal, *my* mother, *my* soul. 'Please!'

His eyes find mine, and in the moment of hesitation, she launches at him. Bites his hand. Hard. 'Agh!' Johne stumbles backwards, blood spilling from his hand. The seal roars. Johne roars too.

'Ye brought this on yourself, Malie,' he says through gritted teeth, raising the sharp-edged shovel.

'No!'

Her eyes meet mine and I know she understands what will happen next. I force myself to hold her gaze, to stay with her in the pain, as the shovel comes down. She yelps, and staggers towards him. Slinks to the ground. My own feet are heavy and impossible to lift. Johne raises his arm again, bringing his shovel down on the seal once more. I cry out. And then Henrye is on top of Johne, prying the weapon from Johne's grip. They rumble and tumble across the rocks, and only then do my legs move. I rush to her side.

My fingers trail her skin, fur layers moulting away. She moans. Skin like my mother out of the sea. Skin like mine. I cradle her head in my lap and she sighs. Salty tears fall from my face to hers. Her blood pools around me. 'I'm so sorry,' I cry.

'Get off her!' Johne is back on his feet. Blood smeared across his cheek, down his arm, and his hand.

'How could you?' I shout at Johne.

'It's too late,' Johne heaves. 'This is all because of what you did, helping that selkie woman. Gettin' in the way of the pups. Swimming! You defied me one too many times.'

He is right. I shudder with pain, anger and grief. I cared too much and I let him see how much she meant to me. It is I who endangered the seals. I put her at risk. *But* I did not hurt her. That was all Johne. He wielded his power in the worst possible way. I cannot let him take it all.

'You know what this means,' I say, in a steely voice. Her pulse slows under my touch. 'You will suffer for this, Johne. Grave misfortune comes from taking the life of a seal.'

Fury flares in his eyes, but there is fear too. He's afraid of me. I am bloodied and rounded like the seals sprawled out around me. Johne stumbles backwards. Many seals have escaped but there are dozens of bodies about, moaning.

Bessie materialises out of the mist and delivers the final blow. 'You will forever be cursed for this, Johne Gray.'

He clutches his bloodstained shirt. 'Witch!' He is fearful of her wildness. Just as he fears mine.

'Let's go,' Father says to Johne, ignoring me. 'We have enough.' I take in all the seals lying on the rocks. More than ten, perhaps twenty. Some are mutilated and cannot be sold for skins. Proof that this was never just about the boat: it was revenge. Father strides away and my brothers follow him. Johne, clutching his hand, looks right at me. His top lip snarls and then he storms off after my brothers. They load some of the bodies onto the boats, ready to transport them back to the port.

Bessie and Henrye stay with me. I hold my mother seal's head in my lap; her breath is laboured. Warm breath on my stomach. A sob erupts. She will never see her pup again. She won't be here when I give birth. She won't be here for any of it. Her pup will be all alone. I will be alone. Again.

Henrye's hand rests on my shoulder and he crouches down beside me. 'Malie.' His voice breaks. My heart breaks. 'She's suffering.'

As I stroke her face, her human-like eyes hold my gaze. Bessie retrieves the scrap of cloth from my coat pocket and tucks it into my hand. 'So she passes quickly, lass,' she whispers. I clutch it tight in my fist.

I can't bring myself to look at Henrye but I signal to him with a nod. I am ready for what must be done. I flinch but I do not break eye contact with my mother seal as Henrye rests the knife against her neck. I hold her gaze, her pain, her soul until her eyes glaze over and there is no life left.

The sky darkens and weeps, and still, I remain.

Forty-Three

Malie

In the early weeks of spring, I stay with Elinor and Adame. The bairn is due any week now. The days lengthen and there is heat behind the sun's rays. As I tend to my brother's garden, hen harriers dance in the sky. Flocks of seafowl have returned to the shores to breed. The last of winter sheds, like my skin; everything sheds and yet nothing is renewed. Mother is gone. Kûna is gone. My seal is gone.

I am gone.

The peedie one is not. She grows strong, stretching and groaning under my skin day after day, but I cannot bring myself to talk to her. I told Father I would not see Johne, and he has bade my husband to stay away from me. I would not go back home. They seem to think I will change my mind when the bairn comes. How can I look at him after what he did? He disgusts me. All of them do. Repulsive.

The only brother I have not shunned is Adame, who was deliberately absent from the cull. Elinor too. We have not spoken about what happened but I know he is concerned that our father planned to kill the seals with no regards as to whether our mother was among them. I didn't have the heart to tell him that Father has told us lies our whole lives.

I am told other seals washed ashore, dead, following the massacre, injured on sharp rocks as they fled, or from fear. They are vulnerable to illness and cold seas when moulting. No live seals have returned. I can't bring myself to visit the Point or expose myself to the jeers of the men who have meat and blubber and seal skins to store and trade for many seasons to come. Father will get his beloved boat.

I think of Mother's seal skin, dusty and abandoned in a hole under Father's bed. How he stole the one thing that connected her to her people, her home. He got away with it for a long time. Until now, that is.

I have needed this time to recover. Like the seals I must haul out to regain strength after a storm. Adame and Elinor join me in the garden. 'Are you ready?' Elinor asks, Nicholas on her hip while her abdomen swells with life once again.

I dust off my knees and drop the spade. 'Aye.'

When we arrive at his cottage, we find my father in the peat bogs with Johne and my three older brothers. My husband's hand is bandaged and his face is pale. It's early in the season but it was a cold winter and the fuel stores for our homes are low. Johne holds the shovel awkwardly due to his injury. Good. *I hope you never forget that bite and how she fought back. How I fought back.*

Father straightens when he sees Adame, who shifts his weight beside me. He too has always done what he was told, but now there is a wound in the family, one that was bandaged tight while it festered away underneath. I can't pretend any more.

'Are you here to help, or just watch?' Father says to Adame. He does not look at me. Adame shakes his head. Patrik, Jerome and William slow their movements, cautious. Johne approaches and stands beside my father.

'Malie has something to say,' Adame says. Elinor shifts behind him, using him as a shield.

Father snorts. 'I have nothing to say to her. She chose the seals over her family.' He spits on the ground. 'She is just like her mother.'

'You're right, Father,' I say, finding my voice. 'I *am* like Mother.'

Johne's face pales and the power feels both good and terrible at the same time. His fear goads me on. I lean into the power like Mother did. She went along with the stories that were told because it would ultimately explain her escape. She outsmarted them.

'Ye should go home with your husband and prepare for the bairn. We'll deal with you then,' Father mutters.

'No. You mistake me, Father. I am like Mother but not in the way that you think. I have been kept from the sea, from my heritage, my whole life. You did that to her, too.'

I step forwards; my abdomen should make me feel vulnerable but it adds to my bulk and for once I don't feel small and intimidated. 'I am not a selkie and neither is Mother. That was just a tale you told us to make it look like she chose the sea over us. But what she really wanted was to escape *you*.'

Anger sparks on his face. He launches at me but just as he reaches me, his eyes flicker to my stomach, and he hesitates. '*Yer* telling tales, Malie.'

I prop my hands on my widening hips. 'So, you're saying our mother found her missing seal skin, transformed into a seal and was never seen again?'

'That's exactly what happened,' he says. My elder brothers circle us like a shiver of sharks.

'Malie, that's enough,' Patrik says and it saddens me that he is most like Father. He believes all the lies.

I turn to Elinor and retrieve the one thing that will unravel Father's lies. 'You mean this seal skin?' I ask, holding up Mother's pelt that I retrieved this morn. Patrik pales. 'The one I dug up from underneath your bed, Father? This one?' My voice is loud and the vibrations wake my peedie bairn so she tosses and turns within me.

'That's not hers—' Father protests.

'No more lies, Father,' Adame says in a low, controlled voice. 'No more.'

'What is going on?' Patrik asks Father. 'Is this Mother's?'

I sigh. 'Patrik, our mother is not and was not ever a selkie. Like Kûna, she washed ashore from an island far away. Greenland. She was separated from her people, her family, her home. Father may have helped her heal and regain her strength but he also held her captive. She had no way of returning to her homeland. Until one day, she did.'

'That's ridiculous. Then why would she leave us?' Patrik asks.

'She wasn't leaving *us*. She was escaping *him*.' I point to my father and he withdraws as though I have hit him. Jerome and William mutter under their breaths.

I caress my stomach, feeling a surge of protectiveness towards my unborn bairn. 'I don't think she wanted to leave us. I think she wanted to take us with her, but he wouldn't allow it. Mother loved us and I know she wanted to protect us. I feel it with my own bairn, and she's not even here yet.'

Father shakes his head. 'Nae. You're wrong.' His face is drawn, creased and hardened. He looks old and frail. Or maybe I just see him clearly now. 'No,' he repeats with less vigour.

Adame clears his throat. 'Father, I may have been too young to make sense of things but I know you were not kind to her. She was sad. You took away the one thing that made her happy.'

'So where is she, Father?' I demand. 'Where did my mother go?'

After a moment, his expression transforms from anger to remorse. He sighs and his entire body slumps. 'You are right, Malie. Your mother left because of me, but I didn't lie to protect myself: I did it to protect all of you.'

The blood rushes from my face. 'Where is she?' I repeat, trembling with fear.

His gaze tracks my face and each one of my brothers. 'I'm afraid she did not make it off the island. As you said, Malie, she is not a selkie. I discovered her body that evening, washed up on the rocks at the Point. She didnae survive.'

My heart twists. 'She's dead?'

Father dips his head. 'She's dead.'

I keel over; the baby kicks my ribs. Adame chokes back a sob; he hurls himself at Father and pummels him with his fists. 'You kept this from us.

All these years.' For the first time ever, Father does not fight back.

I sense Johne's approach and his heavy hand lands on my shoulder but I shrug him off, stumbling away.

Och, she is dead. All this time, I've been at the Point looking for her without knowing it was the place she took her final breath. I held out hope I would see her again. Hope that there is a way out of this life. But if my mother couldn't have it, then how can I?

I reach for Mother's seal skin, throwing it around my shoulders. I stumble down the track, away from the peat bog. They call my name, whispers in the wind. I press on, through the fields, over the grassy banks, onto the sandy shores. Here I let the seal skin drop to the ground. Shed my skin. Shed the lies, the tales that have been told.

She's dead. How could I not know? All this time, she has been gone. My feet drag me into the crisp water. It sends a thrill through my body. I am numb and yet alive. I step into the swell and the water rises around me. The tide is going out, the serpent breathes in, but for the first time ever I don't care if it takes me away, pulls me out to sea until I am lost like my mother.

Forty-Four

Henrye

She is graceful like her mother. Even with the bairn in her belly, she glides through the water, doesn't struggle against the waves. Her long hair floats about her. Henrye recalls Malie's mother, Nava, doing the same. He's a peedie bit older than Malie, so he remembers and can see, even now, with clarity, how different her mother looked and sounded from the rest of the islanders. But she was kind and would smile when she caught him watching her. He'd been in awe of the way she was in the sea. His pa had never allowed him to swim. They were fishermen so they were made for land or boats.

It was dark when she came to their door that evening in late spring. Nava was in a state, tear-stricken, her eyes flickering back and forth like a skittish rabbit. Henrye was dozing off when she arrived; Pa was quick to the door and they spoke in ushered tones.

She asked for the boat but Pa shook his head. 'It's too dangerous.'

'Please,' she said. 'Take me away from here. Help me and my children, please.' Her face was blotchy and bruised.

Pa dragged a palm across his forehead. 'I can't. Neill will have me by the balls.'

Her chest puffed up. 'And what will he do to me?'

They stared at each other until finally his father succumbed. 'All right. Meet me at the boat at dawn.'

For a moment it looked as though she was going to protest but then she sighed and held Pa's hands. 'Thank you. I will never forget your kindness.'

It was the last time they saw her alive. Henrye and his father set off at dawn with ample provisions and went down to their pier to meet Nava. They waited until the sun rose high in the sky, the birds swooping overhead while the grey seals frolicked in the waves. They waited and waited. There was no sign of Nava.

Later in the day, they came upon Neill in a panic. He paced the shores and stormed at them. 'Have ye seen her?'

Henrye thought, *Now, or last night?* Pa shook his head and he wondered at the time why his father didn't say any more. Henrye, sensing Neill's mood, remained silent.

Neill's hands were in tight fists. 'She's left. Taken her seal skin. She's gone.'

'I'm sorry to hear that,' said Pa after a moment. Neill eyed them warily and then strode back up the beach towards his home. Henrye's father did not look concerned but relieved. He thought she'd managed to escape after all.

When they learned of her death, Pa regretted not leaving the night she came to their home. They shouldn't have waited until dawn, but crept back to the house for the children and set sail in the dark. He knew the sea was dangerous at night, but he had underestimated the dangers on land.

As Henrye watches Malie, he wonders about her mother. The tales she's been told. How at ease Malie is in the sea. He thinks about the thunder of her husband's fists. Will she disappear like her mother? Will the sea take her like it did Beatrice? Henrye had confided in his wife about Nava's fate, unable to carry the painful secret alone after Pa's death. He put Beatrice in danger: it was a secret Neill forced them all to keep. Henrye has lived with the guilt ever since.

He was planning to take Malie on Joseph's ship in June, but he knows now he must leave before she births. He must get her away from Johne – and her father – so she doesn't meet the same fate as her mother. He wants to give her the chance to start over. To live the life her mother would have wanted for her. He couldn't save Nava, or his own wife, or even Kûna. But there is still time to help Malie. He is sure of it.

Forty-Five

Malie

The sun warms my face and the air no longer bears a winter bite. I adjust Mother's seal-skin coat around my shoulders, wrapping it tighter around my protruding stomach as I wander back along the moorlands to Adame's home. I scrubbed the pelt clean over several days and laid it bare on the stone in the sun to dry. It is silky, soft and glossy once more. It feels wrong to be wrapped in the skin of an animal I love so dearly, but it also makes me feel close to them. I know my mother: her people would not have culled seals out of fear, only necessity. Out of respect, we use every part of the seal. The skin for clothing and boots, the oil used to light lamps, the meat for eating.

I feel a pang of guilt for not returning to retrieve the body of my mother seal. But Henrye told me he would take care of that; she wouldn't be sold to sailors like the rest of the pelts. I try not to think about her and the hole she left in my soul. I stumble as my abdomen tightens, stealing my breath for a moment, then another, before relaxing once more. It happens daily now.

Voices trickle out of my brother's home, a baby cries, waves crash in the distance. Inside, Elinor jiggles an alert and active Nicholas in her arms while Adame sits at the stone table with someone. 'Henrye? What are you doing here?'

Relief flickers across his face. My chest tightens. The men are afraid. Johne is afraid of me; my father was afraid of my mother. Henrye is afraid of losing me just as he lost his mother, his wife and Kûna. I feel guilty that I have not reached out to him since the massacre. What he did for me and my seal was no easy thing to do. I do not hold him responsible for her death. He spared her the pain.

'I came to speak to your brother and his wife ...' His voice trails off as though he were no longer certain why he came.

Elinor, who is pacing about the room, stops abruptly. 'Malie, Henrye has made a generous offer.'

'It's too dangerous,' Adame says, running his hand through his hair. 'We can't risk it.'

'Staying here is dangerous,' Elinor rebukes and Adame pinches his nose.

'What is too dangerous?' I shuffle away from the doorway, massaging my lower back.

I slip out of the seal skin and feel Henrye's eyes upon me. The room quietens, the air stills as it does in the moments before a storm. 'What is it?'

Henrye swallows. 'I will take you off the island, up to Hildaland or a skerry until you have your bairn and can travel further north.'

He told them our plan. The bairn shifts in my womb: there's mounting pressure on my pelvis. I place my hand on my abdomen and the pressure settles her. 'How? When?'

'Bessie will go with you – she'll help you deliver the bairn,' Elinor says in a rush.

Excitement buzzes through my body but there's something else, too. I hesitate. Is this not what I wanted? What I have been fighting for since I discovered the truth about my mother? Och, it's exactly what I wanted. To go to Greenland and be reunited with her. But what is out there for me now? Mother is gone.

It's true the situation with Johne has worsened and the thought of having a bairn here and being trapped on the island like my mother ... I am scared. But leaving? I'd not just be leaving Johne but my brothers and their wives, my home. Henrye.

'Henrye, this will be dangerous for you. Think of James. If Johne or my father discovers that you're helping me—'

'I just want you safe.' He sighs. 'My father tried to help your mother but it was too late. I won't make that same mistake.'

I approach the table, place my hands on the cold stone to steady myself. The bairn kicks my ribs. 'My mother?'

Henrye offers me his seat. 'Aye, sit.' I lower myself ungracefully and he kneels before me. 'She came to us the night before she disappeared. She asked my father to take her out on the boat, help her escape.'

Mother's voice revives me. I am taken back to our final swimming lesson together in the sea. *It's time, Malie. And so, I must.* My breath quickens. 'Henrye, what happened?'

Henrye swallows and a grave expression passes over his face. 'My father asked her to meet us at the boat before dawn, but when we went there, she was nowhere to be seen. We waited until midday and that's when we discovered her missing. We thought she had found another way off the island.'

Adame lets out a long, shaky breath. 'Malie confronted our father and he admitted she was afraid and wanted to leave him. He searched for her all day and discovered her body by the rocks. She had not made it.'

Henrye's gaze darts between us. He stands. 'What else did he say?'

'That he told us the stories about the selkies to keep us out of the sea, protect us from drowning as she did,' I say.

Henrye clenches his jaw and looks away.

'Is there more?' I ask.

Henrye looks at his feet. 'We don't have much time.'

'Malie,' Adame says, gently. 'Think about this carefully. If you leave here, you won't ever return.'

'What will it be, Malie?' Elinor asks in a whisper.

I lift my chin and square my shoulders. I must be brave, like my mother. I must do what she could not. 'I'll go. It's time and so I must.'

~

Elinor and Bessie help with packing what I'll need for the journey while Henrye and Adame cart peat down to his boat. I will need the fuel for fire to keep the bairn and me warm in our new home, wherever that may be.

'You'll need blankets and a basket for the baby,' Elinor says. 'Here, take this cap. Nicholas has outgrown it.' She places the small scrap of linen in my hand and my chest flutters.

'But you'll need it for your next one. I made some things for the bairn over winter.' It was the only thing that helped pass the time on those long, dark days with my husband.

She shakes her head. 'Never ye mind: I'll make another.'

I press the cap against my chest. 'Thank you.' Tears spring in my eyes.

Elinor pats my arm. 'You'll be all right, Malie. You're braver than all of us. If anyone will survive this, it's you.'

I try to summon Mother's strength but I can't quite reach it. I sniffle and take in my surroundings. The crashing sea in the distance, the salty breeze that has greeted me every day of my life. I swipe away the tears – I can't let Adame or Henrye know I am nervous. I must push on before I lose my nerve. As I collect linen clothing and bedding, I experience another tightening.

Bessie locks eyes with me. 'Och, we must hurry.'

Just as I begin to accept my fate, boots crunch along the stone path. 'Malie!' Father's deep voice booms through the cottage. His gaze lands on the baggage by my feet. His fists tighten. 'Johne needs you.'

'I—'

'He's ill!' Father shouts. 'That blasted seal bit his finger'n his whole hand has swelled up. He has an infection and a right fever.'

Coldness hits me. 'He's ill?'

Father lowers his gaze. 'Gravely so.'

Elinor and Bessie watch me wide-eyed as a scrap of linen slips through my fingers.

'Malie.' Bessie rushes forwards and whispers to me: 'This may be your only chance of escape.'

'That blasted woman put a curse on your husband. She should be punished,' Father bellows. Bessie steps behind Adame but I squeeze her hand. 'There is still time,' I say, even as the bairn sits heavily in my pelvis. I think there's still time. 'We'll get away from here.'

'You should be arrested,' Father spits at Bessie.

'I will come,' I tell my father, who holds my gaze for a beat and then, satisfied, retreats. He has discovered our plan and will get in our way. At least if I go, the others can get everything ready.

Adame and Henrye come back as I am to leave with my medical supplies tucked into the caisie. Elinor quickly updates them. They protest but I hold up a hand to quiet them.

'He's my husband and I am the only one who can help,' I tell Adame, unable to bring myself to look at Henrye. Bessie would be better at it but they would not accept her help; nor would she offer it. 'Bessie, go with Henrye. I will come as soon as I can.'

'You could let him suffer,' Adame says quietly.

My heart beats at a strong, fast rhythm. 'Adame?' His face is fierce and the unwanted image of Johne, wounded, stumbling down the path comes to mind. The hook lodged in his leg. They'd blamed the Finnman, the selkies. Was that another tale?

'He has made *you* suffer enough, Malie. You should leave. You should do what our mother could not,' Adame pleads. 'I couldn't live with myself if you and the bairn didn't make it.'

'Malie, remember what I told you,' Bessie adds. 'What I saw. Leaving now could save your life.'

I am unnerved by this. Leaving could make it worse, especially if I fail. But I've already been on the brink of death and returned – besides, Johne is in no state to hurt me. My father, on the other hand ... 'Please don't worry about me, Adame. I will help Johne and then I will leave with Bessie and Henrye. All right?'

I cannot bring myself to look at Henrye, though I feel his eyes trained on me. The tension in his body. He will risk his life to help me escape my husband and it feels like a betrayal to choose my husband over him right now. But I will not let the men make a monster out of me.

'Adame, take me to my husband.'

Forty-Six

Malie

'I must remove his thumb,' I say. Johne's hand is swollen like a bloated fish. 'Perhaps his entire hand.' A cut runs along his thumb and the surrounding flesh is blackened and decayed. The infection is spreading. The room, previously silent, erupts with roaring men.

'You can't—' Jerome protests.

'How will he fish?' demands William.

I groan. These men and their fish!

'There must be another way,' Father mutters more to himself than me.

Adame stands mute by the open door, letting in a cold draught.

Johne's head lolls back, his face sweat-stricken and as hot as a peat fire. He's in a far worse state than during the ordeal with the hook.

'Quiet!' I say and my brothers startle. I lean into the power of being the only one who can help Johne. With the secret knowledge of my escape plan, I feel braver than ever before. 'The infection is spreading. If we don't, he will die.' I cradle Johne's hand in mine, inspecting the infection line and the swelling.

Father inspects Johne's hand. The thumb is swollen and slightly bent with redness extending across the entire hand and wrist. 'It's true: I have seen this affliction take the lives of men.' He stands up and sighs. 'Back when culling seals was a more common practice.'

There were many men at sea who had died of the infection or impromptu amputation after skinning a seal. Killing seals brings misfortune, a terrifying but true adage told to us as children. This is penance for hunting the seals. Bessie warned them.

'Malie, it must be done,' Patrik says and prepares. 'What do you think?' he asks, a shovel in one hand, a bandage in another. Is this the weapon used by Johne to hurt my seal?

I press my lips together, feeling the weight of responsibility. I won't let him die. 'I believe we can save his hand. I'll remove the thumb.'

Johne groans. Jerome tilts my husband's head back and gives him a snifter of whisky. Johne coughs and moans and drags his gaze up to mine. 'Do what must be done.'

'Are you sure?' I ask.

As Father steps away, Johne speaks at barely a whisper. 'I deserve it. I deserve it all, Malie.'

Tears sting my eyes. It is not the first time Johne has lamented his behaviour but it is the first time I think he truly means it. The bairn kicks my ribs and I poke her back.

A pained laugh comes from Johne. 'Is she moving?'

I guide his hand to my stomach. 'Can you feel her?'

'Aye.' For a moment, his face is content but then he erupts into a coughing fit and his eyes glaze over once again. More whisky is poured down his throat.

So much has happened since the last time I stood beside my injured husband. And here I am again, his life in my hands.

'All right.' I pat my stomach and the movements stop. 'This must be done quickly. One clean, fast cut, or else we risk him bleeding out. Understood?'

My brothers nod eagerly.

'Who will do it?' I ask and my brothers blanch. Father closes his eyes.

I point to my stomach. 'Well, I can't very well do it, can I?'

Patrik steps forward. 'I'll do it. Tell me what to do and I'll do it, Malie.'

I'm not surprised: Patrik is the biggest and strongest of my brothers and he is also the one who can cut off any emotion when needed. Not ideal in our sibling relationship but a quality well suited to the task at hand. I mark a line above the joint and instruct Jerome and William to hold Johne down. Father presses firmly on his hand – Johne cries out – then leans on his upper arm and shoulder to keep him still. 'That devilish witch is to blame,' Johne spits. The warmth and remorse he just showed are now gone. 'She put a curse on me. She must be punished.'

'Aye,' Father says, holding him with a firm grip. His eyes fixed on me. 'I'll take care of that.'

My heart thumps loudly in my chest. Could it be true? Bessie's warning ... was it really a curse? I swallow back the lump in my throat. Bessie must get off this island. One thing at a time. Focus. To Patrik, I say, 'One clean cut. You must cut through skin, muscle and bone at the same time. Do you understand?'

Patrik draws in a deep breath and, even though my instinct tells me to close my eyes and turn away, I mustn't. Patrik lines up the shovel to my mark, raises it up over his shoulder and flicks his wrists. The shovel hits bone. Crunch. Johne screams. My brothers struggle to contain him. The bairn kicks me. Patrik jostles the shovel until it is a clean break. Blood spills out and I rush to wrap the wound.

'Here,' says Father, a steaming bowl of blubber oil in his hands. Our eyes meet and I breathe out. We're not done yet. I lean against the bench as my stomach squeezes: there's a deep pain in my pelvis and lower back. It takes my breath for a moment and feels as though half a minute passes before I can breathe again. This is the longest, most intense one yet.

'You all right, Malie?' Patrik asks.

I swallow. 'Och, just the bairn kicking.' I blow out three fast breaths. 'You must hold him down.'

Patrik grabs Johne's hand and I release the wrapping. Blood spills out again. I am handed a knife and I use it to neaten the saggy flesh between the thumb and the wrist. The wound is stitched, and then dipped into the boiling oil. Johne passes out. Jerome runs from the room and retches outside. William too heaves as the smell wafts around the room. I swallow back my own bile. Adame has left the room. I must focus.

Father removes Johne's hand from the oil and then I wrap it in a clean cloth. The oil will slow down the bleeding and help repair the damage. At least, I hope so. Bandaged and then covered in blankets, Johne sleeps fitfully. There is nothing more to be done.

As I slink into Mother's seal skin, Father's expression hardens. 'You must stay 'ere, with yer husband.'

I lift my chin. 'I will return to Adame's so I can rest. I can do no more here.'

He sucks his teeth. 'There is something you should know about your friend Henrye.'

My senses are on alert. 'Henrye?'

Father turns his back on my brothers and lowers his voice. 'He was responsible for his wife's death.'

I flinch. Surely not. My abdomen tightens again, and a low pressure builds in my pelvis. 'What do you mean, Father?'

'It was no accident, that's what I'm saying. He took her out to sea and drowned her.'

I am disoriented, dizzy. 'No.'

'Aye, it's true. I saw it myself. You should be careful.' He pokes my collarbone. 'Just in case you get any thoughts in your head about leaving this place, Malie. It didn't work out well for yer mother and it won't work out well for ye. You best stay here with yer husband.'

Could it be that Bessie did not have a premonition but an insight into the past? She said a woman is strangled on the beach. Was it Beatrice? I push past my father out into the cold air. He follows. 'He knew your mother was dead and he never told you. Didn't care enough to tell you. So, if you must be angry with me, then you should be angry at him, too. He's no friend, Malie. He's no good, just like his father.'

'He knew?' My vision blurs. 'Henrye thought she'd found another way off the island, that's what he told me.'

'Aye, and your good friend Beatrice knew, too.'

'Nae. Nae, that can't be.' I stumble backwards. There's a heavy feeling, a pain, pulling downwards from my stomach to between my legs. They all knew Mother died, and didn't tell me? I don't know what to believe. Are these more lies? Or does my father tell the truth now? Can I really trust *any* of the men on this island? Men's hearts have never been my speciality; what do I really know of what goes inside them? My stomach constricts and I keel over in pain. Not now, please. Not now.

Forty-Seven

Henrye

The sun dips low on the horizon and still she has not come. Henrye and his son stand beside the boat and wait. Bessie has gone back up to Adame's in search of her. It takes him back all those years to when he waited with his own father only to discover Nava was dead the whole time. They were too late.

His heart rate spikes. Nae, he can't think about that. She'll be here. Malie wants to leave and she'll make it happen. But as time passes, he wonders if something has happened to her. Neill may have prevented her from leaving. Perhaps something went wrong with Johne. Could he have hurt her? Or has she simply changed her mind?

The uncertainty plays on Henrye's mind and he decides he will not accept her absence, not like his own father did. His interactions with Malie, and even Kûna, had livened up his home and given both him and his son something to look forward to. It has been so long time since he felt this way. He doesn't want to lose Malie once more.

'Pa, where are we going?' James asks.

'We're going to find Malie, son. Let's go.'

They trek across sandy shores and grassy banks to Adame and Elinor's cottage, where he knows Malie is staying. He has worried about her since the cull. Swimming brazenly in the sea, her behaviour more erratic, placing her at further risk of danger from her male kin. He knows what Neill is capable of, he saw it with his own eyes – he just wishes he'd been honest with her from the beginning. Wishes he told her the truth years ago. If he had, maybe they'd already be at sea, on their way to Hildaland, to safety. As they near the dwelling, muffled voices carry on the breeze.

'Malie, you must leave *now*,' Elinor insists.

'I can't leave now. I must stay,' Malie growls back.

'Take it easy, love,' Bessie placates her.

Henrye glances at his son and they both rush forwards, panting as they reach the door. Malie's eyes widen upon seeing him. 'Henrye.'

'Yer not leaving?' he asks but he can see from the expression on her face he already has the answer.

She lifts her chin, in a gesture she reserves for her husband and father, the men she despises. Now she turns it on him. 'Nae, I must stay. You must take Bessie off the island. Now. She is in danger. They blame her for what happened to Johne, and many other things, too.'

The accusations of her witchery had become louder and more frequent. He has no doubt Johne will seek revenge on Bessie. 'Malie,' he pleads. 'You can't stay here. It's not safe.'

‘That’s what I said,’ Adame mutters. ‘She just chopped off Johne’s bloody thumb. Ye think he’s going to forgive ye for that? Or how he got bitten in the first place? He will never change, Malie. You will always be in danger.’

She huffs and Elinor strokes her arm. ‘Malie, this is your chance to be free.’

‘They’ve lied to me,’ she cries. Betrayal and anguish are written on her face. ‘Beatrice and Henrye both knew my mother was dead. They didn’t tell me.’

‘Malie,’ Henrye groans. ‘I was trying to keep you safe.’

‘I might not be safe here,’ she says, narrowing her eyes at him. ‘But I don’t believe I’d be safe at sea with you, either. After all, your wife ...’ She hesitates. ‘My friend drowned out there.’

Henrye clenches his fists. ‘I had nothing to do with that, Malie. You can trust me. I will protect you.’

She shakes her head. ‘Father told me you were responsible for Beatrice’s death. You drowned her.’

Henrye stumbles backwards. Malie pales as her gaze lands on James, who darts away from them. ‘James!’ Henrye turns on Malie. ‘How can you say such a thing? I loved my wife! I had nothing to do with her death. Your father has done nothing but lie to you your entire life and you take his word over mine?’

She looks uncertain for a moment but she draws the seal-skin coat tightly around her. ‘Do you deny it?’

‘Of course I deny it. It was a tragedy – while I may be partly responsible for her death, I did not harm her. I’d never harm a woman. You must know that!’

Malie clucks her tongue and her dismissal cuts through him like an axe through soft peat. 'Your father ...' Henrye stops himself. He must be honest with her. 'Your father still hasn't told you the truth about what happened to your mother, has he? What he did to her—'

'You knew all along that Mother had died and you listened to me go on about Hildaland and Greenland knowing I wouldn't find her there! Knowing I'd never see her again.'

Regret slams into him. 'Malie—'

'That's enough,' Malie screeches and as she does, she cries out and falls against the stone wall, clutching her stomach. Bessie rushes to her side.

Henrye recognises the early signs of labour, the constriction of the abdomen, the way it takes a woman's breath away. It was a long, drawn-out business for Beatrice. He recalls every minute of it. He knows it is too late. Malie cannot leave now. Malie will have her bairn on the island. He has failed, again.

Bessie waves him out the door and Henrye stumbles into the cool dusk air. His son is nowhere to be seen.

Forty-Eight

Malie

'Agh!' Another contraction surges through my body. Like the tide coming in, it rolls and crashes, again and again, giving me little time to catch my breath.

Bessie is beside me, rubbing my back with whispers of encouragement. I miss my mother now more than ever. She should be here to help me birth. I moan. As my body relaxes into temporary calm, my thoughts stray to Henrye. How could he? I cannot rely on him. Anyone! Only myself.

'He's a good friend, Malie. A good man. He did not hurt his wife, you must know that,' Bessie whispers. 'I would've seen it if he had.'

I shake my head. 'Your premonition is wrong, Bessie. What you saw has already happened, not what is to come. Beatrice was so sad before she died. Well, angry. She was avoiding me too. Maybe Henrye treated her poorly or he kept her from telling me the truth.' Maybe Henrye is just like

Johne, only he hides it better. How can I truly know someone?

Bessie sighs. 'Oh, Malie. You cannae really believe that.'

My chest tightens. 'What are you saying, Bessie? Are you saying Beatrice chose her fate?'

'Nae. What I'm saying is Beatrice discovered something that changed everything. Aye, Beatrice was not herself. But there's more to the story about your mother. Henrye was trying to protect you.'

'Protect me from what? The truth?!'

'Your father.' Bessie grips my hands. 'Malie—'

'Agh!' I succumb to another wave: my body tenses, my stomach squeezes tight and I steady my breath waiting for it to pass. A ferocious surge erupts within me. 'Tell me, Bessie! What do you know?'

She takes my hand in hers. 'It was your father. He killed your mother.'

I draw back, gulping back air.

'Stop this nonsense!' Father bellows. He is here and so are Patrik and three of the fishermen crew, Angus, Bernard and Duncan. They stand wide-legged in the wind, eyes narrowed, not on me, but Bessie.

Behind them is the Reverend. He reveals a scroll and speaks in a firm and calm manner. 'Mrs Bessie Johnston, you are indicted and accused of the devilrous practice of witchcraft.'

'No!' I shout, gripping my stomach. Another contraction, more intense and longer this time. The Reverend's eyes widen but he continues as Bessie rubs my back. 'It's all right, lass,' she whispers. 'Just breathe. It'll be all right.'

'In the first, you are indicted and accused of coming to the home of Mr Johne and Malie Gray with the wicked, devilish and malicious intent to cast witchcraft and sickness upon them. Johne was injured and you laid your hand upon him and then uncovered his leg and said witchcraft charms. You placed three stones, one at the door, one by the hearth and one under his leg. You dropped these stones into a vessel of water and then washed Johne with the water. After two days Johne was able to sit up and was fully recovered.'

'She helped him!' I howled into the wind. 'She saved him, how can she be punished for that?'

The Reverend drops his gaze. 'She used witchcraft and summoned the Devil.'

'No!'

Father holds up his hand. 'Do not interrupt him, Malie.'

The Reverend clears his throat. 'In the second, you are indicted and accused of patting a lamb and cursing it at the residence of Mr Patrik and Anne MacDuffie and the next day it was found dead.'

'Absurd!'

He continues. 'In the third, you are indicted and accused of being on Johne's property near his sheep. You looked up at an eagle in the sky and muttered witchcraft spells under your breath. That night, the eagle returned and took the lamb.'

'Oh, that's rubbish,' Bessie mutters. She tucks the silver cloth in my pocket just as my father pulls her away from me. She protests but he holds her firm.

'In the fourth, you are indicted and accused of assisting a selkie woman, an unbaptised woman, escape the island. You also brought the storm that nearly killed all the men at sea.'

'No,' I say, groaning against a contraction. 'That's not true. She was not a selkie.'

'In the fifth, you are the last known person to visit the residence of Mr Fergus Grahame who was otherwise in good health and the next day he was found dead.'

I struggle to focus as I am hit with another contraction.

'In the sixth, you are indicted and accused of putting a curse on Mr Johne Gray when he slaughtered a seal. Not a week passed before he was overcome with insufferable pain and infection. He has suffered, at your hands, permanent disfigurement.'

The Reverend continues to read aloud the long list of allegations. The pain becomes so loud: louder than the waves that become a distant whisper in the background. The lies. I can no longer listen to these lies.

'You will be answerable to God, his Majesty and your Counsel,' the Reverend says with finality. Father's fishermen step forwards, eyeing Bessie warily. She spits at them and mutters something that will surely at least be taken as a curse. They grip her upper arms and hurl her roughly away.

'Bessie! No, you can't do this. I need her. I need her to help me with the bairn. Please, Reverend.' Please, don't take another woman from me.

He lowers his gaze. 'I am sorry, Malie; it is for the best. She will get a fair trial.' I trust his words but I do not trust my father or Patrik or those three men pulling Bessie up the grasslands, heading towards the kirk.

I want to follow but the pain is so loud, growing within me. The distant sound of waves against rocks calls to me. Seal songs and sea breezes. I must get to the water. I stumble forwards and follow the call of the sea. I ignore the frantic cries of Elinor and Adame. In the moorland another contraction takes hold and I drop to my knees, onto the soft growth, waiting for it to pass. Eyes stare out at me from the grass. I peer closer and something emerges from a cocoon. It's an emperor moth. It unfolds its striking golden wings, marked with four distinct eye spots. It has not seen daylight in nine months and has transformed into a stunning creature, one that bears no resemblance to its previous self. It flaps its wings, hops a little and then takes flight. It is free.

The sky darkens, the clouds roll in. Everything around me – the sky, the sea and the land – becomes hazy as the pain turns my focus inwards. My feet touch the sand and then something explodes from within me and a gush of liquid splashes at my bare feet. I groan as another contraction takes hold; this time there's a new, corkscrewing squeeze with it. I keel over on the sand. The bairn is coming.

Not here. Nae. I need the strength of the sea. I stagger along the sand to the foamy edge. I'm almost there. My seal skin drops in a heap on the ground. Under the moonlight, cool air blasts upon my heated skin. I tear off my dress, my linen shirt and stockings. I want to feel the water on my naked skin. Wading into the sea, salty water stings the throbbing sensation between my legs. A contraction takes hold and I succumb to the squeeze and push with it. The water squeezes around me, caresses me. The ache in my lower back eases. I squat down.

I howl to the sky, the sea and the land. Images of my mother birthing come to mind; they tangle with the birthing seal and fluffy pup. Pecking seagulls. Wild mothers. I draw on their wisdom, knowledge and animal instincts.

I am not alone.

Flesh stretches and stings; time slows down. Water laps at my skin. When the next contraction comes, I bear down and feel the baby's head crown between my legs. I blow out short, rapid puffs of air. Wait for the next contraction. When it comes, I push down with all my might, howling, as my body opens to the sea. Then she slips from me, into the water, into my hands. I fall to my knees, water lapping at my waist, and cradle my newborn to my chest. She is slippery and soft and silent.

Until, at last, she cries.

Forty-Nine

Henrye

They find her naked in the shallows. Her back to them, whitewash lapping at her waist and a tiny body clutched to her breast. Her hair is tangled and wild. Elinor gasps and hands Nicholas to Adame. Henrye averts his gaze, collecting her seal skin from the pebbles. He dusts it free of sand and, when he looks up across the shoreline, he sees his son, perched on the rocks near the pier where their boat, rigged, sways back and forth with the swell. Henrye passes the seal skin to Elinor and she rushes towards the new mother.

Henrye tries to get his thoughts together as he treads across the sand to his son, but he has never been good with words. 'James?'

'Is that Malie's bairn?' he asks.

'Aye.'

He wipes his damp eyes with the back of his hand. 'Is it true, Pa?'

Henrye chokes. 'Son.'

He blinks. 'Did you really hurt my mother?'

Henrye crouches down beside him. 'Nae, son. Of course not.'

'What really happened to her?' James asks, blinking at Henrye in a way that makes him feel they're on the brink of change. Something they can never go back from. Like three years back when he'd said, 'Son, I'm afraid I have some terrible news. Your mother has passed away.'

Now, Henrye's throat prickles as if he has swallowed a razor clam. He says, 'Son, your mother drowned in the sea, that part is true.' He pauses. 'I should have taken better care of her.'

'Didn't she want to be my mother any more?' James blinks up at him and his heart breaks for James but also for the boy he himself once was. Motherless and lost. Henrye cannot tell him all the truth, not yet. He swallows the lump in his throat. Licks his lips, feels parched. 'Of course she did, James. She loved you. She loved you so much.'

James scoots over to Henrye and wraps his arms around his father. They sit there together, eyes glazed over as the sea crashes against the rocks. In the distance, seals bob up and down. Henrye wipes his tears away.

It's silly to think Beatrice may have come back as a seal but, as silly as the thought is, it has brought him hope. And, like Malie, he has come to the sea, hoping to see signs of her. He understands why the stories are told. They are a way to revise tragic endings.

Malie was told her mother went to the sea and became a seal and she believed the fairytale. She believed it her whole life. It gave her hope. But with the concealment of truth, Malie became trapped in the same life as her mother. He hopes that now she knows what happened, she can have a different life. Make a different choice. He has one more chance to convince Malie. This time he must tell her everything.

Henrye disentangles himself from James' arms. There is no hope for Bessie but there is still time to help Malie. 'Stay here, son. While I speak to Malie.'

'Pa, are we still going to Hildaland?'

'We'll soon find out.'

~

The peedie bairn is nestled against her chest, protected from the breeze by the warmth of her mother and the seal skin draped upon them. Nava's motley seal skin. As he approaches, Malie looks up. 'Henrye.'

Her eyes twinkle and it surprises him to see the tension and anger in her has fallen away. She is soft and exhausted. Elinor whispers something to her and then retreats up the grassy banks.

His voice, when he finds it, is unsteady. 'She's real bonnie, Malie.'

'Aye.' Malie strokes her daughter's cheek. He drops to the ground beside them. He feels heavy and light at the same time. As if he is both treading water and drowning at once. Weighed down with the secret he has carried since he was a boy.

They stare at the horizon at the first glimpse of the sun, rays of light spreading across the sea like tentacles. She draws in a deep breath. 'Henrye, I'm ready for the truth. All of it.'

Henrye rubs his beard and then palms his entire face as if he can wipe away the grief and pain of the last two decades.

'Tell me,' she prompts, her gaze steadfast on the sea.

Henrye closes his eyes for a moment, recalling the unwanted images. The ones he's tried to pretend he never saw. 'It's true my father and I waited by the boat for a long time. Your father came to us asking after her: he stormed up and down the coast. We went home but then Pa began to worry. What if she had left on her own? We went to the Point and we saw her. She was washed up on the rocks.' Henrye eyes Malie but her gaze remains on the sea. He continues. 'At first it looked like she'd fallen but when we got closer we saw she couldn't be saved. That's when we saw ...'

'Saw what?' she asks.

'The marks on her neck.' He feels rather than hears her intake of breath. The baby murmurs and Malie strokes her head. The bairn's hair is light and fluffy like a seal pup's fur.

'Father killed my mother?' She exhales. 'So that's what Bessie saw.'

Henrye makes a sound at the back of his throat. 'Aye; he didn't want her to leave.'

Malie clucks her tongue. 'And then the next morning her body disappeared, just like the boat, and Father span tales no one dares refute.'

'Aye, Neill is good at hiding things.' He kicks the sand to do something with all the tension in his body. 'There's something else.'

Malie peers at him under damp lashes. 'Something else?'

'Aye,' Henrye says again. He tries to find the words to say what he has never said aloud. To speak of it is to risk his and his son's life. Once he tells her, he must leave the island, whether she comes with him or not.

'What is it? Is it to do with Beatrice and how she died?'

Henrye nods. 'I carried the knowledge of your mother's death my whole life. When my father died, I was the only person, apart from Neill, who knew. It was eating away at me. Malie, I wanted to tell you, I wanted to tell everyone. But he killed your mother and I was scared. I knew what he was capable of. He knows Pa found her body and he threatened him. Tried to say she slipped on the rocks and fell. He didn't know I'd seen her too. I thought it best to keep quiet: that's how I'd keep us all safe.'

Malie stills his trembling hand with her own. 'Go on.'

He swallows. 'At a low point, I confided in Beatrice. I told her everything. I gave her my burden, and I shouldn't have done that. She loved you so dearly—' He can't go on, but he must. 'She really did, and she was far braver than I. She went straight to Neill and confronted him. Demanded he tell you what had happened or she would.'

Malie sucks in a breath and squeezes his hand.

'I found her in the shallows the next morning.' A sob escapes him and the bairn guzzles louder at her breast. 'It's my fault she's dead. I am so sorry, Malie.'

Henrye drops his face into his hands and shudders. 'Your father killed your mother, and I think he also killed my wife.'

Malie blows out a breath. 'No one else will believe you, Henrye, but I do. I believe you.' She drags her gaze from the sea and he feels the weight of her contemplation.

'Malie, what will you do now?' he asks.

'Henrye.' Her hand rests on his arm. 'I must do what my mother could not.'

Henrye's stomach flutters. 'Aye?'

‘I must leave this island with my bairn. You and James must come, too.’

The bairn sniffles. ‘Are you certain, Malie? Once we leave, we can never return.’

She nods. ‘Prepare your boat, Henrye. It’s time and so we must.’

Fifty

Malie, Greenland, 1701

Outside the illu, Nava and I watch orange fingers claw out of the frozen sea. The coldest decade is behind us, the climate is warming, and the fish have returned to the northern seas. This coastline is mostly rocky, and there's a lot of it. Soon, we can take our first swim of the season. I will teach my daughter, make her strong like her mother and grandmother.

I named her Nava, like my mother. Turns out it is a tradition here, to name a bairn after a lost loved one. Nava is short for Navagiaq. A name used in the legend where a woman travels from animal to animal as a soul and ends up crawling into a woman and becoming born again among humans. Like Mother, my daughter has travelled from the sea, crawling onto this land for a new life. She wears the skin of my lost seal mother. Kûna made a coat and boots for my bairn, so that we will all be connected forever, and Mother's death is not in vain.

Elinor wrote from Orkney. Bessie was escorted to Marwick's Hole, the dungeon beneath St Magnus's Cathedral in Kirkwall, to await her trial. She never made it to trial. They heard her casting spells and muttering witchcraft in the cell. The next morning, she was nowhere to be found. In her place, they found three stones. One was as hot as a peat fire.

Hildaland isn't quite the magical land I was led to believe. Access was problematic due to strong tidal surges and we four were almost thrown from the boat on two occasions. The island is flat, without any rodents or animals, but there is an abundance of birds and seals. Like home there is old red sandstones, a layer of peat, in addition to an abandoned church where we sought shelter until we could set sail on to our real destination. I was relieved to find a whole thriving colony of grey seals. James loved it. There was one young female seal who followed me around for weeks. She had the same motley coat as my mother seal.

Joseph's ship came through in June and from there we covered twelve hundred miles in four weeks, spending nights at sea paddling by the light of the midnight sun. In Greenland, the land is flat and treeless with whipping winds. It's a lot like my island in that way. Though here, winter is bitingly cold, and the island is plunged into complete darkness. It's why emerging into the first rays of light in spring, the first dawn, is so remarkable. So precious.

'Mama?' Nava's soft voice breaks me from the sun's trance.

'Aye, peedie one, what is it?'

'Can you tell me the story about my grandmother?' she asks. 'Who became a seal?'

I smile and tuck her in close like my father once did as he told stories around the peat fire. I tell the story the way Father did. It is only the ending that changes.

'... and she stayed on land for seven years, until one day she discovered her seal skin hidden away under her husband's bed. She felt betrayed, furious. But finally, she also felt free. She slipped into her seal skin and reclaimed her identity. Her true self. Her soul.'

'And then what happened, Mama? Did she ever see her true love again?'

I fondle the labradorite that Henrye gifted me. The rock shines like the northern lights. My thoughts drift to the men I left behind: Johne, Father and my brothers. And the man who set me free: Henrye. He was recruited by the Hudson's Bay Company and James secured a place with them too. They agreed to serve for five years. James is now thirteen and has become a fine young man. Beaver pelts are in high demand and their voyages have kept them busy. They spend a lot of time at sea, but they visit Greenland often.

I smile, because my daughter knows the ending. 'She did. While her husband was out on a fishing expedition, her true love called for her. Her true love: the sea. She gathered her children, and they made their way to the shore. The woman slipped into her seal skin and transformed from human to seal.'

Nava gasps. 'Aye.' I kiss the top of her head. 'The children were in awe, but she called to them and they all went into the water with her. At first, they were scared because they couldn't swim very well, but as they went into the sea, their arms and legs became flippers. They transformed into seals too! The mother seal dove under the water, and they followed her, into the depths. Until, finally, they reached a kingdom at the bottom of the ocean called Finnfolkaheem. It was the most magnificent kingdom they had ever seen.'

Nava sighs. 'Did they live there forever?'

'Nae. It was their winter home. They couldn't live there forever,' I say and my attention strays to a figure approaching us. Kûna kisses Nava's head and settles beside us. I miss Adame and Elinor but I am grateful to have Kûna, who is now like a sister.

Nava leans against me. 'Why couldn't they stay?'

I look sideways at Kûna. 'In summer she migrated to an island above the water known as Hildaland. But she wanted her children to have a choice, and after some time, they returned to the island where they were born, back to their grieving father.'

'Ohh,' Nava grumbles. 'That's so sad.'

'I suppose it is.' I chuckle and stroke her hair. 'In some ways. But Nava, the selkie, she gave her children the greatest gift of all.'

She frowns 'What was it, Mama?'

'She gave them the land *and* the sea, so they must never choose.' Nava sinks into my lap, her head nestled in my chest. 'It's not the end of the story, peedie one,' I assure her, touching the silver cloth tucked into my dress.

'It's only the beginning,' Kûna says. She hugs us both and points to where seals lounge in the waves. Beyond them is the mirage of a ship's masthead.

Author Note

The psychoanalyst Clarissa Pinkola Estés says, 'Everyone becomes snagged by land commitments. Yet, the old one out in the sea calls everyone. Everyone must return.'

As a daughter, and a mother of two daughters, in addition to working for over fifteen years with mothers in my clinical practice, I connect deeply with this statement. Motherhood can be all-consuming. We grow and expand, but we may also retreat and shrink. Dry out. Pinkola Estés says, 'When we become dried out, we try to walk all crippled up in order to make it appear that we are handling everything, that all is well, and just so.' We become disconnected from our true nature, our soul skin. To replenish, we must return 'home'. We all know our way there; no matter how long it's been, we can find our way.

I've often asked my clients over the years: what grounded you or regulated you before you had children, that you no longer make time for now?

Pinkola Estés goes on to say, 'For some, home is the taking up of an endeavour of some sort. Women begin to sing again after years of finding reason not to. They commit themselves to learn something they've been heartfelt about for a long time. They seek out the lost people and things in their lives. They take back their voices and write ... For some, home is a forest, a desert, a sea. In truth, home is holographic ... When you focus with soul-eyes, you will see home in many, many places.'

In writing my first novel, *All the Bees in the Hollows*, I sought out 'home' in the forest. In *The Woman in the Seal Skin,* I sought 'home' within myself. The push-pull of family vs self, of being present and nurturing vs solitude, was evolving as my girls grew. I wrote this story as I was finding my way back to my own seal skin, soul skin.

'The seal woman returns to the sea, not because she just feels like it, not because today is a good day to go, not because her life is all nice and tidy – there is no nice and tidy time for anyone. She goes because it is time, and therefore she must.'

Like Malie, I hope you find your way 'home': wherever and whatever that may be.

Lauren x

Acknowledgements

Aboriginal and Torres Strait Islander peoples are the land's first storytellers. I wrote this book on Dharawal and Gundungurra Country. I pay my respects to elders past, present and emerging.

The book is loosely set around Stromness, Orkney – though I have taken creative liberties with the size and landscape of the island to make it a more insular setting for my characters.

The Woman in the Seal Skin is in your hands because of all the following amazing people and sources.

I sincerely appreciate the encouragement and support of my publisher, Kelly Doust. Thank you for your enthusiasm about this book before it was even complete – and for continuing to show enthusiasm for my inarticulate and bizarre book pitches! I extend my thanks to the entire team at Affirm Press for giving me my first break and then my second. I do not take for granted the amount of work you do behind the scenes in publicity, marketing, sales, editing and so on. Thank you Susie, my editor Liz, Ari, Jasmine and Alistair.

Kate O'Donnell: you are amazing! It was a pleasure to have you as my copy editor again.

Emily O'Neill: for a STUNNING book cover!

On a practical level, thank you to my research sources:

- The Arctic Exhibition in the Nationalmuseet (National Museum of Denmark) and its display of Inuit tools, clothing and the infamous kayak.
- The book *Interviewing Inuit Elders: Childrearing Practices* by Naqi Ekho and Uqsuralik Ottokie for the beautiful knowledge and beliefs around pregnancy, birth and childrearing that informed Malie's experience.
- Oqaasileriffik – The Language Secretariat of Greenland, especially Minik Jeremiassen, for sharing with me some old Greenlandic words and the meanings behind them.
- Thank you to the 'Old Boys' of Orkney Historic Boat Society for sharing your expertise on 1690s Orkney Yoles and boats.
- The research papers about sightings of 'Finnmen' off the shores of Orkney in the late seventeenth century. One hypothesis is that these 'Finnman' may have been Inuits who had travelled greater distances because of the extension of ice sheets into the Atlantic during the 1690s. Another theory, which I draw upon in this book, is they were Inuits that had escaped capture. It's abhorrent but it did happen. Kidnapping of Inuits was outlawed in the early 1700s across Nordic countries.
- Sadly, it didn't end there. In 1897, an American Explorer brought a group of Inuit to New York as live specimens for research, as retold in the book *Minik: The New York Eskimo* by Kenn Harper.

- The book, *The Little Ice Age: How Climate Made History 1300-1850* which helped my understanding of the 1690s being the coldest decade in Europe that century.
- The book, *Witchcraft and Witchcraft Trials in Orkney and Shetland* (Folklore History Series) by GF Black.
- My friend Amber Neilson for her modern-day nursing expertise which I reassigned to a seventeenth-century fishing injury.
- Clarissa Pinkola Estés, author of *Women Who Run with the Wolves: Contacting the Power of the Wild Woman,* whose insightful, psychoanalytic interpretations of the selkie myths were heavily leaned upon in this book.

Any errors that stem from these research sources are my own – or creative licence!

My early readers – Inga Simpson, Kyra Geddes and Sanchana Venkatesh. A big thank you to the entire Debut Crew 2024 for your support, encouragement and comradeship over the past two years. What an absolute honour to be part of such a wonderful author community!

The sea doesn't call to me, but writing does. A heartfelt thank you to my husband, Ryan, who knows when I must return 'home'. For accepting my need to write and my need for solitude which allows me to recharge and be present with my family. To my girls, Neroli and Finley: you are the most imaginative and creative people I know.

To my readers, thank you for choosing to read my book.

Book Club Questions

- Malie's family tell her selkie lore to explain her mother's disappearance. In times past, what purpose did folklore serve in explaining tragedy?
- Seals are prominent in Malie's life. What do they reveal about the nature of her character?
- For much of the story, Malie is powerless in her relationships. Where does Malie find power in her world?
- The island community are living in hard times, a cold climate, storms, famine and crop loss. How does this affect the men? Why?
- Do you think Henrye was right to keep so much information back from Malie? Does this make him a bad person?
- Do you think that Henrye and Adame, who cared for Malie and tried to protect her, could've done more to help her?
- How did Malie evolve as a person throughout the story?
- What did you feel was the most remarkable or shocking scene or twist in the story and why?
- Johne is the 'villain' in the story. Do you believe Malie got justice?
- Bessie is tried for witchcraft. What makes women like Bessie a threat to male power and the established social order?

AN EXTRACT FROM *ALL THE BEES IN THE HOLLOWS*

PRAISE FOR *ALL THE BEES IN THE HOLLOWS*

'There's a murder and a sweet touch of romance, but at its heart this is a story of a mother and daughter who learn and grow closer together while grappling with a changing world where the old ways are seen as dangerous.' – Kate Forsyth

'A novel that delivers a murder mystery, wrapped in a domestic drama, wrapped in a Grimm-like fairytale.' – *The Age*

'Stunningly written, with evocative descriptions of the forest, seasons and beekeeping life. Marytė and Austėja are two strong women, battling against both nature and society's expectations, and their chafing against limitations is sensitively and believably portrayed.'
– Good Reading

'Beautifully constructed … Within the opening lines you will be transported back in time to a place where the rules of living are clear yet brutal, where religious mania dominates and where women's lives are always under threat … A perfect read for those who need to escape completely into another time of fantastical beliefs, and yet also be comforted by the rule of nature.' – Readings

'A stunning debut novel that has moments of being beautiful and moments that sting.' – Hundred Acre Books

'A mystical and suspenseful debut.' – *Australian Women's Weekly*

'A pleasing mix of genres and a fascinating exploration into a way of life that has been changed utterly by our modern world.'
– Final Draft Book Club

ALL THE BEES IN THE HOLLOWS

LAUREN KEEGAN

Glossary of Lithuanian words

Motina: Mother

Tėvas: Father

Senelė: Grandmother

Marti: Maiden

Bičiulis: Friends

Bičiulystė: Friendship by means of beekeeping

PART I

HIBERNATION

CHAPTER ONE

1557

Musteika, Alytus County

Grand Duchy of Lithuania

Austėja

The bitter air strikes my cheeks as I stumble from the gloomy house into the snow-dusted field. When I breathe in, my chest expands fully for what feels like the first time in weeks. The pressure has elbowed its way in, sharp and stabbing, since my tévas became sick. Outside the suffocating house, some of that pressure eases. The expanse of forest soothes my aching heart. I glance back: smoke drifts behind the house, sifting out through the vent above the hearth. The door is closed. No one has followed me. I don't know if it is relief I feel or disappointment.

I lift my skirt above my ankles and run. Get away. It's all I can think of doing. Get away from home and Senelė's wails, Motina's solemn and silent expression and Danutė's worried face. I can't be there right now, in that room, with all that sadness. There is nothing we can do.

An extract from *All the Bees in the Hollows*

The waiting is unbearable.

The forest beckons me. The cool air prickles my nose, is sucked in, snags on the lump in my throat. I slow down and skim the edge of the swamp on my way to the forest. It's safer this way. I don't want to look at the iced swamp, but my gaze is drawn there anyway, and I wonder what is concealed beneath. What creatures lie stagnant, stuck? Waiting for spring to crack open the ceiling and let in the light.

The clouds hang low, dark and heavy. With each step, I close in on the forest, break free from the tenuous marsh and into the solid, fixed, pine groves. Distance. The gap between me and home stretches with every heavy tread. The space fills with spruce and pine, lichen and the odd oak. Beech and alder too. Close-knit and familiar, they lean on each other, as my family does now. Only I am leaning away, like the wildflowers in spring that tilt towards the light of the sun. My family are huddled around an ashen bed while I scamper away. Pine needles shake off snowflakes, dusting my hair and coat.

My body is heavy with the bulk of the boots, the winter's-end snow and the weight of grief surging through me. I force myself to focus on the fallow deer footprints in the thickening snow, which sits more densely between the trees than back in the clearing. A capercaillie bird canters, echoes through the forest, and my shoulders tense. Spring is closer than I'd thought. It won't be long before these birds perform their spectacular courtship and hungry beasts awaken from their slumber.

Again, I run, scanning the snow for traces of the deer, but the track vanishes. I crash into the trunk of an oak, falling into the slushy undergrowth, moss and rotten leaves hidden beneath. It is here, leaning into the oak's sturdy torso, that I feel closer to him. It is only with this distance between us, between me and the bed where my father lies, where he wheezes and gasps and mutters, that I feel connected with him once more.

Before the coughing disease, he was tall and strong and solid. Much like this oak. Even as his seasons turned and his leaves fell, he remained standing. Before this illness, he never let me down. Now, however, he lies weak and small, his spirit ready to leave his body. It will drift on up to the High Hill, where he will join my older brother Azuolas, who left us last winter, and my older sister, who left before I was born, and Tévas's own parents and brothers. He will exist alongside we who remain, but apart. It will never be the same again.

I lean against the rough bark, run my index finger along the lines that tell of his age, strength and survival. I rely on the oak's deep connection to the earth, the roots anchored into the ground below my feet. I inhale the mixed scent of wet earth and must, the smell of my father. I will not walk this forest with him again.

I should pray. I want to. Motina would want me to. The new priest will expect this of us. But the words won't form when I open my mouth. I tighten the linen headscarf at the nape of my neck and glance up through the barren oak canopy to the mottled sky. I plead with the forest; I don't know what. Please. Save him. Keep his spirit here with us. Please.

Beneath the warmth of my coat, a shiver passes down my neck and trickles down my arms. Like an escaped gasp, the breeze sucks in around me. The crisp air constricts my lungs and immobilises me as the snow softens beneath my boots. The trees fall silent but my heart raps like a tree hollow being chiselled out by a woodpecker.

Senelė says the wind, Vejas, is the knowledge of the world. She says it is curious and determined. If it wants to see the bottom of the ocean, it blows the water from the sea and causes a flood. Well, if Vejas is here now in the forest, she is having a breather.

In the silence a cuckoo call echoes. Hoo Woo. Hoo Woo. Hoo Woo.

And the vibrations shatter my body. I squeeze my eyes shut. And then my chest expands, and the forest breathes once more. I slip, no longer held by the sturdy oak torso but shaken off at the foot. My legs are tingly and unsteady as I draw myself up. Home. I must get back, to the cottage, and my family, and the bed. I had been so desperate to escape the den but now my chest aches for nothing more than my family pack. Before it is too late.

I run again; hulking up my dampened skirt, I move as fast as my cold limbs allow me. My ankles are stiff, and I no longer know why I wanted all this distance. I halt at the edge of the frozen swamp. There's no time to skim the edges, I must take the direct route. Slow. Steady. I creep across the tempering ice. This time I do not think about what is caught beneath.

Instead, I think of Tėvas. At dawn he told me in his raspy, gaspy voice that he had one final request. I leaned in close with anticipation. His breath was sweet, honey scented. Honey-tea was all he consumed in the days since the mead ran out. His eyes flickered and then he fell into a deep slumber. What if I am too late? How am I to know of his last request? How can I do this one last thing for Tėvas if I do not know what it is? If I'm too late, I'll have disappointed Senelė. I shouldn't have left.

Crack.

I stop. I'm almost there. At least I think I am – it's hard to be sure with all this white where the swamp ends and solid land begins. My back foot slides away and my boot plunges into the water. Whoosh.

'Ahh.' Only shin-deep, but the shock of the cold paralyses me. I remain still, and the trickle of water beneath the ice directs my attention outwards. Deep in the forest, a wolf howls, and a breeze follows, sending shivers down my neck. I will myself to ignore the rush of adrenaline within and the worries of what might have happened if the ice had cracked when I was tiptoeing across deeper waters, and what may still happen if the frozen slab beneath my other foot cracks and crumbles too.

I set aside the fears, dust them off as if they are snow upon my coat. My focus is on getting home, to Motina, who will be angry when she sees my sodden boot. It will take near a week by the fire to dry completely.

I pick up my heavy skirt again. My arms reach out to balance as I lift my foot out of the water, and I drag one foot in front of another. Driving forwards. Almost there.

As I reach the cottage, my younger sister Danutė throws open the door. Her face is red and tear streaked. 'Tévas—'

'He's gone,' I say. The bird's call echoes in my ears. The knowledge in the icy wind left a sting on my cheek, and yet I desperately want my sister to tell me I'm wrong.

'How did you know?' She looks down at my saturated dress and boot.

My stomach drops. I push her aside, entering the cottage, and realise I am wrong about my father's scent. He no longer smells like must and earth, not like the forest at all. The air is thick and heated, and it catches in my throat. Not in the same way of the icy air outside, not in the way that reminds you you're alive. I turn back to the door, but Danutė has closed it. Maybe if I don't look at him, the smell will go away. I can hold on to the scent of the damp forest and the promise of spring, of life.

My stomach falls further, if that is possible, and I drag my feet through the dirt ground. I do not know Tévas's last request of me. It is said that if you don't grant the last wish of a dying person, misfortune will visit the person who ignores it. What happens to those who did not choose to ignore, but simply did not hear?

'Austėja,' Motina says and her low voice catches.

I turn and face my mother. Disappointment is evident in her deeply furrowed brow and the downwards pull of her lip. I have let her down – though she does not understand. I am not like her; I cannot just sit here calmly and watch him leave. I had to move, run, breathe in fresh air.

'Come,' she says, and her tone is gentle. I can almost believe she does not resent my getaway. Almost.

I feel the internal pull to be beside Motina, beside Danutė and my grandmother Senelė, to be at my tévas's bed, but my feet won't move. The chill and dampness seep into my bones. The grief sits heavy in my heart.

I swallow. 'Did Tévas say anything?'

Motina's eyes narrow and her head twitches, and my cheeks flush in shame. It is not the right time to ask. And yet I do not know if this slight movement of her head tells me he said nothing or not to ask this question of her now. I was not with my father when he took his final breath, but I endured it in the forest, alone.

I step closer.

My motina sniffles, Danutė sobs and Senelė weeps. Her weeps become wails, louder and intense. And then she cries with words.

'Oh, my dear son, why did you have to leave us? Oh, why did you have to take a trip up to the High Hill?'

A white scarf is wrapped around my grandmother's plump face. She dabs her nose and eyes with a tattered cloth. Her words are pleading; she sucks in breath. Sobs. Gasps. Tévas is in a very deep sleep, and she pleads with him to wake. According to our old beliefs, there is still time to convince him to come back to us. Though Motina does not believe this, it is not the Christian way.

'If only you had a look at your two daughters and wife, if only you had stayed here and brought them up. If only you came back to your old mother. My dear son, do you not hear your mother speak?'

I am drawn forwards to Senelė's lamenting, to my father's bed. His face is no longer strained or pained, but slack. It no longer holds his character, his warmth, his cheerful disposition. His spirit.

'If only you hadn't flown away to the High Hill. Ask the earth to let you go, to open the windows and let you fly. Travel back along the high road and come back to me. Follow the bright sun: she will show you the way.'

Danutė slips her hand into mine. She darts a nervous look between Senelė and me. I squeeze her hand. She's worried the new priest will come. He may not tolerate the old ways like the former priest did. She needn't fear, though; the forest shows no sign of visitors. He will not come today.

'Ask those pied cuckoo birds to lend their speckled wings. Oh, my dear son, fly back to us. Come to the window, so I can see you once more. Oh, we can cuckoo together, maybe that would wake you up. Oh, my dear son, you've forgotten the road. You've forgotten your daughters and your family. You've gone to the High Hill. You've gone to the High Hill without knowing anything.'

Senelė's voice grows weary, and the words cease. She rocks back and forth, her arms around her torso. We stand together around Tévas's bed and yet I feel lonelier than ever. She looks to me, but I can't find my voice or the words, and so silence descends. Shame too. I was not here when my father left, and I am not strong enough to carry the ancient traditions.

I look up because I cannot look at Tévas or my family. It is too painful. The roof is made from the bark of spruce. Tévas layered the dried vegetation with his own hands.

He told me of the way he'd collected fallen conifers, including one from a lightning strike, in winter when the moisture in the air was at its lowest. Conifer was the best material, he explained. He selected mostly spruces to keep his mother happy. Senelė once told me that you build a house made of pine for positive energy but to absorb negative energy you build a house from spruce. It seems obvious to me that you build a house that radiates positivity. Why would you build a house that allows bad things to happen at all?

My gaze sweeps from the hardened dirt floor to the clay and rock, compressed to leave no gap where the first log lies and all others stacked up on it. Will the gloom in the air be absorbed by these spruce logs?

A thud on the roof and a melodic call. Hoo Woo. Hoo Woo. Hoo Woo.

Senelė's gaze darts to the window.

Danutė gasps. 'Cuckoo!'

An extract from *All the Bees in the Hollows*

I bring my gaze to Tévas and wish he were still here to make us whole again, to connect us, the trunk to all us branches. Without him we are not joined. If Tévas were here he'd laugh off this cuckoo, but he is not and I'm afraid I'm the only one to sense the shift in the room. Danutė closes her eyes and tilts her chin up. To her the cuckoo will signal Tévas's receival in heaven. Senelė will see her son in the cuckoo's call and will think she can convince him to come back from the High Hill.

I know it is just a bird, making a sound, just as it did in the forest. It does not know what has occurred within the timber dwelling beneath its claws.

Hoo Woo. Hoo Woo. Hoo Woo.

Or does it? It is sometimes said the cuckoo's song freezes the actions of people, turning them to fate. My family are in mourning, and so mourning will be our fate for the year to come.

I don't need a cuckoo to tell me of this misfortune.

Motina's frown lines soften, and she no longer cries. Senelė squeezes her shoulder, thinking she believes the cuckoo is her husband communicating with them. But I know Motina: I see the way her lip twitches, and I know how she thinks. To her, the cuckoo's call does not freeze her in mourning, nor is it a message from Tévas.

To Motina, the bird call is the first sign of spring. The cuckoo is here to sweep away the last of winter. She's thinking of the work that lies ahead. The work she will now do alone.

With renewed encouragement, Senelė's wails erupt again. They slice through the room as cleanly as Tévas's axe into a felled pine.

'Oh, my dear son, stay here with us. Ask the earth to release you from the High Hill and come back.'

Motina looks down at my father's hand, clutched within hers, but I can't pull my gaze from her face. The cuckoo has given Motina hope. There are now two reasons for my mother's impatience for spring's arrival. The first is to bury my father's body in the thawed earth and let him rest in peace.

The second is to welcome the bees.

CHAPTER TWO

Marytė

Upon her husband's death, there is only one place in which Marytė feels compelled to go and that is to the hollows. She is not absconding, in the way of her daughter. Marytė feels sick knowing Austėja was not there for her father's passing, but it also does not surprise her that in that final moment of need Austėja thought only of herself. No, Marytė does not flee. While her mother-in-law wails, Danutė sobs and Austėja's heart fills no doubt with guilt, Marytė finds the strength to rise, disentangle her fingers from her husband's cool hands and do her duty. There is always work to be done.

The master is dead and so she must tell the bees.

Marytė marches through the dense woodland until she arrives in a clearing and heaves the rope higher on her shoulder. It is around one hundred feet long, heavy but durable. Flax fibres retted, hand-twisted and spun by Marytė herself. A small woven basket is attached securely to her waist to carry her trusted tools: carving knife and hand axe.

The river remains frozen but crackling sounds echo through the forest. It is unsafe to cross. Austėja's sodden boot is evidence of this. She should've known better. Marytė gathers fallen branches and clusters them together, positioning them across the frozen river to the opposite escarpment.

She is pleased with her makeshift bridge. It is no medgrinda, wooden road, but it will allow her to safely take passage. Her bridge, a kamšos, is a less expensive, simpler version. She's heard the men of Darželiai, a village six miles north, are building medgrindos stretching for miles and wide enough for carriages to pass, for the arrival of the Duke and the new priest. Winter's end is not a safe time to travel through Lithuania because of the numerous wetlands: rivers, lakes, marshes and swamps. In winter it is like a freeway, a direct route across the ice, but in spring, travel is more treacherous.

It was three springs ago the Duke last visited them and so he'll want to be here for the beginning of bee season, she presumes. Her chest tightens, as her thoughts drift to her husband Baltrus and how he will not be here to greet the priest or the bees. There is some relief buried in her chest too. Baltrus is no longer in pain or struggling to breathe. He is now at peace.

At first, Marytė steps cautiously across her makeshift bridge but her pace quickens as she nears the other side. Putting distance between herself and the river, she enters the ancient part of the forest. A mile from home, where the trees are centuries old, there is little human interference. She breathes in clean, fresh air. She knows she has made the right decision to come.

It was not easy to leave the cottage or meet her older daughter's outraged expression. Austėja looked at Marytė with those grey-wolf eyes and silently pleaded with her to stay.

'They are šeima,' Marytė said.

Austėja lifted her chin in that way she often does now when she believes she knows best. 'No, Motina, *we* are šeima.' We are family.

Marytė was in no mood to argue with her daughter, and besides there was no time. It is her duty as a beekeeper to extend the news of Baltrus's death to their bee family. Austėja knows of the consequence if Marytė fails in this: if she does not awaken the bees, they will fly away with Baltrus to heaven. Or worse, they will die of heartbreak, Senelė would say. And what will happen to her daughters then?

Marytė cannot see how her daughter can have been part of this small but active community for eighteen winters and not know the importance of their work. It has been in Marytė's family for many generations, and in her husband's for even longer. It is in her blood to be a beekeeper, and yet Austėja turns away from it.

Her contempt reminds Marytė of the unpleasant odour emitted by the black and white striped Hoopoe bird to deter threats. Only it's not a bad smell that Austėja emits, but a bad attitude to their precious way of life. Austėja is this way with any responsibility that she has not chosen for herself. Why can't she see? Marytė is a beekeeper, and so, once married, her daughters will be too. This is the way they do things.

Marytė sighs as she wrangles her way through the forest. Perhaps Austėja will change her mind when she marries. Marytė just needs to find the right son-in-law – when the timing is right, of course.

When Austėja became of marriageable age, a Marti, Baltrus was keen to take in a son-in-law, but as his health declined it became a lesser priority. Austėja, from what Marytė could gather, was keen to marry too – the prospect of finding her unique purpose in life enticing – but she rejected every potential candidate among their bičiulystė, beekeeping comrades, in Darželiai, to the north. Senelė insists they make a match for Austėja from a different village. Laima, the goddess of fate, blesses these types of marriages and sends misfortunes to pairs who come from the same village. Marytė doesn't allow herself to be too caught up in Senelė's superstitions, but she also does not want to tempt fate, particularly on the eve of her first beekeeping season as a widow. Whether the son-in-law joins their family from near or far it is only customary that Austėja finds a suitable husband among bičiulystė.

While Baltrus had been training Azuolas to continue their traditions, Marytė passed her knowledge on to Austėja. A woman, as she has come to learn, should not rely solely on her husband for her livelihood. Embodied in her future hopes she'd spun the word austi into her oldest living daughter's name, meaning 'to weave'. An ode to the woven-like fabric of the honeycomb.

Unlike Danutė, Austėja is steadfast and will make a good beekeeper, if only she lets herself become one.

Sometimes Marytė does not know what her daughter wants, and she wonders whether her daughter knows either.

The snow is thick in the depths of the forest but there is birdsong, somewhere, in the white-dusted pine needles of the spruce and pines.

An extract from *All the Bees in the Hollows*

They stand bulky and firm among the lofty, bare-canopied birch and lindens. Like her, the forest is poised for spring.

Marytė pauses at a lime tree and glances up at the first hollow. The hole is covered with a piece of wood to protect the bees and honey from animals. Bears and woodpeckers are the main threats to the hollows.

She runs her fingertips over the marking her husband engraved on the tree. Axe bites, two lines with another overlapping, to signal that this hollow is owned by her family. More than fifty trees in the forest bear the same mark. She wishes he were here, that they could be together for another season.

It seems only fitting, with the cuckoo's call and Marytė's struggling thoughts of potential bridegrooms, that the lime tree be the first she will climb with her grave news. The lime, or linden, is the sacred tree of Laima. This is where she makes her decisions as a cuckoo.

'Hello,' she whispers, leaning her cheek against the smooth surface.

The hollow is twenty feet above ground and so she prepares her rope, doubling it over and wrapping it at waist height around the base of the trunk. She winds the end through, pulls it firmly and then repeats the process at shoulder height. On the lower loop, she secures her right foot and pulls herself up and then slips her left foot into the higher loop. She is now three feet from the ground and her muscles work hard to keep her body upright, with one arm wrapped around the trunk for balance. Her feet are protected by her well-worn boots with a stiff wooden sole. She is the only woman, wife, in Musteika to climb the trees. Marytė was taught beekeeping by her own father, and when she married Baltrus, he always encouraged her to use the skills she'd learned. After all, it made for quicker work at harvest time. It is the reason they could manage more hollows than most of the other families in the settlement.

Smilte, having three grown sons, none of whom have been wed, will now have the advantage, given there are no men left in Marytė's home. She does not feel envious of her friends, though; she has no doubt Smilte will send her boys around to help if needed. It is the way of bičiulystė. Like the bees in a hive, the families in the settlement work together, respect each other and put the needs of the community before their own.

Marytė feeds the rope over her shoulder until she has enough slack to whip it around the trunk at her new shoulder height. Again, she loops and tugs the rope, then slips her right foot in, levering herself up so that she creates a foot-loop ladder up the trunk of the tree. Her blood pulses through her body, the familiar rush of scaling a tree, rising above the forest, the same as men. It is almost as intoxicating as Baltrus's honey mead. Thinking of Baltrus and his mead-making reminds her of another responsibility she will inherit. Honey, wax and mead are how they paid their taxes, and if they don't pay their taxes, they will lose their right to tree beekeeping. They will lose their livelihood, not to mention their traditions.

A shudder erupts through her body. No, I will never let that happen. She would not allow her daughters to feel the same kind of despair and hopelessness she felt following her own father's death.

By the third loop, she is eye-level with the hollow. The wood covering will be sealed shut by the bees but she prises it open so in spring they can take flight. Marytė's chest feels lighter as she reflects on her role as a beekeeper. Inside the hollow, there remain the bark and moss she left after removing the honeycomb they harvested last autumn. The extra padding keeps the bees warm in winter.

The bees are still here, humming evenly; the sound of their chatter is beautiful to listen to. She ignores the ache in her thighs and arms as the heaviness in her chest gives way to coming home. She doesn't take too long to bask in the sound of her family: she has an important message to deliver.

Marytė taps on the hollow three times. 'Bee family, your master has left.' Her throat tightens and she draws in a cool breath. 'I am your new master, and I will care for you.'

She exhales, slowly, feeling some of the burden ease. And this is when it dawns on her. For the second time in her life, first at the death of her father, and now with the death of her husband, Marytė will inherit the hollows. A wave of panic and exhilaration pulses under her skin. She has never been good at relying on others, but Baltrus made it easy for her to learn. She will mourn her husband for the rest of her life, but she will not let it consume her. Her daughters and their future are too important for that. Beekeeping is like the blood in her veins: it keeps her alive and functioning.

She may undergo another change in name, from Marytė wife of Baltrus to Marytė widow of Baltrus, but she will always remain a beekeeper.

Perched upon the branch, Marytė spies a dark-headed figure in the pale landscape. And she knows that figure and his well-worn coat, but she does not know why he is in the forest now. The bees have not yet taken flight, and so she cannot think of any particular reason to explain the presence of the Hollow Watcher.

CHAPTER THREE

Austėja

As night falls, I worry. From the log-house doorway, I scan the shadows, but there is only forest in these shapes and none of them are Motina. She has been gone all day.

'Keep the door shut, Austėja. You're letting out the warm air.' Senelė stresses my name, so that it heats and crackles as if it were the fire in the hearth. Another quick sweep of the forest, but there's no sign of movement, so I shut the door on the crisp air and my mother. It's a familiar sensation, closing myself off from Motina. It happens deep inside me, even if it's the last thing I want.

Sometimes it happens when she moves towards me, arms open and welcoming, and I turn away. Or when her voice softens, gentle and caressing, when she sees me in a low mood. My voice is harsh in return.

My body rigid. I don't know why but it feels good in that moment to see her composed face crumble. But after that my stomach coils and my thoughts return to that moment, churning it over and over. Considering all the ways I could have responded differently but didn't.

It was never like that with Tévas. Everything was so easy. I knew where I stood with him, and he knew where he stood with me. The only emotion I can be certain of with Motina is her persistent frustration with me and mine with her.

I am a terrible daughter.

Just this morning, Motina announced that she was off to tell the bees. There was a brief pause, anticipation buzzed in the air like her beloved hollows, but I avoided eye contact. She turned and left; unspoken words hung in the air. There are more than fifty hollows in the forest with our family mark. More than fifty trees to climb. I know Motina and she'll stay out there all night until the work is done. My throat feels thick. Perhaps I should have gone with her. Then again, she did not ask me to come. I suspect this is the kind of task she prefers to do alone.

I return to my straw-weaved bed and pick up the needle and thread. A moment passes and then there's stomping outside the door, the loosening of snow on boots. Motina's boots. The door swings open and when I see her face, tired and slack, I want to run to her and bury my head in her chest. Tell her I've been worried about her. I've missed her.

Danutė launches herself into our mother's arms, but I remain where I am. A younger version of myself would've given in to this temptation. But I am not a little girl anymore.

I miss Tévas.

An extract from *All the Bees in the Hollows*

Motina lets out a low cough, as if something is wedged in her throat. It reminds me of Tévas's cough last winter.

Her movements are stiff and laden with fatigue as she pulls off her coat and dusts it down, hanging it by the door. There is something else etched into the creases around her eyes – something other than fatigue.

'Ow.' The needle pierces my fingertip. It tastes sweet as I press it against my tongue. I hold up the white flax linen that is to be my new dress. I have outgrown the one from my brother's mourning and so Danutė will have it, with some alterations. Senelė insists I make this one myself: focus my attention on the repetition of threading needle and not on Tévas. It makes no sense to me, as this dress, this white dress, will forever remind me of him.

There is a blood spot on the corner.

I sigh. I am no good at this.

'You are getting better at this.' Motina pauses at my bedside. She peers closer, eyes narrowing on the bloodstain. She presses her thumb against her tongue and then swipes it across the linen. The stain weakens in colour but swells in size. My jaw clenches. She has taken one vivid speck and made it bigger and horrible.

She doesn't look at me, doesn't want to see my agitation, or doesn't notice it's there. She adds a log to the fire. It hesitates and then rears up, crackling like a threatened asp.

I press my bloodied thumb against the spot Motina has paled, to revive it. But the blood smears on the damp linen, swelling beyond the parameter in a way that reminds me of the riverbanks in early spring. If Motina thinks my sewing skills are good now, then what does that say about my earlier efforts? Why must we do these things when we are no good at them? Why can't we focus our attention on things we do well?

'Austėja,' Senelė says, watching me from across the room. She is sewing the shirt and pants Tėvas will wear at the burial. 'Head down.'

And so, I put my head down, because Tėvas is dead and everyone is sad, and it is best to do what is expected of me.

A sob erupts from my sister's bed. Danutė is lying facedown, her shoulders shaking. I lower my thread, but Motina is there first. She whispers something in my sister's ear and caresses the back of her head, running her pale fingers along Danutė's loose hair. Irritation rises again. Motina never comforts me in this way. Would I let her?

It is not Danutė's fault: she is young, and she needs her mother. I am old enough to be wed, to be a wife, a woman of my own household. I do not need my mother in this way anymore. But how long has it been since she ran her fingers through my hair? Was I eight winters old like Danutė? I cannot picture the moment in my mind, but there is a vague memory that pulses through my veins, a memory of how it feels to have a mother's soft touch.

I suppose I am no longer her youngest daughter. Danutė will always hold that title. I am not the youngest daughter, and I am also not the oldest, but born in the shadow of a lost daughter: I am the second, the middle, not earliest, not latest, somewhere in between.

The oldest has never lasted long in my family.

Tėvas remains in bed, in a deep sleep, now cocooned in blankets. Tomorrow our bičiulystė will visit. The priest has not yet arrived in town. There is rain to come and so he will be delayed. Tėvas will soon be moved to the threshing barn until the coffin is built and the earth is soft enough to dig.

Worry. That is the emotion etched on Motina's face: the creases are deeper now that she sits beside my sister. Did she see something in the forest? Will spring come soon, or not soon enough? I hope the bees do not take flight as we put my father to rest.

'This is enough for now.' Senelė sits on my bed beside me. She unstitches the last few lines and sets it aside. 'Come back to it tomorrow morning with fresh eyes.'

'Senelė?' I pose the question before I can think it through. I steal a glance at Motina, but she isn't listening. 'Did Tévas say anything, anything he meant for me to hear before he left?'

'What happened in the forest?' she asks as if she has not heard my question. 'When your father went to the High Hill?'

'The forest?'

How can I explain to Senelė what I felt when I do not understand it myself? Senelė clings to the old ways, but it is discouraged. Our family is Christian, and we must hold on to our faith, especially now. 'I don't know. Perhaps God sent me a message?' I say, but my voice is weak and Senelė frowns.

'You didn't answer my question.'

I swallow. 'I needed fresh air, to be in the forest. I just wanted a break; I didn't mean to be gone when he—'

Her hand rests on my leg. 'It's okay. Go on,' she says.

'I was running, following the fallow deer marks in the snow and then I fell ... into an oak tree and ... it's like the air stopped moving. Everything was still. Quiet. And then ...' I look to Motina, who does not like to hear of the old beliefs. Tévas would've laughed. I do not mention the cuckoo. 'And then the forest breathed again. I think I knew then, in that moment, and I ran all the way home.'

'Vejas,' Senelė mutters under her breath. 'I always thought you would have the gift.' Her smile is strained, and she eases herself off the bed. Gift? I want to ask her about this, but I fixate on the pull of another thread.

'Wait, Senelė,' I say, and she turns. '*Did* Tévas say anything about me?'

She pauses and inhales through her nose; when she exhales it whistles. 'He did not say anything to me,' she says, turning from me and climbing into her bed.

I lie on my back, waiting to feel relief. Instead, the worry edges in. Senelė didn't exactly answer my question.